**Can marriage**
**ever be put right?**

*New York Times* bestselling author

weaves her spell in

## LOVING

Jay Fraser felt he'd been
trapped into marriage....

## INJURED INNOCENT

Lissa knew Joel felt
nothing but contempt for her....

## THE SIX-MONTH MARRIAGE

Sapphire actually considered remarriage to ease
her dying father's mind....

"Jordan's record is phenomenal."
—*The Bookseller*

Dear Reader,

Romances featuring marriages of convenience have always been some of my particular favorites—both to write and read—and I know I am not alone in this predilection. Georgette Heyer even entitled one of her romances *The Convenient Marriage*.

Quite why such romances are so universally popular, I don't know. Perhaps it has something to do with the fact that somewhere inside us all is that desire for things to turn out well—for love to conquer and for a couple that we, as writer and reader, can see are so ideally suited for one another to recognize this themselves.

Whatever the reason, I hope that in these books you, like my characters, will find that special something called love and that you will get as much pleasure from reading about my marriages of convenience as I did in writing them.

So let us celebrate together the special excitement of a *Marriage of Convenience*.

Penny Jordan

# Penny Jordan

## Marriage of Convenience

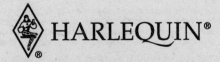

# HARLEQUIN®

TORONTO • NEW YORK • LONDON
AMSTERDAM • PARIS • SYDNEY • HAMBURG
STOCKHOLM • ATHENS • TOKYO • MILAN • MADRID
PRAGUE • WARSAW • BUDAPEST • AUCKLAND

HARLEQUIN BOOKS

by Request—MARRIAGE OF CONVENIENCE

Copyright © 2000 by Harlequin Books S.A.

ISBN 0-373-20181-8

The publisher acknowledges the copyright holder
of the individual works as follows:
LOVING
Copyright © 1986 by Penny Jordan
INJURED INNOCENT
Copyright © 1985 by Penny Jordan
THE SIX-MONTH MARRIAGE
Copyright © 1985 by Penny Jordan

This edition published by arrangement with Harlequin Books S.A.

Visit us at www.eHarlequin.com

**Printed in U.S.A.**

# CONTENTS

# Loving

# CHAPTER ONE

'MUMMY, CAN HEATHER come home and play with me and then stay for tea?'

Looking down into the pleading blue eyes of her six-year-old daughter, Claire once again blessed the totally unexpected inheritance from her unknown great-aunt that had made possible her move away from the centre of London to the small village of Chadbury St John.

Lucy had blossomed out unbelievably in the short month they had been here. Already she seemed plumper, healthier, and now she had made her first 'best friend'. The huge block of council flats they had lived in before had not led to any friendships for either mother or daughter. They had been living an existence that had virtually been hand to mouth, and with no way out of the dull misery of such poverty.

And then, miraculously, almost overnight everything had changed. How on earth her great-aunt's solicitors had been able to track her down was a miracle in itself, but to learn that she had inherited her cottage, and with it a small but very, very precious private income, had been such a miraculous event that even now Claire sometimes thought she was dreaming.

'Not today, Lucy,' she told her daughter indulgently. 'Heather's mummy won't know where she is if she comes home with us now, will she?' she reminded her crestfallen child gently.

'Heather hasn't got a mummy,' Lucy informed her quickly, speaking for the brown-eyed little girl clinging to her side. 'She only has a daddy, and he goes away a lot.'

Another quick look at the little girl standing close to her own daughter made Claire aware of several things she hadn't noticed before. Unlike Lucy's clothes, although expensive, Heather's were old-fashioned, and too large. Her fine brown hair was scraped back into plaits, and the brown eyes held a defensive, worried look.

Another victim of the growing divorce rate? Claire wondered wryly. Even here in this quiet, almost idyllic village twenty miles from Bath, they were not immune to the pressures of civilisation.

Everyone in the village seemed to accept her own status as that of a young widow. Her great-aunt had apparently not been born locally but had retired to the village after her many years as a schoolteacher, and had, according to what gossip Claire had picked up in the local post office, been the sort of person who believed in keeping herself very much to herself.

Would she have approved of her? Claire's soft mouth twisted in a tight grimace. Probably not. She had learned over the years that people drew their own conclusions about young girls alone with a baby to support, and that they were not always the right ones.

It had been hard work bringing Lucy up alone, but once she had been born there was nothing that could have induced her to part with her. The love she felt for her child was the last thing she had expected... especially...

'Mummy, please let Heather come back with us.' Lucy tugged on her jeans, demanding her attention.

'Not today,' she responded firmly, smiling at Heather to show the little girl that her refusal held nothing personal. 'I'm sure that there's someone at home waiting for Heather who would be very worried if she didn't arrive, isn't there, Heather?'

'Only Mrs Roberts,' the little girl responded miserably. 'And *she* won't let me have soldiers with my boiled egg. She says it's babyish.'

Compassion mingled with amusement as Claire surveyed the childish pout. Boiled eggs and soldiers were one of Lucy's favourite treats.

'Mrs Roberts is Heather's daddy's housekeeper,' Lucy told her mother importantly. 'He has to go away a lot on—on business—and Mrs Roberts looks after Heather.'

'She doesn't like me.'

The flat statement was somehow more pathetic than an emotional outburst would have been. And the little girl did look unloved. Oh, not in any obvious way— her clothes were expensive and clean, and she was obviously healthy—but she was equally obviously unhappy. But surely the blame for that rested with the child's father, and not with the housekeeper? Perhaps he was too involved in his business—whatever it was—to notice that his child was miserable.

It was the look of stoic acceptance on the child's face as she took Lucy's hand and started to walk away that decided her.

'Perhaps, if Heather doesn't live too far away, we could walk home with her and ask Mrs Roberts if she could come to tea,' she suggested.

Two small faces turned up towards her, both wearing beaming smiles.

What manner of father was it who would allow his five-year-old daughter to walk home unescorted? Chadbury St John was only a small village, but it was also a remote one. Children disappeared in Britain every day…were attacked in the most bestial and horrible of ways… She…Claire shivered suddenly, things she didn't want to remember obliterating the warm autumn sun. She had been eighteen when Lucy was conceived. An adult legally, but a child still in so many ways, the adored and protected daughter of older parents who had never taught her that the world could be a cruel and hard place.

They had been killed in a road accident shortly after her eighteenth birthday. She had lost everything then—parents, security—everything.

It had been their intention that she would go on to university after school, but her father's pension had died with him, and the small house they lived in had had to be sold to pay off their small debts. There hadn't been much left. Certainly not enough for her to go to university, even if that had still been possible, but an eighteen-year-old girl struggling with the knowledge that she was an orphan and pregnant doesn't have much time or energy to expend on studying.

Of course she could have had an abortion. That was the first thing the doctor had told her after he had got the truth from her. She had wanted to agree—had intended to—but somehow, when it came to it, she couldn't.

And she had never once regretted her decision to bear and then keep Lucy. Of course, pressure had been put on her to give her up, but she had withstood it. In those early days she had still had some money left from the sale of the house, but that hadn't lasted longer than the first twelve months of Lucy's life.

The council flat they had been given, its walls running with damp, its reputation for violence and vandalism so frightening that some days Claire had barely dared to go out—these were all in the past now. She felt as though she had stepped out from darkness into light, and perhaps it was her own awareness of what suffering could be that made her so sensitive to the misery of the little girl standing at her side.

The three of them walked to the end of the village, Heather hesitating noticeably once they had left the main road behind.

'Heather lives in that big house with the white gates,' Lucy informed her mother importantly.

Claire knew which one Lucy meant. They had walked past it on Sunday afternoons when they explored their new environment. It was a lovely house, Tudor in part with tiny mullioned windows and an air of peace and sanctuary. One glance into Heather's shuttered, tight face told her that the little girl obviously didn't find those qualities there.

They walked up the drive together, but once they were standing outside the rose-gold front of the house, Heather tugged on Claire's sleeve and whispered uncertainly, 'We have to go round the back. Mrs Roberts doesn't let me use the front door.'

There could be any number of reasons for that, but even so, Claire frowned slightly. It was, after all, the child's home.

They had to skirt well-tended, traditional flower borders and walk along a pretty flagged path to reach the back door.

There was a bell which Claire rang. They waited several minutes before it was answered by a frowning, grey-haired woman, her lips pursed into a grimace of disapproval as she opened the door.

'Mrs Roberts?' Claire began before the other woman could speak. 'I'm Claire Richards. I've come to ask if it would be all right for Heather to come home with us and stay for tea.'

The frown relaxed slightly. 'I suppose it will be all right,' she agreed grudgingly, summing up Claire's appearance. Her faded jeans and well-worn tee-shirt didn't make her look very motherly, Claire thought wryly. She had been working in their small garden this morning, and she suspected that some of the dirt still clung to her jeans. 'Mind you, her father's expected back this evening, so she mustn't be late.'

'Oh no…of course not. He'll want her to be here when he gets home.'

'Oh, it isn't that,' the housekeeper contradicted with what Claire thought was an appallingly callous lack of regard for Heather's feelings. 'No, he'll be bound to be busy when he gets back and he won't want to be bothered with *her*…' her head jerked in the direction of Heather. 'Course, her mother should have taken her really, but her new husband didn't want her it seems, so Mr Fraser got lumbered with her. I've told him more than once that she's too much for me to cope with, what with the house as well. He should get married again, that's what he should do. He needs a wife, a man like him. All that money…' she sniffed and glowered at Heather. 'Still, I suppose it's a case of once bitten, twice shy. Nuts about that wife of his, he was. Neither of them had much time for *her*…' Again she jerked her head in Heather's direction, and Claire, who had been too appalled by her revelations to silence her before, placed an arm protectively around each child and stepped back from the door.

'I'll bring her back after tea. If her father returns before then I live at number five, the New Cottages.'

She was shaking slightly as she bustled the girls away. Both of them were subdued. Claire glanced briefly at Heather. The little girl's head was turned away from her, but Claire was sure she could see tears in her eyes.

Of all the thoughtless, cruel women! And by all
accounts Heather's father was no better. Oh, she
could imagine that it was hard for a man to be left
alone to bring up his child, but that did not excuse
his apparent lack of love for her. Mrs Roberts had
described him as wealthy, and certainly Heather's
home had borne out that assertion. If that was the
case, why on earth didn't he hire someone who was
properly qualified to look after the child?

They were half way back towards the village when
Heather said suddenly in a wobbly little voice, 'It
isn't true what Mrs Roberts said. My daddy *does* love
me. She only says that because she doesn't like me.
My mummy didn't love me, though. She left me.'

Claire had absolutely no idea what to say. All she
could do was to squeeze the small hand comfortingly
and say bracingly, 'Well, you and Lucy are in the
same boat, aren't you? You don't have a mummy and
she doesn't have a daddy.'

She had little idea, when she made the comforting
remark, of the repercussions it was to have, and if she
had she would have recalled it instantly. Instead, she
saw to her relief that Heather seemed to have taken
comfort from her words, and by the time they had
reached the cottage both little girls were chattering
away so enthusiastically that she couldn't get so much
as a single word in.

She let them play in the pretty back garden while
she watched from inside. A bank statement which had
arrived that morning lay opened on the kitchen table,
and she frowned as she glanced at it. Her inheritance

meant that she was no longer eligible for state benefits, and her small income barely stretched to cover
their day-to-day living requirements. Next year she
would have rates to pay, and the old stone cottage
needed new window frames; there was also, according to her next-door neighbour, a problem with the
roof. If only she could get a part-time job? But doing
what exactly? She was not trained for anything, and
even if she had been, there were no jobs locally; she
would have to travel to Bath.

Pushing her worries to one side, she started preparing the girls' meal. Her small garden boasted several fruit trees, and she had spent the weekend preserving as much of it as she could. Now, when she
had least expected it, she was finding a use for the
old-fashioned homely skills her mother had taught
her. Her mother. Claire stilled and stared unseeingly
out of the window. What would she think if she could
see her now?

Claire had not arrived until her mother was in her
early forties and her father even older. They had surrounded her in their love, and then with one blow fate
had robbed her of that love. When the police came to
tell her about her parents' accident she had hardly
been able to take it in. They had been going out to
dinner with some friends and the car which ran into
them and caused the accident had been driven by a
drunken driver.

She thought that she had endured as much pain as
life could sustain, but six months later she had learned
better.

'Mum, we're hungry...'

Lucy's imperious little voice was a welcome interruption, and although she pretended to frown, Claire
soon got both girls seated at the kitchen table and
watched in amusement as they demolished the boiled
eggs and thin strips of bread and butter.

Real nursery fare. Her mother had made it for her,
too. Just as she had made the deliciously light scones
and the home-made jam that Claire too had prepared
to follow their first course.

'Mrs Roberts never makes any cakes,' Heather
complained, happily accepting a second scone. 'She
doesn't even buy them. She says sweet things are bad
for me.'

Mrs Roberts was quite right, Claire thought wryly,
but she prided herself on the methods she used to
adapt her mother's recipes to fit in with her own more
up-to-date awareness of what was healthy and what
wasn't.

She considered that children at six years old still
needed the calcium supplied by unskimmed milk, and
she poured them both full glasses, watching the childishly eager way they gulped it down. Heather spilt
some and instantly her small body froze, her eyes
widening in fright and tension, fixed on Claire's face.

'Don't worry about it, it'll soon wipe up,' she told
her cheerfully, trying to hide her shock at the little
girl's frightened reaction. Wasn't she ever allowed to
spill anything? She was, after all, only a very little
girl, but Mrs Roberts hadn't struck her as the type of
woman who would make allowances for a six-year-

old, and by all accounts Heather's father was too engrossed in his business to notice or care what was happening to his child.

Mentally she contrasted Heather's life with Lucy's. Lucy might lack things in the way of material possessions, but her daughter had never doubted that she was deeply loved. Watching Heather, Claire was fiercely glad that she had never allowed herself to be persuaded to give her child up. Both she and Lucy had lived in poverty, and it had been very hard, but Lucy had never looked at her with such fear and dread in her eyes, and she promised herself that she never would.

Heather was a much less stalwart child—shyer, and more withdrawn; in Lucy's company she seemed to blossom, but whenever Lucy moved out of sight she withdrew into herself again, staring wide-eyed at Claire while she moved about the kitchen.

'Lucy, you've got a spare toothbrush,' she instructed her daughter briskly when they had finished their meal. 'Take Heather upstairs and both of you wash your hands and clean your teeth.'

The cottage was only small, with a sitting-room and a dining-kitchen. Upstairs they had two bedrooms and a tiny bathroom, but after the grimness of the London flat it was sheer bliss to look out of the windows and see the mellow lushness of the Cotswold countryside. They fronted right on to the main road through the village, but even that was a pleasure to look out on to. The cottages lining the village street had been built during the eighteenth century, in mellow cream stone; all of them had small front gardens, filled with cottage garden plants.

As yet the village hadn't been discovered by commuters, but Claire suspected that that state of affairs wouldn't last long. Most of the younger generation had moved away looking for work. All of her neighbours were old—her great-aunt's generation; the village had no industry, other than the land; there was one general store, the post office and a pub. There was talk of the authorities closing the school, but since it took children from two neighbouring villages also, and was well attended, Claire was hoping that this wouldn't happen. If it did, no doubt Heather's father would be able to send her to a private boarding school, but she... She was frowning over this when she heard someone knocking on the front door.

She opened it and looked at the man standing on her front doorstep. He was very tall, so tall that she had to tilt her head back to look at him. The immaculate tailoring of his pale grey suit made her lift nervous fingers to her tangled chestnut hair. She hadn't so much as brushed it since coming in with the girls. His own hair was black, and very thick. His eyes were grey and totally expressionless. They were studying her assessingly, and she felt herself blushing hotly as she realised how closely her old tee-shirt and jeans clung to her body.

It had been such a long time since a man looked at her like that she had lost all awareness of her own sexuality. Now, recognising the way his hard glance rested on her breasts, she felt her whole body tense with immediate rejection. He felt her tension too, she could see it in the way his eyes narrowed thoughtfully on hers.

'I believe you have my daughter here.'

His voice was cool, as though warning her off, but warning her off what? For a moment she was so bemused that she couldn't think.

'Your daughter...'

'Yes.' He sounded impatient now, his eyes sharp and cold, as though he had judged her and found her guilty of some unknown crime. 'Mrs Roberts, my housekeeper, informed me that you...'

'Oh yes, yes...of course. You're Heather's father.' Why on earth was he making her feel so flustered?

'Jay Fraser,' he agreed smoothly, watching her. 'And you are...'

'Claire Richards.'

'Mummy, we've cleaned our teeth and...'

Lucy galloped down the stairs, coming to an abrupt halt at Claire's side, and staring at the man standing in the doorway. Now it was her daughter's turn to be tongue-tied and wide-eyed, Claire saw, while Heather, who had been behind her, raced up to her father, her face alight with pleasure.

'Daddy, this is Lucy, my best friend,' Heather explained to her father importantly, dragging Lucy forwards for his inspection. 'We had boiled eggs for tea and soldiers, and Lucy's mummy made scones...' The babble of chatter suddenly dried up and Claire saw Heather's eyes suddenly go wide and tearful as she added huskily, 'Mrs Roberts told Lucy's mummy that you don't love me, but that's not true, is it?'

It most indisputably was not, Claire recognised, watching the mixture of rage and anguish that darkened the grey eyes as Jay Fraser bent down to pick up his daughter.

Over Heather's head, Claire said impulsively, 'I know it's none of my business, but why don't you get someone else to look after her? She needs—' She broke off when she saw the expression on his face.

The grey eyes had frozen. He stepped inside the small hall and put Heather down.

'Why don't you and…and Lucy, go outside and play for a little while while I talk to Lucy's mummy.'

Obediently both little girls did as he instructed leaving Claire with no alternative but to invite him into her small sitting-room.

Once inside the room, he dwarfed it. He must be well over six feet, Claire thought absently, watching as he took the chair she indicated, sinking down into it in a way that suggested an exhaustion his face did not betray. How old was he? Somewhere in his early thirties, probably. What did he do for a living? He certainly wasn't her idea of a businessman. He looked too fit, too physically hard for that…

'I'm sorry you've been landed with Heather,' he said distantly at last, reaching inside his jacket and extracting his wallet. 'If you will…'

He was intending to give her money? Claire could hardly believe it. Instantly she was furiously outraged. Why, the man was positively feudal!

'It was no trouble,' she told him tightly. 'Lucy wanted to invite Heather back for tea. I thought it best to check with your housekeeper before I agreed.'

He put his wallet away, but his hard expression didn't relax. 'You're a single parent, I believe,' he said tautly, the sharp question making her frown.

'Yes, but...'

'Let's get one thing straight then, Mrs Richards. I don't care what Mrs Roberts may have told you; I'm not in the market either for a mother for Heather, or a second wife for myself.'

It took her several shattered seconds to assimilate the meaning of what he was telling her, but once she had, Claire felt her face flame with furious resentment. What on earth was he trying to imply? Surely he didn't think that she had invited Heather to come and have tea with Lucy as a... As a what? As a step towards getting to know him better, and through that...

But yes, he had. She could see it in the bleak grey eyes watching her with hard determination. He was a wealthy and successful single man with a young daughter to bring up. No doubt he had been the victim of *some* degree of matchmaking, but that was no reason for him to think that she...

The red tints in her chestnut hair weren't there for nothing; her temper, normally well controlled and kept in check, refused to be subdued. She opened her mouth to tell him just what she thought of him and his insinuations, but found the hot words stifled in her throat as he suddenly forestalled her and demanded icily,

'Have I made myself clear, Mrs Richards?'

He was standing up now. Business concluded, interview over, Claire thought acidly.

'Explicitly,' she told him in a voice as cold as his own, a spark of rage intensifying the greeny gold of her eyes. Although she didn't know it, her anger had left a soft flush staining her cheekbones, and had brought a slight quiver to her mouth. She looked more vulnerable than fierce, but since she could not see her own expression she was unaware of the reason for the cynical and faintly brooding expression in those cold grey eyes,

However, even if she didn't know the reason for it, she knew that it existed and that was enough to make her say bitingly, 'I assure you you have nothing to fear from me. I'm no more in the market for a husband than you are for a wife, Mr Fraser. Believe me, a man in my life is the very last thing I want. Lucy and I are perfectly happy as we are.' Her flush deepened betrayingly as she saw the way he looked around her small and rather shabbily furnished sitting-room, and instinctively her fingers curled into her palms. One of the disadvantages of being only five-foot-one was that people sometimes tended to forget that she was a fully grown adult. The look Jay Fraser was turning on her now was one he might have given a slightly dim adolescent. Maybe her home wasn't much by his standards, but she loved it, and whatever he might choose to think there was no way she would ever want to change it for something like Whitegates.

Her resentment against him incited her onwards.

'If you must know, I invited Heather to come back and have tea with us because I felt sorry for her.'

She had got him on the raw there, she saw with a pleasurable stab of satisfaction.

'Oh, I can see you find that hard to believe, Mr Fraser. Heather might have all the comforts a wealthy father can provide, but a busy businessman doesn't always have time for the little cares and worries of a small child. Mrs Roberts didn't strike me as a particularly sympathetic mother-substitute...' She took a deep breath and then rushed on, 'In fact it seemed to me that Heather is frightened of her.'

She saw from the white line of rage circling his mouth that he was furious with her.

'Heather doesn't need your pity,' he told her sharply, 'and now if you wouldn't mind calling her in for me, I think it's time that both I and my daughter left.'

It was perhaps unfortunate that Heather chose to give her a brief and very shy hug before she left, but there was no way she was going to reject the little girl's hesitant affection, Claire told herself as she bent down to hug her back. She didn't like the bitter glance that Jay Fraser gave her as he took Heather's hand and led her away, but if he thought he could simply walk into her house and insult her the way he had...

It was perhaps just as well that tomorrow was Saturday, she reflected later, listening to Lucy's chatter

as she got her ready for bed. The little girl was full
of her new friend and all the things they were going
to do together, happily oblivious to the fact that her
new friend's father was probably telling his daughter
right at this moment that the friendship was over.

In a way his insinuations were almost laughable.
Any sort of involvement with any man was so totally
opposite to what she wanted…

There had only ever been one sexual experience in
her life, and that had led to Lucy's conception, and
while Claire loved her child with all her heart, the
manner of her conception was something that still
caused her nightmares. She had no desire for any sort
of intimacy with a man; quite the opposite, and so for
her, marriage was something that was completely out.
Her fear and abhorrence of sex went very deep and
was something she normally avoided thinking about.
It was less painful that way.

After Lucy's birth her doctor had suggested some
sort of counselling, but she had refused. She hadn't
been able to bear to discuss her feelings with anyone.
She couldn't even examine them in the privacy of her
own thoughts.

On Saturday morning Claire had to call at the post
office to buy some more eggs. They were delivered
fresh each day from one of the local farms, and were
a relatively inexpensive and nourishing source of
healthy food for both her and Lucy. Fortunately the
little girl adored them, and Claire left her examining
the treats on the sweet counter while she went to pay
for her purchases.

She was just moving away from the counter when she recognised one of her neighbours standing in the queue behind her—nothing moved quickly in the post office; it was the local centre for receiving and sorting gossip.

Her neighbour was an overweight, untidy woman in her late sixties with a faintly overbearing manner. She had come round to introduce herself just after they had moved in, and had almost immediately informed Claire that she was likely to have a problem with her roof. It seemed that most of the cottages had had their roof timbers and slates replaced the previous winter, and that Claire's had been one of the few that had not. She herself had already noticed several loose slates, and she was still worrying about the horrendous expense that would be involved.

Now Mrs Turner smiled eagerly at her and commented in a loud voice, 'Wasn't that the little Fraser girl I saw you with yesterday? Poor little scrap; I feel so sorry for her, poor little mite, rattling around in that great big house, with no one but Amy Roberts for company. And she's never been one for children. Of course, her father really should get married again. She needs a mother, that's as plain as the nose on your face.'

Speculation gleamed in the pale blue eyes, and Claire had to fight down an impulse to be rude to her.

'Heather and Lucy are at school together,' she said instead, forcing what she hoped was a careless smile. 'You know how it is with little girls of that age: a new "best friend" every week.'

She knew quite well that the entire queue was listening, and she only hoped that they picked up the message she was giving out. She could just imagine Jay Fraser's reaction if it got back to him that they were the subject of village gossip.

Luckily Lucy had grown bored with the sweet tray, and so Claire was able to escape from the shop.

It was a pleasantly warm late summer day and she intended to spend it working in the garden. The old lady who lived next door to her had complained during the week that she no longer had the energy to maintain her own garden, and Claire had tentatively offered to take charge of it for her.

In response, Mrs Vickers had thanked her and agreed, but had insisted that Claire had her pick of the raspberries and plums.

For lunch, Claire had made Lucy's favourite ice cream with some of their own strawberries, and on an impulse she took a covered bowl of the sweet round to her older neighbour.

Knowing how proud and independent older people could be she was touched by the enthusiasm with which Mrs Vickers accepted her gift.

'Home-made ice cream—I love it,' the old lady told her with a shy smile. 'My stepmother used to make it for us...' She sighed faintly. 'Why is it that the older one gets, the more one returns to the past? There were five of us, you know, three girls and two boys. Our mother died having a sixth. When our father first brought Mary home and told us she was going to be our new mother I hated her. She was less

than fifteen years older than I was myself, but she
was so patient with us, and so kind. Very modern in
her ways too. She insisted that my father let us girls
stay on at school, and never made us do more in the
house than the boys—and housework was hard in
those days. She had three children of her own to look
after as well as us five. All that washing…and the
cooking! My father used to come home for his lunch,
and he expected a three-course meal on the table…and another at night. But she was always cheerful. I see you had young Heather Fraser round yesterday. Poor little thing. If ever anyone needed
mothering it was her.'

Claire, who had been listening to the old lady's
reminiscences with interest, tensed slightly.

'Heather has a mother, Mrs Vickers,' she pointed
out coolly.

'She has someone who calls herself her mother,'
corrected Mrs Vickers stubbornly. 'Never gave a
thought to her from the moment she was born, she
didn't. Always off out, leaving the baby with anyone
she could get to look after her, and once she met that
American… Many's the time her father's come into
the village to buy the poor child something for her
tea because her mother'd gone out without feeding
her.'

'I really don't think you should be telling me any
of this, Mrs Vickers,' protested Claire, softening the
words with a smile. 'Mr Fraser didn't strike me as
the kind of man who would like the thought of people
gossiping about him.'

'Gossip is part and parcel of village life; when you get to my age it's one of the few pleasures left. He did take it very hard when she left, though, and that's a fact. Never seemed to have seen it coming like the rest of us. Of course, with him being away so much… He has a manufacturing company in Bath and they do a lot of business abroad. I'm not sure what they make, but she was the sort of woman who needs a man's constant attention, and when he wasn't there to give it to her she looked for it somewhere else. She never struck me as the sort who was suited to village life—or to marriage, come to think of it. Little Heather was only a few months old when they moved in. That father of hers ought to find someone better to take care of her than Amy Roberts, though. Not keen on kiddies, isn't Amy…'

That was the second time today that someone had made that observation, reflected Claire a little later as she returned home, and it was one she agreed with. However, the person they should be telling wasn't her but Heather's father. It seemed ridiculous that one brief visit should give the village the idea that in some way she was responsible for Heather's welfare. Nothing like this had ever happened in the block of flats; no one cared or noticed there who went in or out of someone else's front door. But here it was different…people did care, and they certainly noticed!

# CHAPTER TWO

CLAIRE HERSELF HAD not expected that Lucy would receive an invitation to have tea with Heather, but it was very difficult to explain to her little girl why she could not bring her new friend home with her every afternoon.

'But Mummy, Heather likes it with us,' Lucy protested one afternoon when Claire had gently but firmly refused once again to allow Heather to come home with them.

'Lucy, Heather has her own home, and her daddy will be waiting for her.'

Privately Claire thought it was appalling that the little girl should be left to walk home from school on her own, and she had got into the habit of walking Heather to her own gates first and then taking Lucy home. From her own point of view she was more than happy to feed Heather *every* tea time; she always had plenty, and the two little girls played happily together. She didn't want Lucy to grow up as a lonely only, and since she herself was never likely to have any more children, friends were something she wanted Lucy to have plenty of.

It tore at her heart to see the woebegone and hurt

expression in Heather's eyes, but how could she explain to a six-year-old that she couldn't encourage her visits because her father would put the wrong interpretation on them—not to mention half the village. She did notice, however, that Heather was losing weight and gradually becoming worryingly withdrawn.

Two weeks after her confrontation with Jay Fraser, Claire relented and agreed that Heather could stay to tea the following day, provided that Mrs Roberts agreed.

Everything went very well until it was time to take the little girl home, and then to Claire's dismay Heather burst into tears and clung to her, sobbing pitifully.

'I don't want to go back,' she wept. 'I want to stay here with you and Lucy!'

'But Heather, your daddy…'

'He's gone away again. I wish I could come and live with you and Lucy and then you could be my mummy and Daddy could be Lucy's daddy…'

'Yes Mummy, don't you think that would be a good idea?' Lucy piped up. She had gone very quiet when Heather started to cry, but now her brown eyes sparkled excitedly, and the unmistakable contrast between her bright, happy daughter and the little wan face of the child burrowing into her lap caught at Claire's tender heart.

She tried to tell herself that it wasn't all Jay Fraser's fault—a man had to work—but surely he could do better for his daughter than to leave her in the care of someone as plainly unfeeling as Mrs Roberts? Even she herself had quailed a little before the older woman's sternness, and she could well imagine the effect it would have on someone as shy and insecure as Heather. She suspected that Mrs Roberts wasn't above bullying the little girl, and, like all bullies, the more frightened Heather seemed, the more bullying she would become.

'Please, can't I stay here tonight?'

If only she could say yes, but she couldn't, and neither could she explain why not.

'Not tonight, Heather,' she refused gently, softening her refusal by adding, 'perhaps another night, if your daddy will let you. Come on now, let's dry those tears and then we'll take you home.'

She could tell that Heather was reluctant to go, but what could she do? She saw her safely inside the gates, but didn't go up to the house with her, mainly because she didn't want to run the risk of running into Jay Fraser, should he have returned.

Later she was to curse herself for that bit of selfishness, but as she watched Heather's small figure trudging miserably towards the house she had no premonition of what was to happen, only a tender-hearted sadness for the little girl's misery.

The following day, when she went to meet them from school, Claire found that both little girls seemed rather subdued. She left Heather after seeing her safely inside the gates to her home, and although Lucy was quieter than usual, there was nothing in her small daughter's silence to worry her.

They had almost reached their own cottage when
Lucy suddenly asked, 'Can Heather come and live
with us, Mummy instead of with Mrs Roberts?'

Sighing faintly, Claire shook her head. 'Heather's
daddy would be lonely if she came to live with us,'
she said by way of explanation. 'Just as I'd be lonely
if you went away from me.'

'But Heather's daddy is always away, and she
doesn't like Mrs Roberts. She didn't like her mummy
either; she was always cross and smacking her.'

Claire was too aware of how Jay Fraser would react
if he ever learned that his daughter had been passing
on these confidences to encourage Lucy to say any
more. His comments to her on the one occasion on
which they had met still stung.

She hated the thought that other people besides
himself might consider that she was on the lookout
for a husband. A man in her life was the last thing
she wanted, especially a man with the legal right to
share her bed and her body. She felt herself tense, the
familiar sense of nausea sweeping through her.

After she had had her tea, Lucy asked if she could
go and play in the garden. Claire agreed readily
enough; Lucy knew that she was not allowed to go
outside its perimeters.

Mrs Vickers had commented to her earlier in the
day that soon it would be autumn. She had remarked
on the likelihood of autumn gales and the damage
they might do to the cottage roofs. Her cottage, like
Claire's badly needed re-roofing, but unlike Claire it
seemed that she had enough money put on one side

to cover this expense. She had mentioned a sum that
had frankly appalled Claire, who had not realised that
the age of the cottages and their country setting meant
that they had to be re-roofed in the same traditional
hand-made tiles as had been originally used.

She hadn't realised how long she had been sitting
worrying about the roof until she heard the church
clock chiming seven. She went to the back door and
called Lucy, frowning slightly as she scanned the garden and realised there was no sign of her daughter.

She was just wondering if Lucy could possibly
have slipped round to see Mrs Vickers, when she suddenly appeared.

The guilty look on her face was enough to alert
Claire's maternal instincts. It was her private and
most dreaded fear that the same thing that had happened to her might happen to Lucy, and it was because of this nightmare dread that she was so strict
about not permitting her to stray outside the garden.
Now, however, the guilt in her daughter's eyes made
her hesitate before getting angry with her. Her 'Where
have you been?' brought a pink flush to Lucy's face.

'I went for a walk...'

'Lucy, you know I've told you never to go out of
the garden without me. Come on now, it's bedtime.'
How on earth could one describe to a six-year-old the
perils that lurked behind the smiling mask of friendly
strangers?

'Don't be cross, Mummy.' An engaging smile, and
a small hand tucked in hers, made her sigh and decide

that her lecture would have to await a more propitious occasion.

It was only when she was making Lucy's supper that she noticed that her cake-tin was almost empty. She frowned slightly. She had never forbidden Lucy to help herself to food if she wanted it, but neither had she encouraged her. Lucy was not a greedy child, and rarely asked for food between meals, but she could have sworn that that cake-tin had held far more home-made buns last night than it did now.

NORMALLY HEATHER WAS waiting for them outside the school gates, but this morning there was no sign of her, and Claire couldn't help feeling concerned. Was the little girl ill? Heather wasn't her responsibility, she reminded herself, and neither her father nor Mrs Roberts would thank her for interfering, and yet she knew that if Jay Fraser's reaction to her had been different she would have called at the house on her way home and checked to see if Heather was all right.

She knew that Heather was perhaps becoming too attached to her, needing a mother substitute, and while she had scrupulously tried to avoid encouraging the little girl to depend on her in any way at all, she knew that she herself was growing very attached to her. Heather wasn't her child in the way that Lucy was, but there was something vulnerable in Heather that cried out for love and attention.

Several times during the morning she found herself worrying about her, remembering her wan little face. Heather was frightened of Mrs Roberts, and while she didn't think the housekeeper would go as far as to physically maltreat the child, there were other ways of inflicting pain and fear on children.

She had almost decided that after lunch she would call round at Whitegates and brave Jay Fraser's wrath if he found out, when she heard her doorbell ring.

The sight of Jay Fraser standing on her doorstep, flanked by the village constable and a young woman in police uniform, was so shockingly unexpected that she was robbed of breath.

It was the policewoman who spoke first.

'Mrs Richards. I wonder if we could come in for a moment.'

Conscious of the curiosity of her neighbours, Claire hurriedly agreed. Her small sitting-room had never seemed more cramped. The local policeman, although not as tall as Jay Fraser, was still quite large. He was an older man, married with two grown-up sons, and he seemed pleasant. Now however, he looked worryingly grave, and Jay Fraser, who had refused her offer of a seat, looked almost ill. The tan she had noticed on his first visit now seemed a dirty yellow colour. His immaculate white shirt was unbuttoned at the throat, his tie askew, and his hair ruffled.

'Mrs Richards, I believe your little girl is very friendly with Mr Fraser's daughter.'

A terrible sense of foreboding overcame her.

'Yes, yes, she is,' she agreed in a husky voice. 'They're…they're best friends.'

All that she constantly dreaded for her own daughter suddenly filled her mind, and it was as though

Heather was actually her own child. She sank down into a chair, her body trembling.

'Something's happened to her, hasn't it?'

Sergeant Holmes grimaced slightly. 'We're hoping not, Mrs Richards. We do know, however, that she's disappeared. Mr Fraser's housekeeper reported it to us late last evening.'

'Late last evening?'

'Yes, after the little girl didn't come home from school.' The sergeant frowned, and looked across at Jay Fraser. 'It's probably none of my business, sir, but that's quite a lonely walk home for a six-year-old…'

'Mrs Roberts had strict instructions to take Heather to and from school,' Jay said tightly.

In that instant Claire felt for him, truly understanding how he must be feeling. No doubt he had given the housekeeper her instructions, never imagining that they would be disobeyed. More out of compassion for him than anything else Claire said huskily,

'I…I…used to walk home with her. I didn't like the thought of her walking alone. It wasn't far out of our way…'

Instantly the sergeant's frown disappeared, and he said eagerly, 'And did you walk back with her yesterday, Mrs Richards?'

'Why, yes. I always walked her to the gate and saw her safely inside. I…'

She heard the sound that Jay Fraser made and felt her own throat muscles lock in a mingling of pity and fear.

'Then you must have been the last person to see her.' The sergeant frowned. 'Mrs Roberts says that she didn't come home from school last night.'

And the woman had waited how long to report that she was missing? Inadvertently Claire looked across at Jay and saw the same emotions she was feeling reflected in his eyes.

'Mmm. I was wondering if we could talk to your little girl, Mrs Richards. Children sometimes confide things to their friends that they don't tell adults. We won't say anything to frighten her,' he added, correctly interpreting her expression.

'She and Heather were very close,' Claire admitted. She bit her lip and glanced apologetically at Jay. He wasn't looking at her. He was staring down at the carpet, his face set and hard.

'I don't know if it's important, but I know that Heather was...well, she didn't get on very well with Mrs Roberts.'

She caught Jay's roughly expelled breath, and hurried on. 'Of course it might not mean anything...and I'm not suggesting that Mrs Roberts was in any way unkind to her...but Heather is a very sensitive child.'

'And you think that perhaps she might have said something to upset the little girl? Children of that age get odd notions into their heads,' the sergeant agreed. 'I'll never forget when our boy decided to leave home. All of five he was, and luckily a neighbour found him pedalling down the road on his trike.'

'If Heather had walked off like that someone would have seen her,' interrupted Jay roughly. 'God—she's

only a baby...' His voice was full of anguish. 'She's
been gone all night...nearly twenty-four hours!'

Claire felt for him, but she suspected that the last
thing he would want would be her sympathy. He must
be in hell right now, she thought compassionately.
What parent wouldn't be?

'Have you informed her...her mother, sir?' Sergeant Holmes asked.

Jay shook his head. 'She wouldn't want to know.
I would have given her custody of Heather, but she
didn't want her.' His back straightened, his face suddenly bitterly angry, as he read the expression in the
policeman's eyes. 'I love my daughter very much,
Sergeant,' he told him curtly, 'but that doesn't stop
me thinking that a little girl of Heather's age needs
her mother. I can't be there all the time for her. God,
when I think I deliberately looked for an older woman
to look after her, thinking that she would be likely to
be more responsible! I have to be away a great deal—
there's nothing I can do about it, at least not at the
moment...'

'No one's blaming you, sir,' Sergeant Holmes said
quietly. 'All of us here are parents, and we all know
what kids are like. Half the time you just don't know
what's going through their heads.'

'If she was so frightened of Mrs Roberts, why
didn't she tell me? If anyone's touched her...hurt
her...'

He couldn't put his fears into words, and Claire felt
her body clench on a wave of nausea and pain. That
was the way *her* father would have looked if he'd

known…but he'd been dead then and she'd been alone… She sent up a mental prayer that somehow Heather would be safe. If she was, no matter what her father had to say about it Claire intended to give her as much love and attention as she wanted. She felt almost as much to blame as Jay. She had known that Heather was unhappy, but because of her pride and her determination not to give Jay the slightest cause to think she was trying to attract him, she had deliberately backed off.

'I normally go and collect Lucy from school about now,' she told the sergeant. 'Do you want to come with me, or shall I…?'

'It's best if you go alone; we don't want to frighten her. Try and act as naturally as possible with her, Mrs Richards. Children get some weird ideas in their heads. If she does know anything we don't want to frighten her into keeping it to herself.'

The sergeant's words made sense, but they were hard to put into practice. Claire could feel her voice turning croaky with anxiety as she casually asked if Heather was at school, already knowing what the answer would be.

Lucy shook her head. As Claire looked down at her she saw that her daughter was avoiding her eyes.

*Did* Lucy know something about Heather's disappearance? Striving to seem calm, she said, 'Oh dear, Heather's daddy's waiting for us at home. He thought Heather might be coming home with you.'

No reaction, but Claire felt the small hand tucked into hers clenching betrayingly.

She took Lucy into the kitchen and settled her with a glass of milk and a biscuit before going into her sitting-room.

'I think she knows something,' she told Sergeant Holmes worriedly.

'Will you let me talk to her?' he asked. 'I promise I won't frighten her.'

Knowing what was at stake Claire could hardly refuse. She took the two police officers into the kitchen and made sure that Lucy knew who they were before leaving her with them. She sensed that the sergeant was more likely to learn something if she was not hovering anxiously at his side.

As she opened the sitting-room door she saw that Jay Fraser had slumped down into one of her chairs, his head in his hands. He looked up as she walked in, and she saw the dread and the pain in his eyes.

'I pray to God that we can find her.'

Instinctively she placed her hand over his, shocked to feel its fierce tremble. 'I'm sure Lucy knows something...she looked so guilty. Perhaps Heather's...' she broke off, his eyes widening as she suddenly remembered Lucy's disappearance and the missing cakes.

'What is it?'

'I think Heather might have run away,' she said unsteadily. 'Last night Lucy disobeyed me and left the garden...I found some cakes missing, I...'

Before she could say any more the sitting-room door opened and Sergeant Holmes appeared, holding a tearful Lucy in his arms.

'I promised Heather I wouldn't tell Mummy...' her bottom lip wobbled. 'She wanted to come and live with us, but you said she couldn't and Mrs Roberts was very cross because she'd come here for her tea. Heather wanted her daddy, but he wasn't there...'

Oh, the anguish of that innocent double indictment! Over the tousled brown curls, grey eyes met green, both of them mirroring their guilt and anguish.

'It seems that Heather spent the night in one of the huts on the old allotments down by the railway,' Sergeant Holmes informed them. 'She made Lucy promise not to tell.'

'Mrs Roberts smacked her,' Lucy whimpered, 'she made her cry...'

'I was wondering, Mrs Richards—if WPC Ames here stays with Lucy, would you...'

Claire didn't even think of refusing. After hugging and kissing her daughter and reassuring her that no one was cross with her, she was half way out of the door as Jay opened it.

It was less than half a mile to the allotments, but none of them spoke. All of them must surely be thinking of the terrors that could be inflicted on a small girl of six on her own.

As they reached the allotments, the Sergeant suggested softly, 'I think you'd better be the one to go first, Mr Fraser. If she's still there, we don't want to frighten her.'

From the white look on Jay's face, Claire knew that nothing on earth would have prevented him from going first. Hands clenched, her body tense with dread, she waited as he walked towards the tumbledown hut.

He opened the door and went inside. Claire held her breath, all sensation suspended as she prayed harder than she had ever done in her life before. It was illogical to feel this depth of emotion for someone else's child, but she knew the horrors that could be inflicted on the innocent—oh, how she knew—and in that aeon of waiting there was an emotional bonding between her personal anguish and the fear she felt for Heather that coalesced in a wave of love so strong and intense that when Jay walked out of the hut, carrying his daughter in his arms, nothing on earth could have stopped her from stumbling across the distance that separated them to take the sobbing child in her arms.

Small arms clung to her, heaving sobs swelling the childish chest. Jay looked white and stunned—lost, almost.

'She was frightened of me!' Claire heard him say disbelievingly. 'She was frightened...'

'Let's get her home now,' Sergeant Holmes suggested, 'time for questions later.'

As Jay leaned forward to take her from Claire, Heather clung to her, and wept piteously. 'I want to go to Lucy's house, Daddy. I don't want to go home!'

Claire avoided looking at him. She could sense everything that he was feeling. If he had resented and disliked her before it must be nothing to what he was feeling now.

They took Heather back to the small cottage, a look

of relief and guilt mingling on Lucy's face as they walked in.

'I think we should leave her with Mrs Richards for a few minutes, sir,' Sergeant Holmes suggested to Jay.

Busy trying to soothe Heather's tears, Claire was absently aware of Jay stepping back from them and allowing the sergeant to take him into the kitchen.

It was a long time before Heather calmed down enough to be coherent, and the story she told left Claire shaking with rage and appalled by the enormity of what could have happened.

She took her upstairs and put her in the spare bed in Lucy's room, knowing from experience that such an outburst would soon result in sleep. She was emotionally and physically drained, poor little mite, and even in sleep she clung to Claire's hand, not wanting her to leave her.

She went down to the kitchen, where the sergeant was entertaining Lucy by reading her a story.

'She ran away because she was frightened of Mrs Roberts,' Claire told them tiredly. 'It's partly my fault.' She looked at Jay Fraser and saw that his face was shuttered and remote. Who knew what he was thinking behind that iron mask? 'She wanted to have tea with us the other day and I...I refused. I said she must ask Mrs Roberts' permission. The next day she said she had; I didn't check—I...' She couldn't look at Jay Fraser; surely he must know why she hadn't felt able to speak to his housekeeper. 'Apparently she hadn't asked at all, and after I took her home that evening Mrs Roberts was very angry with her—the poor woman must have been out of her mind with fear when she didn't turn up from school. Apparently she shut Heather up in her bedroom and told her she was going to tell her daddy what she had done. Mrs Roberts told Heather that her father would be very cross.' Claire bit her lip, wondering if she ought to suppress the next bit, and then, deciding that she could not, 'Apparently Mrs Roberts threatened to leave and told Heather that if she did, Heather would have to go into a home because neither her mummy nor her daddy wanted her.' She heard the sound Jay made and steeled herself against it. 'That's why she ran away. She was frightened.'

'I never knew!' It was agony listening to the torment in his driven voice. 'I trusted the woman. I thought she was reliable! I had no idea.'

'It happens to the best of us, sir,' said Sergeant Holmes gruffly. 'Try not to blame yourself. I've known Amy Roberts for years. I knew she didn't like kids, but I'd never have suspected...'

'I'll have to dismiss her, of course.' Claire felt that he was talking more to himself than to them. He looked directly at her for the first time and she was shocked by his haggard expression.

'Could you...would you let her stay here tonight? I'll...'

'I'll leave the two of you now, sir. No need for us to stay any longer...'

Tactfully the sergeant and his colleague left. Lucy was sitting down in front of the television in the sit-

ting-room when Claire peeped in to check that she
was all right.

She went into the kitchen. Jay Fraser was standing
by the window, his arms rigid against the rim of the
sink. He looked up at the entrance and stepped back
from the unit, his movements jerky and uncoordinated. He walked like a man who had had too
much to drink, and suddenly he swayed, his face
tinged with a frightening pallor.

'The bathroom,' he muttered thickly.

Numbly Claire told him, trying to blot out of her
mind the sound of him being violently sick. Shock
affected people in many different ways, and she could
almost feel the bitter combination of pain and anguish
that made up his.

When he came back down he moved like an old,
old man. Leaning against the kitchen door, he said
slowly, 'I owe you an apology.' He shuddered suddenly. 'God, when I think of what could have happened to her...I had no idea how she felt, no idea at
all.'

She could hear and see the anguish of a parent
suddenly realising how it had failed its child. Ridiculously, she wanted to comfort him, but what could
she say?

'You did your best. It can't be easy...'

'No, I didn't do my best,' he said savagely. 'If I'd
done my best she'd have a proper mother.' His eyes
suddenly focused on her and darkened. 'Someone like
you. Have you any idea what it does to me to know
that you know more about her feelings and her fears

than I do…? That you cared enough to make sure she got home from school safely, while I…'

'You didn't know. You couldn't know. In your shoes I'd have opted for an older woman.'

'I should have known there was something wrong. Hell, I *did* know,' he said savagely. 'She never stopped talking about you, but I wouldn't listen. It's been one hell of a bad year for me,' he added slowly. 'The divorce became final eighteen months ago. I suppose you've heard the story: the neglected wife leaving; having an affair with her husband's business partner right under his nose. Susie never wanted children. She wanted to abort when she discovered she was pregnant…'

He was telling her things he'd normally never dream of telling anyone, Claire sensed; his defences were relaxed by shock and fear. He needed the release of talking, even if he barely realised who he was talking to. She wasn't a person to him right now, she was just a presence…someone to listen.

'She never cared for Heather, and Heather seemed to sense it. I was glad when she said she didn't want her. She's my child and I love her,' he said fiercely as though she had voiced a doubt. 'But after my experience with Susie I swore I'd never marry again; never allow another woman to entangle me in that sort of emotional mess. It isn't that easy, though. Human beings have certain needs.' He wasn't aware of how Claire froze. 'And I soon discovered there are plenty of women willing to share a man's bed, especially when they think he's vulnerable. I've lost count of the number of women who've told me that Heather needs a mother.'

He knew who she was now, Claire recognised, catching his oblique glance.

'I misjudged you and I'm sorry for it, but I'd just spent a fortnight in the States, trying to fend off half a dozen or so attempts at matchmaking from the wives of my business colleagues. Heather might need a mother, but I don't want a second wife.' He pushed one hand through his hair. 'What the hell am I going to do?'

What could she say? 'I don't know.'

'Neither do I,' he said grimly.

She heard him sigh as he levered his shoulders off the door. Even now, exhausted with anxiety and tension, there was a magnetic attraction about him that she recognised and recoiled from. She saw him frown as she stepped back.

'Look, I really am sorry about what I said to you. There was no call for it. Put it down to tiredness and the frustration of having to fend off my friends' matchmaking efforts. To have you repeat what they had been saying to me—that Heather needed a mother—'

'Made you leap to the instant conclusion that I had myself in mind,' said Claire wryly. 'Yes, I can understand that, but you were quite wrong. A husband is the last thing I'd want.'

She saw him frown. 'My remark was crass and uncalled for.'

A silence stretched between them, but it wasn't an

uncomfortable silence. In fact, it was oddly companionable.

'I'll come and see Heather later, if I may. Will it be all right if she stays here with you?'

She could see how much he hated having to ask, and that was something else she could understand from her own experience of single parenthood. It bred in one a fierce pride, a determination to manage alone without having to ask for help—but help was sometimes needed, and it wasn't in her nature to be anything less than generous. Pushing the heavy weight of her hair off her face, she said firmly, 'Heather can stay here as long as she wants to. I'm genuinely very fond of her, you know,' she paused, searching for the right words, 'she's so vulnerable…and…and wanting. Nothing like my independent little Lucy.'

'Perhaps because she hasn't experienced the same security and love.' Jay's voice was clipped, his eyes edged with bitterness. 'I've got to go back now. I want to have a few words with Mrs Roberts. I can't blame it all on her, though; *I* should have known. But she seemed so responsible. She had such good references!'

'As a housekeeper, perhaps,' said Claire gently, sensing his frustration and guilt. 'But a woman who's a good housekeeper isn't always a good…'

'Mother? No,' he said bitterly. 'I can see that— now. I'll just go up and see Heather before I leave.'

He sounded uncertain and awkward, and Claire didn't go with him. Some things were too private to be witnessed by anyone else.

'She's still asleep,' he told her when he came down. 'I'll come back later.' Claire walked with him to the front door. As she opened it he turned to face her.

'I haven't thanked you,' he said huskily.

'There's nothing to thank me for.'

And she didn't feel there was. If she hadn't been there perhaps Heather might never have thought of running away. She hadn't meant to encourage the little girl to love her, but how much damage had she inadvertently done?

# CHAPTER THREE

BOTH GIRLS HAD had their supper and were bathed
and pyjamaed when Jay Fraser came back. They were
sharing Lucy's room, but Claire took her own daughter downstairs so that Jay and Heather could be alone.

She had barely been downstairs with Lucy for more
than ten minutes when Jay Fraser's dark head suddenly appeared round her sitting-room door. He
looked unexpectedly vulnerable for such a very hard-
edged man, his mouth set in a grimly despondent line.

'Can you come?' he asked quietly. 'Heather seems
to have cast me in the role of angry parent; I can't
get it through to her that she isn't going to be pun-
ished.'

Claire had always been acutely sensitive to the feelings of others and it was for that reason that she kept
her attention fixed on a point to the left of his shoulder rather than on his face. She didn't need a crystal
ball to know that he was finding it very hard to ask
for her help.

When she got upstairs Heather was curled up in a
small ball, crying. The moment she saw Claire she
flung herself into her arms, cuddling up against her.
Over her dark head Claire looked at the grimly set

face of her father. Strange to think that less than a
month ago she had viewed a second meeting with this
man with both apprehension and dread. Now she was
seeing him stripped of his masculine arrogance, a human being with fears and doubts, and ridiculously she
wanted to reassure him that everything would be all
right, and that Heather would eventually come round.

Instead, she stroked her soft dark hair, and said
quietly, 'It's all right, Heather, your daddy isn't cross
with you. He was very worried about you, we all
were.'

'Mrs Roberts said he would lock me in my bedroom without anything to eat.'

The harsh exclamation smothered in his throat
drew Claire's eyes back to Jay's face. She wasn't enjoying witnessing his suffering.

'Mrs Roberts is gone now. Your daddy is going to
find someone else to look after you…when you go
home.'

'I don't want to go home!' Although they were
muffled against her breast Heather's words were quite
clear, her voice shrill with a mixture of fear and stub-
bornness. 'I want to stay here with you. I want you
to be my mummy.'

Claire didn't dare look at the tense figure standing
by the door. What on earth was he thinking?

Swallowing the lump in her throat she said huskily,
'Heather, you know that I love you very much, but
I'm not your mummy…'

'But I want you to be.' Tears weren't very far

away, and Claire gnawed tensely at her bottom lip. What on earth could she say?

The bedroom door opened and Lucy came in, frowning. 'What are you doing up here?' she demanded. Her question was directed at Claire, but she was looking at Jay with a mixture of assessment and fascination in her eyes. To Claire's amazement she went up to him, tilting her head back so that she could look at him. For a little girl who had had virtually nothing to do with the male sex, she was amazingly at ease with him.

'Can Heather stay here with me?' she asked him. 'My mummy could look after her, and we could play together...'

Across the room green eyes met grey. 'Lucy, I think it's time that you and Heather were both in bed.'

Claire had a suggestion to make, but she wasn't going to say anything in front of the girls, just in case Jay Fraser rejected it. She wasn't going to be accused of putting him in a position where he couldn't do so.

She tucked Heather up in bed, and bent down to kiss her. Lucy climbed into the other single bed, and after she too had received her goodnight kiss she looked across at Jay and demanded, 'Aren't you going to kiss us too?'

Claire hid a small smile at the expression in his eyes, but he acceded to Lucy's request easily enough, kissing her first and then Heather, who shrank away from him slightly.

Downstairs in the sitting-room she offered him coffee, but he shook his head.

'More stimulation is the last thing I need right now. I've got a feeling it's going to be hard enough to get to sleep as it is, and in less than forty-eight hours I've got to fly back to the States. I'm more in need of a stiff whisky than caffeine.'

'I'm sorry, I don't have any.' Claire apologised, but he shook his head again.

'I couldn't drink it anyway, I'm driving.'

She wished that he would sit down; he made her feel nervous standing over her like that. It gave her an unpleasant sensation in the pit of her stomach to be alone with him. She always felt like that with men, no matter how harmless they might be. As he moved restlessly she stepped back from him, biting her lip as she saw his frown.

'I didn't want to say anything when the girls could overhear us, but...if it would help I could have Heather until you find someone to take charge of her.'

Complete silence followed her offer, and Claire felt the colour crawling over her skin. Surely he didn't still think she had an ulterior motive for making the offer? She risked a look at him, but could read nothing in the slate-grey eyes and hard mouth.

'Look, I assure you that I don't want...a husband...if that's what you're thinking...' She could have cried at her own gaucheness. What on earth must he be thinking? She told herself it didn't matter and that Heather was the prime concern here.

If Jay Fraser had been a woman there wouldn't have been the slightest degree of awkwardness in her making the suggestion, but with his remarks about a second marriage and involvement very much to the forefront of her mind, Lucy hoped that he wouldn't misconstrue her offer.

The silence stretched from seconds into minutes, while her heartbeat picked up to an almost unbearable speed. What on earth was he thinking? Why didn't he say something, even if it was only a refusal?

When he did speak he sounded very abrupt. 'You make me feel very ashamed of myself,' he told her. 'You're being far more generous than I deserve. Almost every other woman I know would have enjoyed making me eat humble pie and beg for the help you've just offered. It's an art at which my ex-wife was an expert.'

'Do you...do you still love her?'

Claire felt her face flame with embarrassment. What on earth had got into her? She looked away from him, and said indistinctly, 'I'm sorry, that was unforgivable.'

'It's all right. You aren't the first to ask. No, I don't still love her. I don't think any man can love a woman who rejects his child. To be honest with you, I no longer believe that passionate love exists. Sexual desire, yes, and non-sexual love of the kind I feel for Heather. And you...do you still love Lucy's father...?'

She went white and stepped back from him, her eyes huge with pain. It was a natural enough question and he couldn't know how she felt about the man who had fathered Lucy, nor could she tell him. She couldn't tell anyone.

'I...'

'Forget it, I shouldn't have asked. I take it there's no chance of the two of you getting back together.'

He had obviously completely misread her reaction, and like someone in a dream Claire said thickly, 'I...he's dead...'

'Oh, I see. I'm sorry.'

'It...it was a long time ago. Before...before Lucy was born.' She was lying. She had no idea whether Lucy's father was alive or dead, or where he was. Or even who he was, a small voice reminded her, but she shuddered with the onset of familiar pain and loathing, forcing her mind to shift from the past to the present, before her memories could overwhelm her. 'About Heather?' she added.

'If she can stay with you for the time being I'd be more than grateful. I'm going to have to get someone to replace Mrs Roberts, of course.'

'There's no need to rush. I'm very fond of Heather.'

'Yes, I can see that.'

'There's something about her that reaches out to me. A need that Lucy doesn't have, a loneliness.' Claire broke off, suddenly conscious of what she was saying.

'Yes, she is lonely,' he agreed bitterly. 'Susie was never much of a mother to her. She never wanted her at all...' He too broke off, and Claire sensed that his marriage and his daughter were normally two subjects that he did not discuss with anyone.

It seemed that a strange bond had been formed between them, a bond that at the moment was very tenuous and fragile, and which instinctively Claire feared. She knew that sexually she had nothing to fear from him. A man like Jay Fraser did not need to force himself on a woman.

She watched him as he got up, aware of the way his shirt clung to his shoulder and tapered down to his waist. He was a very masculine man, and the knowledge made her shiver with distaste as she instinctively averted her eyes from his equally masculine stance.

'While Heather is living with you, you must let me make some contribution to your household budget,' he said.

'No.' Her refusal was immediate and firm. 'No, I can't let you do that.'

He frowned and Claire knew that he was a man who did not like to be beholden to others in any way at all.

'If you won't accept money from me, I'll have to find a way of repaying you in kind,' he said at last. He glanced at his watch. 'I'd better go; I'm expecting a call from the States. I'll come round and see Heather tomorrow, if I may?'

Claire saw him to the door, watching as he slid his lean length behind the wheel of his car—a long, lowslung Jaguar sports car. He gave her a brief nod as he fastened his seat belt, and she went inside and closed the door. She was tired now and very drained, but too on edge to sleep. If anything had happened to Heather... It was almost as though the little girl was her own child. She mustn't get too attached to her or, more importantly, allow Heather to get too attached to her. No, she must gradually reassure her that her father both loved and wanted her; she must instill in her enough self-confidence for her to go back to her father happily and gladly.

When Jay called the following day, she deliberately left father and daughter alone together, but it was Lucy who chatted away to him, demanding that he play, while Heather clung anxiously to her side.

'I was going to suggest that if you could let me know when you're likely to be home I could arrange to bring Heather back to you for those weekends?'

'You think you can manage that, do you?' he asked sardonically, 'It seems to me that I'm featuring very much as the cruel father at the moment.'

'Only because of what Mrs Roberts has been feeding her. She's been using you as a threat to frighten her. She'll get over it. She does love you, Jay.'

It was the first time she had used his name directly, and she wondered what had caused his eyes to change form light to dark grey like that.

'I'll ring you from the States before I come back.'

It was Lucy who ran up to him for a goodbye kiss, and Heather who had to be gently pushed. Claire's tender heart ached for him, for, despite his controlled smile, she knew that inside he was hurt.

Two MONTHS SLIPPED BY without Jay being able to find a suitable replacement for Mrs Roberts, and during that time Heather blossomed. She was always going to be a more vulnerable child than her own daughter, Claire thought, but now she looked forward to her father's return, running to him eagerly, and Claire hoped that she had banished the spectre of Mrs Roberts' threats.

October was a cold, wet month with high winds that disturbed the shaky tiles on her roof. Several came crashing down one night as she lay in bed, and she wondered how on earth she was going to pay for them to be replaced.

Jay was due home on Friday. She must remember to go up to Whitegates and turn on the central heating; he had given her a key to the house several weeks ago, but she was scrupulous about using it only when she had to. She had fallen into the habit of checking on the contents of his fridge when she knew he was due back, but she had never ventured further than the kitchen when he was not there, nor did she linger when she delivered Heather to him, despite his suggestions that she and Lucy stay and have a meal.

He didn't make her feel nervous as other men did; she wasn't frightened of him, and she didn't know really why she was so anxious to remove herself from his vicinity. Perhaps it had something to do with their very first meeting and her determination that he would never be able to accuse her of running after him. It was, after all, the last thing she was likely to do! Her mind might be able to accept that he was a very attractive and masculine man, a man with an uncommon degree of sex appeal combined with that aura of power that women find so sexually stimulating, but she wasn't *like* other women; his sexuality made her cringe. She found conversation with him stimulating and interesting, but only if she could manage to blot out his masculinity. She was glad that he wasn't the sort of man who liked to touch. She didn't think she could have endured that.

Mrs Vickers was opening her gate just as Claire went past with the girls on the way to school.

'Gales forecast for tonight,' she warned Claire. 'Hope our roofs will stand up to it.'

Claire did too. When she got back from school she saw that the row of elms on the opposite side of the road were swaying fiercely in the strong wind. All the leaves were gone now, and the branches looked starkly bleak. Winter would be early this year.

She spent the morning baking, more for the therapeutic properties of the task than for any real need to provide the girls and herself with sustenance. When she collected them from school, they went first back to the cottage, where Heather sniffed the warm scented kitchen aroma eagerly.

'Have you made an apple pie?' she asked Claire, surveying the fruits of the afternoon's labours enthusiastically.

She had, using the apples from their own tree.

'It's Daddy's favourite. Perhaps we could take him some?'

On the face of it there was no real reason why they should not; Claire always made something extra when she baked which she normally took round to Mrs Vickers; the three of them on their own would certainly not get through everything she had made—but even so, she hesitated, knowing all too well the construction that Jay could place on her gift of food. However, she knew equally that it was not something she could explain to his six-year-old daughter.

Hating to wipe the happy look of pleasure from Heather's face, she suggested instead,

'Perhaps next time. I made this one for Mrs Vickers. It's *her* favourite too,' childishly she crossed her fingers behind her back as she mouthed the small fib, 'and you can help me make it,' she told Heather. 'I'm sure your daddy would like that.'

'I'll help too,' Lucy chimed in. 'I could make him some of my gingerbread men.'

Claire stifled a grin at the thought of Jay's expression should he be presented with these tokens of her daughter's regard. She knew enough about him to know that he would eat the proffered gift whether he wanted it or not, but as yet Lucy's enthusiasm for the task of baking far outweighed her skill.

An hour later, both girls raincoated and wellingtoned against the heavy rain that had started to fall, they set out for Whitegates.

As Claire opened the front door, the wind shipped it from her fingers, shrieking malevolently and making her gasp for breath. Both little girls clung firmly to her hands as they hurried down the deserted village street. Luckily the wind was behind them, otherwise Claire wasn't sure how they would have managed to walk. It had increased tremendously in velocity since she had fetched them home from school, and the heavy, rain-sodden clouds darkening the sky promised a very unpleasant night. Already there was evidence of the storm's havoc in the branches that had fallen from some of the trees, reminding Claire that she would have to find someone to prune her own fruit trees.

Icy flurries of rain stung their faces; the girls' hooded coats kept them fairly dry, but Claire's raincoat had no hood, and one look at the weather had convinced her of the folly of trying to use her umbrella. She could feel the rain soaking into her hair, releasing its errant curl, and the walk down the country lane to Whitegates, which was normally such a pleasure, had become more of an ordeal.

The house was warm, thanks to Claire's foresight in turning on the central heating when she had called earlier with the shopping. She made both girls strip off their wellingtons and coats in the kitchen, hanging them up to dry.

Jay's flight should have landed by now, but the bad weather might have delayed it. She glanced at her watch and frowned. It was barely five o'clock, but already it was very dark outside.

Having checked that both girls had put on their slippers, she agreed that they could go into the sitting-room to watch television.

Despite the expensive furnishings, the house always struck Claire as being very unwelcoming. She had always been very sensitive to atmosphere, and it sometimes seemed to her that the house was rejecting its inhabitants in the same way that a child will reject those it senses do not give it love.

The kitchen was fitted with every electrical device known to man, or so it seemed; the units were undoubtedly very expensive and stylish, but Claire found the white and grey décor of the room distinctly chilling. It was not a kitchen she could ever imagine herself enjoying working in. It was too glossy and sterile, looking more like something out of a magazine advertisement than part of a home. She always felt faintly uncomfortable in it, afraid almost of leaving so much as a fingermark on the brilliant worktops.

What she had seen of the rest of the house was the same: sterile and cold. She often wondered who had chosen the décor, Jay or his wife. It seemed inconceivable that any woman with a small child would opt for off-white carpet and white leather furniture, but then neither could she see Jay choosing the thick white goatskin rugs in the drawing room.

White was the colour of purity; it was also the colour of snow, and that was how Claire perceived the house's décor, cold and frigid, unwelcoming, and unliveable-in.

She turned on the oven and took out of the fridge the casserole she had brought with her earlier in the day. She didn't normally prepare a meal for Jay, but tonight was an exception; no doubt he would be feeling both cold and tired when he did arrive.

Both she and the girls had eaten at the cottage. She didn't like the thought of them spilling anything on that sterile white marble kitchen table, or those immaculate grey tiles that covered the floor.

Jay had managed to find an agency who had agreed to take over the cleaning of the house, but as yet he had found no one who could care for his daughter. Secretly Claire was glad, and she knew that when the time eventually came she would miss Heather very much indeed. Lucy, with her sunny practical nature, was not the slightest bit jealous or resentful about sharing her mother with her friend.

As she moved automatically about the kitchen she frowned, wondering what the future held for Heather: a succession of nannies, perhaps, followed by boarding school? There were doubtless many children for whom such a regime would lead to a perfectly happy and well adjusted adult life, but Heather was so sensitive and withdrawn already. It was none of her business what arrangements Jay might choose to make for his daughter, Claire reminded herself firmly, but no amount of logic or reason could cancel out the bond of love that had built up between Heather and herself. When she lost her, it would in some ways be like losing her own child. Ridiculously, especially in the circumstances, she was already worrying about whether someone else would know how much care and cherishing the little girl needed. And that wasn't her only concern. She was also worried that Heather would see her withdrawal from her life in the manner of a betrayal, or worse, and although she had scrupulously tried to prepare her for their eventual parting, she sensed that Heather was too young to genuinely comprehend what lay ahead.

It was gone seven o'clock when Claire eventually heard Jay's car draw up outside.

Lucy came dashing into the kitchen almost before the engine had died.

'Jay's back!' she called out excitedly, pouting a little when Claire grasped her firmly by one arm and reminded her,

'Jay is *Heather's* daddy, Lucy.'

But for all her encouragement, Heather made no attempt to rush to the door and give Jay the exuberant welcome Lucy always favoured him with.

Claire saw the moment that the kitchen door opened that he was tired. He dumped his overnight case by the door and grimaced faintly across the kitchen.

'Sorry I'm late, but the plane was delayed.'

'Yes, we thought it might be.' She gave Heather a little push towards her father, releasing a faintly tense breath as the little girl gave him a slightly shy hug.

Lucy had no such inhibitions, flinging herself against his knees and lifting up a shining little face for his kiss.

With one little girl in his arms and the other clinging to his side, he still managed to retain the aura of the male predator rather than that of domesticity.

His hair had grown, Claire noticed idly, and he seemed to have lost a little more weight. It was stupid and totally unnecessary for her to worry about him;

if he knew, he was more likely to be irritated by her concern than anything else.

'Something smells good.'

'It's a casserole. I thought you might be hungry.'

'I am. Have I got time to shower and change?'

Claire nodded her head.

'Good. How about someone bringing me a drink?' he suggested, putting Heather down and smiling at her.

'I'll do it,' Lucy piped up instantly, and Claire suppressed a faint sigh.

'Why don't both of you do it?' suggested Jay diplomatically. 'I shan't be long,' he promised Claire. 'About ten minutes.'

Of course she was the one who poured out the whisky and soda she knew he liked, warning Heather to be careful as she carried it upstairs. She knew which was Jay's room, but she had never been inside it; there was no need. And yet as she stood at the bottom of the stairs watching her charges' careful progress she had an instant's appalling awareness of Jay's lean body as he divested it of the civilisation of clothes.

She shuddered tensely, closing her eyes to blot out the image, and when she opened them again she was trembling violently. She had never seen a naked man, not really, and she had never wanted to, so why that brief, illuminating image?

Jay was as good as his word, returning downstairs within ten minutes, dressed in jeans and a checked wool shirt. His hair was still damp, and the clean male

scent of his soap mingled with the aroma of the casserole, cutting sharply through the domestic atmosphere of the kitchen, bringing in an alien and pred-
atory note that made Claire's body tense as she
moved automatically away from him.

She saw him frown, his mouth tightening as though
in some way her reaction displeased him.

'You should know by now that I'm not going to
pounce on you, Claire.'

Her face flushed. 'I know that.'

'Then why the so-obvious retreat?'

'Perhaps I'm just one of those people who likes a
lot of personal space.'

'Maybe, but you must have allowed it to be invaded at one time,' he retorted, glancing meaningfully
at Lucy, just in case she should be unaware of what
he was saying.

Claire gnawed nervously at her bottom lip, wondering what on earth she could say, but to her surprise, Jay made a sound of wry self-disgust and apologised quietly,

'I'm sorry. It's been a hell of a fortnight, and the
delay in landing didn't help matters. That doesn't excuse me taking my frustrations out on you, I know.
It's good to come home and find you here, Claire,'
he added slowly, totally confounding her.

'I...we really ought to be leaving.' She placed his
meal in front of him, avoiding his eyes. 'It's getting
late...'

'You're not walking back on a night like this. I'll
run you there after I've eaten.'

To drag him out again on a night like tonight, when he was plainly so tired, was the last thing Claire wanted, but she sensed that to argue would only harden his determination.

'I'll make you some coffee,' she suggested instead.

'You know, delicious though this is, it's a little bit off-putting to eat it all alone. Next time, why don't we all eat together?'

Taken thoroughly off guard by his statement, Claire stared at him. She had scrupulously avoided doing anything that might even hint at any degree of intimacy between them, and for him to suggest that they all ate together, almost as though they were a family unit...

To save herself from pursuing her thoughts any further she said quickly, 'I don't like letting the girls eat in here. Everything's so spotless,' she told him, seeing his uncomprehending frown. 'I'm always afraid they'll make a mess.'

She saw his attention focus on the kitchen and sweep round it, as though he were seeing it properly for the first time.

'Susie was responsible for all the decorating and the furniture.'

'It's very sophisticated and luxurious,' Claire hurried to say, hating the thought of him thinking she was criticising his ex-wife, 'but...'

'But it's also sterile and clinical,' he supplied for her in a clipped voice, surprising her with his perception. 'Unlike your cottage, it isn't a home, is it?'

She bit her lip, unable to look at him.

'It's the woman who makes a place a home, not the furnishings...'

He pushed his plate away suddenly, and Claire wondered if he was thinking of his ex-wife. Despite his claim that he no longer loved her, did he perhaps miss her more than he allowed anyone to know?

It was just gone eight o'clock when Jay drove away from Whitegates. The two girls were in the back of the car, Claire sitting in the front next to him.

She thought as they drove down the village street that there seemed to be a good deal more activity than was usual, but it was only when they turned the corner that Claire saw why, and then all she could do was to sit motionless in shock and stare out of the car window.

One of the huge elms had lost a heavy main branch during the storm. It had crashed across the road and smashed down on the house opposite—her house, Claire acknowledged in shocked comprehension. She couldn't speak; she couldn't do anything but lift appalled eyes to Jay's grim face. Why was he looking like that? An expression of shocked disbelief in his eyes that was surely far too intense, bearing in mind the very casual nature of their acquaintanceship. And then it hit her—Heather could have been in there with Lucy and herself; Heather could have been asleep in that front bedroom where she could now see a gaping hole in the wall.

'I...' Hardly aware of what she was doing, Claire struggled to open the car door. A crowd of people were standing outside the house staring up at it.

'You stay here.' Jay's hand on her arm held her rigid in her seat, his voice unusually harsh. 'I'll deal with it. You look after the girls.'

She wanted to protest that it wasn't his problem, that somehow she would cope alone as she had coped with so many other things, but she wasn't given the opportunity to say anything. He was out of the car and shouldering his way through the massed crowd before she could open her mouth.

He was only gone for ten minutes. Claire could see him in conversation with another man. Both of them glanced up at the house from time to time as they spoke.

Slowly the reality of what had happened was seeping into her. That was *her* home with the gaping holes in the roof and front wall where the heavy branch had crashed through. Her house...her home... She started to shake with shock; silly, really unimportant things, such as the fact that she had only just done the ironing and everything would now need washing again, preventing her from taking in the full enormity of what had happened.

It took Lucy's anxious, 'Mummy...where are we going to live?' to alert her to it and then she could think of no answer to give her daughter. Her thoughts ran round and round in frantic circles as she tried to grapple with the shock of what had happened. Perhaps Mrs Vickers would put them up. Thank God they hadn't been inside when the branch had fallen...

Jay came back and slid into the car beside her.

Claire struggled with her seat belt.

'I must go and ask Mrs Vickers if we can stay the
night with her. I...I must go inside and find our
clothes, I...'

'For God's sake, you're not going anywhere. The
house is unsafe!' Jay told her grimly, his voice so
angry that she actually focused her eyes on him, unaware of how vulnerable and young she looked in her
jeans and sweater, her hair curling wildly round her
small face.

'I've just been talking to someone from the council.
He says the house is unsafe. You can't go back inside.'

'But our clothes. My...'

'Damn your clothes!'

She hadn't heard him swear before, and the violence in this voice shocked her. In the darkness of the
car her eyes widened, her body shaking suddenly with
the drenching onset of reality.

'You're coming back with me,' Jay told her flatly.
'There's plenty of room at Whitegates.'

'Mrs Vickers...'

'For God's sake, Claire!' he exploded tensely.
'Why are you always so damned independent? You
hate me doing the slightest thing for you. You didn't
even want me to run you home tonight, did you? Did
you?'

How could she explain to him that she hated being
reliant on anyone? Suddenly it all seemed too much;
she could feel the tremors of reaction building up inside her. She wanted to cry, but she couldn't let herself, not in front of Jay and the girls.

'You've done me enough favours,' he reminded her grimly. 'Surely I'm allowed to do you one small one in return? You and Lucy will stay at Whitegates tonight, and every night until your own home has been repaired.'

'That could take weeks,' protested Claire, her eyes darkening bleakly as she looked back at her small house.

'The council are going to put some men in to make sure it's safe; when they have we can come back down and collect your things. You realise that the council won't pay for the repairs, don't you—even though the tree is on council-owned land?'

She hadn't thought that far ahead yet, and she looked at him blankly. Her mind seemed to be working very slowly.

'But surely my own insurance…'

For some reason Jay's mouth compressed grimly.

'Maybe,' he agreed at last, 'but most insurance companies class something like this as an "Act of God".'

When he saw that she was looking uncomprehendingly at him, he explained tersely,

'It isn't one of the risks they cover—they won't pay out under the policy. You'll have to find the money for the repairs yourself.'

Claire had too much pride to let him see what she was feeling. She turned her face away, so that he wouldn't see her shock. If the insurance company wouldn't pay out, what on earth was she going to do? How could she possibly afford to pay for the restoration work herself? A terrible, icy sense of fear engulfed her. A vision of the cramped council flat she and Lucy had lived in before they moved to the cottage rose up in front of her and wouldn't go away. She couldn't go back to that, not now that she had had a taste of the pleasure that life could be in attractive surroundings. Fate couldn't be so cruel, surely?

Jay had set the car in motion, but she was barely aware of it. If only tomorrow wasn't a Saturday. It would be Monday before she could get in touch with the insurance company, before she would know where she stood. Surely Jay was wrong? The house must be covered for this kind of accidental damage.

Round and round her thoughts went in a feverish dance that took her no further forward and did nothing to alleviate the horrendous sense of oppression hanging over her.

# CHAPTER FOUR

'I EXPECT YOU'LL WANT TO go down to the village and look at the cottage. I'll run you down there if you like.'

All four of them were having breakfast in the grey and white kitchen, which now looked lamentably untidy.

Claire had barely slept at all last night and breakfast was the very last thing she had wanted, but nothing seemed to impair Lucy's appetite, and she owed it to Jay to at least make some attempt to repay his hospitality. And anyway, it helped to keep busy.

'There's no need. I don't mind walking.'

'No, I'm sure you don't,' Jay's voice was dry, 'but you're going to want to collect some clothes for yourself and Lucy, and you can hardly carry them back with you.'

She wanted to protest that there was no need for him to involve himself in her affairs in this way, but the words stuck in her throat. She still couldn't totally comprehend what had happened. Last night in the bustle of making up beds for herself and Lucy, and getting both girls settled for the night, there hadn't been time to dwell on what had happened. Later, alone in bed, in the austere off-white bedroom Jay had suggested she use, there had been too much time, too many worries crowding into her mind for her to be able to sort things out into any sort of order.

As she sipped her coffee she stared out of the kitchen window. The sky was a perfect pale blue, the sun palely gold; last night's gale had died out and it was hard to look at the beautiful perfection of the crisp autumn day outside and remember what last night had been. Part of her stubbornly wanted to pretend that it hadn't happened at all.

'Mummy, can we go and play outside?'

Nothing seemed to daunt Lucy. This morning her daughter was her normal cheerful self, but Lucy didn't realise, as she did, exactly what effect that falling branch was likely to have on her life. Every time she thought about the future she could feel the panicky, helpless feeling swirl through her. She put down her coffee, knowing that her hand was trembling.

'Yes, yes, but put your wellingtons on, and no going outside the garden.'

Her response was automatic, her eyes barely even focusing on the two small jean-clad figures as they opened the back door.

As soon as they had gone she stood up. The intimacy of the kitchen with only Jay and herself in it made her feel uncomfortable. 'I...'

'Sit down.'

His voice was harsh, and she obeyed it automatically, looking at him with shocked, bewildered eyes as he poured her a fresh cup of coffee and brought it over to her.

'You've had a bad shock,' he told her curtly, 'and you're feeling the effects of it. It happens to all of us at times.'

'I'm all right.' Her lips pressed tightly together, panic surging through her at the thought that he was aware of her weakness.

'For God's sake, what is it about you that won't allow you to turn to anyone for help? Independence is fine, Claire, but there is such a thing as taking it to extremes, or is it just *me?* Is it the thought of *me* helping you that makes you react like this?'

'I...' Her throat seemed to have seized up. She swallowed and managed to say painfully, 'I don't like being beholden to anyone.'

'I don't believe I'm hearing this! Beholden? It's positively Biblical! I'm the one who's *beholden* to you, Claire, not the other way round. When I brought you back here last night, I felt as thought I were dragging you here against your will; every time I come within arm's length of you, you cringe away as though you think I'm about to commit rape!'

He stopped when he saw her face. Coming on top of everything else it was too much. She started to shake so violently that she spilled her coffee.

'What is it? What did I say?'

Jay took the cup from her, careful not to get too close to her, but she was barely aware of him.

'Claire, what is it? Surely you don't think I'd hurt you in some way, do you?'

She shook her head.

'Then what is it?' He frowned. 'Lucy's father?' His eyes narrowed. 'Is it your husband, did he…'

She felt the bubble of hysterical laughter well up inside her like a painful lump.

'There was no husband… I was never married… Lucy… I was raped on my way home from school when I was eighteen. My parents had just died… I was still living in the house. I never saw his face; he came up behind me and knocked me out. When I came round I was in his car. I tried to stop him, but he…' She shuddered tensely, trying to stop the memories coming back. 'Afterwards he pushed me out of the car and drove off…'

'Oh my God! The police?'

'I never told them. I couldn't tell anyone. Only the doctor when I realised I was pregnant…'

'I would never have guessed. You love Lucy so much.'

'I didn't know if I would, not until she was born. But it wasn't her fault.'

'And that's why you don't want a husband, is it, Claire—because of what happened?'

'I don't like men coming anywhere near me. I don't want any sort of intimate relationship with them. I can't explain it, I…' Claire shook her head, trying to dispel her disturbing memories.

'You don't need to,' Jay told her curtly. 'I'm not totally devoid of imagination.'

'I don't think I can bear it if I lose the cottage. Before we came here Lucy and I had a council flat…'

She shuddered again, suddenly feeling intensely cold. What on earth had prompted her to break down like that? She had never, ever confided to anyone other than her doctor the true circumstances surrounding Lucy's conception. She had never wanted to tell anyone before. The events of that night were something she thought she had locked safely away.

It was the shock of what had happened to the cottage, of course; but that didn't mitigate her sense of self-betrayal.

'I shouldn't have told you,' she muttered, trying to stand up. 'I...'

'You hate revealing anything of yourself to others, don't you, Claire? Well, I can sympathise with that.' Jay stood up too, reaching out to steady her as she trembled. 'It's a fault I think I share, but I had hoped that you and I were becoming friends. Friends trust one another; I want you to feel that you can trust me. You think that what you've just told me makes you vulnerable to me,' he added, watching the give-away expression on her face. 'But I've been equally vulnerable to you—more so, possibly, and your strength and kindness when Heather was missing are something I will never forget, and never be able to repay,' he added quietly. 'Now go upstairs and get your coat, and then we'll drive down to the village and see what the situation is with the cottage. Oh, and Claire,' he added, as she headed for the door, 'I want you to know that you and Lucy can stay here for just as long as it takes to get things sorted out, and before you say a word, it won't be all one-sided. While you're living here, I'm getting a housekeeper and a nanny for Heather all rolled into one.'

She couldn't dispute the truth of what he said, but his other comment—that they could be friends, that they were equally vulnerable to one another—how true were they?

As she went upstairs she felt curiously empty, as though by telling him about Lucy she had somehow lost a part of herself. Why *had* she told him? To make him angry? To shock him? To gain his pity? She didn't know the reason.

She wasn't gone very long, and when she came back down she opened the kitchen door so quietly that it was several seconds before he realised she was back. He was standing in front of the window and she could see his expression quite clearly. There was a bleakness about his mouth that made something deep inside her ache, and then he saw her, and his expression changed, the bleakness hidden away.

'Ready? Come on, then. We'll collect the girls on our way.'

Not even the sparkling perfection of the blue and gold autumn day could alleviate the stunning shock of seeing the cottage by daylight.

Darkness had somehow softened the reality of the carnage the falling branch had caused, but now, in the bright sunshine, nothing could disguise the huge hole in the roof, or the smaller one in the front wall. A pile of shattered roof slates lay in the front garden, the whir of saws as council workers busied themselves clearing as much of the mess as they could blurring into a dull, numbing sound as Claire stared helplessly at her home.

'Wait here a moment.' For once she didn't move away as Jay touched her arm. 'I'll check to find out if it's okay to go inside.'

It was too much of an effort to protest that he had no need to do these things for her—that she was perfectly capable of doing them herself. Instead she simply stood numbly where he had left her. Mrs Vickers came out of her house.

'Thank goodness you weren't here!' The old lady shook her head. 'My daughter came round last night after it happened. She wanted me to go home with her, but I wouldn't. I've lived here all my life and I'm not moving out now.'

Jay came back. 'It's safe to go inside, just as long as we're careful. I'll come with you.'

Something strange had happened to Claire. She felt too numb to object to his assumption of control. Mrs Vickers offered to keep an eye on Lucy and Heather, and so, trying to conceal her inner trembling, Claire followed Jay into the house.

A film of dust covered everything, particles of it still swirling in the air, making her gasp for breath.

On the far side of the room was the small desk where she kept all her important papers. Her insurance policy was in it, and yet she found herself reluctant to move towards it.

'You'll need enough clothes to last you for quite some time. Pack as much as you can,' Jay told her.

'I'll wait down here for you. Just give me a shout if you need help.'

Even in the midst of her shocked anguish Claire recognised his awareness of her need to be alone. She wanted to thank him, but somehow the words just wouldn't come.

Her suitcases had once belonged to her parents. They were old and battered, and she filled them automatically, emptying drawers. Luckily most of Lucy's clothes were stored in her own room.

Lucy's room. Like a sleepwalker she dropped the pile of underwear she was putting in the case and walked slowly towards the other bedroom. The door was slightly open; she pushed it and walked in.

The two small beds were broken, crushed beneath the weight of the heavy branch. Dust and debris covered the once immaculate duvets that she had made with such love and care. Half a dozen or so slates had fallen through the roof and ceiling on to the beds.

She must have made a sound without being aware of it, because just as the full horror of what might have happened struck her and her body started to convulse in shocked waves of reaction Jay pushed open the bedroom door.

She had a fleeting glimpse of that same bleak expression on his face, intensified this time, and then she was in his arms, her face pressed against his shoulder.

'Come on—it's all right. They're both safe, Claire. Nothing happened.'

She wasn't aware of him as a man in those moments as she let her body absorb the strength of his; he was just someone who shared and understood her anguish.

'But it could have done. I knew the roof needed attention. I... If something had happened, it would have been my fault!'

Hysteria built up inside her. She started to cry, hard, gulping sobs that tore painfully at her chest. She hadn't cried for years, not since her parents died, but there had been no one to comfort her then, no Jay to hold her in his arms and tell her that everything was all right.

'If you hadn't been coming home this weekend! If...'

'Stop it! I know what you're going through. Do you think I didn't go through hell myself when Heather went missing; do you think I didn't hate and blame myself? Come on. Finish packing your things and then we'll go.'

Suddenly she felt acutely self-conscious, and her body tensed within the protective circle of his arms. As though he sensed her feelings he released her immediately, stepping back from her.

As he turned away he added casually, 'If you know where your insurance policy is it might be a good idea to collect that as well. I could get my broker to have a look at it for you if you like. Sometimes they're in a better position to bring pressure to bear than we mere individuals.'

He was being tactful, Claire knew, giving her time to recover herself. This emotional side of her nature was something she had held rigorously in check since the death of her parents, and the trauma of being raped and then discovering that she was pregnant had forced her to become even more self-sufficient. She and Jay shared that need to protect themselves from being hurt, she recognised as she finished her packing; in many ways they were alike, each sensing within the other a deep-rooted fear, hers of physical intimacy, his of emotional intimacy.

He was waiting for her when she went back downstairs. 'Okay now?'

She nodded her head. 'Yes, I'm fine. Fate seems to be smiling on the pair of us recently,' she added wryly. 'If you can call losing the roof over your head that.'

'Well, they say good things go in threes.'

Claire grimaced. 'I can hardly wait.'

An odd expression that she couldn't define crossed his face. What was he thinking about? His ex-wife? What business of hers was it if he was?

'SO YOU DON'T THINK the insurance company will pay up?'

They were sitting in Whitegates' elegant, but to Claire's eyes sterile, drawing-room. Lucy and Heather were upstairs in bed, and she and Jay had just gone over her insurance policy.

Her heart sank as he shook his head gravely. 'I don't think so, but of course, I'll get my broker to check.'

Claire shivered, hugging her arms round her slim

body. Without any money from the insurance company, how on earth was she going to pay for the damage to be put right?

'Of course, you know that you and Lucy are welcome to stay here for just as long as is necessary.'

It was a kind offer, but she didn't feel at all at home in this elegant, sophisticated house. She was terrified that Lucy might break something or leave muddy footprints on the off-white carpet. No wonder Heather was considerably less exuberant than her own daughter!

'I have to go back to Dallas on Wednesday. I'll give my broker a ring first thing Monday morning and see what he can sort out.'

Claire immediately felt guilty. 'You've got enough problems of your own without taking on mine as well.'

'It's no problem...and I owe you a few favours.'

'How long will you be away this time?'

'Only a few days. I'm hoping to get a final signature on a very large contract.'

Claire knew now that Jay's firm created reproduction Adam-style mouldings and Tudor-style panelled interiors, replicas in every detail of those made by master craftsmen in the past. There was a booming market for his products in America, especially in Texas, where they were enjoying a vogue, but the partner who had left the firm when he married Jay's ex-wife had been the salesman of the team, and Claire knew that Jay was now looking for someone to take his place—preferably an American with an entrée into the sort of society where the company's products found their best market.

'Once that's organised I can get down to doing some interviewing. I need an American-based rep, then I can concentrate on the manufacturing side of the business over here.'

'Have you thought of setting up a factory in the States?'

'Yes, but it wouldn't work as well. The fact that our products are British gives them an added cachet. We're not just selling Adam-style décor, or Elizabethan libraries, we're selling something our customers can boast about to their friends.'

It was pleasantly relaxing sitting here with him like this. Claire found him fascinating to listen to and was genuinely interested in the way he had built up his business, so that when he said casually, 'Claire, I want to talk to you…about…about the man who raped you,' she was taken completely off guard.

'No, don't run away.' His fingers curled round her wrist, holding her in her chair as she tried to stand up. 'I'm not prying or asking out of any prurient curiosity. I just think it would help you to talk about it.'

'Therapy, you mean? Thanks, but no thanks. I don't want to talk about it.' She tried to pull away but did not succeed.

'Have you ever tried?'

How could she? There had never been anyone to talk to about it. Her parents had been killed; her shock and horror after it had happened had been so great that she had simply gone home and shut herself in her bedroom for days, not eating, not sleeping, not doing anything. And then afterwards, when the reality of it had sunk into her, she had been too... Too what? Ashamed? Yes, there had been a sense of shame and of guilt, although why she had no idea. She had done nothing to encourage the man, nothing at all. He had physically abducted her, raped her and then thrown her out of his car like a used doll.

'I haven't pried into your private life, Jay, and I...'

'I'm not prying. Before you were raped, had you had any sexual experience at all?'

Claire's shudder gave her away, and this time when she stood up he stood too.

'I don't have to stay here and listen to this, Jay.'

'No, you don't, but one day you're going to have a teenage daughter who's going to want to talk to you about sex. How are you going to cope with that, Claire? Do you want her to inherit you inhibitions and fears?'

She swallowed hard. How on earth had he known how much that very dread haunted her: that she would infect Lucy with her own sickness?

'What is it about what happened that you find hardest to come to terms with?'

'My own guilt.'

The words were out before she could stop them, an expression of anguished despair flooding her eyes as she realised what she had said.

'You don't have anything to feel guilty about. You know that.'

Rationally perhaps she did, but emotionally...

'And because of that sense of guilt you've refused to allow yourself to feel any emotion for any other man—is that it?'

It was part of it; the major part, perhaps.

'You're a young and very attractive woman; haven't you ever wondered—'

'No.'

Her sharp denial cut across what he had been going to say.

'I wasn't about to make you a proposition,' he said grimly.

Claire looked at him. 'No, I know that. It's just that I can't even talk about the intimacy of a physical relationship with someone without remembering *him*.'

'Because what he did to you patterned your sexual responses,' Jay told her quietly. 'Claire, there's something I want to talk to you about.'

What on earth was he going to say? She watched as he walked over to a cupboard and poured them both a brandy.

She took a sip when he handed her the glass, feeling the raw spirit slide down her throat.

'When I said I wasn't going to proposition you, I meant it, but I do have a proposal to put to you. Neither of us, for differing reasons, wants the intimacy of a marriage based on the current concept of what marriage should be—neither of us want the physical or emotional commitment such a marriage involves. But there are other types of marriages: marriage entered into between two people who have other things to offer one another. Recently I've been giving it a lot of thought, and I believe that you and I could make such a marriage work. No, listen to me,' he demanded, when she started to protest. 'I need someone to look after Heather, but whoever I found could never give her the love she's already getting from you. I admit that when I first realised how attached to you she was getting I resented it, but you can give her something I can't and I can give you and Lucy something you can't—security financially.' He paused. 'I'm not going to ask you to give me your answer now, but I want you to think about it while I'm away. I can promise you that sexually you'll never need to fear anything from me.'

Claire stared at him. He didn't strike her as a man who lived like a monk, and as though he had read her mind, he said sardonically, 'I had an extremely satisfying sexual relationship with Susie, Claire, if that's what you're wondering, and if I want sex there are plenty of women who will oblige me. You needn't worry that I might embarrass you by indulging in a series of affairs, either; I won't.'

No, he wouldn't do that. All those overseas trips would no doubt provide more than adequate opportunities for relieving any sexual frustration he might experience.

'I don't know what to say...'

She knew what she ought to be saying if she'd any sense. She ought to be telling him that what he was suggesting was unthinkable.

'I don't want you to say anything right now. I want you to think about what I've said, that's all.'

'If…if I agreed. Would we…would we live here?'

Now what on earth had made her ask that? It made it sound as though she was seriously considering his outrageous proposal.

'Yes.' Jay frowned. 'Don't you like the house?'

'It's very lovely, but I have nightmares every time the girls come in with muddy boots on.'

'Oh, that!' Instantly his face cleared. 'Yes, it is rather impractical. Susie chose the décor; someone once told her that white was her colour. Well, of course you can change it if you wish.'

It surprised Claire that he appeared so uninterested. In her experience, after the break-up of a relationship the partner who retained the house always either threw out everything connected with the relationship and started again, or clung desperately to every last thing that had been bought or chosen together; Jay fell into neither of those categories.

'Personally, I've never been all that keen on it,' he said. 'It looks lifeless.'

'You could always employ a nanny to take care of Heather, you know,' Claire felt bound to remind him.

'She loves you, and besides, a nanny couldn't give the same sort of permanence that would result from our marriage. Lucy needs a father just as much as Heather needs a mother, Claire. I like your daughter very much. I promise you I would always treat both of them equally.'

She knew that he would, and that he was right. Lucy was already becoming very attached to him. On the face of it marriage between them would be the ideal solution to all their problems, but human beings were irrational creatures and marriage was such an irrevocable step—at least to her.

'Think about it,' said Jay, drinking the last of his brandy. 'I promise I won't mention it again until I come back from Dallas. That should give you time to weigh up the pros and cons.'

'But what if you should meet someone else… someone you could fall in love with…?'

His mouth compressed. 'I won't.' he told her starkly. 'I made that mistake with Susie and I soon learned that a woman only wants a man just as long as he remains out of reach. Once she knew I loved her that was it: she lost interest in me, emotionally if not sexually.'

He saw her expression and smiled grimly.

'Oh yes, there are women like that, Claire, women who enjoy sex uninhibitedly for sex's sake alone— and Susie was certainly one of them. She married me because she was expecting my child. She didn't want to, but I persuaded her. She thought I was a wealthy man; when she realised I wasn't, the marriage began to go sour, but even at its worst we still slept together, right up until the day she left with Brett. I learned after she'd gone that Brett hadn't been her only lover—he was just the richest. You see, his partnership with me was only one of his business interests. His father is a millionaire.'

He was still very bitter over the betrayal; Claire could also see it so clearly. She could also see exactly why a marriage that was merely a business arrange-

ment would appeal to him. But would he feel like that
for ever? Might there not come a time when he was
ready to love again, and when he did, what would
happen to her?

Why was she even thinking about it? Surely a marriage between them was out of the question? But was
it? Sitting talking to him tonight she had felt completely relaxed, and even happy, at least until he had
brought up the subject of sex; she could live with him,
she knew that, and more importantly, if she married
him she would be bringing stability into the lives of
both Lucy and Heather.

'Think about it, Claire,' he urged again.

# CHAPTER FIVE

SUPPRESSING A FAINT SIGH, Claire replaced the telephone receiver. The news from Jay's insurance broker, that the insurance company had no liability under her policy, had not come as a total surprise, but even so...

Pushing her depression to one side, she stood up and walked over to the drawing-room window. Through it she could see Lucy and Heather playing in the garden. A faint flush of excitement coloured Heather's pale skin, her happy laughter mingling with Lucy's.

'Let's have no illusions between us, Claire,' Jay had said before he left, when she had tried to point out to him that it went against everything she herself believed in for her to escape her financial problems by marrying him. 'We both have something the other needs. I know you well enough to know that you aren't the mercenary type, if that's what's worrying you.'

'But practical considerations alone are surely no secure base for something like marriage,' she had protested, and instantly his expression had hardened, his eyes shadowed and cold as he demanded in a clipped voice, 'What do you consider to be a sound base? Love? Is that what you want, to fall in love with someone and share your life and your body with him?'

She had sensed that he had been deliberately reminding her of what marriage really was, and she had flinched away from him.

'I need you in my life, Claire, and I'm not too proud to tell you so,' he had continued. 'I need you as a mother for Heather, and perhaps later on, if you feel up to it, as a hostess for my business colleagues. If this contract with Dallas gets off the ground, several of the company's executives will be wanting to come over here and see how our operation works, but entertaining them isn't something I'd want to press on you if you felt you couldn't cope. I'm not ashamed to say that I need you, and if you're honest you need me too. We both know that you can't afford to have the cottage repaired. You don't want to go back to the sort of life you lived before you inherited it. I'm not buying you, Claire, and you're not selling yourself into marriage with me; we're entering a mutually beneficial arrangement.'

'You make it all sound very businesslike.'

'Isn't that what you want?' His expression had unsettled her. 'Or are you secretly looking for a Prince Charming to release you from your repression with the magic of his kiss?'

Her body tensed as she recalled the mockery in his voice as he delivered those words. Until that moment she had not even known herself how strong a hold that sort of foolish daydream had on her deepest and most private thoughts. Even so, she had denied it vigorously to him, and now, within a few short days he would be back, expecting an answer to the proposition he had put to her.

The girls' laughter reached her through the thick glass. Outside it was cold, frost riming the edges of the lawn where the sun had still not touched. Inside, the house was comfortably warm; pinching economies like needing to keep a check on central heating bills did not feature in Jay's world. Did she have the moral right to deprive Lucy of all that Jay could provide—and not just in the more obvious materialistic terms? There were other, more important considerations, such as the fact that already Lucy was becoming attached to Jay, that through him she could have the sort of education that would give her the very best sort of start in life, and that she and Jay together could give both girls the kind of stable, calm background that she sincerely believed gave untold benefits to the children who received them.

And it wasn't just her own child she had to consider. There was Heather as well. Heather, who was only just now starting to come out of her shell; Heather who clung to Claire at bedtime when she kissed her goodnight, who would appear at her side, almost out of nowhere, as if to check up on the fact that she was still there. All these considerations tipped the scales in favour of Jay's proposal.

And against it? What was there? Her own stubborn desire to remain self-supporting? Her dislike of any tag being attached to her that might label her as a mercenary, scheming woman taking advantage of a lone male with a small child to bring up? Her very deep-rooted fear of the state of marriage, of the powerful position in her life that it would give to Jay? But she already had his word that their marriage would be a business relationship only, and she knew that she could trust him. She had no illusions about Jay's sexuality. Even she could see that he was the sort of man whose passion was a powerful motivating force in his life—but he was also good-looking and male enough not to need to coerce any woman where sex was concerned. Putting it at its most cynical and logical, what would be the point in him wasting his time trying to coax her into a sexual relationship when, doubtless, there were countless number of women only too eager to have that privilege? No, she had nothing to fear from him in that way.

But there were other dangers. Claire bit her lip, gnawing anxiously on it. She already knew how vulnerable she herself was to emotional bonding. Witness the way her feelings for Heather had grown to the point where her love for the little girl was almost enough on its own to make her accede to Jay's proposal.

Jay was a very charismatic and genuinely fascinating man. A man, moreover, who took the trouble to talk to her as an equal—a man whom it would be very easy to come to depend on, in a way she had not had someone to depend on since the death of her parents. Yes, there was a very real danger there, but surely the mere fact that she was aware of it would make her wary and careful. She would not burden Jay with an emotionalism he wouldn't want, even if it was only the emotion of friendship rather than sexual love.

Both of them, in their separate ways, had been crippled emotionally by life; both of them together could build a secure home for their children that would enable them to put down the strong roots every living thing needed to grow.

'WHEN WILL JAY BE BACK?'

'Later on this afternoon,' Claire responded.

'Can we go and meet him at the airport, please, Mummy?'

Claire shook her head firmly, ignoring Lucy's cry of disappointment. As always, fortunately, her daughter's attention proved fairly easy to distract. She was unlike Heather in that respect, who would worry and brood over something until it was sorted out to her satisfaction.

Jay's return coincided with the half-term holidays. Claire had made tentative plans to take the girls to Bristol, mainly to buy them both new clothes, and she had also rashly promised a brief visit to the zoo.

How long would Jay wait before demanding an answer to his proposal? Not long, she suspected. He was a decisive man who would not tolerate shilly-shallying in others. Inwardly she knew that her decision had been made, but even so, actually telling Jay that she was prepared to marry him was something she wasn't looking forward to doing. Actually saying the words made it seem so final. She guessed that he wouldn't want to wait very long after her agreement before legally formalising their marriage.

Partly because Lucy had pleaded with her and partly to avoid being left alone with him, Claire had agreed that the girls' evening meal could be delayed so that they could share it with Jay.

She had no real idea or knowledge of his culinary preferences, but knowing the delays that could arise both during the flight and after it, she had made another casserole, a slightly more glamorous one this time: chicken breasts in a special sauce, which she intended to serve with duchesse potatoes, and fresh vegetables. She suspected that after several days in Dallas Jay would be heartily sick of prime steak, and so the chicken should be a welcome change.

Leaving both girls happily occupied in the kitchen with their crayoning books, she went upstairs to check on Jay's room.

Shortly after he had left she had entered it for the first time to strip his bed, and as it had then, when she opened the door and walked into it, its almost monastic austerity surprised her. She didn't know what she had expected, but it certainly hadn't been this coldly plain room, so empty of any personal possessions that it might have belonged to a hotel. The large bed was covered by a plain, dull spread. The bedside tables held only a telephone and an alarm clock. A bank of fitted wardrobes and cupboards presented a plain cream front to her cursory glance.

Brown curtains hung at the window to tone with the neutral-coloured carpet.

All in all, the room was spectacularly uninspiring and, unlike the rest of the house, did not reveal the decorative hand of Jay's ex-wife.

Claire wondered why. She already knew from Heather which room had been her mother's, and although she had not as yet ventured inside it she had assumed that Jay must have shared it with her. She could well understand him choosing to sleep in a different room after the break-up of the marriage, but what she couldn't fathom out was why this one room out of the whole house had not been redecorated.

Arming herself with clean sheets, she set about making the bed. Jay had his own private bathroom off his bedroom, and she was just on her way out when she remembered he would need fresh towels.

The telephone rang, distracting her. She hurried to answer it, surprised to hear Jay's voice as she picked up the receiver.

'I just thought I'd let you know I'd landed. I'm calling in at the factory on my way back. I should be home for about six.'

He didn't say anything else. Claire had no opportunity to ask him about the contract. He had sounded tired, and he had made no mention of his proposal—but then he wouldn't, of course.

'What are we going to have for pudding?' Lucy asked her as she walked into the kitchen.

'You could make an apple pie,' suggested Heather eagerly. 'It's Daddy's favourite.'

Telling herself that it was what she had, after all, planned to make, Claire cleared the table and started making pastry, carefully checking the enthusiastic assistance of her two 'helpers'.

Baking was something she had always found therapeutic, and somehow one thing led to another. The mouthwatering aroma of cooking pastry and fruit mingled with that of the chicken, and Claire was just putting a final dollop of mixture into some bun tins when she heard the sound of a car.

'It's Jay,' shrieked Lucy eagerly, scrambling down from her stool, and rushing for the back door.

Jay reached it first, his eyebrows lifting slightly as he walked in.

'You're early?' For some reason Claire felt oddly shaky. He looked so alien standing in the kitchen, in his immaculate business suit and his crisp white shirt.

'Yes...and we've been making your very favourite—apple pie,' Lucy announced.

A sudden awareness of pastry-sticky fingers and flour-smeared hands made Claire dart forward to pick Lucy up before she could inflict any damage on his immaculate suit, but Jay forestalled her, swinging Lucy up into his arms, so that she shrieked with delight.

'Jay, your suit...' She reached up automatically to brush off the floury marks left by Lucy's hands and then realised to her mortification that her own were equally floury.

'Stop fussing, it will clean.'

He put Lucy down and held out his arms to

Heather. As always she clung to Claire's side. Bending down, she gave her a little push. 'Go and kiss Daddy hello.'

Over Heather's dark head Jay gave her a wry look.

'Odd, isn't it? *Your* daughter can't wait to fling herself into my arms, whereas mine…'

'Give her time,' Claire urged in a low voice. 'She's such a sensitive child, and she's had too many upheavals in her life. She needs to learn that she can trust you always to be there. She needs stability…'

'Yes, she does.'

The look he gave her was direct and determined, and ridiculously, Claire felt hot colour sting her face.

Lucy's impatient tug on her skirt caused a welcome diversion. 'Mummy, what's a woman?'

Claire was perplexed. She looked down at her daughter. 'I'm not sure what you mean, Lucy.'

'Well, when you were talking to Mrs Vickers after school yesterday and Heather and me went in the post office, Mrs Simmonds was there and she said that you were Lucy's daddy's woman.'

Over her daughter's auburn curls Claire's shocked eyes met the grim expression in Jay's.

'I…'

'It means that your mummy and I are going to get married,' Jay announced, ignoring the choked sound that emitted from Claire's throat.

'You mean like real mummies and daddies?' Lucy was plainly ecstatic about the idea. 'And we'll live here for always?'

'Something like that,' he agreed urbanely. He was

still watching her, Claire realised, a hard purposeful-
ness in his eyes that warned her that he had made her
decision for her, and he wasn't going to let her back
out of it.

She ought to have been furious with him for his
high-handedness, but in reality it was a relief. Her
decision had in fact already been made, but the
knowledge that their relationship was the subject of
village gossip and speculation wouldn't have made it
any easier for her to communicate it to Jay.

Feeling rather feeble, she said unsteadily, 'Lucy,
you're covered in flour; why don't you and Heather
go upstairs and clean up?'

As Jay put her down, Heather put her hand on
Claire's arms and looked up at her. 'Are you really
going to be here for always?'

The expression in her eyes wasn't something Claire
had the strength to withstand. Going down on her
heels so that her face was on a level with the little
girl's, she asked huskily, 'Is that what you want,
Heather, for me to be here for always?'

'Yes...yes...' A fierce hug accompanied the emphatic words.

'Then I will be.'

Although she was speaking to Heather, Claire knew
that her words were meant for Jay. As she stood up
she looked at him and caught an expression on his
face that puzzled her. He looked like a man who had
been under almost unendurable pressure and who had
now found it relaxed.

Claire waited until both girls were out of the kitchen before speaking to him.

'You had no right to tell them that.'

He didn't argue with her, simply flexed his body as though it ached. 'It saves you from making any decision though, doesn't it?'

Claire's mouth compressed as she caught the tinge of contempt in his voice. Did he really think she was incapable of deciding for herself? On the verge of telling him that she had already decided to marry him for herself, she caught the words back, and said instead, 'I shouldn't have thought a little bit of village gossip would worry you to that extent.'

'It doesn't,' he agreed flatly. 'At least, not on my own behalf, and especially when there are no grounds for it—but I don't want either of the girls to be subjected to the sort of sniggered whispers that go the rounds of every school playground. Okay, right now they're too innocent to understand what's being said, but for how long?' He looked at her, and for the first time Claire saw the exhaustion in his face. 'Before we go any further, can I take it that since you didn't contradict what I said to the girls about our plans for the future, you are going to marry me?'

'It doesn't seem that I have much choice now, does it?' Claire responded tartly.

Almost instantly his face closed up, his mouth going hard. 'No, it doesn't, does it?' he agreed with more than a hint of acerbic grimness. 'And since that's settled, if you don't mind, I'd like to go upstairs and have a shower.'

Seeing the weariness in his tense back, Claire wished her own part in their exchange unsaid. The problem was that she had been so shocked by Lucy's innocent revelations that things had got out of hand. She had had everything carefully planned—a family meal over which she and Jay could relax in one another's company, and then a quiet evening with the girls, followed perhaps by a chat together in front of the sitting-room fire, when she would have felt relaxed enough to convey her intentions to him. Now, abruptly, all her plans had been swept away, and far from being relaxing, the evening looked like being extremely tense indeed.

Still, looking at it from Jay's point of view, it had hardly been a good homecoming. She could remember how tired and tense her father used to be after dealing with a difficult business meeting, and Jay had had a whole series of them. It could hardly have helped his frame of mind to be greeted by the artless announcement, the moment he stepped through the door, that the whole village was gossiping about them.

She was just about to clear the kitchen table when she suddenly remembered that she had forgotten to put clean towels in Jay's room.

The airing cupboard was full of clean towels, and she selected a pile at random, pausing outside his bedroom door to knock.

She heard him call out, 'Come in,' and pushed open the door with her hip.

'I just remembered that you don't have any towels…' She froze, her voice locking in her throat as she realised that she had interrupted him while he was getting undressed.

He had discarded his suit jacket and his shirt. The latter lay on the floor, a puddle of white cloth. She stared at it for what seemed like a long time, as she fought to control the rapid rise and fall of her chest.

She couldn't look at him again. One brief glance at that tough, muscle-hardened torso with its rough shadowing of hair had been enough to freeze her where she stood.

Obliquely she was somehow aware of her own body as though she had stepped outside it. She could feel the rapid pulse of her blood along her veins; she could hear the frightened thud of her heart. She knew that her eyes had dilated with the shock and that her breathing sounded raspy and painful.

The room was warm, and yet somehow she could feel the soft movement of air against her skin like an icy embrace, as Jay moved.

'It's all right, Claire, it's all right…' She knew that he was aware of what had happened to her and that logically there was nothing for her to fear, but while her mind could comprehend it, her body could not. She saw him reach past her for his shirt and tug it on. All the time he was talking soothingly to her, but she barely heard him. She couldn't comprehend anything other than the maleness of his body; that blocked everything else out. She shuddered as he fastened the buttons, remembering that dark arrowing of hair disappearing beneath his belt.

'Claire, it's all right.'

He stepped towards her, taking the towels from her numb arms and putting them down on the bed. 'It's all right.' His hands gripped her arms, and felt their clenched muscles. He started to massage them, easing the frozen tension out of her.

'I…' Somehow she managed to unlock her tongue, a tide of fierce heat enveloping her as she realised how stupidly she had behaved. She was shaking violently now, perspiration breaking out all over her skin. Where she had been cold, now she was hot.

'It's all right…don't try to say anything. Come and sit down for a moment.'

Numbly she let him lead her to the bed, and gently push her down on to it. Now, with the raw evidence of his maleness concealed from her, she was able to get herself back under control.

'Is it always like this…?'

'Always?' She looked blankly at him.

'Mine can't be the first naked male chest you've seen, Claire,' he reasoned, catching the train of her thoughts.

That was true, but the others had been sanitised by their surroundings: on television, on the beach… Never, ever in the intimate confines of a bedroom; never, ever so close to her that she had seen the faint stickiness of sweat dampening the silky chest hair, or been aware of the musky male scent of a man's body.

'I…'

'Mummy, I'm hungry…when are we going to eat…?'

'I'm hungry too.'

Lucy and Heather stood in the open doorway.

'Will you and Daddy both be sleeping in here when you're married?' Heather enquired innocently.

Above her Claire heard Jay catch his breath. 'No,' he said roughly.

'You and Mummy didn't sleep in the same bed either, did you?'

'No,' he agreed. 'Claire's like your mother. She wants her own bedroom.'

'Why do you want your own room?' Heather asked her.

Claire got up and walked towards the door.

'Because she likes her privacy,' Jay answered for her. His voice sounded unfamiliarly harsh, as though something had hurt his throat. It couldn't be anything to do with her. A reaction perhaps to the memories Heather had unwittingly stirred up by mentioning her mother?

IN SPITE OF EVERYTHING, supper was a convivially relaxed meal, any conversation gaps left by the two adults more than compensated for by the excited chatter of the two girls.

'Can we tell everyone at school about you and Mummy getting married?' Lucy asked Jay.

'If you think they'd be interested.'

An announcement like that was bound to cause more gossip than it squashed, at least until they were actually married, Claire reflected as she cleared away their plates and got out the pie.

'Claire's made apple pie for you 'cos it's your favourite, Daddy,' Heather told her father with a beam. 'She made it specially because you were coming home.'

'Did she? That's very kind of her.'

Against her will Claire found herself turning to look at him. In a low voice that neither of the girls could hear, he said softly, 'I think I'm going to like coming home to a wife who makes apple pies especially for me.'

For some extraordinary reason Claire felt herself tremble. To compensate for it she said sharply, 'Didn't Heather's mother...'

'No... No, Susie wasn't much of a cook,' said Jay sardonically. 'Her talents lay in other directions.'

Yes, and she knew what those were, despite those separate bedrooms. Her face grew hot as she thought about the likely outcome had his ex-wife happened to walk into his bedroom when he was half naked.

'What's wrong?' asked Jay.

'Nothing.' How on earth had he come to have such long thick lashes? she wondered absently, fighting to disentangle her glance from his. They looked so soft, so at odds with the harsh angles of his face.

'Mummy, may I have some pie?'

Hurriedly Claire turned towards her daughter.

Much to her surprise, Jay joined in the girls' bedtime preparations. Heather was much more relaxed with him now, she noticed as she briskly handed both girls clean nightdresses.

'Clean your teeth and then straight into bed.'

'And then will you come and read to us?'

That was Heather, the dreamer. Claire was reading *The Secret Garden* to them, reliving her own child-hood pleasure in the magic of the book. Out of the corner of her eye she caught the expression on Jay's face.

'Not tonight, it's Daddy's turn,' she said firmly, not letting herself respond to Heather's agonised expression.

That brief awareness between them when she had sensed Jay's feeling of rejection had gone, but she had been aware of it, just as she was aware of his pain whenever Heather turned from him to her.

He was upstairs for a long time. Claire busied herself in the kitchen, knowing that when he came down they would have to talk, but reluctant to do so.

He came in quietly, but she was still aware of him. She turned to look at him and was struck by the air of exhaustion that clung to him.

'You look tired.'

'It's been a long week. Heather still seems to see me in the guise of some sort of ogre. I can't believe that Mrs Roberts alone is responsible.'

Claire didn't either, but she had to choose her words carefully. 'She's a very sensitive child; she hardly knows you. You've been away such a lot. From what she tells me she hasn't spent much time with either you or her mother...'

'No. And if you're trying to tell me that in those circumstances it's hardly surprising that she wants to reject me, I know it, but that still doesn't stop me from… Every time I reach out to her she retreats from me, but with you…'

'Some little girls do respond better to their own sex, especially at that age,' she soothed. 'I know how you feel, though,' she added in a low voice. 'I feel equally guilty when I see how enthusiastically Lucy goes to you. It had never even occurred to me that she might miss having a father, even though I was very close to mine.'

She heard Jay sigh.

'I'm sorry I forced your hand earlier on.' He leaned back against the wall tiredly, hands pushed into his pockets. The material strained across his thighs and her attention was concentrated like a fly trapped in honey on the strong play of muscles there. Desperately she wrenched it away.

'I had already decided to accept your proposal,' she told him huskily. 'I've been trying all week to convince myself that you're right and that we'd each be contributing equally to the marriage, but…'

'But you still haven't managed to do it?' He made a small explosive sound in the back of his throat as he levered himself off the wall and came towards her.

'You know what your trouble is, don't you, Claire? You're too damned proud! Do you honestly think that money can actually compensate for all the things you can give Heather that I can't? No! When I walked in here tonight she actually smiled at me. Do you know how long it's been since she did that? Since I came back to this house and found anything like a welcome, in fact? To walk in here tonight after a week spent arguing over the final details of the contract...' He made a brief gesture that encompassed without words what he was trying to say. 'Susie wasn't much of a homemaker. She never wanted to get married. She was a model when I met her, and she bitterly resented being dragged down here and buried alive in the country, as she called it. If I hadn't stopped her, she'd have had Heather aborted. Sometimes I wondered if...'

'No... No, you mustn't think that!' Claire's voice shook with anguish for him. Without even thinking about it she reached out and touched his arm lightly.

It was strange to feel his living flesh beneath the fabric of his shirt and her fingertips lingered briefly before she realised what he was and hurriedly withdrew.

'Let's go and sit down,' he suggested. 'We've got a lot to talk about.'

In the sitting-room he poured them both a drink. Claire sat on the edge of her chair, nursing hers tensely. Jay shivered slightly as he sat down.

'It feels cold in here.'

'The central heating's on, but I suppose it was much hotter in Dallas.'

'Mmm... I suppose it was, although I never got beyond my air-conditioned hotel room, or an equally air-conditioned suite of offices.'

'But you got the contract. I wish I'd known; I could have made a special celebratory meal.'

There was a moment's odd silence that for some reason made her skin prickle warningly, and then Jay

said in a husky voice, 'I wish you'd known too. I
think I could quite easily get used to being spoiled
by you, Claire... This room is cold,' he added
abruptly. 'I've never liked it. It's too cold and sterile.
So is the whole house, come to think of it, but I was
desperate to find somewhere at the time, and Susie
was no help, complaining that she hated everything
we saw.'

Claire longed to tell him that there was nothing
wrong with the house and that it was the décor that
was at fault, but instead she said tactfully, 'I was wondering if you would mind if I changed things a little
after we're married, Jay. Oh, nothing too expensive.
It's just...'

'Make whatever changes you wish. And Claire...'
She looked at him. 'Don't worry about what it costs,
provided you aren't intending a wholesale refurnish-
ing exercise with antiques.'

'I was wondering about using some of the company's products,' Claire suggested cautiously. An
idea had taken root in her mind, but she wasn't sure
what Jay's reaction would be. 'You did say that we
might have to entertain American executives from the
Dallas company, and I was thinking some of the
rooms here could be redecorated using some of your
products, as a sort of...'

'Showcase!'

Jay had been lounging back, his head resting
against the cream leather of the settee, and now he
sat upright, his eyes alert.

'Yes, it's an excellent idea, but it would involve

you in a lot of extra work, Claire—workmen in and out of the house, as well as taking care of the girls—and I'd have to leave all the planning and design to you as well. Initially, until the orders start moving smoothly, I'll be fully occupied keeping tabs on them.'

'I don't mind.' She didn't. She would welcome anything that would change the house from its present austere state to something a little more homely.

'Well, if you're sure, I'll get you some of our brochures and you can browse through them and see if there's anything you can use. In fact, I'd like to make the arrangements for the wedding and get it over with as soon as possible. I was thinking we could get married in Bath; if you like we could spend a couple of days there and I could take you round the factory.'

'It would be even better if you could organise it to fit in with half-term,' Claire suggested. 'I have promised to take the girls to Bristol Zoo—and they both need new clothes…'

'Fine, I'll organise something. You're going to need to do some shopping for yourself as well.'

It was lightly said, but even so, Claire flushed. She knew that her clothes weren't glamorous—far from it—but there had never been any money to spare to spend on herself.

'I…I don't need anything, Jay,' she lied.

'Yes, you do,' he corrected evenly. 'Claire, if you're going to act as my hostess, you're going to have to dress the part. American women are very clothes-conscious, especially Dallas women, and believe me, if the men are coming over here, their wives are going to want to come with them. It might even be worthwhile looking into ways and means of keeping them occupied—you know the sort of thing: a tour of Bath, and a couple of stately homes. Afternoon tea in thatched cottage villages.'

Surprisingly, instead of feeling daunted by what he had outlined, Claire felt a surge of interested excitement. She had never had a career, never really worked in the sense of being employed, but she had done well at school, and knew that she had a lively intelligence. To take on the role Jay was outlining would be a challenge, and one she felt she could respond to. And he was right—clothes; the right sort of clothes, would be an important part of that role.

'If it's the fact that I'll be paying for your clothes that's worrying you, then don't let it,' he advised her. 'Believe me, Claire, if I had to pay for a full-time nanny for Heather, plus a cook and housekeeper of the high calibre that you are, plus a social secretary-cum-hostess, it would cost me far, far more than you're ever likely to spend on clothes.'

'Ah, but that's why you want to marry me, isn't it?' she said lightly. 'So that you don't have to do that…'

'Partly. But more important is the stability and permanence you're going to bring to Heather's life. It's just as well that Lucy is such a sunny-natured child. No problems there with any incipient jealousy, I hope?'

'No, none at all. Lucy is a very well-adjusted little girl, luckily; I often wonder...'

'Who she gets it from?' he said evenly. 'It's not my affair, Claire, but what are you going to tell her when she's old enough to start asking questions?'

She took a steadying breath. 'I can't tell her the truth.'

He seemed to consider for a moment and then said, 'No, perhaps not. So what will you tell her?'

'That I loved her father. That he and I were at school together... That he was an orphan...' she bit her lip. 'I thought I could tell her that he was killed in...in an accident...'

'Thus effectively making sure she won't go looking for him or for anyone connected with him. Mmm, I suppose it could work.'

His question led to one that had been bothering her. Putting down her half-empty glass, she stood up and walked nervously towards the window, before turning to face him.

'Jay, what will you do if your...if Heather's mother ever wants her back?'

'She won't.' His voice was harsh, corrosive almost. 'Susie made that more than clear. Besides, I took the precaution of getting her to sign an agreement giving me total responsibility for Heather. Do you honestly think I would allow a child as sensitive as Heather is to be torn apart between two parents?'

'If Susie changed her mind and decided that she wanted to...to come back, you...'

'I what? Wouldn't be able to resist her?' He

laughed bitterly. 'Don't you believe it! Sexually she could still turn me on, I suppose, but emotionally—no...that's all gone, and besides, she won't come back. She's got what she wanted, now that she's the wife of Brett Brassington the Third.'

There was no mistaking the cynical bitterness in his voice, and Claire's heart ached for him. It was impossible for her to comprehend the sort of relationship he had had with his ex-wife, and as though he knew it, he said savagely,

'Our marriage was never the sort of marriage you can visualise, Claire. I loved Susie, yes, but it was an obsessive physical love that didn't last much longer than the honeymoon. I married her because she was carrying my child which she had threatened to abort, and she married me because she was twenty-six years old, and for a model, that's old. She could never accept or understand the amount of time I had to give to the business. Sexually she knew all the tricks there are to know; she knew exactly how to make me ache, and she enjoyed making me beg. You heard Heather: we had separate rooms—Susie's idea not mine,' he added brodingly. 'She kept me dangling on a thread for so long that after a while I just lost interest. Things weren't going well with the business. I was tired of arguing with her; tired of being made to pay and beg for sex; something inside me just seemed to shut off.' He laughed derisively. 'She couldn't believe it; she thought I was trying a few tricks of my own...' He broke off when he saw the confused look Claire was giving him, and explained rawly, 'Too much strain overloads the system, Claire; I lost the ability to respond to her in any way at all. Once that happened I think we both knew the marriage was over, and I know I was never her only lover, not even in the early days when I genuinely thought she did care. I tried to keep the marriage going because of Heather, but it wasn't any good. And when Susie found out that I was able, to put it bluntly, to respond to other women in a way I could no longer respond to her, that was the end. Her pride couldn't take it.'

Jay was saying that he had been impotent? Claire stared at him, totally unable to comprehend such an eventuality; to her, he seemed such a physical man. Her eyes widened and she looked at him, unable to hide her thoughts.

'You don't believe me?' He laughed again, this time properly. 'Thanks for the vote of confidence, but believe me, it's true. Even now...' he shrugged powerful shoulders and said lazily, 'suffice it to say that you need never worry that any brief flings I might have will damage our marriage. It's too important to me for me to risk it in any way.'

She did believe him, but she also wondered how on earth he had ever confused the obvious physical infatuation he had for his ex-wife with love. His own description of his feelings had been so lacking in that emotion that Claire had been both shocked and saddened by the emotional paucity of their relationship.

'I...I think it's time I went to bed.'

He glanced at his watch. 'Mmm, me too. Oh, by the way...the cottage...'

## CHAPTER SIX

'RIGHT EVERYTHING'S arranged. We get married on Thursday in Bath. I've booked us into a hotel for a couple of days—that should give us enough time to get the girls and you re-equipped and to do a little bit of sightseeing.' He put down the briefcase he had brought from the car and opened it, the fabric of his suit jacket stretching taut across his back. Perhaps it was because the only other man she had ever lived with had been her father that she was so constantly aware of, and caught off guard by, the essential maleness of him. Perhaps she had lived too long in the softer world of women, and it was that which made her so conscious of the hardness of his muscled body.

'Here you are; I brought these back for you to browse through,' He handed her a pile of glossy leaflets. 'We don't have a design department as such, but if you feel you want to engage an interior designer...'

Claire shook her head decisively. Whitegates was going to be her home, and besides, she was looking forward to the challenge of re-planning it herself.

'Well, just as long as you don't start worrying about keeping costs down,' Jay warned her. He grimaced faintly and looked round the kitchen. 'While

you're at it, how about doing something in here...
something...'

'Warmer?' Claire supplied dryly.

'Mmm. And Claire, don't forget you're going to
need to adapt some of the bedrooms into guest suites,
complete with *en suite* baths.'

Claire laughed. 'It sounds more like I'm going to
be running a hotel than a home!'

'Mmm, talking of which... This is the hotel I've
booked us into in Bath. I've organised a suite with
three bedrooms—the girls can share. It's just on the
outskirts of the town and has its own leisure complex,
complete with swimming pool. 'Can Lucy swim?'

'Yes. Can Heather?'

'Yes.'

NEWS OF THEIR IMPENDING marriage had spread
through the village grapevine faster than an epidemic
in a slum, and Claire had got used to being stopped
in the street and discreetly pumped for more information. Overall, she gained the impression that the
village thoroughly approved.

'It is such a nice arrangement,' Mrs Vickers innocently told her. The village apparently did not approve of such modern things as 'living together', and
she gathered that Jay's ex-wife had not been particularly popular. Indeed, no one seemed to know much
about her at all, other than the fact that she had run
off with another man, leaving her small daughter behind.

Naturally, both little girls were wildly excited, anticipating the dual treat of the wedding plus the visit to Bath. Jay proposed that they leave after breakfast on the Wednesday morning, which would give Claire plenty of time to get all her shopping done before the Thursday afternoon ceremony.

A backlog of work at the factory kept him late there most evenings, although he always tried to get back in time to read the girls a story. Heather was slowly starting to relax with him, and once or twice Claire even thought she saw a glimmer of anticipation in the little girl's eyes when he walked through the back door. And Lucy was uninhibitedly in favour of the marriage. Jay was her hero, and she worshipped him with an unashamed adoration.

Already it was November. Christmas loomed on the horizon, and unless she wanted the house to be in a total state of uproar over the Christmas holiday she would have to get a move on with her plans for the house, Claire realised as she picked up the brochures Jay had brought for her.

After supper Jay disappeared into his study, and Claire curled up on the leather couch, her feet tucked up underneath her as she browsed through the leaflets. There was a range of Victorian reproduction sanitary-ware, which she thought was bound to impress the Americans, and she put the details on one side, turning to concentrate on the photographs of various types of reproduction plasterwork.

The large drawing room would lend itself very nicely to that sort of embellishment, and although not strictly Georgian, the house was old enough, the rooms high-ceilinged enough to take that sort of decorative detail. The thought struck her that she could probably get some sort of inspiration as to how to use the mouldings to best effect by studying photographs of original Adam-style rooms.

Jay had pointed out to her that although several firms manufactured similar products, they prided themselves on genuinely making an effort to reproduce even the finest detail of the original plasterwork, just as modern furniture makers were now using the original pattern books of men such as Chippendale and Hepplewhite, so that they could reproduce furniture which was comparable in quality and workmanship with the original. There was nothing either cheap or tacky about their products, Jay had told Claire, and the methods they used to make them reflected as far as possible the workmanship which had gone into the originals.

It seemed to Claire, as she studied the photographs of various mock room-settings, that both the drawing-room and dining-room could become showpieces for Jay's products, while the panelling could surely be an attractive addition to Jay's study?

As she worked through the literature, she made various notes, jotting down ideas that occurred to her for new colour schemes. Here in the sitting-room she had set her heart on a comfortable country house atmosphere with deeply cushioned settees in modern chintz, and colour-washed walls. A pretty, soft golden yellow perhaps...something warm and sunny. She wanted a room that people could be at leisure in.

Somewhere where the girls could play, and Jay could relax.

She glanced at the clock, stunned to see that it was almost half past eleven. It was time she went to bed. She tidied up the papers, and then got up, yawning.

As she took her coffee cup to the kitchen she saw that there was still a light on in the study. On impulse she knocked briefly and opened the door.

Jay was sitting behind his desk, his tie loose and the top buttons of his shirt unfastened. His hair looked as though he had been pushing his fingers through it.

'Hello, still up?'

'Mmm. I got rather involved in my room planning. I'm going to bed now, though. Do you fancy a cup of coffee?'

'Yes, please. I've got quite a lot to do yet; I could do with something to keep me awake. Did you come to any conclusions—about how we could use our products?'

'Oh, yes, I've got loads of ideas…while we're in Bath I'll have to look round at fabric shops, that sort of thing. What is worrying me, though, is finding someone to install it properly.'

'Oh, we've got our own team to do that. We don't take the risk of having it installed by anyone else. I'll take you down to the factory while we're in Bath and you can meet them.' He frowned suddenly and picked up his pen, fiddling with it.

It was an unusual gesture for him. He was normally so very decisive and assured.

'What is it?' Claire asked.

'I was just thinking. If you're re-planning the bed-rooms, it might be an idea for us to have intercon-necting ones—I don't want any of our male guests getting the wrong idea.'

He meant that he didn't want his male pride hurt by others knowing that they didn't have a sexual re-lationship, Claire surmised, but she realised she was wrong when he said harshly, 'I don't want a repeat performance of what happened with Susie, Claire. I don't intend to lose you as well. If we have rooms at the opposite end of the house, you're bound to get some opportunist who's going to think that sexually you're as available as Susie was. Neither of us wants that.'

She felt uncomfortably guilty when she realised that his concern had been as much for her as for him-self. Every day, it seemed she learned more about him, and the more she learned, the more she won-dered how on earth Susie could have not loved him. Surely, if a woman could love a man it must be this one: he was caring and kind, attractive, considerate—and strong enough to lean on if one was the leaning type.

But he no longer wanted a woman's love, she re-minded herself as she went to make them both a cup of coffee, so really it was just as well that she was incapable of giving him it.

IN THE SRAMBLE TO GET the girls and herself ready for an early start, mercifully Claire hadn't had much time to worry about the commitment she was about to make.

However, once she was inside the car, she had all the time in the world to worry about what she was doing.

Jay was a skilled but careful driver; the girls were both occupied with giggles and private chatter in the back; the music drifting from the stereo was designed to calm and relax; yet as the miles went by Claire found herself growing more and more tense, more and more convinced that she was doing the wrong thing, that she was, in fact, mad even to consider marrying. How on earth could it work?

'Stop worrying; everything will be fine, you'll see. Just think, in twenty-five years from today, you and I will be celebrating our silver wedding.'

His uncanny ability to divine her thoughts unnerved her. Unlike her, Jay seemed to have no doubts about the wisdom or the stability of their marriage, but then he already had something to compare it with, something to work towards, while she…

It was too late for second thoughts, Claire told herself firmly. She had already made a commitment to Heather, even though she hadn't yet made one to Jay, and on that count alone it was too late for going back.

Even so, she still found it hard to relax. Panic cramped through her stomach, an apprehension quite unlike any of her previous experiences enveloping her.

All the local weather seers had predicted a bad winter, and looking at the rolling countryside, held fast in the iron grip of a frost which turned the golden stubble monochrome, and lay across the bareness of the hedges like icing sugar, Claire could well believe that they were right.

In summer it was pretty countryside, but now the lavish display of autumn leaves had gone, and without the starkness that made harsher countryside look magnificent and awesome in winter, the bare fields only looked melancholic—or was that simply her imagination?

Just outside Bath, Jay turned off the main road, and drove in through an imposing gateway. Only a discreet plaque set into one of the brick pillars supporting the wrought iron gates betrayed that this was a hotel.

Beyond an avenue of bare trees Claire saw the house: soft cream Cotswold stone, the precision of a Georgian facade.

A high wall joined what Claire suspected had originally been the stable block to the main building, and Heather called out delightedly, 'Look...it's just like *The Secret Garden!*'

'Look, Mummy, horses!' Lucy, wide-eyed, tugged on her sleeve as she pressed her nose to the car window. In a paddock opposite the house several horses had gathered by the fence.

'There's a riding school here,' explained Jay. 'Lessons can be arranged for the guests.'

'Does that mean that we can ride?' breathed Lucy expectantly.

Since their removal to the country, Lucy had de-

veloped an intense passion for horses and ponies, and
Claire suppressed a faint sigh. 'Riding lessons are
very expensive, Lucy,' Claire cautioned, 'and besides,
Heather might not want to ride.'

'Yes, I do. I'd like a pony of my own. We both
would.'

'I think we're the victims of a two-pronged attack,'
Jay murmured *soto voce* to Claire, but she saw that
he was smiling. 'We probably won't have time for
riding lessons while we're here,' he told them, ignoring the protests of disappointment. 'But maybe...
maybe...if you're both very good, Father Christmas...'

It was enough to produce ecstatic sighs of anticipation, and to keep them quiet as Jay stopped the car,
and got out to go round and open Claire's door.

'Don't worry about the luggage. Someone will
come out for it. Come on, you two,' he called to the
girls as they paused to give wistful glances in the
direction of the paddock.

'Heather's growing,' he murmured to Claire.

'Mmm. They both are,' but because, obviously, no
one had paid any attention to Heather's wardrobe for
quite a long time, her skirt was well above her small
knees. 'It's going to prove an expensive couple of
days,' Claire warned Jay. 'Both of them need new
school clothes. Of course, I'll pay for Lucy's, but...'

'No.'

The sudden, unexpected pressure of his fingers on
her arm shocked her into immobility. He was close
enough for her to see the fine lines fanning out from

his eyes—eyes that had gone cold and dark with anger. When he was like this he could be very forbidding indeed, she thought, noticing the way his mouth had hardened.

'No, Claire,' he said in a softer tone. 'I told you that from now on, financially, Lucy would be my responsibility, and I meant it. That's part of my contribution to our marriage; please don't deprive me of making it. I don't want to feel beholden to you any more than you do to me, you know. We're partners in this—equal partners.'

She knew that he was right.

He released her arm and she shivered suddenly, missing the protection of his tall body as he moved away from her, and a cold wind bit through her thin jacket.

'Come on, let's get inside; it's cold out here. Come on, you two,' he called to the girls. 'You can admire your new friends later.'

It was an odd sensation to have someone concerned for her comfort after being independent and alone for so long, even if he was only being courteous.

Inside, the hotel retained much of its countryhouse flavour. A smiling receptionist handed Jay a key, and called for a porter to show them the way to their suite. She was a pretty girl with blonde hair and nice teeth, and the way she smiled at Jay reminded Claire of just how sexually attractive he was. That knowledge seemed to heighten her own sense of inadequacy reminding her sharply of all that she wasn't and never could be.

But it was because of the things that she *was* that Jay was marrying her, she reminded herself firmly, and not the things she was not.

Their suite was magnificent: a sitting-room and three bedrooms, each with its own private bathroom, co-ordinated throughout in toning shades of French blue and terracotta. Here were several ideas she could copy for their own guest suites, and for the house itself, Claire reflected, making a closer examination of some decorative faux marbling on the door frames.

'What do you think of it?' Jay asked her, strolling over to join her as she studied the attractive décor of the sitting-room.

'It's lovely!'

'Yes. It certainly should be; they've spent a fortune on renovating the place.' He moved past her to look more closely at the delicate plasterwork on one of the walls, and instantly Claire realised.

'It's yours, isn't it? The plasterwork...'

He was grinning hugely, looking almost carefree.

'Yes, and the columns that have been marbled. I like the way they've done this, don't you?' he asked her, indicating a panel on the wall where the decorative plasterwork inside it had been delicately tinged in a soft terracotta fading to palest peach. 'I wonder how they do it.'

'By putting on the colour and then wiping it off.' Claire told him promptly. 'That way, only the most raised parts of the design get the paint.'

She saw his eyebrows lift and explained. 'It's something I'm very interested in, and last winter I got several books from the library on the subject. We could try something similar in the drawing-room, if you like, it's certainly large enough to take it.'

'Mummy, which bedroom is going to be ours?'

Lucy's impatient question distracted them both, and Claire suggested to her daughter that she and Heather should share the room with the two single beds in it.

While she was talking to them, the porter came up with their luggage. Jay tipped him and then glanced at his watch.

'It's gone twelve o'clock. How about an early lunch and then shopping this afternoon?' To Claire he added, 'We won't have time now, but later I'll show you the sports centre they have here. It's very luxurious, and we supplied the plaster columns that surround the swimming pool. We were called in after they had a bad fire eighteen months ago, and we had to replace and match a lot of the original plasterwork. This hotel is part of a small but very prestigious group which specialises in these country-house settings. We're in the process of negotiating a contract with them for work in other hotels owned by the group.'

He broke off suddenly and frowned, his voice brusque. 'I'm sorry, you don't want to hear all about that. It's boring...'

'It isn't boring at all,' Claire contradicted him quickly. 'I think it's fascinating.'

Jay gave her an odd look, and for the first time she saw in him Heather's vulnerability. She reached out to touch his arm in the same comforting way she would have done one of the girls, and as she touched him, he stopped dead and stared down at her. Immediately Claire withdrew from him, her face scarlet.

'I'm sorry, I...'

'Don't be. There's no need.'

The way he was looking at her made her feel quite odd, breathless and slightly light-headed, and then the lift arrived and he looked away, and everything returned to normal.

They lunched in what had once been the Victorian conservatory, now beautifully restored and replanted.

The menu, although not vegetarian, featured recipes chosen with healthy eating in mind. Claire and Jay both chose a vegetable mosaic in broccoli mousse to start with, while the two girls opted for a fresh fruit platter.

'What would you like for your main course?' Jay asked her.

'I think I'll have the chicken in cheese sauce with vegetables, and the same for the girls.'

'Mmm. I'm going to have the poached fillet of steak.'

The food, when it came, was deliciously light, leaving Claire feeling virtuous enough to opt for crème caramel for her sweet.

Jay had ordered wine with their meal, and over coffee Claire found herself slowly relaxing as the alcohol spread through her body.

'It's just gone two now,' said Jay, glancing at his watch. 'It will take us about twenty minutes to get into Bath, so—if you're ready?'

At half past two exactly, he was skilfully parking the car in the centre of Bath.

It was only a short walk from where they had parked to the main shopping area, but Jay directed them instead to what Claire soon realised was a far more exclusive area.

'I'm told by my secretary that we're far more likely to find what we want here,' was the only explanation he gave Claire, as he shepherded them all into one of the exclusive boutiques.

The woman who came forward to serve them was wearing the most elegant casual clothes Claire had ever seen, and her heart sank. It would cost a small fortune to buy anything here. Jay probably didn't realise. But Jay was already explaining to her that she, Claire, needed a complete winter wardrobe, including evening wear.

'There's a couple of toy shops further along here,' he added to Claire. 'I'll take the girls there and they can start thinking about what they'd like Father Christmas to bring them. We'll come back in, say, an hour.'

Whereas when he had calmly announced what he thought she needed to buy she had felt almost resentful, now, conversely, she felt as though he were deserting her, and wanted to beg him to stay, but he and the girls were gone before she could raise any protest.

'What a sensible man your husband is,' remarked the saleswoman when they had gone. 'Choosing clothes is difficult enough, isn't it, without the added distraction of an impatient family?'

'He isn't my husband,' Claire said weakly. 'At least, not yet. We're getting married tomorrow.'

Now what on earth had made her say that? The woman's semi-formal manner relaxed immediately.

'Oh, how exciting! Have you already chosen something to wear? Of course, I suppose you must...'

When Claire shook her head, she positively beamed.

'Well, you couldn't have chosen a better time to look, because we've just taken delivery of our winter stock. Let's get the basics out of the way first, shall we, and then we can concentrate on the "fancies". What does your own taste run to? Any particular make?'

Claire shook her head, unable to tell her that it was so long since she had bought herself anything that hadn't come from a chain store that she had no idea what to ask for.

'I like the outfit you're wearing,' she managed at last. 'But I'm afraid...'

'This is an Escada, and they do a lovely range. It's one of my favourites. I'll take you into our separates section and you can have a look. I'd say you were only a size 10, if that, so you won't be hard to fit.'

Half an hour later, Claire had chosen a slim-fitting grey skirt with a beautifully detailed silk satin blouse in cream, with padded shoulders that gave her a silhouette that she privately thought was almost film-star-ish. To go with it, the saleswoman suggested a sweater with a bird motif on it, in toning greys and creams, with a touch of blue to go with the very 'county' tweed jacket in the same range of colours.

Clare loved them all.

'It really is a "go anywhere" outfit,' the saleswoman told her, and Claire knew that she was right.

Having settled on them, the woman produced half a dozen day dresses in a variety of styles and colours, and Claire allowed herself to be persuaded into one in bright red, with a diamanté-speckled bow at the throat and rows of demure pintucking down to a dropped waist and slightly flared skirt. It would be a lovely Christmas day dress, and luckily it was the kind of red that she could wear. As this, too, was added to the growing pile, she tried to stifle her growing feeling of guilt. Surely Jay had never meant her to spend so much money, but it seemed that he had, because now the saleswoman was directing her towards the evening clothes section of the shop, which stretched a long way back from its small shop window.

'I think this would suit you,' she told Claire, producing a pretty blue knitted dress with a design on it in sequins and bugle beads. 'This Frank Usher is dressier—great for parties, and then we've a range of cocktail suits.'

In the end Claire found she had added three more outfits to the growing pile.

'Now, all that's left is your wedding outfit. Had you anything in mind?'

When Claire shook her head, she smiled. 'Well, I have! I'll show it to you.'

She came back with an outfit which she showed to Claire. It was pure silk, with a pleated skirt and a blouson top, and a ribbed waistline and cuffs. On the white background was printed a design in soft blue and terracotta, and Claire fell instantly in love with it.

'Try it on,' the woman urged. 'It really is lovely.'

It was. The pleated skirt swayed and clung with every step; the buttons up one side finished mid-thigh so that every movement gave an enticing glimpse of leg. The knitted cuff on the waistband of the top ensured that it fitted snugly, and bloused properly, and Claire knew that if she searched for a month she could never find anything as attractive. But the price...

She was just about to refuse it when Jay and the girls walked in. She saw Jay in the mirror and noticed the way he came to an abrupt halt and just stared at her.

His stillness worried her, and she turned quickly to the saleswoman. 'It's lovely, but I'm afraid it's too expensive. I...'

'No. She's having it,' contradicted Jay flatly. 'I don't care how expensive it is,' he told Claire when she started to object. 'You're having it.'

'You looked very pretty in it, Mummy,' Lucy informed her when she re-emerged from the changing room. 'Didn't she, Heather?'

'Yes.'

'We've been in a toy shop, Mummy, and they had a doll's house, and teddies…and everything…'

'I seem to have spent an awful lot of money, Jay!' confessed Claire.

'I should hope so. That's why I brought you here. Dressing well will be part of your new role, Claire. If I couldn't afford it, you wouldn't be here. You'll need to get shoes, now, won't you and…'

'If I might recommend somewhere,' the saleswoman suggested, overhearing. 'There's a very good shop not very far away, and for good underwear, if I could suggest "Understudy"—it's only four doors away. They specialise in couture underwear.'

Claire could feel the heat crawling up under her skin. It was ridiculous to feel so embarrassed, but she did.

'Right, then,' said Jay when everything had been packed and the bill paid. 'First underwear and then shoes.'

'Jay, you've spent so much already; I don't need…'

'What is it? Are you frightened that I might demand some sort of payment?'

She felt the blood leave her skin as Jay muttered the angry words in her ear.

'No…no, of course not. It's just…'

'Look, I've already tried to explain to you once, Claire: once you're my wife, you'll be expected to look the part. Susie always wore designer fashion; she…'

'I'm not Susie!'

Claire wasn't sure which of them was most surprised by her vehemence. Jay's mouth compressed slightly, his eyes flinty.

'No,' he agreed in a hard voice. 'You're not. And I wasn't making comparisons, if that's what you thought.'

Her small spurt of temper died as quickly as it had been born and Claire shook her head tiredly. 'No, I'm sorry. It's just that I feel so...overwhelmed...'

'Try and think of it as buying a uniform for a new job,' he told her wryly. 'That might help.' They were outside the underwear shop already, and he pulled out his wallet and gave her a sum of money that made her eyes widen in shock.

'I think I can manage to keep the kids occupied for another half an hour. That should be long enough, shouldn't it?'

It was and when she re-emerged with several parcels, Claire marvelled at how quickly she had disposed of such a large sum of money.

'Shoes, and then somewhere to have a cup of tea before we start on the girls' things,' Jay pronounced as he took the packages from her. 'Don't worry, I'm not going to look,' he added drily, correctly interpreting her anxious look. It made her feel gauche and silly.

No doubt Susie had enjoyed not just buying but wearing wisps of lingerie for him. But their marriage wasn't going to be like that, she reminded herself, forcing down the panic that built up inside her every time she compared herself to his ex-wife. There was no need for her to worry. He didn't want another Susie...that was why he was marrying *her*.

# CHAPTER SEVEN

'WAKE UP, MUMMY; it's time for breakfast.'

Claire opened protesting eyes and saw Lucy and Heather, both still in their dressing gowns, perched on her bed.

'Jay said we weren't to put on our new dresses until after breakfast.'

Wise Jay, Claire thought, struggling to sit up. Those delightful grey velvet dresses with their white collars and maroon velvet bows would not be enhanced by the addition of breakfast cereal. They had been shockingly expensive, but Jay had insisted on buying them, 'to wear for the wedding,' and then there had been those irresistible tartan dresses with white collars and matching bows that she hadn't been able to resist for Christmas Day; a red one for Heather with her dark colouring and a green one for Lucy who had inherited her chestnut hair.

'The man brought breakfast on a special table,' Lucy chattered on.

'But Daddy said we had to come and ask if you wanted a cup of tea,' added Heather.

'Ah, so you are awake!'

Jay stood in the doorway. He was wearing pyjama

bottoms and a towelling robe—perfectly respectable articles of clothing, but nevertheless Claire felt her stomach clench and contract in response to the sight of him. He must have had a shower, because his hair was still damp.

'I believe it's tradition for the bride to have her breakfast in bed on her wedding day.'

'Not this bride,' Claire assured him firmly. 'I'm getting up. Come on, you two,' she told the girls, 'off the bed.' Her dressing gown lay just out of reach on a chair, and although her cotton nightshirt was perfectly respectable, she felt reluctant to get out of bed in front of Jay.

She was almost frozen with horror when he casually walked over to the chair and picked up her faded dressing-gown, holding it out to her.

As clearly as though she had spoken her anguish out loud, he came over to the bed, and said in a low voice so that the girls couldn't overhear,

'I'm not going to touch you, but there are going to be times when we're going to have to act the part of an apparently normally married couple. Children are very quick, and we don't want either of them worrying that something isn't right about our marriage. They'll accept the fact that we have separate rooms much more easily if they can see that we're on reasonably intimate terms. And the time to start establishing that is now, unless you want to be the object of village speculation and gossip.'

Claire knew that he was right. Even so, she wished he would move away from the bed, and more than that she wished that he would put down her robe and go away, but he wasn't going to. So she had to push back the covers and swing unsteady legs to the carpeted floor, trying to appear as casually relaxed as Jay was himself as he handed her her robe. As she turned to take it from him, his fingers rested on her arm, his mouth brushing a light kiss against her forehead. She could smell the clean mint freshness of his breath, and the soapiness of his body.

The reality of him was so different from her deeply suppressed memories of her attacker that it held her tense with surprise.

She heard him say her name, but wasn't aware of the harsh undertone to his voice until his grip on her arms tightened and she focused on him.

His eyes were brilliant with an anger that made her recoil sharply. 'No…Claire…' His grip prevented her from breaking free. 'I'm sorry. The look on your face brought home to me what could have happened to Heather. I think it takes being a father to bring home to a man how vulnerable and unprotected women are. I think if any man hurt either Heather or Lucy I would tear him apart with my bare hands. I wish I could turn time back for you and wipe out what happened, but I can't…'

'No… And at least I have Lucy,' Claire said unsteadily.

The emotion in his eyes and voice had been so unexpected. His fingers still dug into her arm and she covered them gently.

'I'm sorry, did I hurt you? I...' He sounded almost dazed.

'It doesn't matter.'

Heather and Lucy had disappeared into the sitting-room, but now Heather came back, hovering uncertainly in the doorway, eyeing them both with an anxiety that tore at Claire's heart.

'Susie never liked her interrupting us,' muttered Jay huskily when he saw Claire's frown. 'In some way she almost seemed to be jealous of any attention I gave her.'

Understanding the reason for the little girl's hesitation, Claire smiled at her. 'Come on, let's all have breakfast,' she suggested cheerfully. 'After all, we've got a wedding to go to.'

Contrary to all her expectations, the civil ceremony, far from being austere and unmeaningful, took place in a small, prettily decorated room. On the registrar's desk was a bowl of fresh flowers, and Claire had the feeling that everything that could be done had been done to make the room attractive and welcoming. The service, simple though it was, was very moving, causing even Lucy to remain silent in awareness of the solemnity of the occasion.

Jay didn't kiss her, and she was glad of that. Her nerves were too tightly strung to endure much more.

A cold wind knifed through her thin suit as they all walked outside. Claire saw Jay frown and put out an arm as though he intended to draw her close to his side to keep her warm, and she moved away from him automatically, shivering as she felt the wind bite.

'You need a coat.'

'I've already got one,' she told him lightly. It was true, she had; an ancient duffle-coat which she had bought second-hand but which was excellent at keeping out the cold.

'Now that you're married, will Jay be my daddy?' Lucy demanded irrepressibly as Jay led the way back to the car.

Over her head Jay looked at Claire. Stooping down to the little girl's height, he asked her quietly, 'Would you like me to be your daddy, Lucy?'

Her emphatic 'Yes,' would have made Claire smile at any other time.

'And Heather wants you to be her mummy,' she told Claire firmly.

Claire bit her lip and looked helplessly at Jay. Heather already had a mother.

'I think it will be easier all round if we let both girls call us "Mummy" and "Daddy",' he suggested softly.

'But Heather...'

'I want you to be my mummy,' Heather protested, clinging to Claire's arm and gazing up at her, and Claire didn't have the heart to deny her.

Whatever happened though, she promised herself, if Heather ever wanted to talk about her mother, and to see her, she would do her utmost to ensure that she did. Maybe now, with Susie's rejection of her very much to the forefront of her mind, she didn't want to know about her natural mother, but later, when she was more adult... It was something she would have to discuss with Jay, Claire admitted to herself, but not right now.

'Who's hungry?' asked Jay, lightening the emotional mood. 'I've booked us into a local restaurant for lunch,' he told Claire. 'I felt we should do something to celebrate, but I also thought you might not like the idea of the hotel staff knowing that we'd just got married.'

His sensitivity, so unexpected in so tough a man, made her eyes sting with emotional tears. It seemed unbelievable that a man who had so many demands on his time already should make the effort to arrange a celebratory luncheon for what, after all, to him was merely a business arrangement.

The restaurant was in a small village several miles outside Bath. The chef had trained with the Roux brothers, Jay informed Claire as they drew up outside.

The restaurant had once been a farmhouse, and a huge log fire burned in the enormous hearth, throwing out a welcome heat. The furniture was simple and cottagey, the beamed walls colour-washed a soft cream, the old rose carpet on the floor enhancing the intimate atmosphere of the place.

They were shown to a table slightly secluded from the others, a deferential waiter ceremoniously unfolding the crisply starched pink napkins and placing them on two grey velvet laps, much to the awed delight of the girls.

'I've already ordered our meal,' Jay explained. 'So if there's anything you don't like...' He broke off as another waiter advanced with an ice bucket and two glasses.

'Champagne,' he told Claire quietly. 'I felt it was appropriate.'

Champagne! It was the last thing she had expected, and she sipped the golden wine nervously, gasping as the ice-cool liquid bubbled down her throat.

'Like it?'

'It's lovely! I've never had any before.' She flushed, wondering what on earth Jay must think of a woman of her age who had never tasted champagne, but he looked more sombre than amused.

'You can drink it with your first course,' he told her, 'I'll order wine to have with the main meal.'

'Mummy, what's that you're drinking?' Lucy demanded, and when Claire told her, she said eagerly, 'May I have some?'

She was just about to refuse, when Jay summoned a waiter and said something to him. Within seconds he returned and put down two glasses of fresh orange juice, to which he added a very small amount of champagne before handing them to the girls.

Watching Lucy's beatific expression as she sipped her drink, Claire could only marvel at how much Jay had enriched their lives already.

'You're spoiling them. You're spoiling all of us,' she remonstrated.

'A little bit of spoiling once in a while never did anyone any harm.'

It was mid-afternoon before they left the restaurant. Claire had eaten caviare, and truffles, and vegetables so perfectly fresh that the flavour had been indescribable. It was a meal she would never forget, even if it had not marked their wedding ceremony, and she shuddered to think how much it had all cost.

'Feel like a quick trip round the factory before we go back to the hotel, or would you prefer to go straight back?'

'I'd like to see round the factory,' Claire told him eagerly. The more she saw of Jay's work, the more eager she was to see how it was produced.

Jay's factory was situated in a purpose-built modern building on the edge of an industrial estate. His small work-force treated Claire deferentially but with reserve until they realised that she was genuinely interested in their work, and then it was as though the floodgates had opened.

These were craftsmen, Claire realised, listening to them—men who took a pride in what they were doing, and who believed that what they were creating today would be the heirlooms of tomorrow.

'You haven't forgotten that you're taking us to the zoo tomorrow, Mummy, have you?' demanded Lucy sleepily later on that evening after she and Heather had been put to bed.

They had all dined together in the suite, and then they had watched television together.

At first Claire had felt uncomfortably aware of her changed status, but Jay's manner towards her was so calm and matter-of-fact that her tension had gradually gone. Now she felt pleasantly tired.

'I don't know about you, but I feel that an early

night is in order,' he remarked easily when she went back into the sitting-room.

'I agree, especially bearing in mind tomorrow's trip to the zoo!'

Jay had stood up as she walked into the room, but he made no move towards her as she walked across to her own bedroom.

'I'll say goodnight, then,' she said gravely, pausing outside it.

'Yes. Sleep well.'

So now she was married, Claire thought flatly as she closed her bedroom door behind her. What was Jay thinking right now? Was he comparing tonight to his first wedding night—comparing her to Susie?

Stop it, she chided herself. Jay married you because he doesn't want another relationship like the one he had with Susie.

THEY HAD A FORTNIGHT of relatively uninterrupted peace, with Jay commuting daily to the factory, and then he came home one night and announced that he had to go back to the States.

'Apparently there are a couple of points in the contract they want to discuss. I shouldn't be gone for too long. I might even pick up some additional business! Apparently my client's sister wants to talk to me about remodelling her indoor swimming pool and its surroundings, using our stuff. If all goes well I ought to be back by the end of the week.'

They all went with him to the airport to see him off, and then Claire got a taxi back to Bath. With nearly a whole day to spare, she was determined to make a start on her plans for the house.

The blue and terracotta colour scheme at the hotel had fired her imagination, and already she had a few tentative ideas of what she wanted to do, but first she needed to find someone to help her, and she remembered seeing a small shop in Bath which had advertised an interior design service.

She found it easily enough and paused outside to admire the window. A bolt of material was draped carelessly over a single chair; an arrangement of toning dried flowers displayed next to it on a pastel-toned kilim rug.

Feeling slightly apprehensive, Claire went inside, warning Lucy and Heather not to touch anything.

A smiling blonde woman came to serve her. Slightly plump, and in her mid-thirties, she looked as elegant as her window.

It didn't take Claire long to outline her ideas, and within minutes of being shown wallpaper pattern books and swatches of fabrics, she knew that she had found someone on her own wavelength.

'What I'd really like is for you to come out to the house,' she confided. 'I don't want to employ an interior designer as such, because I want the house to reflect our own taste. I want it to be a home, not a show place, but I need advice on where I can find the right kind of decorators—you know the sort of thing.'

'Yes, I do, and most of my clients feel the same way that you do. There is a move away from the very traditional interior design service now, to one where we work alongside the client.' She picked up a diary. 'I could come out on Thursday morning if that's any good.'

'That's fine.' Claire gave her directions, and left the shop feeling buoyed up with achievement.

It had occurred to her that since Jay's craftsmen could make panelling and bookcases, they must also be able to craft kitchen units for her, and on impulse, instead of going straight home, she asked her taxi driver to call at the factory on the way.

The foreman remembered her and made her welcome. When Claire explained what she wanted, he readily agreed that it was something they could do.

'Any work in hand would have to take precedence, of course,' Claire acknowledged, 'but what I had in mind was something in antique pine?'

'You're in luck there. Jay recently bought up some old pine doors from a demolition site. I'll have to check with him that he doesn't have something in mind for them, of course.'

Hastily concurring with this, Claire left it that once Jay had returned, and if he was in agreement, some-one could come out to the house to measure up for her kitchen.

She had already decided that in the girls' room she would have fitted walls and cupboards built which could then be painted and decorated with stencils, and that in the guest rooms, the same simple type of built-in furniture could be marbled, dragged or sponged in a variety of paint finishes to create a very luxurious effect.

The displays in some of the shop windows reminded her that Christmas wasn't very far away. She already had a fair idea of what both girls wanted, and she and Jay had already talked over the idea of riding lessons and then possibly a pony to share if their enthusiasm lasted.

This would be the first Christmas that she had not had to scrimp to buy Lucy even the simplest present. She glanced down at her daughter's burnished head. Already she could see the difference in Lucy; she was a little girl who needed a masculine influence in her life, and she adored Jay. Heather, too, had blossomed, and now she chattered as happily as Lucy, as both of them drew her attention to a shop window filled with a cornucopia of childish delights.

The bright sunny day had given way to a frosty evening when they eventually got back to the house. After supper, when Claire was tidying up, the phone rang.

When she picked it up and heard Jay's voice, she was almost too stunned to speak. They chatted for several minutes, mostly about the children, and even though she had not been expecting the call, when he eventually rang off she felt curiously bereft.

What would he be doing tonight? Would he be alone in his hotel room, or, far more likely, would he be out somewhere being wined and dined? And then afterwards, would he...?

Angry with herself, she pushed the thought away. She had no right to question the very personal side of Jay's life. If he chose to go to bed with someone that was no concern of hers. So why was there this unpleasant little ache inside her? Shaking her head, she switched off the lights and made her way slowly upstairs. The house felt empty without him. Already she missed him; she missed his company at supper, missed hearing about his days, missed their chats by the fire after dinner.

He came back at the end of the week, and the whole house seemed to come alive. Both little girls flung themselves at him the moment he opened the door, and Claire saw in the look he gave her over their heads that he was pleased with the change in Heather.

After dinner he told her about his trip. She learned that in addition to the contract which was now due to be signed after the New Year, he had also received commissions from several of his client's friends and from his sister.

When Claire enthused he frowned.

'Yes, it's good for business, but it does mean I'm going to be away quite a lot, although I hope only for the next few weeks.'

'Well, the girls will be pleased,' she remarked drily, 'especially if you keep spoiling them with presents like those you brought back this time.'

The huge patchwork dolls Jay had brought back with him from Dallas were so exquisitely detailed that Claire felt they were more for just looking at than playing with, and she knew, just from the workmanship, that they must have been horrendously expensive.

'Guilty conscience presents,' he explained, frowning suddenly as he added, 'which reminds me.' He got up. 'I won't be a minute. Wait here.'

He was back almost immediately carrying a large manilla envelope which he gave to her.

'Your wedding present,' he told her quietly.

Claire opened it and took out the contents, smoothing them with suddenly tense fingers. She read through the papers once again and then again just to make sure she wasn't making any mistakes.

'You're paying for the work to be done on the cottage! But it will cost thousands! Jay, you mustn't feel you need to do that...'

'I wanted to do it. Let's face it, Claire, I could have offered to pay for the damage in the first place, then you wouldn't have needed to marry me.' He held up his hand when she would have interrupted. 'No, I'm not implying that you married me purely for material reasons—I know how much you love Heather—but you have to admit that it was an excellent lever, and I used it deliberately. In fact, that storm couldn't have come at a better time as far as I was concerned. If you hadn't had to move in here, we would have had to have a long courtship, with all its attendant problems, and for selfish reasons I wanted our marriage accomplished fast. I've already made the mistake of trapping one woman into marriage; I wanted to give you an escape route if you ever felt you needed it. I was going to suggest that when the work is complete you let the cottage—everyone likes to have their own financial independence; it won't bring in much, but at least it will be yours.'

His sensitivity made her want to weep. How long had it been since a man, any man, had shown her such consideration, such care?

Almost without thinking she leaned forward, touching the side of his face with her fingers. 'Oh, Jay, I just don't know what to say!'

He turned his head, his fingers clasping her wrist, and she gasped as she felt the warm pressure of his mouth against the palm of her hand.

The moment she tensed he released her.

'Sorry.' His voice sounded gruff. 'I'd forgotten.'

'It...it doesn't matter. I'll go and make some coffee.' Claire stood up shakily and hurried into the kitchen. How on earth could she have explained to him that her tension had come not from the warm contact of his mouth against her palm, but from her own totally unexpected reaction to it? She had liked it; she had enjoyed the totally pleasurable sensation that had shot through her body.

HE WAS AT HOME FOR FIVE days, just enough time to go shopping with the girls to buy advent calendars, and to keep them occupied while Claire sneaked their carefully chosen presents into the house. And then he was gone. Back to Dallas to discuss the final details of the contract.

The American client was a builder, specialising in prestigious new houses, for which he wanted only the finest craftsmanship. Of a neo-Georgian design, their proportions lent themselves well to the reproduction plasterwork Jay's company produced, but the American lawyers were finicking over every detail, and so Jay and his solicitor had to fly out once again.

It worried Claire how much she missed him. She oughtn't to have done; after all, she had never wanted a husband—but Jay wasn't just a husband, he was a person who made her laugh, who treated her as an equal, who filled out and warmed her life in a way she could never have believed possible.

She went with him to the airport, where he was meeting his solicitor, and was surprised by the sudden surge of desolation that struck her as he walked away. She wanted to cling on to him, to… Abruptly her body tensed as she watched his retreating back. Confusion and panic replaced desolation. What was happening to her? She mustn't become emotionally dependent on Jay as well as financially dependent on him.

The days flew by, excitement mounting as the girls opened door after door on their advent calendars. They were both in the school play—nearly everyone in the school was involved in it in one way or another. Claire went to see them, and took Mrs Vickers with her because Jay was still away.

The last few days before Christmas trickled away far too fast. Jay rang three days before Christmas Eve to warn her that he could only get home at the last minute. Claire, who had put off buying and dressing a tree in the hope that he would be home in time, took the girls to the local garden centre and they chose one together, but it wasn't the same as it would have been if Jay had been with her.

After Christmas, work would start on the house, but until then she had warmed up the sitting-room with deep pink and blue satinised-cotton-covered cushions and a large, toning rug.

But without Jay in it the house lacked something Claire recognised; she missed his vibrantly masculine presence. A trickle of awareness ran down her spine, a sense of danger and unease. She didn't want to miss Jay, to be so conscious of his absences. She dismissed her thoughts as foolish, but something lingered, some faint frisson of knowledge that she determinedly forced into the back of her mind to think about later— much, much later.

# CHAPTER EIGHT

THE NIGHT BEFORE Christmas Eve, they decorated the tree. Claire sat looking at it after the girls had gone to bed, watching the soft dazzle of the tiny pinpoints of light. Everything was ready: the presents were wrapped, including the appallingly expensive desk filing system she had bought for Jay, the turkey was keeping cold in the garage, all the shopping was done, and for once even the weather was in tune with the season. It had been cold all day, and now the night sky had a dull glow that presaged snow.

Everything was ready, but Jay was not here to share it with them. She told herself that she was disappointed for the girls, that it was because of them that that small ball of pain lodged deep inside her wouldn't go away.

She stretched tiredly and got up to tidy away the debris from the tree decorations. Perhaps if she made some mince pies that might help relax her.

She went into the kitchen and was soon busily engaged in the ritual of making pastry. Through the window she saw the first flakes of snow fall, and was unable to resist the childish impulse to watch. Thick, fat snowflakes fell from a midnight blue sky, whirling and dancing in a pattern that mesmerised her. A fine white blanket covered the ground before she managed to drag herself away.

Snow for Christmas. She finished making her mince pies and put them in the oven.

It was still snowing half an hour later when the pies were cooling on a rack and she had finished cleaning the kitchen. It was too early to go to bed, but she felt too keyed up to sit down and watch television or read a book.

She was just about to make herself a cup of hot chocolate when the back door suddenly opened.

'Jay!' She said his name unsteadily, unable to believe it was him. The snow must have muted the sound of his car. Snowflakes clung to his hair and jacket.

Somehow, without knowing how it had happened, she had crossed the kitchen floor, her face alight with pleasure.

She touched his arm and grimaced. 'You're all cold and wet!' She was standing so close to him that when she looked up she could see the dark irises of his eyes. As she looked his expression changed and she felt a strange tension grip her.

'You're...you're back early...'

Her voice sounded rusty, and she seemed to be having difficulty breathing.

'I managed to get an earlier flight; Christmas is no time to be away from home. Girls in bed?'

'Yes. Over an hour ago.'

For some reason she felt oddly flat. She moved

away from him, checking as he laid his hand on her arm.

'Claire.'

She turned towards him, her eyes widening as he bent his head and she felt the warm brush of his mouth against her own. It was an odd sensation, that soft touch of warm lips. It made her quiver inside, and realise on a searing wave of pain that never once in her life had she been kissed properly.

The sudden shocking hiss of boiling milk spilling on to the cooker jolted her back to reality, her body stiffening with rejection and fear. Immediately Jay released her.

'I'm sorry.' He sounded weary. 'For a moment I forgot....'

What had he forgotten? That he wasn't coming home to Susie? 'It doesn't matter...'

She just caught the expression of grimness tightening his mouth before he turned away.

'I was just making myself a cup of chocolate. Would you like one...or something to eat?' she asked hurriedly.

'These smell good.'

He had obviously recognised her conciliatory offer and was trying to respond to it, Claire realised as he picked up one of her mince pies and ate it.

'Chocolate will be fine, and then an early night, I think. I ate on the plane.'

'Shall we drink it in the sitting-room?'

Those few moments of strained intimacy might never have occurred. On the surface all was as it had always been, but beneath the surface Claire was just beginning to realise that there lurked some very treacherous waters indeed.

What would have happened if the milk hadn't boiled over? Would he have gone on kissing her? Would she have let him…? It was too uncomfortable an avenue of thought for her to pursue.

'You go through; I'll bring the chocolate in a minute.'

The faintly sardonic look he gave her made her face burn. Did he realise how odd his proximity was making her feel? She felt that she needed to be alone to get herself back to normal. That brief pressure of his mouth against hers had unleashed a series of sensations she was still having difficulty coming to terms with.

It hadn't been dislike or fear she had felt in those few seconds before reality had intruded, far from it. So, what had she felt? Shock, grief for all that was missing from her life, and also a frisson of pleasure so delicate and new to her that even now she wasn't sure if she had experienced it or merely imagined it. But surely it was impossible to imagine something like that—something she had never known before in her life, or dreamed of knowing? Now she had known it.

Shaking herself free of her confusing thoughts, she put the two mugs of chocolate on a tray and added a plate of mince pies, quickly making some sandwiches from the ham she had roasted that morning.

Jay was sitting on the settee when she walked in,

his head relaxed against the cushions. 'I like the tree,' he commented, getting up to pull up one of the small coffee-tables for her to put the tray on.

The room had an open fireplace with an immense cream marble surround, part of the original Victorian architecture. Susie had had the fireplace blocked off, and one of the first things Claire had done was to have it re-opened and an attractive coal effect gas fire installed. She switched it on, and paused for a moment to watch the flickering flames.

'Mmm…very cosy.' An expression of sadness seemed to cloud Jay's eyes.

'The girls wanted to wait until you came home to decorate it, but I thought you might be too late.'

'There's nothing on the top.'

'I couldn't reach,' Claire confessed. 'There's a fairy in the box that the girls chose.'

'I'll put it on for them tomorrow. Mmm, these are good.'

He was eating one of the sandwiches she had made. Without his suit jacket and his shirt open at the throat he looked less formidable. He was tired, she realised.

'How did it go in Dallas?' she asked.

'Come and sit down here beside me and I'll tell you.'

She sat next to him on the sofa.

'What an excellent wife you are, Claire: caring, obedient…'

At first she thought he was mocking her and she flushed painfully and started to move away, his hand on her arm stopping her.

'What's the matter?'

'I know...I'm not Susie,' she said painfully. 'It can't be much...fun for you coming home to me, Jay...'

'Fun?' His mouth twisted bitterly. 'Is that what you think Susie and I had, Claire? There's nothing fun about coming home to find your wife's out enjoying herself with another man, while your child is left all alone. There's nothing fun about knowing she's being unfaithful, about knowing she doesn't give a damn. I never caught an early flight to come home to Susie, Claire, because I never knew what I was coming home to. If you want the truth, I dreaded coming home.'

His mouth compressed, his eyes focusing on the leaping flames of the fire, as he looked back into the past.

'Don't ever thing I'm comparing you with Susie— there is no comparison.'

No, there wasn't, Claire realised. He had loved and desired Susie, while she was just someone whom he had chosen to marry because of Heather.

'I have to go back to Dallas after the New Year, and I want you and the girls to come too. John and his wife want to meet you.'

'Me—but...?'

'It's the American way,' he told her laconically. 'They're throwing a big party to celebrate the signing of the contract and we're invited to be their house guests. It will be during the school holidays, so it shouldn't be too much of a problem.'

Jay moved to pick up his mug of chocolate, the muscles down his back and arm tautening. His skin where it was exposed by the collar and cuff of his shirt was brown and firm, his wrist very sinewy in comparison to hers.

'This will be Heather's first real Christmas; Susie always preferred to go away somewhere.' He put down his empty mug and relaxed back against the cushions. Somehow he seemed to have moved closer to her, but she felt no compulsion to move away.

'You look tired.'

He turned his head and she saw the small darker flecks in his eyes. 'I am,' he admitted. He closed his eyes and sighed. 'It was quite a shock to come home and find snow.'

'My first white Christmas.'

He made a sound in his throat that might have meant anything and Claire turned to look at him. His eyes were closed and she sensed that he was on the verge of falling asleep.

She got up to take their cups to the kitchen, and when she came back he was fast asleep, sprawled out against the sofa. She leaned over him shaking him gently.

'Jay...'

'Mmm.'

The shock of his arms coming round her and pulling her down against the relaxed warmth of his body was totally unexpected. Her knees had caught against

the edge of the sofa so that she had collapsed on to
him, and now he was burrowing his face into the
curve of her neck, his breath triggering off tiny con-
vulsive waves of sensation where it touched her skin.

After her initial moment of panic, what she felt was
nothing like the terror and disgust she had experienced before. Being held in Jay's arms was so totally
different from that. She felt at once both safe and yet
deliciously trembly, her body fitting softly against the
hard planes of his.

He was cuddling up to her in much the same way
that Heather held on to her teddy, she thought with
shaky amusement, and she had no doubt that he was
totally oblivious to what he was doing. It would have
been the easiest thing in the world to wake him up
and break out of his hold of her, but for some reason
she felt no compulsion to do so. Instead she raised
her hand tentatively and touched the stubbly line of
his jaw, held deep in thrall to a curious need to know
more of the alien maleness of him. He muttered something in his sleep, releasing her momentarily as he
raised his hand to cover hers, his head turning so that
he could caress the soft skin of her palm with his
mouth. The sensation that shot through her was so
totally unexpected, so thoroughly unnerving, that she
jerked back instinctively.

Instantly Jay was awake, his eyelids lifting, although he didn't move. His cheekbone pressed hard
against her shoulder, and she was acutely conscious
of him in a thousand previously unknown ways. As
though some deep inner part of her was waking from

a long sleep, she felt the first stirrings of what she sensed instinctively was her suppressed sexuality.

Fear, joy, an exhilaration beyond anything she had previously known quivered through her; she felt as though she wanted to get up and dance, to burst out into a song of pleasure, to open her heart to him and tell him about the miracle his touch had somehow achieved. Because to her it was a miracle that for the first time since she was attacked she had felt like a woman.

A great flood of joy filled her. She wanted to reach out and touch him to communicate to him in all the ways there were her sense of release and freedom, but already he was withdrawing from her, his expression shuttered, as he said curtly,

'Sorry about that, Claire. I didn't mean to touch you.'

It was like someone cruelly puncturing a gaily coloured balloon. One moment it was a thing of joy and beauty floating free; the next it was gone. She came down to earth with his curt words ringing in her head, and she shivered violently, suddenly realizing her own folly.

Jay had married her because she wasn't a sexual woman, and she must not let herself forget that. He didn't want the complications of any sort of emotional relationship with her, and for her a relationship in the physical sense would have to contain an element of emotional commitment as well.

A physical relationship? What on earth was she thinking? Her face went white with the shock of the realisation that hit her. She licked her lips nervously, unaware of her state of frozen tension or of the interpretation Jay was putting on her stiff silence.

'Look, Claire, it won't happen again. It was a momentary aberration, nothing more.' He got up and paced the floor tensely. 'Try and put it out of your mind.'

What was he saying to her? Her confused mind tried to sort out the meaning of the words, and failed.

'I…I think I ought to go to bed.'

She got up, still trembling wildly, retreating from him when he reached out to help her.

Jay watched her as she fled from the room, and then walked over to the fireplace, to stare moodily out of the darkened window. In front of it the tree glimmered softly in all its finery, but he didn't see it.

A frustrated bitterness glittered in his eyes as he turned to face his own reflection in the giltwood mirror above the fireplace.

'Damn!' he swore savagely, bringing his fist down on to the marble with a force that threatened to crack the bones. 'Damn…and damn again…'

ON CHRISTMAS MORNING they were up early, despite the fact that Claire and Jay had attended Midnight Mass the night before.

Both girls had had small stockings filled with little presents left at the bottom of their beds the night before, but Claire had already stipulated that the rest of the presents, which were piled beneath the tree, were not to be opened until after breakfast. She suspected that was the only way of making sure that Heather and Lucy got something inside them.

There had been another fall of snow, and there had been a magical quality to their walk through the village to the pretty Norman church the night before. Jay, in a fit of impulsive extravagance, had insisted on buying a huge red wooden sledge for the girls on Christmas Eve, and that too was now wrapped up beneath the tree alongside the dolls' pram Heather had asked for, and Lucy's bike.

Claire had spent almost every evening in December knitting small woolly garments for the golden-haired doll who was to occupy the pram, and against her better judgment both girls were to receive the much desired, and to Claire's mind, quite revolting pastel-haired plastic ponies they had both ecstatically requested.

Tastes change, she reminded herself, as she heard the squeals of pleasure coming from their room, and no doubt she had pleaded for things that her parents had found equally incomprehensible.

She was still smiling about this when her bedroom door opened, but it wasn't the girls who came in, it was Jay, a towelling robe belted over his pyjama bottoms, a cup of tea and some digestive biscuits on the tray he was carrying.

The awkwardness she had anticipated having to cope with after the evening of his return had never materialised. In the morning Jay had been as casually relaxed as he had always been, and she had been too busy to give more than a passing thought to her own reaction to him. In fact she had begun to think she had imagined it, but the way her heart jerked like a stranded fish just because he walked into her room told her better.

'You're looking very flushed,' he commented, completely misreading her vivid blush. 'Not sickening for a cold, are you? Those boots you were wearing last night...'

The boots in question were old ones, but they were good enough for the snow.

'I'm fine,' she told him, watching him put the tray down on her bedside table, before he perched himself on the edge of the bed.

'Mmm. You were looking very perky when I came in. You were grinning like a Cheshire Cat!'

'I was thinking about those awful ponies we bought for the girls and wondering if I ever wanted something that appalled my parents.'

'Well, I know I did,' confessed Jay. 'My parents were both members of CND, and one year I asked Father Christmas for a tank and sub-machine gun. It says a lot for their understanding that I got both—I also got twelve months' worth of lectures from my mother, pointing out the savagery of war.'

He didn't often talk about his family, possibly because the subject had never come up, and Claire had not liked to question him.

'What happened to them?' she asked now.

'My mother was killed in a rail accident in France and my father died of a heart attack not long afterwards. I was the only one, and away at university at

the time. I missed them, of course, but I think it's
only when one becomes a parent oneself that one real-
ises the true depth of parental love.'

'Yes. They say, don't they, that it's the mark of a
successful parent to be able to send out one's young
to enjoy the world without them having to give you
a backward glance. The security of a loving background—'

'Helps to create a child who is healthily selfish in
its attitude to its parents. Yes, I know. You've done
wonders with Heather,' Jay added quietly. 'She's a
different child.'

'She just needed more self-confidence. Heather
knows I love her, and because of that...'

'She can love herself...' He broke off and grimaced
as two small bodies came hurtling into the room.

'Downstairs, the pair of you,' he told them. 'We're
going to make breakfast for Mummy this morning.'

They were wearing their new tartan dresses, and
Claire felt her throat lock with emotional tears as she
saw the matching tartan bows tied in their hair. Both
of them wanted to grow their hair, and for school she
made them wear it plaited. This morning both of them
sported rather drunken bows.

'Heather put my ribbon in my hair for me,' announced Lucy cheerfully, darting past Jay to climb on
to the bed.

'And Lucy did mine.' Heather, not to be outdone,
climbed on the other side, still clutching her stocking.

'Look what Father Christmas brought me...'

'And me...'

'Something tells me if I want any breakfast, I'm going to have to make it on my own,' smiled Jay.

'I'll be down in a minute,' Claire assured him, shooing both girls off the bed.

'Mummy, have you got a new dress to wear too?'

She was going to wear the pretty red one she had bought in Bath. The girls' excitement was infectious, and Claire felt it bubble up inside her as she showered and dressed.

When she got down to the kitchen, Heather and Lucy were happily tucking into bowls of creamy porridge. Jay had made the coffee, and the rich smell of it floated aromatically on the air.

'Can I leave you in charge while I go up and get dressed?'

'Don't be long, will you, Daddy?' Heather demanded impatiently.

It was impossible to keep the girls at the table after they had finished eating. They had already seen the pile of brightly wrapped presents surrounding the tree, and Jay and Claire exchanged amused looks over their heads as they hurried Jay to finish his toast.

'You're looking very festive,' he murmured to her as they followed the girls to the sitting-room. 'Red suits you.'

He was wearing a pair of mid-blue trousers that clung to the hard muscles of his thighs. His checked woollen shirt was open at the throat, the softness of the cashmere sweater he was wearing over it touching Claire's skin as the girls dashed past them and she was forced to move closer to his side.

If having one child at Christmas time was fun, having two was more than double the pleasure. As she remembered her pathetic attempts to make something special out of Christmas for Lucy when she was a baby, Claire thought wistfully of the delight it would be to be able to watch that wide-eyed joy and bewilderment now, in these warm protected surroundings.

Lucy's first Christmas had been in the cold damp of their flat, her first Christmas tree one Claire had salvaged at a jumble sale. Expensive presents didn't make Christmas, she knew that, but warmth, comfort, security; these all added an indefinable lustre of pleasure to this special time of year.

For a few seconds there was pandemonium as sheet after sheet of wrapping paper was shredded in their wild attempts to discover what was inside, but Claire had deliberately given them the much desired ponies first, and once they had assured themselves that Father Christmas had not been remiss in this regard, they settled down quite contentedly to savour the rest of their booty.

Claire, who had not been expecting any presents at all, was surprised to discover that she had quite a pile, two of them very inexpertly wrapped, and decorated with stick-on home-made Christmas trees.

'We made those for you,' Heather told her importantly. 'Daddy helped us.'

It brought a lump to her throat to think of Jay finding precious time to assist with the choosing and wrapping of her presents. Another man could quite easily have carelessly ignored the sensitive feelings of two very feminine six-year-olds and had them gift-wrapped instead. Even though she prided herself on being practical, Claire knew quite well that those lovingly made wrappings would find their way into the large cardboard box in which she hoarded all her sentimental treasures.

This was the first year Lucy had had someone to assist her with such a task, and as she looked into her daughter's shining eyes as she unwrapped the soap and bath oil she had chosen, she felt a tremendous surge of gratitude and joy.

This marriage was right; right for Heather and Lucy and right for her. But was it right for Jay? a tiny inner voice asked her. Would he come to regret his selflessness in putting Heather's needs before his own?

'Smell it, Mummy,' urged Lucy. 'I chose it specially, because it reminded me of you.'

Rather cautiously Claire took the top off the bath oil, and was surprised to discover that despite its rather virulent colour it smelled pleasantly of roses.

'Now mine,' Heather instructed, watching her with anxious eyes as she carefully unwrapped her second untidy parcel.

'We saved up with our spending money,' Lucy explained importantly. 'Daddy saved it for us, didn't you?'

Although Heather had been calling her 'Mummy' for some time, and had indeed anxiously asked to be allowed to do so, this was the first time Lucy had referred to Jay as 'Daddy'.

Wondering if Jay was as aware of this completely

natural acceptance of him as she was herself, Claire
glanced across at him, and saw that he shared her
feelings.

In a moment of shared intimacy and awareness they
continued to look at one another, and Claire experienced a closeness to him that made her feel both ex-
alted and humble.

'Look at mine,' Heather urged her impatiently, tugging on her sleeve. 'Look at mine!'

The moment was gone, but Claire knew that she
would remember and savour it later.

Heather had bought her body lotion and talc to go
with Lucy's soap and bath oil. Overcome with emotion, Claire held out her arms to both of them, hugging them tightly. Lucy, as always, was the first to
break free.

'Daddy hasn't opened his present yet,' she said severely.

'Something tells me that Father Christmas has been
extremely active on my behalf this year,' drawled Jay,
looking at Claire. It was true that she had found several small things to add to her original present, and
then of course there was the girls' contribution. They
had bought him a leather wallet from their combined
savings, and on impulse Claire had taken them both
to have their photographs taken wearing their new
velvet dresses.

In addition to the large photograph which she had
had framed and which was now waiting to be unwrapped amongst his other presents, were two indi-

vidual small ones, just the right size to go in his wallet.

She held her breath as he opened their present, but she needn't have worried; his reaction was everything that was necessary to delight both girls.

It took another hour for them to fight the way through the rest of their presents, while Claire tidied up and collected the discarded wrappings.

She had kept back the filing system she had bought for Jay until last. He had already opened the Roger and Gallet toilet water she had bought him and unwrapped the navy jacquard sweater with its design in olive and maroon, and she held her breath as he now unwrapped her last gift.

For a moment the expression on his face confused her. He looked so strange that she wondered if she had somehow angered him.

'If you don't like it...' she began, tentatively, but he shook his head.

'I love it,' he said simply. 'Come here.'

She got up unsteadily, wondering what it was he wanted. Was he perhaps going to kiss her, the way he had done the girls? Her heart thudded shakily at the prospect, but when she reached him, although he took hold of her hand, it was just to tug her down beside him.

'Here's my present to you,' he said softly, handing her a long rectangular parcel.

Claire frowned. She had already received several presents from him, including one of perfume, and an American cookery book, that a brief glance had told her she was going to enjoy. There had also been a much coveted decorators' directory she had glimpsed in the window of an exclusive book shop in Bath, and, rather surprisingly, a silky camisole in softest peach, lavishly trimmed with lace.

'Open it!' demanded Lucy impatiently.

All they had left to open were their large presents, hidden behind the tree, and so, bemusedly, Claire started to unwrap her gift. Inside the paper was a dark leather-covered jewellers' box edged in gold. Claire felt her stomach clench in shock as she fumbled with the fastening and got it open. On the bed of dark velvet lay a necklet of milky pearls, supporting a heart-shaped emerald surrounded by diamonds. It was the most exquisite thing she had ever seen, and she touched it tentatively, too stunned for words.

'Jay...it's...' She looked up at him and swallowed. 'You shouldn't have bought me this! It must have cost a fortune!'

'The emerald reminded me of you,' he said quietly. 'Cool, and as clear and honest as a mountain spring that refreshes and revives. Beautiful and rare.' He saw she was abut to interrupt and said softly, 'You are all those things to me, Claire, and if it had cost ten times what it did, it still wouldn't be adequate recompense for all that you've done.'

Recompense. She tasted the word and found it bitter. She didn't want to be recompensed. She wanted...she wanted to be loved, she realised shockingly, unaware that her face had lost all its colour, or that her eyes had a blind terror in their depths.

She heard Jay's sharply indrawn breath, but didn't connect it with her own reaction to his gift, and then Lucy was saying excitedly, 'Aren't you going to kiss him, Mummy?' And somehow, reacting automatically, she was touching her cold lips to his warm skin, and feeling his sharp recoil with a pain that hurt so much, she couldn't believe she had ever thought she had known pain before.

It was a relief to escape to the kitchen to see to the lunch. Jay took the girls outside on their new sledge, while she worked like an automaton, wondering why it was that she should be condemned to loving a man who could give her only gratitude. And he wouldn't even want to give her that, if he knew the truth. In that moment she knew that she must conceal for ever how she felt about him. If she didn't…if she didn't their marriage would be a nightmare. He wouldn't divorce her for the girls' sake, but if she told him how she felt she would lose his friendship, lose those precious confidences he gave her, those evenings together when he talked to her about his work, when she felt as though they met as equals. She would lose all that, without any hope of ever gaining what she really wanted. And what did she want? For him to love her, yes, but how—in the way that he loved the girls, or in the way that he had loved his first wife?

Did she want his tenderness or his passion? She didn't know, she had only known in that blinding moment of revelation that she loved him totally.

# CHAPTER NINE

'WELL, HERE WE ARE, LADIES—Dallas!'

The faint air of constraint that had sprung up between them after Christmas Day still lingered, despite her forcedly cheerful attempts to dispel it and appear normal, and Claire couldn't help noticing how careful Jay was not to touch her as they disembarked from the plane that had brought them from Heathrow.

She didn't think Jay had actually guessed how she felt about him, but she knew that he sensed something. She often found him watching her in an assessing, almost withdrawn way. Assessing and finding wanting, perhaps? A cold fear dug icy fingers into the pit of her stomach.

'Are you all right?' he queried.

'Just getting used to feeling firm ground underneath my feet again.'

The Goldbergs had sent a chauffeur-driven car to pick them up, and as they drove from the airport and through the city itself Jay pointed out several landmarks to them. It was the flatness of the countryside and the expected and yet awesome vastness of everything that she noticed most, Claire thought as she listened to the girls' excited chatter.

She knew that the Goldbergs owned a house on the outskirts of Dallas and that it was here that Jay's firm had done the work which had won them the contract for John Goldberg's prestigious building developments.

The Goldberg house was built in what Jay had described as a Neo-Colonial style, and featured a large enclosed patio in the manner of the French Créole houses of St Louis. Claire was looking forward to seeing it, but the ten-foot-high brick wall and the security guard on the gates came as rather an unpleasant shock. The man was cordiality itself as he let them through, but Claire couldn't repress a small shiver as she noticed the gun he was wearing.

'John's a millionaire,' Jay told her quietly, 'and these days I'm afraid that means taking certain security precautions.'

Claire knew that the Goldbergs had two almost grown-up children: a son at Yale and a daughter at Vassar.

The long drive curved through immaculately kept gardens, with sprinkler systems to keep the lawns green and fresh, and the house stood at the end of the drive, its long, symmetrical windows gazing out over the grounds.

A double flight of marble steps led up to the colonnaded Palladian-style entrance. The car stopped, and the chauffeur opened the doors. Claire noticed how subdued the girls were as the four of them climbed the steps.

'I had no idea it would be so big!' she whispered to Jay as they approached the front door.

She just had time to catch his grin, and to hear him whisper in a mock American drawl, 'Honey, this is Texas,' before the massive double doors were opened.

The couple who came out to greet them could have starred in any glamorous American soap opera. John Goldberg was tall, his face tanned, his hair just touched with distinguished wings of silver. Celeste Goldberg was petite and blonde. Her silk pants and top shrieked Milan, and there could be no doubting that those pearl and diamond earrings she was wearing were real. Even so, her smile of welcome was warm and genuine, her manner towards the girls, instantly putting them at ease.

They were ushered into a rectangular hallway; a flight of marble steps at the far end rose to a galleried landing. The soft, green-washed walls were embellished with gilded plasterwork, which Claire instantly recognised.

'It looks wonderful!' she told Jay impulsively.

'We certainly think so,' said Celeste. 'And so do all our friends. We've given you a suite of rooms overlooking the patio; I'll show you to them now. I know you must be tired.'

Claire was. In fact, she was finding it hard to understand why sitting still for so long should be able to induce such numbing exhaustion.

'It's this way.'

Claire and the girls followed their hostess upstairs, while Jay lingered to talk to John Goldberg. At the top of the stairs a pair of double doors in white and gold opened out on to a galleried walkway that went all the way round an unroofed quadrangle.

'All the bedrooms have access to the pool and patio area from this gallery,' Celeste told Claire, indicating a flight of steps that went down to the ground below.

As she gazed over the iron railings, Claire could see the rich blue shimmer of the pool. Built in a traditional shape, it was ornamented with a piece of marble statuary, and the patio itself was flagged in white marble diamond-shaped tiles, interspersed with smaller dark blue ones to match the tiles in the pool. White marble columns supported the walkway and a wide variety of exotic climbing plants curled green tendrils around them. The whole effect was one of cool richness, right down to the birds Claire could not see, but could hear singing.

'It's a recording,' Celeste told her, laughing when Claire commented on it. 'John wanted to create the old St Louis-style family patio, but I drew the line at caged birds, so this was a compromise. We do have a much larger pool and barbecue area in the grounds, of course; but we only use it when we're having large parties. John had a tented pavilion area made next to it where we can put down a dance floor and serve a buffet. Ah—this is your suite here.'

She was way, way out of her depth here, realised Claire, marvelling at her hostess's casual acceptance of her possessions and life-style.

Celeste opened a door. 'I've given you two rooms, and a small sitting-room.'

All three rooms were decorated with French Empire-style furnishings and fitments; all three were luxurious and glamorous, as were the two *en suite* bathrooms, but it was not the luxury of her surroundings that made Claire go tense with shock; it was the realisation that Celeste had given her and Jay a bedroom that possessed an enormous king-sized bed.

The girls' room had two twins, but she could hardly suggest that she and Jay sleep in there, and there was certainly no question of anyone sleeping on the delicate chaise-longue at the bottom of the bed.

'Dolores will unpack for you; she and her family have been looking after us for the last ten years. It was Thomas, her son, who drove you here. We don't have dinner until eight, and you'll want to rest before then. Shall I send up some tea for you now, and leave you to settle in?'

Claire was too strung up now to rest, so she shook her head. 'I'm tired,' she admitted, 'but if I let the girls sleep now, they'll never want to go to bed.'

'Well, if I'm any judge, the men will be talking business in John's den. We'll go down there and rout them out, and then we'll have tea in the courtyard. The air-conditioning keeps it lovely and cool, and the fact that it's enclosed protects it from the dreadful winds we get here.'

As they went back downstairs, Claire learned that this evening they would be dining alone with their host and hostess, but that for the rest of their stay the Goldbergs planned to entertain and introduce them to several of their friends.

'John is so thrilled with the work Jay has done for him. Initially he was worried that such a small company wouldn't have the manpower to cope with a large contract, but Jay's dedication and know-how has finally convinced him. I think it was the news that Jay had remarried that finally convinced him,' Celeste added with a brief sideways look at Claire. 'John is a keen advocate of the benefits of a secure and strong marriage. I think it's very romantic how the two of you met and married.' She looked meaningfully at Lucy and Heather, who were preceding them down the stairs. 'And anyone can see how happy those two little girls are. I scarcely recognised Heather. She used to be such an unhappy, withdrawn child.'

'You've met Heather before?'

'Only briefly, when John and I were visiting London. Jay invited us back to the house for drinks, only when we got there it was plain that Susan wasn't at all pleased. Poor Jay—I felt terribly embarrassed for him, and we weren't really surprised when he heard that they'd split up, but John believes that divorce has a very unsettling effect on a man; it stops him from concentrating totally on business.' Celeste added the last few words with a wry grimace. 'I'm afraid my husband is something of a workaholic, but having said that, I wouldn't swop him for anyone else. Come on, we'll go and rout them out of John's den.'

As she listened to the conversation flowing around her, Claire could see what Celeste meant about John being a workaholic, but at least he did not, as many men did, presume that because they were female they could have no conceivable interest or worthwhile comments to add to the conversation, and she could see that he valued Celeste's opinion.

It had been rather a shock to hear Celeste describing their marriage as 'romantic'. Did she think that she and Jay were wildly in love, then? Obviously she must do. Even more disquieting, though, had been her innocent revelations about John's views on men and marriage. Was it possible that Jay had married her not just for Heather's benefit, but possibly for his own?

It was too late by a long time to start querying his motives now, she told herself, and anyway, what did it really matter? It mattered because, having discovered that she loved him, she found that it hurt to think that to him their marriage was just a sensible business manoeuvre. She had thought, before Christmas, that there was a closeness developing between them, a closeness which she had foolishly cherished.

'I think I'll take the girls upstairs now. It's gone six o'clock and they're both beginning to look tired.'

'They'll want something to eat...' began Celeste, but Claire shook her head. 'No, the sandwiches they've just eaten and the food they had on the plane will be enough. If they have another meal now, they won't sleep.'

'I'll come and give you a hand.' Jay smiled easily at John Goldberg. 'I miss out so often on saying goodnight to them that I like to share their bedtime whenever I can.'

'Yes, they grow up all too quickly,' John Goldberg

agreed. 'I often regret that I didn't have more time to spare for our two when they were kids.'

Claire was surprised by Jay's behaviour. After all, this was essentially a business trip, even if the Goldbergs had specially wanted him to bring his family to meet them, and she had expected Jay to remain downstairs talking to John while she got the girls into bed.

She said as much as they went to their suite, careful to keep her voice down so that Lucy and Heather wouldn't overhear her.

'We're here for four days,' Jay pointed out. 'Plenty of time to discuss business matters, and besides, John's already told me that his advisers have finally agreed the contract. I'm not the sort of man who wants to sacrifice everything on the altar of material success, Claire. Oh, I enjoy my work: I like producing something that I know is good, and I like the success of selling it—but it isn't the be-all and end-all of my existence. I don't want either Lucy or Heather growing up thinking of me as a casual participant in their lives who can be relied on for expensive presents and not much else. Parenting is a dual role.'

They had reached the outer door to their suite. Claire hung back while the two girls rushed eagerly inside. Reluctantly she followed them.

'Jay...' she began.

'Mmm?'

'Celeste has only given us one room—with a king-size bed.'

His eyebrows lifted, and he asked in amusement, 'For all four of us?'

Claire could feel the hot colour flooding betrayingly over her skin. 'No, of course not.'

'Don't worry about it.' Suddenly for some reason his voice sounded clipped, angry almost. 'If I know anything about American beds, it will be large enough for us and at least half a dozen bolsters.'

Claire felt her mouth compress. It irritated her that he should be able to treat the matter so casually, and yet, what had she expected? Horror at the thought of having to share the bed with her? Pleasure?

'Mummy, come and look—this bath is big enough for Lucy *and* me!'

Distractedly Claire pushed aside her disturbing thoughts and went through to the girls' bathroom.

'No, TRULY, I COULDN'T EAT another mouthful.'

In point of fact, she was totally exhausted, realised Claire, as she refused another helping of sweet. Jet-lag was obviously catching up with her. In contrast the other three, including Jay, all seemed unfairly wide awake.

Not even two cups of coffee in the white and gold drawing-room that overlooked the sweep of lawns at the front of the house could lighten her heavy eyelids and Jay, catching sight of her smothering yet another yawn, said quietly, 'Why don't you go up to bed? John and I still have one or two things to discuss, and I can see that you're tired.'

'Yes, please don't stand on ceremony, honey,' insisted Celeste, 'and don't worry about having a lie-in in the morning. We've all suffered from jet-lag at one time or another, and we all know what it's like.'

Having been assured that her host and hostess wouldn't think her rude, Claire went gratefully upstairs. She was so tired she could barely walk.

She almost fell asleep in the bath, a huge affair with an in-built jacuzzi effect that she was too exhausted to try.

It was sheer luxury to find that all their luggage had been unpacked and put away. After a couple of attempts she managed to locate her nightdress—in the same drawer as Jay's silk pyjamas—and ridiculously, her last muddled thought as sleep claimed her was to wonder on which side of the bed Jay preferred to sleep. Well, it was too bad if she had chosen the wrong one, she thought grumpily; he would just have to wake her up.

He did, but only very briefly and only because she was an extremely light sleeper.

It was the bedroom door opening that brought her out of a strangely confused dream to the odd knowledge that she was feeling extremely cold. She said as much, very crossly, to Jay as he apologised for waking her, and heard him laugh.

'It's probably the air-conditioning—it's still on, and the temperature does drop quite a lot at night.'

She was almost asleep by the time he came out of the bathroom, one small part of her registering the fact that he was sliding into bed beside her.

As though he sensed her awareness of him, he said

calmly, 'Go back to sleep, Claire, there's nothing to
be afraid of...'

Nine-tenths asleep, she mumbled back, 'I'm not
afraid, I'm cold.'

He laughed again, and the sound held a faint hint
of indulgent affection. 'If you were the little girl you
sound like I could cuddle you until you get warm,
but...'

He caught her sharply indrawn breath.

'Claire, what is it? You surely don't think I...'

'The last person to cuddle me was my father, and
then he died, and...' She was wide awake now, shivering with a mixture of cold and pain.

She heard the noise Jay made deep in his throat—
somewhere between a growl and a groan—and she
felt him move, but didn't know why, until she felt her
body being turned and held close to his own, one arm
holding her gently, while his free hand stroked the
nape of her neck comfortingly.

'Part of you is still a frightened little girl, isn't it?
Poor little Claire!'

She wasn't a little girl, and it was ridiculous for
him to assume that she wanted him to treat her as
such. She wanted to be strong and cool, and to push
him away, to freeze him off, and make him regret that
he had dared to trespass into her most private feelings,
and yet the way he was holding her, comforting her,
brought back memories so long suppressed. This was
what she had craved and longed for after her parents'
death—someone to hold and comfort her—but there
had been no one, no one at all, and then after-

wards…after…him…the thought of anyone touching her had been so abhorrent that she had forgotten that she had ever felt like this.

Instinctively, without being aware of it, she snuggled closer to him, unaware of his sharp intake of breath, or the tension invading his body. He felt warm and safe, and he smelled…nice…she thought woollily, burying her face against his skin and breathing in the scent of it with the voluptuous innocence of a small child. He was only wearing pyjama bottoms, and she liked the sensation of his flesh beneath her hand, where it rested against his chest. She wriggled closer.

'Claire…' She froze as Jay moved away from her, his hands clamping round her wrists. 'I'm sorry—I shouldn't have touched you.' His voice was hard and remote.

What he meant was that he didn't want her to touch him. Claire's face burned as she realised what she had done. Instantly she retreated to the other side of the bed, feeling as bruised and rejected as only a woman in love can feel when the man she loves physically repulses her.

'Claire… Look, let's talk about this.'

She heard the tentative, gentle note of enquiry in his voice but ignored it. She wasn't in the mood to have a reasoned discussion on what had happened.

The very fact that Jay thought it was something they could talk reasonably about was enough. If he had been here in bed with Susie… The instant the treacherous thought formed she tried to suppress it, but it was too late. Jealousy seared her, leaving her raw and vulnerable, prey to emotions she had never known existed. Despite her exhaustion it was hours before she finally fell asleep.

WHEN SHE WOKE UP, THE SUN was shining and she was alone. She glanced at her watch and blinked. Half past ten. She really had overslept.

She got up and padded through into the girls' room. It was empty. They must all be downstairs. Putting clean clothes and underwear on the bed she went through into the bathroom, shedding both her night-dress and her robe. She was just about to step into the shower when she saw it. The most enormous spider she had ever seen! And it had seen her—she was convinced of it, convinced that it was staring at her with malevolent glee.

She opened her mouth and screamed in pure panic-reaction, totally unable to drag her attention away from the soft, pulsating body and horrid mass of hairy legs.

Her scream had been pure instinct, and the last thing she had expected was for the bathroom door to be flung open.

'Claire? Ah...I see... It's all right, come on.'

She was hardly conscious of Jay's hand on her arm as he gently tugged her out of the bathroom and back into the bedroom. It was only when he closed the door, firmly locking the spider inside that she actually dared to breathe again. Jay released her, but she clung to him, shaking.

'It's all right. I just want to get your robe for you.'

For the first time she became conscious that she was naked, and her whole body turned a delicate shade of pink as Jay stepped away from her and then turned to look at her.

There was something strangely driven, reluctant almost in the way he studied her naked body. No doubt compared to Susie she was very ordinary indeed, but there was nothing wrong with the smooth suppleness of her skin, she thought proudly and her waist was narrow enough for Jay to span with both his hands if he wanted to do so. Her breasts weren't particularly large, but they were firm.

She forgot why they were here like this as Jay stared at her; a curious and very intense ache throbbed through her body. Her nipples swelled and hardened into deeply rosy nubs of flesh.

Jay was watching her with a darkly intense absorption. Her stomach muscles fluttered a nervous protest, and she touched startled fingertips to her skin.

'Claire, for God's sake!'

Jay's harsh protest exploded into the silence engulfing them. She looked at him with innocent, hesitant eyes, caught up in a mass of conflicting sensations and emotions.

Her face was flushed, his eyes glittering between narrowed lashes. He swallowed, and she followed the movement of his throat, seeing the tiny beads of per-

spiration dampening his skin. His shirt was open at
the throat, revealing a dark tangle of soft hair.

'Claire...' His voice was tight with anger; and
rough with something else; a kind of raw, aching pain
that caught at her heart strings and made her move
towards him with the jerky, mechanical gait of a doll,
without being aware that she had moved, only knowing that his pain was something she must soothe.

She reached him and wondered at the expression
in his eyes, and while she was assimilating it, he
reached for her with a tortured, smothered sound,
dragging her into his arms, and imprisoning her
against his body, so that she felt its heat and its maleness as his mouth moved hotly over her face, communicating a blind, frantic urgency that seemed to
echo the fierce throb of her flesh.

No one had ever held her like this before, ever
kissed her like this before, and it was like being cast
adrift in an alien sea which swelled and roared as it
threatened to drown her. There was only Jay to cling
to for safety, her nails biting into his skin, as she
trembled and shook with a kaleidoscope of new sensations.

Jay's mouth covered hers, hot with urgency. Her
eyes widened in shock and she felt him check, and
then his hand was in her hair, his fingers spreading
against her scalp, his tongue pressing against the
closed line of her mouth, until with a suppressed
sound of frustration he nipped sharply at her bottom
lip.

Her sharp cry of pain surprised them both. Claire

almost felt him do a double-take as the glittering heat
died out of his eyes and tension invaded his body.

His face was still flushed, but this time with anger.

'Hell, Claire, I'm sorry. I don't know what came
over me.' He released her as carefully as though she
was made of precious crystal, and then stepped back
from her.

He turned round looking for her robe, and she
heard him say in a muffled voice, 'For a moment I
forgot that…'

'That I wasn't Susie?' She felt as though her blood
had turned to ice. No, not ice—if she was frozen she
wouldn't be feeling this appalling, unendurable pain.
In one brief, illuminating moment she had known all
that Jay could have given her if he loved her, but he
didn't love her. She was merely his wife. His second
wife.

She took her robe from him and pulled it on, turning her back on him so that he wouldn't see the agony
in her eyes.

'I'll dispose of the spider and then I'll leave you
to get dressed. We're all down by the pool.'

It took her almost an hour to get ready to face
everyone. She knew that from now on whenever she
looked at her naked body she would be imagining
Jay's hands on it, Jay's mouth. She shuddered deeply,
aware for the first time in her life of the depth and
intensity of her own feelings.

The terror of coming face to face with that horrendous spider—she had always feared and loathed
them—seemed to have broken loose the chains that

had held her in captivity to her sexual fears. She couldn't really explain to herself why it was one minute she loathed anything to do with sex and the next she ached for Jay to be her lover—or had it really happened as quickly as that? Hadn't she slowly been drifting towards this for quite some time, since the start of their marriage, in fact, like a leaf borne unknowingly towards the brink of a weir it didn't know existed?

She couldn't stay here all day, she reminded herself. Sooner or later she would have to face Jay.

'I LIKED IT VERY MUCH in Dallas, Mummy, but I'm glad we're going home now, are you?'

They were circling Heathrow, and soon their jet would land. Absently responding to Heather's question, Claire glanced at Jay. He was sitting on the opposite side of the aisle, looking out of the window. Since that dreadful episode in their room, he seemed to have withdrawn from her almost completely. He was so cold towards her, so meticulously polite, chilly and indifferent, that she ached sometimes to elicit some response from him, even if that response was only anger.

She had been glad that the Goldbergs had organised so many social events for them, otherwise she didn't know how she would have got through the visit. It had been torture sharing that enormous bed with Jay each night, knowing he was there so close to her, and yet knowing that he did not want her.

Claire had learned a lot about herself in the last

few days. She had learned, for instance, that she was a woman who liked to touch. She ached to touch Jay. To run her fingertips over his body, to find out if that dark tangle of body hair felt as silky as it looked. She found herself looking at his mouth sometimes, and wishing she could feel its hard warmth against her own, against…against all of her, she admitted, shuddering faintly as she felt the molten heat run through her body.

She had learned something else. She had learned that she was a masochist; she must be, otherwise she would not torture herself with these haunting images of what could never be. Jay did not even desire her, never mind love her, she knew that—and she also knew that what had happened in the past had made it impossible for her to give herself to a man without mutual love. She wanted Jay's love; she wanted it emotionally, mentally and physically. She wanted the moon. She looked down at Heather who was sitting next to her, and saw trusting eyes looking back at her from the little round face. A wave of love cramped through her: Jay's child. How she would love to give Jay another child. She bent down and gently kissed Heather's dark head. The little girl hugged her back in wordless communication.

'Why are you looking so sad, Mummy?'

Trust sharp-eyed Lucy to notice!

'Oh, I'm not sad,' she lied, 'I'm just thinking.'

'We'll have to go back to school next week, won't we?' Lucy chattered on, and Claire forced herself to listen, glad of the diversion and yet resenting the way

Lucy turned confidingly to Jay, confident of his interest and his care. She was actually jealous of her own child! Bitterness rose in her throat and she had to look away.

The last thing she had expected when she married Jay was that she would fall in love with him. Fate had played a very cruel trick on her indeed.

# CHAPTER TEN

'CLAIRE, AFTER DINNER tonight, when the children are in bed, I'd like to talk to you.'

Over the last two weeks she had barely seen Jay. Ever since their return from Dallas, there had been a kind of armed and guarded tension between them, an atmosphere unlike anything she had experienced before, but which set her nerves on edge so much that she was steadily losing weight.

Jay didn't look too good either, she noticed, turning to look at him. She had avoided doing that recently; it hurt too much. Now she saw that there were deep grooves of tiredness carved along his face, and that his tan had faded, leaving him looking almost sallow. Of course he had been working hard—and late almost every night. They were busy, but she also knew that he stayed away because he didn't want to come home.

What had happened to the comfortable, pleasant relationship they had been building up before they went to Dallas? Her love had happened to it, that was what. She had fallen in love with him, and now she was unable to let herself relax with him because she was mortally afraid of what she might betray.

But it wasn't just she who had changed. Jay had

changed too: he had become remote and withdrawn. Sometimes she found him watching her with a brooding expression in his eyes, and she thought she knew the reason. Whatever he might have said to her, or told himself, he still loved Susie, and it had been that day when he held her in his arms and realised that she was not his first wife that he had discovered this. She was convinced of it.

Now, hearing him say that they needed to talk made her heart bump and jolt with shock and fear. What was he going to say to her? She looked at him out of the corner of her eye and saw that his face was wearing the blanked-off, almost bitter look that had become so familiar to her recently.

'They've gone up to have their baths now,' she told him tonelessly. 'They were both tired tonight.'

Even so, it was over an hour before both girls were settled. 'I'll go down and make some coffee.'

Jay shook his head. 'I'll do that. You do enough.' His mouth compressed slightly. 'You go and sit down.'

She was too nervous to sit down, and instead she paced the sitting-room floor nervously. Next week the workmen were due to start; she had shown Jay the colour schemes she had chosen, but his response had been abstracted and remote. Perhaps he was regretting giving her *carte blanche* with the décor, and that was what he wanted to talk to her about. Perhaps he had now decided that he wanted the house to remain as it was—as Susie had decorated it.

When he came in with the coffee, Claire was staring unseeingly out of one of the windows.

'Come and sit down.' His voice sounded rough and he looked tense. 'Please come and sit down, Claire,' he amended, mistaking the reason for her frozen stance. He ran impatient fingers through his hair and added rawly, 'This is bad enough as it is. When we married I made you certain promises and...'

'And now you're having second thoughts.' She marvelled at her own calm. How cool and controlled she sounded; she was really quite proud of herself. Inwardly she was awash with intense pain and agony. She knew now what Jay wanted to say to her; he wanted to tell her that their marriage wasn't working out, that he couldn't live with her any more because she wasn't Susie.

'How did you *know*?' He was frowning heavily and looked pale. 'I thought I'd...'

'Hidden how you feel?' She smiled mirthlessly. 'Some things can't be hidden, Jay.'

'I see.' His voice was heavy. 'I hadn't realised you'd guessed how I felt. Well, since you have, what do you suggest we do about it?'

'What do *I* suggest?' She stared at him. 'There's nothing I can do, Jay.'

For a moment he just stared back at her, and then his face tightened and he was walking towards her, quickly and almost menacing, his whole body taut with tension.

When his fingers curled round her arm she tried to jerk away, but he wouldn't release her. Instead he shook her, the aura of suppressed violence emanating from him so totally alien to his normal manner that she couldn't take it in properly.

'*Nothing* you can do? Nothing you *will* do, don't you mean?' he grated bitterly. 'For God's sake, Claire, you must know what it's doing to me living with you like this!'

'Of course I know! Do you think I can't see the changes in you? But what can I do? I can't bring her back for you, Jay! I can't be Susie.'

'Susie?' He released her so quickly that she half stumbled against the sofa. 'What the hell are you talking about?'

His face had gone white with rage, the anger glittering in his eyes making her take a step back.

'Jay, you know what I'm talking about. I'm talking about the fact that you're having second thoughts about our marriage because you've discovered you still love Susie.'

There was a long, long silence and then, speaking slowly and spacing the words out as though he was having the greatest difficulty in forming the words, Jay said thickly, 'I don't believe I'm hearing this. Are you for real?' He shook his head. 'You're way, way off beam!'

'But you agreed that you were having second thoughts...'

'About the *terms* of our marriage, not what happened in the past. I've fallen in love with you, Claire,' he told her flatly, 'and I want you in all the ways a man wants the woman he loves. I want to feel your skin against my hands, I want to touch it with my lips, I want to spread your hair out over my pillow and thread it through my fingers. Just the way you turn your head is enough to burn me up, do you know that? I want this, Claire,' he told her roughly, taking her in his arms and bringing his mouth down hard on the softness of hers.

The kiss took her by surprise, her mouth tremulous and soft beneath his, her tongue retreating shyly from the fierce invasion of his. She could feel his heart thudding furiously against her body. She could feel the tension in him—and the arousal, she acknowledged as she shook with shock and disbelief.

Abruptly his mouth left hers and she was free. Free to stare wide-eyed at him, to touch tremulous fingertips to her mouth. She saw his eyes darken and a hot flush of colour burn along his face, and her stomach lifted and plunged.

'But you can't love me...'

'Why not?' he laughed hollowly. 'Because you don't love me? Life isn't like that, Claire.'

'But you didn't love me when you proposed marriage.'

'No,' he agreed, dragging in a lungful of air and fighting for self-control. More calmly he continued, 'No, I didn't, but I did like you very much, both as a woman and as a person. I liked your quick intelligence, your interest in other people, your compassion, your womanliness. A womanliness it seemed a miracle you had kept when I knew what had happened to you. I saw the love and caring you gave Lucy, and

I wanted that caring for my own child—and then for myself. After Susie left me I swore I'd never enter a permanent romantic relationship with any woman again. I knew I couldn't put up with the sort of infidelity and cheating I'd had with Susie. It was my own fault; I should never have married her. I should have let her have her abortion and we should have gone our separate ways, but I couldn't believe she meant it. I couldn't believe she didn't want our child. I thought she was just being independent and proud and that really she wanted marriage. I threatened to tell her parents what she was planning to do if she didn't marry me, and she never forgave me for that—or for making her have Heather. When you told me how Lucy was conceived and how you felt about sex I knew you'd never be unfaithful to me. I knew then that I desired you, but I told myself I could control it. It was only later after we were married that I realised I couldn't, and with that realisation came others, like how much happiness and extra dimensionality you'd brought to my life; like how eager I was to come home to you and the girls; before I knew it, I'd made the transition from liking to loving...'

'And does loving me mean that you want me physically?' Claire asked him.

His eyes didn't waver. 'Yes,' he said gravely. 'I've already told you that. Wanting you, desiring you... those are a part of my love.'

'But in Dallas you pushed me away!'

His eyes narrowed incredulously. 'Pushed you away? For God's sake, Claire, how much self-control do you think I have? You were completely naked, I was holding you in my arms. I wanted to take you to bed right there and then, and show you how I felt about you,' he admitted flatly, adding in a thick and unfamiliar voice, 'although, the way I was feeling, I doubt that I'd have made it as far as the bed!'

She shook visibly with the effect of what he was saying, knowing that he was telling her the truth, but totally unable to take it in.

'What on earth gave you the idea I still loved Susie?'

'The way you rejected me. I thought you were wishing I was her, and then since we got back from Dallas, you've been so distant.'

'So have you,' he pointed out.

'Yes, but...'

'But what? Was it because I kissed you, Claire? Did I frighten you so much that you felt you had to keep me at a distance?'

The anguish in his eyes was too much for her to bear.

'I wasn't frightened of you. I was...I was frightened of myself, Jay, frightened of how you made me feel, of...'

'How *do* I make you feel?'

He had never looked less urbane and in control, and she had never loved him more, she thought achingly, watching the expressions race across his face; dread...hope...need...

'You make me feel...' She broke off and licked her lips nervously. She heard him make a strangled sound deep in his chest and looked at him with wide nervous eyes.

'Claire?' His voice pleaded and begged, and promised terrible retribution if she strung out his torment any longer.

'You make me feel like a woman,' she told him huskily. 'You make me...want you, Jay... You make me love you.'

There was a long, poignant silence and then he said softly, 'Come here.'

She almost ran into his open arms. They closed round her so tightly she could hardly breathe. He kissed her hungrily, running his tongue over her top lip and then the bottom one, probing their softness.

'Open your mouth.'

She shuddered as his tongue touched hers, but not with revulsion. As he felt her shudder, Jay raised his head, his eyes dark with pain. 'It's too soon, isn't it?' he whispered rawly. 'I'm rushing you too much. God knows I don't want to hurt or frighten you. I want to give you all the time there is. I want to cherish and protect you. I...'

She knew all that. She also knew gloriously and freely that she wanted him. Here and now at this moment in time, she wanted to be at one with him in a celebration of their love.

Raising herself up on tiptoe, she leaned towards him, cupping his face, running her tongue over his top lip in the way he had caressed hers, and then beyond it, feeling the faint prickle of his beard. 'Make love to me, Jay.' She interspersed the words with soft kisses. 'I want to be your wife, to bear your child. I want...'

She felt his indrawn breath and shivered heatedly in delight as his mouth opened over hers.

She was drowning in pleasure, floating in a delicious sensuous haze. She felt his hands on her body, and made a soft sound of satisfaction as he stripped it free of clothes. Her breasts filled his hands as though they were made for them, her nipples tight and urgent with desire.

'I think we'd better go upstairs.'

She didn't want to be apart from him, and she twined her arms around him, burying her hot face in his throat, tasting the salt heat of his skin.

'Claire, you're not making this easy for me.'

She didn't listen; she was too busy struggling with the buttons on his shirt. When he helped her with them she murmured a pleased sigh of pleasure, raking her nails gently through the darkness of his chest hair.

It *was* soft. She bent her head and pressed her face against his body. He shuddered and moaned something unintelligible into her ear, his mouth devouring the arched line of her throat and then beyond.

When his lips gently caressed the taut hardness of her nipple Claire thought she would faint from the pleasure. She clung to him as it coiled through her, unashamedly digging her fingers into his back, her body arching supplicatingly.

Somehow they were lying on the floor, supported by the cushions Jay had dragged off the sofa. The power and beauty of his naked body thrilled and aroused her. His hands stroked her skin and she was filled with a wanton delight, giving herself to him easily and eagerly, twisting and writhing against him as his hands and lips brought her to the edge of ecstasy.

It was she who begged him to enter her, sensing that he was fearful of hurting her, but her body welcomed him joyfully, his mouth absorbing her delirious cries of pleasure as they surged together to the glittering tantalising heights and then finally fell slowly back to earth.

'WHAT ARE YOU DOING?'

Claire had fallen asleep after they had made love, but now she was awake, watching Jay pick up their discarded clothes. He was wearing a towelling robe and she was covered in a duvet.

'We don't want the girls asking awkward questions, do we?' He abandoned his task and came over to her. 'How *could* you think I still loved Susie?' he groaned against her mouth, taking her in his arms.

'I don't know.' Claire gave him a smile that was purely mischievous. 'Perhaps you ought to convince me again that you don't...just to be on the safe side... The safe side!' Her face changed, and Jay frowned and stared at her.

'What is it?' he demanded roughly. 'Claire, what's wrong? *Did* I hurt you after all? Did...'

'It's nothing like that. I love you, Jay, and I know you'd never hurt me. It's just...'

'What?'

She coloured delicately and offered with a small laugh, 'Well, I've never done this sort of thing before, and...'

'And?'

'We didn't take any precautions, Jay. I could have a baby!'

'You said you wanted my child,' he reminded her, watching her.

'I do...but you might not...'

'Is that what you really think?' he asked thickly. Bending down, he scooped her up into his arms, duvet and all.

'You're right,' he told her. 'I do have to convince you.'

At the top of the stairs Jay paused and, looking down into her glowing face, asked softly, 'Which room, madam, yours or mine?'

'How about ours?' Claire suggested.

'Ours. Mmm. I think I like the idea of that—we'll buy ourselves a new bed, I think, and it won't be ten feet wide! I want you as close to me as it's possible to be from now on. Close to me in all the ways there are, Claire. I've been so lucky to find you...'

Fate had not been unkind to her after all, Claire acknowledged headily as he shouldered open his bedroom door and carried her over to the bed.

# Injured Innocent

# CHAPTER ONE

SHE WAS IN a very dark, very smoky, very crowded room, crammed with unfamiliar faces, most of them contorted into frighteningly threatening grimaces. Panic surged through her in waves. She wanted to turn and run and yet for some reason her feet remained locked to the floor. Alien sounds and scents filled the air; she was overwhelmed by the despairing conviction that she could never, ever escape from the place of torment her inner consciousness told her her surroundings were, and then miraculously a door opened; light flooded the room and a man stood there his arms open wide to encourage her to run to him, his face in the shadows, but she knew without seeing his features who he was, and his name was torn from her lips on a glad cry as she ran for the haven of his arms.

'Daddy...' She cried his name again, her relief suddenly, horrifyingly turning to terror as he stepped into the light and she saw that he was not her father at all but someone else—a stranger—dark and forbidding, unknown to her and yet somehow recognised by her inner senses...recognised and feared. She screamed, and screamed again, and it was the sound of her own pain and fear that eventually jolted her out of the fantasy world of her nightmare and back to reality.

The nightmare. Lissa shuddered deeply, touching her damp skin with trembling fingers. It was years since she had been tormented by it—well three years at least, she amended mentally…since she had made the break from home and come to live in London. Sighing faintly she glanced at her watch. Six-thirty… There was no point in trying to get back to sleep now. She would have to get up in another hour anyway.

She padded through the bedroom of her small flat and into the kitchen busying herself making a mug of coffee. The fragrant scent of the beans soothed her sensitive nerve endings, the warmth of the drink stealing into her chilled fingers as they closed round the mug. It was still only January and the central heating hadn't come on yet. She shivered violently in her nightdress and pattered back to her room, sliding under the duvet; snuggling its comforting warmth all around her. Amanda would have laughed and said something silly, like the best way to keep warm in bed was to share it with a man. When Amanda said things like that everyone laughed. Her sister had a way of saying the most outrageously suggestive things with an innocence that robbed them of their sting. Even after three years of marriage and two children Amanda still looked like a little girl, with her mop of blonde curls and her large blue eyes. Or at least she had done. Deep shudders of mingled guilt and pain racked her as she sat huddled beneath the bedclothes. Dear God even now she could hardly believe it was true; that that midnight call three days ago had actually happened… That her sister, her

brother-in-law and both sets of parents had been
killed outright when a freak thunderstorm had struck
the light aircraft her brother-in-law had been piloting.

She had not seen much of her sister since her marriage—nor of her parents. There had been duty visits
of course, but there had always been an air of uncomfortable restraint about them. She knew her parents
had never forgotten, nor really forgiven her for what
she had done. It was useless for her aching heart to
protest that she was innocent. They would never have
believed her. Tears formed in her eyes and fell un-
heeded rolling down her cheeks. Was she crying for
her sister, or for herself Lissa asked herself cynically.
She and Amanda had never been particularly close.
There were four years between them, Amanda being
the elder, and to Lissa as a child it had often seemed
that whilst some Fairy Godmother must have looked
down into her sister's cradle and given her the gift of
a happy life; hers had been blighted by the machi-
nations of some mischievous spirit who had ensured
that she was destined always to be in trouble.

It had taken her years of exhaustive self analysis to
understand that she was not to blame; that those
things which she saw in herself as hopeless inade-
quacies because they did not mirror her sister's vir-
tues, were not necessarily that. It was stupid to have
the nightmare now, after so long had passed... Why
*had* she had it? Why? Did she really need to ask
herself that question, Lissa mocked herself. Of course
not. She knew exactly why she had dreamed so hor-
rifically of that party, of that long ago night, of Joel

Hargreaves, her sister's brother-in-law, and now, with her, co-guardian of the two little girls who had been orphaned in the plane crash that had robbed Lissa herself of parents and sister...just as it had robbed Joel of brother and parents.

She had not been able to believe it when she received the phone call from Amanda's and John's solicitors. She had gone to see them immediately, taking time off work to do so, and had been stunned to hear of the tragic accident that had taken place while Amanda and John were visiting John's parents in Miami.

If Joel hadn't been looking after the children that weekend; they too would have been killed. Lissa shuddered deeply again. Even now she could barely take it in. She had had no idea until the solicitors told her that Amanda had appointed her joint guardian of the girls, along with John's brother, but it was not a responsibility she had any intention of shirking, no matter what the solicitors might think. Her mouth tightened slightly as she remembered the carefully worded comments of the solicitor, and his cool surprise that she should not want to extricate herself immediately from any responsibility towards the children. When she had taxed him about it he had coughed in vague embarrassment and then said half apologetically that Mr Hargreaves...Mr Joel Hargreaves, that was, had given him to understand that she would not wish to accept any responsibility for her nieces.

Lissa, who suspected she knew Joel Hargreaves

and the way his mind worked far better than Mr Lawson, had seethed inwardly, knowing that what Joel had been intimating was not so much that she should not *wish* to take on the children, but that he considered her an unfit person to do so.

But she did wish to take on her share of the responsibility. She owed it to her sister and her parents—not to mention little Emma and Louise—but it was not just that, she admitted to herself. There still burned inside a deep seated sense of injustice, an intense need to show Joel Hargreaves just how wrong all his assessments of her were. To prove that the great Joel Hargreaves was not as infallible as he and apparently everyone else liked to believe. And *that* was why she had had the nightmare... That was why she had dreamed so painfully of events which had happened more than six years ago. That was why she could not forget the humiliation she had suffered at his hands.

She sipped her coffee, refusing to allow her thoughts to slide backwards into the past. She had taught herself now to ignore the past... All right, so she could not erase it...could not entirely put it behind her and close a door on it, but she could refuse to allow herself to dwell obsessively on it.

When she had come to London she had vowed to put the past behind her. She had fought valiantly against her own inner sense of inadequacy. She had found herself a good job, which she thoroughly enjoyed, working as a secretary-cum-P.A. to an up-and-coming young architect, Simon Greaves. She had bought her small one bedroomed flat, albeit with the aid of what sometimes seemed to be an extremely onerous mortgage. She owned a little car...took regular holidays. Had a pleasant circle of friends...never lacked dates. All in all, to the casual observer, her life was a very comfortable and modestly successful one. She had come out from behind the shadow of her elder sister, or so she had told herself...but did one ever wholly recover from the traumas of childhood? Wasn't it true that somewhere deep inside herself she still considered herself unworthy; inferior; judging herself as her parents had judged her, simply because she was not a carbon copy of Amanda.

Stop that! She abjured herself, pushing aside the duvet and padding towards the bathroom. She was wide-awake now and might as well get up. She had a very busy morning ahead of her, with a meeting with her parents' solicitors sandwiched in at lunchtime. She had already seen them twice and not been wholly surprised to discover that despite her parents' pleasant life-style they had left behind them few assets. The house had been mortgaged very recently to provide her parents with an annuity, which of course had ceased with their death, but it was not to discuss her parents' few assets that Lissa wanted to see their solicitors. It was to discuss her legal position with regard to her nieces. She didn't need sixth sense to guess that Joel Hargreaves would do everything in his power to have her guardianship of the girls set aside, but Amanda had stipulated that she wanted her as guardian to her daughters, and it was an act of faith and love that Lissa wasn't going to turn her back on.

Despite the fact that Amanda had always been their parents' favourite she and Lissa had always got on reasonably well. They had never been close, but they had always loved one another. In fact Lissa could only remember her sister being angry with her on one occasion. Stop it, she cautioned herself again. Stop thinking about that.

But it was easier said than done, which accounted for the fact that the past still haunted her in the shape of tormenting nightmares, even after all this time. At seventeen she had been so innocent…so naive and trusting, but she had been judged as being wanton and wild, and the scars of that judgment still haunted her.

After she had showered, she rubbed herself dry briskly, grimacing ruefully at her mane of red-brown hair and her tall, slender body. Amanda had been small and cuddly, entrancingly feminine, whereas she as a teenager had been gawky and awkward to the point of being plain. Now when Simon called her elegant and classy, she was tempted to deny his compliments, to make him see that whatever elegance she now had was simply a disguise; armour behind which she could hide all her deficiencies. She herself saw very little to admire in her height, or in the classic bone structure of her face. Her hair which she wore long was probably her best feature, if one overlooked the fact that it was not blonde, just as her eyes were a cool hazel green and not blue. But then hadn't she realised long ago that she was not and never could be another Amanda. She was herself, warts and all. Sighing faintly she made up her face with practiced skill. The grooming course she had invested in when she first came to London at the suggestion of her first employer had taught her to re-assess herself as the person she was, not as a shadow of her sister, but she had stood in Amanda's shadow for too long to be able to wholly accept that she was capable of taking the limelight in her own right. The classic coolness of her demeanour was in direct contrast to her own inner insecurity, but few people guessed that. Not even Simon who was her boyfriend as well as her employer really knew what she hid away from public view.

Simon! Unwittingly Lissa bit her lower lip, marring its fullness with the sharp bite of her teeth. She had worked for him for eighteen months and for the last six they had been dating. She liked and admired Simon; physically he was a very attractive male, tall and blond with a ready smile and easy charm, but when it came to the crunch; when it came to the point of giving herself to him as a woman...of taking him as her lover, she held back. She knew that he found her sexual coldness towards him hurtful, but how could she explain to him that every time she came close to allowing a man to touch her...any man...she was instantly confronted by a mental image of Joel Hargreaves' darkly contemptuous features; and that the image was powerful enough to instantly quench whatever desire she might previously have felt. Joel as the mental guardian of her morals exerted a far more powerful veto on her ability to respond sexually to anyone than the most vigilant of parents. And it was all so ridiculous and unnecessary. The real Joel didn't give a damn what she did with her life; and anyway she was way, way past the age of consent at twenty-three. It was stupid and unnecessary that she was still a virgin. She heartily wished herself rid of the burden of her unwanted innocence, but every time she met a man she felt she could respond to, Joel came between them. She knew quite well why of course. But it was one thing to know, it was another to overcome the mental barriers created by the past.

'Stop thinking about that now,' she ordered herself. She would need all her powers of concentration today when she saw her parents' solicitors. She knew quite well that Joel would try to take the children away from her, to stop her from taking up her role as co-guardian. He had already flown out to Miami to arrange the funerals of Amanda and John and both sets of parents and he had taken the children back with him, all before Lissa had even been informed of the accident. The children were now living with him, and Lissa knew she would have to fight to preserve her own rights towards them. Quite why she was so determined to take up those rights, she found it difficult to say. It was true that she was fond of both her nieces; they were her sister's children of course, but she loved them in their own right. However, if Joel had not been her co-guardian... If John's brother had been a different man...a married man perhaps whom she liked and approved of, wouldn't she have been quite happy to hand the children into the care of he and his wife? Wasn't it partially because it was *Joel* who was her co-guardian; Joel her bitter enemy that she was summoning all her forces, all her rights under the law to oppose his high-handed decision to make himself solely responsible for the girls, by the simple expedient of arrogantly ignoring her co-guardianship?

What if it was? Legally she had every right to share his guardianship. Amanda must have wanted her to do so otherwise she would never have appointed her in the first place. But then Amanda would never have expected to die at twenty-seven. Neither would John, Lissa argued mentally with herself. No…she had every right to take legal advice and discover what steps she could take in the law to force Joel to recognise her rights.

What about the children? an inner voice argued. Was it fair on them to subject them to legal quarrels between their guardians so shortly after they had lost their parents? But if she didn't do so she would be cut completely out of their lives. Joel was ruthless enough to do that, she knew it. He was not married either, so there would be no feminine influence in their lives, if one discounted the string of glamorous girlfriends who seemed to slip in and out of his life, not to say his bed. No, the girls needed her, she was convinced of it…just as they needed Joel. Unlike him she didn't deny that he had his rights.

Simon knew all about her hopes and fears in connection with her nieces and had generously told her to take off all the time she needed to visit her solicitors. This morning she had managed to arrange an early appointment, which meant that she should not arrive at the office too much later than Simon himself, who didn't normally put in an appearance until ten.

The night before last Simon had taken her out for dinner and they had spent most of the evening talking about the children. Sighing faintly, Lissa finished her coffee and collected her outdoor things. Simon was intrigued by her she knew; he found her sexual coldness a challenge he was not used to facing; he couldn't see that her refusal to go to bed with him wasn't just a manoeuvre in a clever game, but a genuine abhorrence of the sexual act. She had tried to tell him…to explain to him why it was she found it so difficult to let him touch her even in the most general way, but as always, guided by some inner caution she had withheld the real truth. That was something she found it impossible to talk to anyone about, and a thin film of sweat broke out on her skin as her mind kaleidoscoped back and she was fifteen again. Clenching her hands together Lissa willed the memories away, but they refused to listen. How ungainly and insecure she had been at fifteen; how conscious of being the family's ugly duckling; of being unloved in the way that Amanda was loved. Her father had wanted a son and not a second daughter; she knew that, but even so, if she had been another blonde moppet like her elder sister she felt reasonably sure that he would have come to terms with his disappointment. As it was her dark red hair and tall uncoordinated frame were so much the antithesis of what her father thought was feminine that he had never been able to reconcile himself to his disappointment. Her mother, like Amanda, was a delicate, fluffy blonde, and Lissa had lost count of the number of times she had heard her mother explaining half apologetically to her friends that she had no idea where her second daughter got her plainness from. 'Not from my side of the family, I'm sure...' Lissa's mouth tightened, and she counselled herself sternly not to blame her parents. A more self-reliant and less intensely emotional child would soon have learned to come to terms with being second best. Her parents were not responsible for the flaws in her personality, any more than she was herself. Over the years she had taught herself to accept that and to make the best of what Nature had given her. There had been many men who if asked would have quite openly chosen her tall, red-headed elegance over her sister's blonde prettiness, but she had never allowed them to do so. Picking up her bag and keys, Lissa made for her front door.

Three quarters of an hour later she was seated in her solicitor's office, listening to his careful, judicial speech.

The question she had asked him was whether Joel Hargreaves could legally deny her access to her nieces.

'Not legally,' her solicitor told her, frowning slightly as he leaned his elbows on his desk and studied her. Her parents had been clients of his for many years, and he felt intensely sympathetic to this quite beautiful girl who he remembered as a rather plain and very frightened teenager. 'But of course, we can't overlook the fact that materially he can give them much more than you can. He owns a large house in the country, unless I'm mistaken?'

Lissa nodded. 'Yes, and he's rich enough to be able to afford a nanny for them...something I couldn't possibly manage... I know I can't have them to live with me on a permanent basis—at least not yet, but visiting rights...weekends...'

Her solicitor pursed his lips. 'Yes...yes... After all it was your sister's wish that you be appointed co-guardian of the girls. You're their godmother as well, aren't you?'

Lissa confirmed that this was so.

'It's just a pity that you aren't married, or at least engaged,' he added thoughtfully. 'Judges are often a trifle old-fashioned in their attitude towards minors. If they can see a ready-made family unit they look upon it very favourably.'

Lissa wanted to point out that Joel wasn't married either, but she did not. After all, unlike her, Joel could afford to buy all the help needed. Joel and John had both received all the benefits of being rich man's sons. Both had gone to a famous public school; Joel had taken over running the family estate when his father retired, while John had run the components factory from which they derived their wealth. The estate was a large one, encompassing several farms, woods, a shoot in Scotland, and Winterly House itself, a Queen Anne gem of a building which Lissa had only visited twice, but had fallen instantly in love with. She had never been able to understand how John and

Amanda could prefer to live in the extremely modern
house John had had built for them, but then Amanda,
unlike herself, had been a thoroughly modern young
woman. Painfully, Lissa dragged her thoughts back to
the present, in time to hear her solicitor saying that
while there was no doubt about her legal rights to the
children, he suspected that Joel Hargreaves intended
to make it extremely hard for her to take them up.

He frowned slightly as he studied the papers in
front of him, a faint tinge of embarrassed colour darkening his skin as he said hesitantly, 'And then of
course there is the matter of…well, reputation…from
the court's point of view…'

He got no further, because Lissa had stood up,
pushing her chair back unsteadily, her eyes darkening
to brilliant emerald as she interrupted bitterly. 'Are
you trying to say that a court might not consider me
a fit person to have charge of the girls? And how will
they prove that I wonder?' Temper had her in its coils
now, burning fever bright, pushing through the barriers of pride and reserve, words boiling up inside her
and spilling volcanic-like from the place deep inside
her where all her pain was buried. 'By checking
through my life? By questioning my friends? By delv-
ing into my private life, searching diligently for every
little grub of dirt they can find?' Two angry spots of
colour burned high on her cheeks as she added finally,
'Perhaps they might even want to subject me to a
physical examination…just to find out how promiscuous I am… What a pity they can't apply the same
rules and standards to Mr Hargreaves…but then of

course, his lifestyle isn't important is it? After all he's rich and important, and I'm neither... Isn't that what you're trying to tell me.'

'My dear...' The solicitor looked and felt embarrassed. What she had said held a faint shadow of truth, although of course there could be no question of any examination of her...physical or otherwise... In the face of her bitter anger he felt unable to defend or even explain the workings of the law...nor could he entirely refute her allegations concerning the court's possible view of Joel Hargreaves. It was wrong and unfair he knew that.

'I won't give them up... I won't...'

Lissa turned round and almost ran from his office, still so angry that she never even noticed the speculative stares of his secretary who had caught her raised voice from inside her boss's office. No wonder she had lost her temper, with a mane of hair like that, she reflected half enviously. Her own hair was a soft mousy brown, and in her fantasy daydreams she had often imagined herself as a passionate redhead.

Lissa was still shaking when she reached her own office. Simon was there already, checking through the post. He smiled warmly at her, checking when he saw her expression. 'Heavens, what's happened?' he questioned her, guiding her into a chair and perching on the edge of his desk. 'You look as if you're about to explode.'

'So would you if you'd just been told that you aren't a fit person to have charge of your nieces because you aren't rich enough to sway the opinion of the Judge.'

She was so overwrought that she was barely aware what she was saying, and unacknowledged, but at the bottom of her agony was the memory of past hurts and humiliations and of one in particular so painful to call to mind even now that the thought of it seared her mind, making her shiver convulsively and grip her hands together.

Gradually Simon got the full story out of her, and then eventually said lightly, 'Well it seems to me that there's only one solution, and that's for you to get engaged to me.' He saw her face; and before she could utter her denial said coaxingly, 'Lissa, you know how much I want you…how I feel about you. Just give us a chance… If we were engaged I'm sure the court would be bound to view you in a more favourable light. Solid, respectable background for the kids and all that.'

He was offering her an engagement ring in exchange for the use of her body, Lissa thought sadly, and who was she to blame him for that? She had made it more than clear that she would never willingly give herself to him physically.

'No, Simon it wouldn't work out.'

Just for a second the mingled anger and frustration in his eyes frightened her. It showed her a Simon she had never seen before. She ought to have remembered that the powerful sexual drive that was in men to possess and dominate her sex could change even the mildest of them into a frightening stranger. She of all people ought to have known that.

'Because you damn well won't give it a chance to work out,' he swore at her. 'Christ Lissa, what is it with you? Anyone would think you were still a timid little virgin.' He saw her face and his expression changed, frightening her again as she saw the male satisfaction and victory in it. Exultation crept into his voice as he said softly, 'That's it isn't it? You are still a virgin? Oh, darling...' He was smiling at her now, coming towards her. Any moment now he would be touching her. Lissa stood up shakily and edged away from him. 'No, don't run away...' He was practically crooning with delight and she felt sickness stab through her. She couldn't move...couldn't do anything to stop his arms coming round her, pulling her against his body. She went rigid at the intimacy of it, loathing him and loathing herself because she felt the way she did.

'Don't be frightened...there's nothing to be frightened of...I'll make it good for you, wait and see...it will be so good...so...'

He wasn't really talking to her, Lissa thought with frigid distaste; he was thinking of his own pleasure; his own satisfaction. Held fast in his arms she felt as though she were two people; the frightened, terrified creature who couldn't break free of his hold; and then another, immeasurably older person who stood outside of her body and watched; censorious and cold, reminding her that she had no one but herself to blame for feeling the way she did. She shuddered with revulsion as she felt his hot mouth pressing against her throat. The outer office door opened and she was dimly aware of someone coming in, and then behind her a familiar and loathed voice drawled softly, 'Well, well…so this is how you spend your time these days is it Lissa… Nothing's changed then.'

Simon released her immediately, pushing his fingers through his hair in a way he had when he was caught at a disadvantage. Tall though he was, the newcomer towered over him. Few men could compete with Joel Hargreaves when it came to sheer masculinity, Lissa thought bitterly, turning round to face her tormentor.

'Joel?' She smiled thinly at him, grateful for the fact that she had somehow recovered her poise. 'As you say nothing's changed… You, I see still have the habit of bursting in on people unannounced. What were you hoping to find this time? Evidence to prove that I'm not a fit person to have charge of the girls?'

The wide male mouth slashed into an open curl of contempt. 'I don't need to go looking for that, Lissa. It's all there, documented and collated and I don't even need to look for a witness do I? I saw the whole thing for myself.'

She wanted to cry out a denial, to hide away from the merciless scrutiny of his hard gold eyes, but she wasn't fifteen anymore and so she tilted her chin and said coldly, 'Your own personal life wouldn't bear too much close scrutiny Joel. People in glass houses shouldn't throw stones should they?'

He had a trick of looking at someone beneath those

heavy lidded eyes that had always made her heart pound with a mixture of fear and apprehension. He did it now, making her feel as though he could see through her forehead and into the farther-most recesses of her brain.

'I want to talk to you,' he said calmly. 'I've got a busy morning but I could see you at lunch time.'

'And deny yourself the opportunity of lunching with your latest ladyfriend whoever she might be?' Lissa snapped. 'Don't bother. I've only one thing to say to you Joel and that is that I'm not giving up my rights to the girls, no matter what you say or do. Amanda appointed me as their guardian...'

'Silly, loyal Amanda,' Joel derided her sister. 'I'll bet when she did it, she never thought you might actually have to have charge of them. Your mother wouldn't have approved.'

It hurt because it was the truth, but Lissa refused to give in to the pain. She had enough experience of Joel's methods of waging warfare to know that he always aimed for his opponents' most vulnerable spots, and he knew hers to a nicety.

'I'm not giving them up, Joel,' she repeated coolly. 'And this is a private office. If you want to communicate with me, please do so through my solicitor.' As she finished speaking she walked past him and into her own office, firmly closing the door behind her. Two minutes later she heard the outer door slam and then Simon walked into her office.

'Phew,' he commented theatrically, raising his eyebrows. 'So that's the fabled Joel Hargreaves.'

Joel was constantly appearing in the gossip press. He had fingers in many financial pies and was known as much for being a highly successful entrepreneur as he was for his womanising. 'Quite a man,' Simon murmured.

'If you like the type.' Lissa managed a thin smile. 'Personally I don't.'

'No, I could see that.'

Lissa had a small smile at the smug satisfaction in Simon's tone. Physically, they couldn't be more dissimilar. Simon although tall was slim and boyish with his shock of sunbleached fair hair and his easy smile. Joel in contrast, was taller, broader, the epitome of everything that was intensely male. His skin was olive coloured, his eyes a glinting rich gold, his hair dark and thick. Once, rather fancifully before she had really known him Lissa had imagined that he might have posed for a statue of Achilles. She had always had an overromantic imagination she thought wryly. Joel was no story-book hero. Far from it. Women fell for him like ninepins and he made full use of the power he seemed to have over her sex. Lissa had watched a procession of women come and go through his life, and if he had ever felt anything more than sexual desire for any of them, she had never noticed it.

'Dinner tonight?'

She dragged her mind back to the present and Simon. Over his anger now, he was a cajoling, eager boy again, but how long would it be before he reverted to type...before he tried to force her into an intimacy she didn't want to share. She sighed faintly. She liked her job and she liked Simon…but if he was going to be difficult… But how could she give up her job now, when she might need to prove that financially she was able to care for the girls, at least on a part-time basis. She knew there was no possibility of them coming to live with her full time at least not now. For one thing her flat had only one bedroom but in a few year's time… If, however, she let Joel bludgeon her into giving up her rights to them now, she would have no chance of re-establishing any relationship with them in the future. She knew that.

# CHAPTER TWO

LISSA STARED at the letter, tapping her nails absently on her kitchen counter as she studied its contents for the umpteenth time. It had arrived three days ago; a coolly worded, imperative demand from Joel that she present herself at Winterly so that they could discuss the girls' future.

Trust Joel to make sure he had the advantage of being on his home ground, Lissa thought wryly. The letter had surprised her; taken her rather aback. After the way they had parted in Simon's office she had expected only to hear from him via his solicitor, but instead had come this command, because that was what it was, to go down to Winterly so that they could talk. She was tempted to refuse, but if she did might that count against her in an eventual court hearing? Her solicitor seemed to think so. She pressed the heel of one hand to her aching temple. Perhaps she ought to take Simon up on his offer and hope that her status as an engaged woman might persuade the court to settle in her favour. But Simon wasn't really interested in the girls; all he wanted was to get her into his bed. She glanced at her watch. Ten o'clock. She had been up since seven, prowling round her small flat, knowing that she must go to Winterly but desperately searching for excuses not to do so.

Chiding herself for her weakness she went into her bedroom, hastily packing enough clothes to last the weekend, and then before she could change her mind, she pulled on a jacket, collected her car keys and carrying her overnight bag marched towards her front door.

There was a freezing wind blowing, driving needle-sharp flurries of icy snow into her face, and Lissa huddled deeper into her jacket as she made for the lock-up garage block where she kept her car.

The traffic through the centre of London was bad enough to need all her concentration. Once on the M4 though she turned on her radio, and listened with grim foreboding to the weather forecast. A drop in temperature and snow, but not until late evening. Well she should be safely at Winterly by then.

Once off the M4 she drove carefully along the familiar country roads. She had spent all her childhood living in Dorset, the names of the villages she drove through composed a familiar litany. Her parents' old home lay only fifteen miles from Winterly. Amanda and John had met at the home of mutual friends, and the tiny village five miles east of Winterly she was now approaching was also the nearest village to her parents' old home. Nothing had changed, she thought with a hard pang of nostalgia as she negotiated the sharp bend in the centre of the town where the Tudor building now housing a bank jutted dangerously into the centre of the road. A sign outside a shop, fluttering in the cold wind caught her eye and she drew up outside it. A cup of coffee was just what she needed right now. Coward, an inner voice chided her as she climbed out of the Mini and locked it. She didn't really want a drink, she simply wanted to put off facing Joel.

The small town was busy with Saturday shoppers, but she was lucky enough to find a small corner table still free. A smiling waitress came to take her order, the familiarity of her soft Dorset burr taking Lissa back in time.

She had just received her order when she heard someone call her name in an incredulous voice.

'Lissa, it is you isn't it?' the feminine voice exclaimed, a pretty plump brunette of about her own age hurrying over to her table, a wriggling toddler tucked securely under one arm.

'Helen…Helen Martin,' Lissa exclaimed in turn, recognising an old school friend.

'Helen Turner now,' the latter laughed. 'Do you mind if I join you?'

'No, please do…'

Aware that Helen was studying her, Lissa strove to appear calm and friendly. At one time she and Helen had been 'best friends', but after…but after she was fifteen they had drifted apart.

'I was sorry to hear about Amanda and John,' Helen said quietly at last. 'It must have been a dreadful shock for you. Joel has got the children hasn't he? Poor little things. They must miss their parents dreadfully.' She pulled a face. 'Somehow I can't see Joel in the role of doting uncle. Has he changed at all or is he still as masterful and macho as ever.'

'I don't see much of him these days,' Lissa said assuming a fake casualness. 'In fact I'm on my way to Winterly now. We're joint guardians of the girls.' She might as well let it be known that Joel wasn't solely responsible for her nieces' welfare.

'Yes, you're godmother to both of them aren't you?' Helen broke off as her son reached for his glass of orange juice, almost tipping it over.

'Are you married yourself?' she asked when she had rescued the glass. 'I remember I always used to think you would marry young and have a brood of children.'

'No, I'm still single,' Lissa told her calmly. It was true that when they were teenagers she had yearned for the security of a loving husband and children, but in those days she had been so ridiculously innocent, wanting without realising it to compensate herself for the lack of love in her own home.

'Umm... Well it can only be by choice,' Helen said frankly, wrinkling her nose as she studied Lissa's smoothly made-up face and immaculate hair. 'You look very lovely and elegant Lissa, I hardly recognised you at first. What have you been doing with yourself? I know your parents sent you away to school...' She grimaced faintly. 'And it was all my fault really, wasn't it? If I hadn't persuaded you to go to that party with me. My parents gave me hell for that, I can tell you. What exactly happened?' she asked curiously.

'Oh nothing much.' Lissa was proud of her cool

offhand tone. 'It was all very much a storm in a tea-cup.'

'Yes, that's what my parents thought,' Helen agreed. 'I remember them discussing it at the time. My father always thought your people were too strict with you.' She giggled lightly. 'All I can remember is you disappearing upstairs with Gordon Salter and then the next minute your folks storming in with Joel Hargreaves, demanding to know where you were.' She rolled her eyes and grinned. 'Funny how seeing someone you haven't seen in a while brings back old memories. You didn't come back to school with the rest of us after that summer holiday did you? Your folks sent you off to boarding school didn't they?'

'Yes.'

Lissa looked down at her coffee cup, gripping her hands together under the table to stop them from shaking.

Helen was looking at her watch. 'Heavens I must fly,' she exclaimed. 'I promised Bill I'd meet him in the DIY centre at one, and it's nearly that now. Come on poppet,' she commanded, picking up her son. 'Nice to see you again, Lissa... Bye.'

She had been gone five minutes before Lissa felt relaxed enough to pick up her coffee cup and drink what was left of her coffee, and then when that was done she simply sat staring into space, unable to drag herself back to the present...too caught up in the memories of the past Helen had unleashed. What Helen remembered as merely an awkward incident had had such far reaching effects on her own life that even now still affected her.

Sighing faintly Lissa leaned back in her chair, willing her body to relax. She had been so excited about that party. Her parents had forbidden her to go, because they didn't approve of her crowd of friends. Why couldn't she have 'nice' friends like Amanda, her mother had constantly harped? Not that there was anything wrong with the crowd she went around with; they simply did not have the sort of moneyed background her parents approved of. This particular Saturday her parents had been dining with John's family. John and Amanda had been on the point of announcing their engagement, and Lissa had spent the afternoon at Helen's bewailing the fact that she was forbidden to attend Gordon's birthday party. Gordon Salter was something of a local Romeo, and Lissa had had a mammoth crush on him for several weeks. 'Why not go to the party anyway,' Helen had urged her. Her parents need never know. She could leave early and be back before they even knew she had been out. Even though she knew it was wrong, Lissa had agreed. After all what did her parents really care about her, she had argued rebelliously with herself. Amanda was the one they loved not her.

It had been surprisingly easy to deceive her parents. They had left home with Amanda a good hour before the party was due to start, leaving Lissa plenty of time to get ready. She didn't have many 'going out' clothes of her own, and on a reckless impulse she had raided her sister's wardrobe, 'borrowing' a mini dress which was rather shorter than short on her much taller frame. Make-up had come next. Some of Amanda's eyeshadow, and thick black liner applied with a rather unsteady hand. Lissa had thought the effect rather daring.

She had arranged to meet Helen at Gordon's house, but when she arrived there her friend had been busy talking to several people she did not know, and feeling suddenly shy she had felt reluctant to intrude. Gordon himself had materialised from the kitchen, and had greeted her with a brief kiss on the cheek. She had been so thrilled and excited that later she could barely remember accepting the drink he had given her, or drinking it. She must have done so though; and she had compounded her folly by drinking two more glasses of Gordon's special punch. That was why she had agreed to go upstairs with him, thrilled out of her mind that he should actually find her desirable. She hadn't been drunk, but what she had had to drink had been sufficient to rid her of her normally stifling inhibitions. She could remember quite vividly the thrills of excitement that had run up and down her spine when Gordon kissed her—boyish, quite inexperienced kisses really. They had been lying together on his bed, doing nothing more than exchanging explorative kisses when the door had suddenly been thrust open and a man Lissa didn't recognise had appeared framed darkly against the light behind him. Even now she shuddered slightly remembering the sickness and fear that had then crawled down her spine. Before she could even move her father was in the room, dragging her off the bed, saying things to her, calling her names...that had numbed her senses and her tongue.

What had followed had all the trappings of the very worst kind of nightmares. Her parents had dragged her home in a thick silence, but once there, the real torment had started. What had she been doing with that boy? her mother demanded. They had questioned her in her father's study with Joel Hargreaves standing impassively by, listening to every single word. Lissa thought now she had never hated anyone in all her life as she had hated him that night. Send him away, she had demanded tearfully of her parents, but her father had refused. 'No, Lissa. I want Joel to know what sort of girl his brother is going to get for a sister-in-law. Had you no thought for your sister when you disobeyed us?' he demanded, adding, 'do you think it fair that she should be tarred with the same brush as you?'

They had questioned her about what she had been doing with Gordon and in vain she had told them they had simply been kissing, blushing bright painful red to admit as much, but they had refused to believe her, saying why should they when she had already deceived them once by attending the party in the first place, and all the time Joel Hargreaves' watchful eyes had been on her, deriding...scorning...making her feel dirty and humiliated.

And her humiliation had not ended there. There had been a visit to their doctor; an examination which had left her racked with anguish and mental agony; and then she had been sent away to school. So that Amanda wouldn't have to bear the disgrace of a promiscuous younger sister, her parents had said.

It had taken years for Lissa to accept that she was not what her parents had called her; but the events of that night and the days which had followed had left her permanently scarred. To allow a man to so much as touch her was to relive again all that anguish; to endure the biting contempt in Joel Hargreaves' eyes when he looked down at her lying on the narrow bed with Gordon, her brief dress exposing all the long length of her legs, her mouth swollen from Gordon's kisses, all her tender, vulnerable adolescent emotions exposed to the cruel scrutiny of his worldliness.

'If you've finished with the table...'

It was several seconds before Lissa realised the waitress was speaking to her and that people were waiting for her to vacate her table. Almost stumbling she got to her feet and hurried out into the bitter February afternoon. Strange how fate worked. If she hadn't been such a coward about facing Joel she would never have come into the café, and then she would never have bumped into Helen; never have revived all those memories she had sought so firmly to conceal. She was literally shaking with reaction as she unlocked her car and a small moan broke from her mouth. Would it never end? Would she ever be able to put the past fully behind her and enter into a normal relationship with a man? Would she ever be able to take and give physical pleasure without the ever-present crushing guilt and self-disgust she now suffered from.

Why it was Joel Hargreaves whose face she saw every time another man touched her and not her father's she wasn't really sure. Her father had been the one to condemn her; to insist that she was lying...but it was the memory of Joel Hargreaves that brought her out in a cold sweat and turned her sleep into horrendous nightmares. Simon had been exultant when he accidentally hit on the fact that she was still a virgin, but he wouldn't be exultant if he knew why. He thought she was clinging to some silly out-moded convention of purity, whereas she knew the truth...that those cataclysmic events during her fifteenth summer had frozen and destroyed some essential female part of her; the pain of her humiliation so intense that it prevented her from allowing herself to feel anything sexual for any man.

By the time she drove through the gates of Winterly, Lissa had regained control of herself. As she stepped out of her Mini and walked towards the main door with long-legged grace no one could guess at the torment of emotional agony she had just endured, least of all the man watching her.

Joel's mouth twisted sardonically as he looked at her. She reminded him of a glossy, elegant chestnut filly he had once owned. There was pride and beauty in every movement of her graceful body, and also a wariness that warned him that she had come prepared to do battle if necessary.

Joel Hargreaves wasn't used to women keeping

him at a distance; very much the opposite. What would have intrigued him in another woman, in Lissa grated on his nerves. He had known her since she was a teenager, and throughout all the years since she had treated him as though he were some vilely contaminated life-form.

He had once tried to talk to Amanda about it, but his sister-in-law had simply shrugged and said that Lissa was an odd girl.

Odd maybe…beautiful and extremely desirable, yes. In the past she had never allowed him to get close enough to know her, but now, dramatically the situation had changed. Telling himself that he was a fool for even thinking of resurrecting what should have been no more than a passing whim he went to let her in.

'Lissa. You decided to come then.'

Lissa inclined her head coolly, praying that she had herself well under control. She was consumed by a wholly unfamiliar and extremely dangerous desire to give vent to the turmoil of feelings bubbling up inside her; to rave and scream at him that he and he alone was solely responsible for the destruction of her femininity…that she hated…hated and loathed him and that nothing…nothing would induce her to stay in his house.

As she followed him inside Joel caught the brilliant gleam of her eyes, and wondered if her anger was because she had had to leave her boyfriend for a weekend. Joel knew all about Simon Greaves. A very personable and persuasive young man.

'I think we'll talk in my study.'

Trust Joel to choose to do battle on his own home ground Lissa thought bitterly as he held the door open for her to precede him. She had visited Winterly on several occasions both when his parents lived there and since they had left, but this was the first time she had been in this particular room. The austerity of its furnishings were initially deceptive until one became aware of the intrinsic beauty of the antique desk and the silken beauty of the Aubusson rug covering the floor. A small display cabinet caught her eye and she held her breath for a moment awed by the collection of jade inside it.

'You like jade?'

Joel was watching her, and for once she saw no reason to conceal the truth from him.

'I love it,' she admitted.

'So do I. I started collecting it several years ago on a trip to Hong Kong.' He moved towards the case and then stopped abruptly as the study door opened and a harassed looking middle-aged woman burst in.

'Mr Hargreaves,' she began without preamble. 'I simply cannot have those children in my kitchen. The moment my back's turned they're into my cupboards, upsetting everything...'

She paused to take a break and Joel inserted smoothly, 'Don't worry about it, Mrs Johnson. I'll soon have everything sorted out.'

'Well I certainly hope so.' Mrs Johnson seemed far from mollified and Lissa fought hard not to burst into impetuous speech and remind the older woman that if the children were being naughty it might possibly be remembered that they had only recently lost their parents and both sets of grandparents.

'If you'll just keep an eye on them for me while Miss Grant and I finish talking,' Joel continued, to his housekeeper. 'I promise you I'll take them off your hands.'

She withdrew but with bad grace, muttering something under her breath about not being paid to look after children. When she had gone Lissa raised her eyebrows and said coolly, '*That* is what you consider doing the best you can for the girls is it?'

She was surprised by the faint flush of colour staining his skin. 'In the past few days I've been trying to get a nanny. I haven't had much success.' He drummed impatiently on his desk for several seconds and then turned to face her, admitting, 'All the more reputable agencies are rather dubious about the fact that I'm a single man, and as for the rest...' His grim expression startled her a little. 'Well let's just say I'm not too keen on the idea of adding an eighteen year old au pair to my other problems.'

Lissa knew she should have felt triumphant, but the emotion uppermost in her heart was pity and concern for the children. She had experienced too much trauma and heartache during her own childhood, to treat the miseries of any other child's lightly.

'When can I see the girls, Joel?' she asked huskily.

'Soon... When we've finished talking.'

'How are they?'

How she hated having to ask him for anything,

even something so mundane as information about her nieces, and she knew it showed in her voice from the twisted smile he gave her, his eyes glinting dark gold as he turned to look at her.

'Poor Lissa,' he mocked watching her. 'Forced to actually ask me for something. How that must hurt. Why are you so frightened of me, Lissa?'

'I'm not.' Her chin firmed and she stared back at him. 'I simply don't like you very much that's all.'

He laughed then, the warm rich sound startling her. What could she possibly have said to make him laugh. It was obvious that he wasn't going to tell, so she insisted coolly, 'The girls, Joel. How are they coping?'

'On the surface, quite well,' he told her. 'Louise of course being older is finding it harder to accept that they're gone. Emma...well I can barely understand a word she says as it is. Louise seems to be able to interpret her chatter all right though. They've been asking for you,' he added abruptly. 'I didn't realise they knew you so well.'

'I've spent quite a lot of time with them.' It was true. She had looked after them for the odd weekend for her sister. Amanda knowing how much she loved children, and not being overly maternal herself had been delighted to leave them in her care.

'You really care about them, don't you?' he said curtly, further surprising her.

Instantly she was defensive, glaring at him from angry emerald eyes as she responded bitterly, 'Why should that be so surprising? I happen to like children...I always have done.'

'And yet you've never given any indication that you'd like to get married and have your own,' Joel put in softly, 'I wonder why?'

Lissa had to turn away from him so that he couldn't read her expression. Her heart was thumping frantically, her pulse beat rocketing way out of control.

'Perhaps I just haven't met the right man yet,' she told him flippantly, hoping he wouldn't guess at her emotional turmoil. How could she ever have children of her own, feeling as she did about sex? It wasn't only the ability to love as a woman he had robbed her of, she thought, hating him, it was also the ability to mother children... And now he even wanted to take her nieces away from her.

'I'm not prepared to give up the girls, Joel,' she told him, pivoting round to face him. 'Amanda left them in my care...and I don't care what you say,' she cried out passionately, 'I can't really believe that any caring judge would rule that the care of strangers— because that's what your nanny will be—will be more beneficial, even with all the material advantages you can give them, than my love. You *don't* love them Joel...not the way I do.' She was close to tears and had to blink them away, horrified when she opened her eyes again to find that he was looming over her, the gold speckles in his eyes igniting with fierce heat.

'Like hell I don't,' he told her thickly. 'You seem to have conveniently forgotten that their father was my brother... I only want what is best for them Lissa...'

'No, you don't. You just want to take them away from me.'

Her voice was high and strained, hysteria edging in under her self-control. She could see Joel looking at her, and she could feel his anger.

'Don't be such a bloody fool,' he flung at her. 'You seem to be developing a persecution complex where I'm concerned, Lissa. Oh yes,' he gritted grimly watching her with cold eyes. 'I'm well aware of the extraordinary lengths you go to avoid my company. I know quite well that Amanda had strict instructions never to invite you to the house when there was any chance that I might be around. Just what have I ever done to warrant such antipathy, Lissa. Tell me?'

She shrugged lightly, struggling for self-control. It seemed impossible that the events that were burned so painfully into her memory should not exist for him. But perhaps it was safer for her that he did not remember, she told herself, her nerve endings jumping tensely when the next minute, he said with silky softness, 'Or can I guess? Does all this haughty disdain you exhibit towards me spring from the fact that I once caught you in bed with your boyfriend?'

The brilliant wave of scarlet flooding her skin gave her away, and she watched his mouth twist in wry mockery, hating him with all the intense passion of her nature when he drawled tauntingly, 'You should be grateful that you were stopped when you were. A teenage pregnancy is no fun...'

God, how she hated him, Lissa thought feeling the nauseous loathing rise up inside her. She wanted to scream and cry…to tear that smooth smile from his face with her nails. She hated him…hated him… Her attention was deflected from her own inner turmoil when she heard Joel saying calmly, 'No, Lissa, I don't think the best thing for the girls is for them to be constantly shuttled between us, as though we were divorced parents. Children, especially children such as Louise and Emma who have already suffered the loss of their parents, need security and stability, and in an attempt to give them both, I've decided that what I need is not a nanny, but a wife.'

Lissa could only stare at him, but hard on the heels of her shock came the knowledge that if he did marry, she would lose her nieces, because surely a judge was bound to favour the suit of a man who had not only wealth but also a wife, above the claims of a girl, struggling alone on a little more than adequate salary.

'No comment?' she heard Joel saying, the words reaching her through a fog of thoughts. 'You don't want to know the identity of my wife-to-be?'

'Why should I?' Lissa managed to croak the denial. 'It's nothing to do with me.'

'On the contrary,' Joel assured her with smooth silkiness. 'It has everything to do with you my dear. You see, I've decided that the very best solution to Louise and Emma's problem would be for you and I to marry thus uniting both their guardians and providing them with a stable background.'

Lissa barely heard his last words. 'You and I…?'

She stared at him, the colour leaving her face on an ebb tide of shock. 'No, I...'

'Lissa, neither of us are foolish teenagers any longer.'

'We don't love one another...we don't even like one another,' Lissa interrupted harshly. 'How can you even think of a marriage between us?'

'Oh quite easily.' He was smiling at her in a way that told her that little though he might like her, he found the shape of her sexually desirable. Shock hit her on a tidal wave, swamping her. Joel desired *her*.

'You see,' he mocked her softly, 'we could have a lot more in common than you think. There is no need for our marriage to be a sterile one, Lissa. On the contrary...'

Lissa felt as though she were drowning in some whirlpool far too frenzied for her to fight. 'But you've always avoided marriage,' she whispered huskily, 'I remember Amanda once saying that she thought you'd never marry.'

'At one time I thought that myself,' he agreed laconically, 'but that was before John died.'

'And if I refuse...?' What did she mean 'if'? Of course she was going to refuse...but a thought had taken possession of her brain...the seed of an idea, that at last she might have found a way to make Joel pay for all the agony and shame he had caused her.

'Then I'll have to look around for someone else,' he told her calmly. 'Make no mistake about it, Lissa. For the girls' sake I intend to marry. I should prefer that my wife is you, but if you refuse, then I shall simply marry someone else.'

'And I'll lose the girls.' She breathed the words softly, but he heard them and shrugged.

'The choice is yours. I'm not, after all, asking you to make any sacrifice I'm not prepared to make myself. We'll both be giving up our freedom…and one thing more, Lissa.' He came towards her standing only feet away, but making no move to reach out and touch her. She felt almost suffocated by his proximity but refused to step back, making herself endure it. 'Our marriage will not be an empty legal bond only, but very real, in every sense of the word.'

'But I don't want you.' She said it through stiff lips forcing them to frame the words, half of her praying that he would take back his proposal; and the other half, the bitter, angry half hoping that he would not.

'How can you know that,' he taunted softly. 'We haven't been lovers yet.'

Nor ever will be, the bitter half of her exulted. Let him marry her…let him think he was going to have it all his own way, but when she lay in his bed and in his arms she would be as cold as ice; as devoid of the ability to give and take pleasure as she had always been, since he had destroyed the feminine core of her. Ignoring all the urgings of common sense Lissa faced him, praying that he wouldn't see the bitterness in her eyes, and that he wouldn't guess exactly why she was marrying him. He was using her affection for the girls to force her into this marriage…a marriage she was sure that would not stop him continuing with his many affairs, but what he did not know was that she was also going to use him...as the instrument of her revenge.

'Very well Joel...I agree to marry you.'

She was surprised to see the heated flicker of triumph burn dark gold in his eyes. He took a step towards her and she backed away, but before either of them could speak the door burst open and the elder of their nieces came rushing in.

'Auntie Lissa...Auntie Lissa...I heard you talking.' The petite four year old ran up to Lissa, clinging tightly to her legs, the blonde head buried in her skirt. 'Are you going to stay here for ever?' Louise demanded when Lissa bent down to pick her up. 'I want you to...so does Emma...'

'Yes, Louise, she's going to stay here for ever,' Lissa heard Joel saying from a distance, and just for a moment she felt a twinge of apprehension at the deep note of triumph in his voice, but then she banished it, telling herself she was imagining things. She was the one who should be feeling triumphant. She had got her nieces, and she had also got the means of repaying Joel for all the years of anguish and pain he had caused her. He might think their marriage was going to be a 'normal' one, but she knew different.

# CHAPTER THREE

LISSA WOKE UP the next morning feeling totally disorientated; initially by the strangeness of her room, and then by the huge weight of depression which seemed to have descended upon her out of nowhere. And then she remembered.

She had agreed to marry Joel! She closed her eyes and groaned, her head falling back against her pillow. How could she have been so stupid? She would have to tell him she had changed her mind. It was her own silly temper and pride that had led into folly; the old burning anger cum anguish she always experienced whenever she was with him. Why oh why after all these years, should Joel still be the one whose contempt and rejection of her hurt so badly? Was it because he had been the one to thrust open that bedroom door and see her? Was it because somehow in her innermost mind she had because of that confused him in some way with her father? They were questions Lissa could not answer; all she did know was that whenever she came in contact with him she was reminded of the way he had looked at her that night...and how for one weak minute she had longed to cry out to him to understand and forgive her...

Shivering faintly despite the centrally heated warmth of her bedroom, she was just contemplating how best to tell him that she had changed her mind and that she was certainly not prepared to marry him; even for the sake of her nieces when the door burst open and the two little girls rushed in, both still in their night-dresses.

Louise reached her first, flinging herself on to the bed and cuddling up next to her. Emma, still very much a toddler needed a helping hand, but there was no mistaking the enthusiasm in her hug when she was finally on the bed with Lissa and her sister.

'You're going to marry Uncle Joel and then you'll be our new mummy and daddy,' Louise announced importantly.

Lissa's heart sank. She felt trapped and desperate. How could she have been so crazy as to allow those old hurts to trap her into her present position. It seemed mediaeval and archaic now, in the cold clear light of a February morning that she should actually have contemplated marrying Joel, simply to even punish him for the pain he had once caused her. That was all over and done with now. But Joel…why did he want to marry her?

That was simple Lissa told herself; he wanted someone to look after the children who was not going to walk out on him. If she backed out she would lose the girls, Lissa reminded herself, looking at the two blonde heads, nestled together against her warmth. As she watched them, a melting, aching wave of love for them suffused her. If she didn't marry Joel, he would find someone who would and the girls would be lost to her for ever. Could she endure that? Looking at them Lissa knew she could not. This deeply maternal feeling she felt towards them was something she had always kept well hidden from others. Only Amanda had been aware of it, wryly amused by her sister's passionate love for her daughters, warning Lissa that when she married she would soon discover the drawbacks to being a mother. 'You want them because this way you can satisfy your mothering instincts without having to endure someone's lovemaking,' an inner voice warned her, but Lissa refused to listen, her fingers curling slightly into the bedclothes as she tried to deny the thoughts. Whose fault was it that she froze every time a man touched her? she asked herself, trying to whip up some of the anger she had that had consumed her last night. Not hers!

Her bedroom door opened again, and she blinked in stunned disbelief as Joel strolled in carrying a breakfast tray, which he put down on the table by the bed.

'Who said you two could come in here?' he demanded of the girls, ruffling the blonde curls and drawing stifled giggles form Louise.

'You and Lissa are going to be our new mummy and daddy, aren't you?' Louise demanded importantly of him, and yet Lissa could see that beyond the child's self-importance was a shadow of uncertainty and fear, and all her inner arguments against what they were doing melted. If for no other reason surely the sacrifice demanded of her was not too great when she thought of what it would mean to the girls. Joel was right; they needed the security and stability of a proper family unit, and if she didn't marry him, Joel would stand by his threat to find someone who would. She loved them too much to let someone else take her place with them, Lissa knew, and as she raised stormy hazel eyes to meet the mocking gold of Joel's, she knew that he had faithfully monitored each and every single thought that had passed through her head since he walked in the room.

'Too late for second thoughts,' he mouthed softly. There were two cups on the tray, Lissa noticed for the first time, and she gaped a little as Joel promptly started to fill them both with aromatic freshly brewed coffee. No doubt he was used to providing breakfast in bed for his legion of girlfriends, she thought waspishly, but he had no right to look so at ease and relaxed as he did so. He was dressed casually in jeans and a soft woollen checked shirt.

'Mrs Johnson's day off,' he explained laconically, handing her a cup.

'Very impressive,' Lissa responded tautly. 'But then I expect you've had plenty of practice.'

She saw his mouth tighten, the good humour that had lightened his eyes going, and a certain hard coldness taking its place. 'I thought we'd agreed to bury our differences and start afresh,' he said curtly. 'Two adults who spend all their time together back-biting at one another aren't going to help these two.'

Lissa knew he was right, and she bit her lower lip in mortification, hating him for putting her in the

wrong and for making her appear selfish. She ought
to be thinking of the girls and not herself. Joel obviously had. There were two beakers on the tray and
he poured orange juice into each of them, handing
them to his nieces. He was rewarded with a beaming
smile from Emma, and a small frown from Louise,
who confided artlessly, 'When Daddy makes
Mummy's breakfast for her, he always gets back into
bed with her. Sometimes he tells Nanny to come and
take us away,' she added importantly.

Lissa could feel the colour stealing up under her
skin, but it was impossible for her to drag her eyes
away from the amusement sparkling in Joel's.

'Blushing.' He ran a teasing finger along the curve
of her cheek as he sat down on the edge of her bed.
'How novel, and why I wonder should the thought of
married sex embarrass you when you yourself must
surely be no stranger to the early morning rituals between lovers.'

Lissa wanted to vigorously deny what he was saying, but how could she without betraying the truth?

'I must go back to London today,' she mumbled,
desperately anxious to change the subject. She was
going hot and cold all over with the onset of a familiar fear. It seemed incredible and she knew that
Joel would never have believed it, but the closest she
had come to real intimacy with any man in the years
since her fifteenth summer was what she was sharing
with him right now. Suddenly she became intensely
aware of the weight of his body on her mattress; the
warm male scent of him as he leaned forward to tickle

Louise. The little girl giggled and moved closer to her, grabbing the soft fabric of her nightdress. It was a fine lawn cotton, and covered her quite adequately, but as Louise grabbed the fabric she was suddenly intensely conscious of the way it was tightening across her breasts. She could feel Joel watching her as thought his glance were burning into her skin.

'London?'

The sharpness in his voice made her tense, and when she managed to compose herself sufficiently to meet his eyes they were cold and angry.

'Joel, I'll have to arrange something about my house…and then there's Simon and my job. I'll have to explain that…'

'I'll do all the explaining necessary,' he told her curtly. 'I want you to stay here with the girls.'

'But Simon…' Lissa expostulated. 'I must tell him myself that…'

'That you won't be sharing his bed any longer?' Joel bit out grimly. 'That he'll be losing a lover as well as a secretary. No Lissa, I'll tell him for you. I don't want you seeing him again, now that you've agreed to marry me. I suppose it hasn't occurred to you that if he'd really thought anything of you, he'd have proposed marriage…knowing how you feel about the girls.'

It was on the tip of Lissa's tongue to tell him that Simon had, but for some reason she suppressed the words. 'What are you so afraid of Joel?' she lashed out instead. 'That if I see Simon I won't be able to

resist jumping straight into bed with him. You always
did have a high opinion of me didn't you?' she finished sarcastically, watching the way his mouth
twisted with bitter derision as he looked at her, and
wondering why she should feel this knife twist of pain
so deep inside herself; why she should lash herself so
unmercifully, when she knew…oh how she knew exactly how much he despised her. Why should she seek
further confirmation of that knowledge so determinedly?

'You've certainly never gone out of your way to
show yourself to me in a good light have you?' Joel
countered. 'In fact I sometimes think you deliberately
want me to think the worst of you, Lissa. I've often
wondered why?'

He got up before she could make any retort, dropping light kisses on the two small blonde heads of his
nieces as he did so.

'Aren't you going to kiss Lissa too?' Louise piped
up instantly. 'Daddy always kissed Mummy before
he went to work.'

'But I'm not going to work,' Joel explained, ruffling her curls. 'I'm going downstairs to make some
telephone calls. However, poppet, just to please you.'
He bent his head, and although Lissa cringed back as
far as she could, until the back of her head was
pressed against the unyielding brass of the Victorian
bedstead, it didn't stop Joel from kissing her, the torment of the warmth of his mouth moving softly
against her own making her shiver with shock and
fear. When he released her he was frowning and Lissa

held her breath, wondering if she had betrayed herself, and if he was now having second thoughts about marrying her. He was a virile man; even she could see that and when he discovered that…that she was neither prepared nor able to be a true wife to him… Tell him, tell him the truth now an inner voice cautioned…but she couldn't…she couldn't lay herself open to the male mockery and contempt she would see in his eyes if she did. And besides she would lose the girls. No, after they were married…after they were married she would tell him that she had changed her mind and that she could not accept him as her lover. After all he would still have what he wanted from her; the children and her service as a stand-in mother. For the rest…well she doubted that he had had any thoughts of being faithful to her in any case… Feeling a little uncomfortable because she knew she was deceiving him, Lissa was glad when he turned his back on her and walked towards the door. Once he was through it and had closed it behind him she let out a shaky breath. Emma took her thumb out of her mouth and stared up at her with golden brown eyes. A huge smile split her solemn little face and she said firmly, 'Mummy.'

Lissa had to dash away tears. Amanda had complained that Emma was slow to speak because she had Louise to translate for her, and it seemed prophetic that she should choose now of all times to start.

'No, not Mummy,' Louise corrected her sister, 'Auntie Lissa…but you can call her Mummy I s'pose,' she said kindly. 'Shall I call you Mummy too…and Uncle Joel, Daddy?' she asked Lissa.

'You must call us whatever you like, Louise,' Lissa told her. She suspected that by the time she reached school age Emma would not be able to remember her parents, but Louise was old enough to do so and the last thing Lissa wanted to do was to try to erase from her memory the reality of her parents. The best thing to do was to let Louise feel free to decide for herself and see what happened, she decided, trying to occupy her mind with the girls' problems and not her own.

She left them playing together on the bed while she showered and dressed, and then wearing comfortable jeans and a soft russet silk shirt that toned with her hair, she shepherded them back to their own room.

Joel had put them in his own and John's old nursery, and while the bedroom with its bathroom and study-sitting room was large and airy the decor was more suited to two teenage boys rather than two small girls. Making a mental note to talk to him about it, and to ask him about the girls' toys and clothes, Lissa helped them to get dressed and took them downstairs.

The sooner a proper routine was established, the sooner they would overcome the trauma of their parents' death. Making another mental note to enquire locally about play groups, Lissa headed for the kitchen, suddenly conscious that Louise was hanging back, a worried frown puckering her forehead.

'Come on darling, you want some breakfast, don't you?' Lissa asked gently.

'Mrs Johnson doesn't like us going in the kitchen,'

was Louise's quavery response. 'She says we're pests and that it's time Uncle Joel make some proper arrangements for us.'

Listening to this artless confirmation that little pitchers did indeed have long ears, Lissa repressed a quiver of anger against the housekeeper. Surely the older woman could have made allowances, knowing the circumstances surrounding the girls.

'Uncle Joel got us a new nanny,' Louise continued confidingly, 'because Nanny Jo's boyfriend didn't want her to come and live here with us, but we didn't like our new nanny...'

Lissa was not surprised that 'Nanny' Jo's boyfriend was reluctant to allow his girlfriend to live virtually alone with a man of Joel's calibre, even she was aware of his powerful, vibrant brand of masculinity, but while other women were attracted by it, she was repelled, she told herself, witness her revulsion when Joel had kissed her. And yet there had been no violence, no domination in his kiss... If anything the first touch of his mouth against her own had been almost tender, coaxing... Shutting such dangerous thoughts away Lissa turned her attention to the task of getting the girls' breakfast, secretly appalled to discover how little there was in the way of food in the kitchen cupboards. She was going to have to speak to Joel about his housekeeper and she grimaced faintly at the thought.

She had just settled the girls at the comfortable farmhouse table with plates of toast and honey, when Joel walked in.

'Any chance of a cup of coffee?' he enquired of Lissa, lifting one eyebrow interrogatively. When she nodded assent, he sat down between the two girls, deftly preventing Emma from dropping her toast sticky side down on to her lap. Watching his easy confidence with the girls, Lissa realised she was seeing a new side of him. In her mind he was and always had been the sardonic contemptuous enemy of her youth; the man who had torn from her all her romantic yearnings and dreams and tossed them back to her blemished and made sordid by his totally unexpected intrusion into the bedroom where she had been experiencing her first tentative and innocent forays into the land of sensual pleasure. Had they been left alone she knew that nothing more than a few fumbling kisses and caresses would have been exchanged between Gordon and herself. For all his image as the school pin-up, his worldly experience had not been more than hers, and with the wisdom of age she realised that both of them would have drawn back before they had gone much further, but the reaction of her father and the disapproval of Joel, the stranger he had brought with him to witness her shame and degradation, had made it seem as though she were more of a nymphomaniac than a shy and rather naive fifteen year old experiencing virtually her first kiss. Now she could accept that her parents had been over-strict with her, much more so than they had been with Amanda, but Amanda had been the image of her mother while she apparently, or so Amanda had once confided, was very much like their father's sister…someone who

was never mentioned at home, and who apparently as
a teenager during the War had led a rather promiscuous life, eventually leaving home and disappearing.
This explained some of her parents' strictness and
even possibly her father's dislike of her, Lissa acknowledged, but surely if they had loved her as they
undoubtedly loved Amanda they would have seen—
known—that she was not the wanton creature they
themselves had branded her.

She could still vividly recall her shock and mental
anguish at discovering from another of the pupils that
the school she had been sent to was for 'naughty'
girls. 'What have you done to get here?' the latter had
asked her.' Boasting, 'I'm here because I hate my new
step-brother.'

The nuns hadn't been actively unkind, indeed some
of them showed an extremely enlightened attitude towards their wayward pupils, but Lissa had felt too out
of step…too alien to respond to them. She had also
felt besmirched…dirty and degraded…defiled in a
way that made her recoil from any human contact.

'Lissa?'

She came back to reality with a start, uncomfortably conscious of the strange look in Joel's eyes as
he looked at her. 'Where on earth have you been?'
he asked softly.

Just for a moment the concern she heard in his
voice touched her and she said huskily, 'To hell…'
bitterly regretting her weakness when she saw first
shock and then caution enter his eyes.

'It's too late now for backing out,' he told her

harshly, revealing that he had totally misunderstood her comment. 'I've already spoken to Greaves and told him that you're marrying me.'

How possessive he sounded, Lissa thought wryly, almost as though telling Simon they were to marry had given him a great deal of pleasure. 'I've also spoken to our local vicar.' He saw her start of surprise and smiled grimly. 'What were you expecting, Lissa—a civil ceremony.' He shook his head. 'My grandparents, my parents and John were all married in our local church. We won't have a large wedding of course…in fact I've arranged a very quiet ceremony; just the Vicar and a handful of witnesses. His wife has offered to have the girls for the afternoon. I've given out that we'd planned to announce our engagement on your birthday, but that because of what has happened, we've brought the wedding forward for the sake of the children.'

Her birthday was six weeks away, and Lissa marvelled at Joel's ability to remember such a trivial thing, just as she was chilled by his ability to reason and plan. It made sense of course—she was the last person to want a lot of speculation and curiosity about why they were marrying.

'And, Lissa, one thing more,' he continued in a quiet voice. 'Once we *are* married I shall expect you to stay faithful to your vows. We live in a very quiet village and…'

'…and a front of respectability must be maintained at all times,' she finished bitterly for him, remembering that this had been her parents' attitude. Almost as though he read her mind, Joel put in curtly, 'You hurt your parents very deeply with your unconventional behaviour, Lissa, but I won't accept it the way they did.'

'Hurt *them!*' Lissa was incredulous…struck dumb by his arrogant charm. He knew nothing about her relationship with her family, nothing at all…

'Yes.' Joel continued as though she hadn't interrupted. 'I can vividly remember your father's shock that night when you deceived him to go to that party. They were dining with my parents and your father developed a migraine. I offered to run them back as your mother couldn't drive. When they got home and found you gone your father was beside himself. Luckily your mother remembered the telephone number of your friend and it was from her parents that they learned where you were… Your mother explained to me later the problems they'd had with you…how wild and uncontrollable you were, how you'd got in with a bad set…I must say at first I was disinclined to believe them, but when I walked into that house with your father and found half the kids in it were put of their minds on drugs and the other half on drink…'

Lissa could have told him that the drugs had come from the older brother of one of the boys there who had brought them home from university, and as for the drink…well most of them had been so young and inexperienced that a couple of glasses of wine had been more than sufficient to go to their heads, never mind the weird punch concoction that had been served.

'But of course you were out for another kind of thrill weren't you, Lissa...? How many others had you been to bed with before him?'

'Does it matter?' She felt literally sick, her body shaking with tension as she saw herself through Joel's eyes. She remembered how the brief dress had ridden up exposing her thighs, the low neckline revealing the curves of her breasts and she shuddered deeply. To bolster herself up she demanded huskily, 'If you disapprove of me so much Joel, why marry me? If I've slipped so far beyond the pale, I'm surprised you're even contemplating it. My morals...'

'It isn't your morals that are at issue,' Joel cut in angrily. 'I don't give a damn how many men you've slept with Lissa. I'm not hypocritical enough to expect a woman to remain chaste while a man does not...no, what baffles me is that you should have so little respect for yourself...so little self-pride. The gift of your body to another human being is exactly that—a gift—not something to be thrown away lightly, but something to be treasured...'

'And to ensure that Emma and Louise treasure theirs, are you going to keep a ball and chain on them while they're growing up, as my father did me,' Lissa hit out blindly.

Joel looked at her, his expression hard to define, but somewhere in it was a pity that lashed at her pride, and made her burn with resentment. How dare he pity her. How dare he falsely accuse her...force her into a set pattern that was not hers and never had been.

'No...I shall tell them that whatever they do in life is by their own choice, and it matters little what it is, or what others think, as long as they can face themselves and keep their own self-respect intact. Self-respect is more important than the opinions of others; than momentary sexual release...'

'And you of course are speaking from experience,' Lissa taunted bitterly.

'I've never made love to a woman I don't both like and honour, if that's what you mean,' Joel agreed with devastating candour.

A bitter smile curved Lissa's mouth. 'Then obviously you're prepared to make an exception in my case.' She could feel tears pricking the backs of her eyes, and hated herself for her weakness. Flinging down the cloth she was holding, she hurried out of the kitchen, conscious of Joel calling her name, but the strident shrill of the telephone prevented him from following her.

It was half an hour or so before she felt able to go back downstairs.

The girls were seated at the now cleared kitchen table, busily drawing on large sheets of paper. Joel was filling the coffee maker and turned as she walked in.

'Let's just put the past behind us, Lissa,' he said in a clipped voice, without looking at her. 'All I want is your promise that you will adhere to our marriage vows; that there'll be no sneaking off to meet the likes of Greaves.'

Was he worried that she might neglect the children? That must be it, Lissa thought subduing a mild bout of hysteria at the thought of her of all people sneaking off to meet any man. If only he knew! But he must not know! Quite why she should feel so strongly that she must keep the truth from him Lissa wasn't sure. She had sensed a compassion and gentleness in his attitude towards the girls that she had once believed alien to his nature and if he knew the truth that compassion might even be extended to include herself. But she didn't want his compassion, she told herself angrily. She didn't *want* to like him...she didn't want him to like her. To stop herself from pursuing this potentially dangerous line of thought she asked sweetly, 'And you Joel, do you intend to keep to your vows?'

'Do you want me to?'

He was challenging her, Lissa knew that, but her eyes dropped away from the golden gleam of his. He laughed softly, and feather light shivers of alarm coursed over her body as he came towards her. 'What an enigma you are, Lissa,' he said quietly. 'What did I say to provoke this?' His fingers touched her heated face and she blushed harder, hating herself for doing so. 'Surely it can't be the thought of me as your lover that makes you so hot and bothered. After all to you what's one more man?'

'Auntie Lissa, come and look at my drawing,' Louise demanded, giving Lissa an opportune excuse for moving away. Her heart was thumping jerkily, her body a melting pot of strange and alien sensations, her nerves stretched like over-fine wire.

'I've got to go out,' Joel informed her. 'I'm interviewing several applicants for John's job.' A shadow crossed his face, and Lissa felt a tug of sympathy for him. He had been very close to his brother, she knew.

Originally Joel had overseen both the estate and the business, but after their father had retired John had taken over as Managing Director of the company, and Joel had concentrated on running the estate, bringing in many new innovative measures, according to Amanda, but he had also been on hand to help and advise John whenever his help was needed. He had other business interests too according to Amanda, with money invested wisely in a variety of enterprises. All in all he was a shrewd and very astute man; a husband many women would be delighted to have; physically he was extremely attractive, his manner towards the children was both gentle and firm. He would make an excellent father, she found herself thinking, swiftly denying the thought. There would be no children for them, and if he didn't like it well then...he would...he would simply have to divorce her... She subdued a bubble of hysterical laughter forming in her throat. How many potential brides were thinking about divorce even before the wedding ceremony took place.

Later on in the day, when she had settled the girls for a nap, having previously taken them for a walk, Lissa had time on her hands to think. She should never have agreed to marry Joel she knew, but having agreed how could she back out now, without losing the girls? Already this one day spent with them had

# CHAPTER FOUR

'WHY AREN'T YOU WEARING a white dress?' Louise scowled, looking uncannily like Joel, as she sat on Lissa's bed watching her dress. 'Brides always wear white dresses,' she complained. 'I've seen them!'

'Yes, darling, I know,' Lissa agreed, 'but this isn't that sort of wedding. Now, you're going to be a good girl for Mrs Chartwell aren't you? She's going to look after you and Emma while Uncle Joel and I get married.'

'She's got a dog,' Louise told her, instantly distracted, excited colour glowing in her cheeks. 'Can we have a dog, Lissa? Mummy said we couldn't because Granny was all…alle…'

'Allergic,' Lissa finished for her, remembering her mother's aversion for any kind of pet. 'We'll see,' she told the little girl. 'I'll have to ask Uncle Joel.'

'Ask Uncle Joel what?'

Lissa felt her stomach muscles tense as Joel walked into her room. He was already dressed for the ceremony in a dark pin-striped suit and a fine white silk shirt. He looked very tall and male, Lissa thought shakily, and for some reason she had the oddest desire to be held against his chest and comforted the way he had comforted Emma the other evening when she fell over and grazed her knee. She wanted her fears and miseries soothed away, the way he had soothed Emma's she thought crazily, stunned by the impact of her thoughts.

'If we can have a dog,' Louise replied promptly, forcing her to take notice of what she was saying, rather than abandoning herself to the enormity of her own thoughts.

'Louise would like a dog,' Lissa cut in shakily. 'I told her she must ask you.'

'I don't see why not...but...only if you're a very good girl,' Joel added cautioningly when Louise started to bounce up and down on the bed, 'and that includes not making Mrs Johnson angry.'

His mention of the housekeeper made Lissa remember her own doubts about the other woman, and saying firmly, 'Louise, be a good girl and go and see if Emma's awake will you?' She sent her out of earshot.

Joel was frowning as the door closed behind her and Lissa said quickly, 'I sent her away because I wanted to talk to you about Mrs Johnson. I don't like her attitude towards the girls—at least I don't like what I've seen of it. I realise that staff can be hard to find but...'

'If you want to replace her you can do so,' Joel surprised her by saying without argument. 'I've had a few doubts myself,' he told her grimly, 'but I've already been accused of spoiling the girls, so I held my peace.'

Spoiling them? By whom Lissa wondered.

'All ready?' His glance skimmed her pale face and then studied the soft cream wool of her suit. The colour was a perfect foil for the richness of her hair, and although Lissa thought she looked far too pale she was conscious of looking good in the outfit—a new one she had purchased for spring and so not yet worn. She had confined her hair in an elegant knot, and on impulse had driven into the nearest town the previous afternoon and managed to find an absurd concoction of feathers and net in a Princess Diana style which made her suit look much more bridal.

'Almost. I've just got to dress Emma and Louise.'

'I'll do that for you.'

Once again he had stunned her.

'Don't look like that,' he told her grimly. 'I do know how to. What's the matter, Lissa?' he mocked. 'Surprised to discover that I'm not quite the ogre you thought?'

His perspicacity unnerved her. He saw far too much, far too clearly.

She managed a light shrug. 'It's just that I find it surprising that you should know so much about child care—you being a single man.'

Somehow she managed to make his caring sound suspect, and was instantly ashamed of herself, but he only said quietly, 'I don't find it at all unmanly, Lissa, and if you do, then I'm very sorry for you…but it's your problem. John was a devoted father and spent a lot of time with the girls. Amanda had a nanny but both of them believed in being with the children as much as possible and I think that is the right attitude. Too many women shut their husbands out of their childrens' lives, especially when the children are very young.'

Once again he had made her feel very much in the wrong…very shallow and unfair in her attitudes. Biting her lip, she turned away from him and concentrated on putting on her lip gloss.

'Don't wear too much of that stuff,' he startled her by drawling. Her eyes swivelled sharply to meet the amusement in his.

'I don't want to get it all over me when I kiss you,' he explained softly, apparently fascinated by the slow crawl of hot colour turning her pale skin pink. Her fingers went instinctively to her lips as though to protect them from even the suggestion of his touch. A thick sound stifled in the back of his throat drew her attention back to Joel. He was standing watching her, with an unreadable expression in his eyes, their gold darkened to a burning topaz.

'You've got all the tricks, Lissa,' he told her bitterly, 'I'll give you that…but you're wasting your time playing the shy bride on me. I know the real you—remember…'

'And knowing—still want me,' she flung at him dangerously. For a moment the tension of his body frightened her and then he seemed to force himself to relax.

'An inexplicable weakness,' he agreed in a slow drawl, 'but one which I suspect time and familiarity will eliminate.'

He was gone before Lissa could retort. She stared into the mirror at her own baffled and furious expression. Had he really meant to intimate that once he had made love to her a few times he would no longer want her? No doubt about it! Her mouth compressed grimly. Oh, she hated him...hated him...

Angry colour sparkled in her eyes as she joined him downstairs, her cheeks still glowing faintly with the heat of her resentment. Both girls bounced excitedly around them as Joel shepherded them out to the car.

'Mrs Chartwell offered to have them for the night, but I didn't think that was a good idea,' Joel told her quietly as he opened the car doors. 'They've had bad dreams just about every night since their parents died, and I don't want to subject them to any unnecessary alterations in routine.'

Lissa managed a casual shrug. 'Well we're hardly a normal bride and groom are we?' she countered.

'What's normal?' Joel held open the car door for her and Lissa shivered remembering what he had said about their marriage. As he closed the car door on her she had a wild impulse to thrust it open and tell him that she couldn't go through with it. The words hovered on her lips, but just at that moment Louise leaned forward from the rear of the car and said happily. 'After today I'm going to call you "Mummy" Aunt Lissa, and I'm going to call Uncle Joel "Daddy", and we'll be together for always won't we? You'll never, ever go away to heaven and leave us will you?' The anxiety in the high childish voice

silenced Lissa's tongue. How could she back
out…how could she subject the girls to more upset
and upheaval?

The answer was quite simply that she could not,
and it was this and nothing else that kept her going
through the brief, tense ceremony that made her Joel's
wife. As he had threatened, once she was he bent his
head to kiss her. The warmth of his breath fanning
her face made her feel faint; but the acute nausea she
was used to experiencing when men came so threat-
eningly close to her never came; nor on this occasion
was she attacked by those flashing pictures that so
often in the past had tormented her; images of Joel
staring down at her dishevelled clothing and flushed
face, Joel disapproving and contemptuous…perhaps
because this time it was Joel himself who was kissing
her, Lissa thought numbly, keeping her mouth firmly
closed as his lips moved over it. She could feel him
checking slightly, anxiously aware of the narrowed
scrutiny in his eyes as they searched hers. Her heart
was thumping alarmingly.

'If you're thinking of reneging on our bargain,
Lissa, then don't,' he warned her softly.

There was no time for him to say anything more
because they were being congratulated by the vicar
and Joel had to turn aside from her to respond to him.

An hour later having accepted the celebratory glass
of sherry the vicar's wife had offered, and collected
the girls, Lissa sank thankfully into the leather up-
holstery of Joel's Jaguar. She felt exhausted, both
emotionally and physically; totally drained by the ef-

fort of maintaining a facade of calm, while inwardly she was a mass of nerves.

Joel too seemed unusually silent as he drove them back to Winterly; even the girls were a little subdued Lissa noticed. Now that the ceremony was over and they were actually man and wife she felt foolish wearing her frivolous hat and the first thing she did as she walked into the house was to take it off, halting with it still in her hands as she observed the determined expression of the housekeeper as she came into the hall. The grim look in the older woman's eyes, plus the fact that she was dressed in her outdoor clothes gave Lissa an inkling of what was to come, and she was proved right. The moment Joel was through the door Mrs Johnson announced curtly that she was leaving. As she made this pronouncement she eyed Lissa with disfavour, adding that she had told Joel when she took the job that single gentlemen were what she preferred working for and that she never worked in households where there were children.

Quickly shepherding the girls upstairs Lissa left Joel to deal with her alone. It was about ten minutes before she heard Mrs Johnson's small car drive away.

''Well I'm afraid it looks as though we're going to have to find a new housekeeper a little earlier than we'd planned,' Joel announced as he walked into the nursery. 'I did try to persuade her to stay on long enough to give you time to adjust, but she wouldn't agree.' He looked rather grim and Lissa wondered if he considered her incapable of looking after the four of them herself. At the convent the girls had had to look after their own rooms, and they had also had to take turns working in the kitchens. It was considered therapeutic, and Lissa had discovered then that she enjoyed cooking.

'I'll get in touch with the agencies after the week-end,' she told Joel, glancing at her watch. 'It's time for the girls' tea. I'll go down and make it.'

She was surprised by the glimmer of amusement she saw in his eyes and blurted out defensively, 'What's wrong...why are you laughing?'

'It's hardly a traditional start to married life is it?' Joel murmured, one arched eyebrow inviting her to share his wry amusement. Lissa refused to respond. He alarmed her when he was relaxed and friendly with her; she found herself having to fight not to respond to him; she preferred it when he was coolly contemptuous and distant. Her fingers curled into her palms as she remembered that she was now his wife...that tonight... She went hot and cold as she remembered the savage fury with which she had accepted his proposal; the reprisals she had planned to punish him for the anguish he had caused her. Now she could hardly believe her own folly. How on earth had she expected to get away with it? Joel wasn't the man to allow her to change the rules of their relationship simply to suit herself. He expected her to be his wife in every sense of the word; to share his bed, and when he discovered that she could not... She shivered suddenly, freezing when he reached out and touched her arm. 'Cold?' He was frowning slightly as though the fact that she might be concerned him. Dear

heavens what would he *say* if she told him the truth?
If she told him that she was as cold inside as perma-
frost and that neither he nor any other man could melt
it? How clearly she could recall her anguish when she
first discovered her inability to respond sexually to
anyone. She had been almost twenty before she had
had another boyfriend—a quite pleasant boy she had
met at work, but the very first time he had kissed her
she had been frozen by the mental image of Joel his
touch conjured up. Shaking her head in an effort to
dispel the past, Lissa managed a brief smile. 'No, not
really. I'll take the girls downstairs and feed them.
What do you want to do? Shall I make something for
us later...'

'What do you have in mind? A romantic candlelit
dinner *à deux?*' His eyes and voice held amusement,
but it was a gentle amusement rather than a mocking
one, and the rueful curl of his mouth showed that he
wanted to share it with her. Against her will Lissa felt
herself responding, a wry smile tugging at the corners
of her own mouth.

'By the time I've fed and bathed these two, I'll
probably be so tired all I'll want to do is fall straight
into bed.'

She had spoken without thinking, lulled by the gentleness of his voice and eyes, and now hot colour
flamed over her skin. Much to her chagrin her embarrassment only seemed to increase Joel's good humour.

'No...don't try to hide it,' he told her softly, when
she tried to duck away. His fingers cupped her face.

'You know, when you blush like that I find it very hard to believe that you're the experienced woman you are. Mind you...' his voice dropped to a tormentingly sensual drawl, 'I find it extremely flattering that you're so anxious to...consummate our marriage.'

She hadn't meant that at all Lissa thought frantically, and he knew it. The fact that he could be so coolly amused over what had already caused her a sleepless night stung her into saying curtly, 'Well I shouldn't be if I were you...after all you know my reputation.'

For a moment he looked almost bitter, and then his expression changed, his voice smooth as he half purred with dangerous silkiness. 'Yes indeed and I shall look forward to discovering if you merit it.'

Lissa turned away, calling to the children. Why, oh why did he always manage to outflank her? She was regretting her impetuosity in agreeing to this marriage more and more with every second that passed, and yet when she looked into the happy faces of her nieces she couldn't entirely regret it. Already she felt a fierce upthrust of protective love for them, much stronger now than it had been when her sister was alive. How could she have allowed Joel to take them completely out of her life? The answer was that she could not, but neither should she have deceived him. When he proposed to her she should have told him the truth; that their marriage would have to be a platonic one.

All the time she was feeding and then preparing

the girls for bed Lissa was conscious of nervous but-
terflies swarming in her stomach. She couldn't bear
that... She couldn't bear to be parted from the children. At that moment he raised his head and looked
across at her. 'You look tired.' The compassion in his
face stirred her senses. For one wild, mad moment
she almost allowed herself to believe that he genuinely cared about her welfare, and then she subdued
the weakness. She had always viewed Joel with a certain amount of awe and dread, but she was coming
to recognise that she had under-estimated his masculine power. She had thought him hard and aggres-
sive and had prepared herself to withstand such macho maleness, but what she had not expected was this
streak of tender concern; this warmth and caring that
completely contradicted the mental image she had always had of him.

'Just a little.' She went across to the girls to kiss
them good night, promising to leave the little night-
light on.

'I'm glad you and Joel are going to be our new
mummy and daddy,' Louise said drowsily, kissing her
back. 'But you won't ever leave us will you?' Anxiety
clouded the blue eyes and Lissa hugged her fiercely.
'No, poppet, I promise I'll never leave you,' she whispered back. Poor little mite; how frightened and insecure she must feel at times. It would be her responsibility and her mission in life to give her back a sense
of security and belonging.

'Dinner...' Joel said firmly, taking her arm and
shepherding her out of the room.

Lissa almost sagged at the thought of having to go downstairs and prepare a meal. The ordeal of the ceremony had taken more out of her than she had realised.

'What would you like?' she asked Joel. 'I'll have a root round in the kitchen.'

'No need,' he surprised her by saying. 'It's all done. All you have to do is go and get changed.'

When he saw her surprise, he grinned, a surprisingly boyish grin that made him look years younger than his thirty-odd and for some reason Lissa felt her heart start to trip in tiny hammer blows that made it difficult for her to breathe. 'Don't look like that. All I've done is take something out of the freezer and put it in the oven. I did it whilst you were feeding the kids. I thought about taking you out to eat, but you look all in.' He glanced at his watch and announced, 'You've got half an hour.'

It took her twenty minutes to shower and change. Joel had been up to London and cleared her flat, and now all her clothes were hanging up in her new wardrobe. Her heart started to thud despairingly as she picked out a soft lilac Jean Muir dress she had bought on impulse. The colour brought out the rich red of her hair and the silky jersey clung lovingly to the sleek lines of her body, but Lissa was barely aware of how she looked, she was too concerned with what lay ahead. Would Joel expect her to move her things into his room or... If only she could just get through tonight... Dare she risk telling him that she could not be his wife? She bit her lip thinking of the promise she had just made to Louise.

'Play it by ear,' an inner voice told her. Joel wasn't a boyfriend after all…he might not even care whether she responded to him sexually or not…he might not even realise that…that she was a virgin and frigid as well? Don't be a fool, she cautioned herself. The man she had always imagined Joel to be might not have cared what she was and might indeed have simply been content to take his own pleasure without giving a thought to her, but the complex, sometimes sensitive man Joel was revealing himself to actually be would hardly be oblivious to the fact that she was not the experienced, almost promiscuous woman he thought her.

Frowning slightly Lissa brushed her hair. Why did Joel want their marriage to be consummated? Knowing the opinion he had of her he could hardly desire her that much, he had certainly never been short of female companionship… The answer lay in his love for Louise and Emma, Lissa decided. Like her he cared very deeply about his two nieces, and like her he obviously did not want a long drawn out legal battle over them.

But that did not answer her question, Lissa reflected thoughtfully. It showed why he might want to marry her; but not why he should want that marriage consummated. Unless perhaps he wanted a son… For some reason that thought made her heart beat faster, her mind's eye all too easily conjuring up the image of a small dark-haired baby with Joel's golden eyes.

Perhaps if she simply said nothing and let him discover… Shivering she pushed the problem out of her mind, coating her mouth with a soft lip gloss and then getting up. The more she dwelt on what lay ahead the more tense she got. If she carried on like this Joel was bound to realise something was wrong. What if he became furious and insisted on having their marriage annulled? Could she bear to lose the girls now?

'Lissa?'

The sound of his voice outside her door made her jump up from the dressing table and hurry across the room. 'Coming,' she called out, huskily, opening the door, coming to a full stop as she realised that Joel too had changed. Her eyes widened a little over the formality of his crisp white shirt and dinner suit, and then colour flooded her pale skin as she realised that he was studying her, his glance lingering appreciatively on the curves the lilac jersey seductively revealed.

'Why the embarrassment?' he asked, touching her cheek lightly with his finger. 'Surely by now you must be used to men finding you attractive.'

'I…I never think of myself that way.' She had made the admission before she was aware of it, adding more to herself than to him, 'I was always so gawky and plain as a teenager, especially compared with Amanda and my mother…'

'…that in an effort to prove to yourself and them that you were attractive you flung yourself into bed with every available male that came along?' Joel finished for her, but there was no accusation in his voice, no contempt either, Lissa noticed. In fact, if anything, the only emotion she could hear was a certain wry sadness. She risked a quick glance at Joel and found that he was smiling at her.

'I...I always felt that my parents preferred Amanda to me,' Lissa heard herself admitting huskily, much to her own astonishment.

'Yes, I know what you mean,' Joel agreed. 'John was always very much my father's favourite and there was a time when I over-reacted against that favour-itism in an effort to draw my father's attention to myself.'

They had reached the top of the stairs and Lissa felt a wave of fellow-feeling towards him engulf her. She turned towards him but he forestalled her questions by saying quietly, 'We must make sure that nei-ther Louise, nor Emma...nor indeed any children of our own we have, suffer that same burden.'

Instantly the rapport between them snapped as Lissa contained a shiver of fear and drew back slightly from him, her eyes unconsciously darkening. 'Who are you thinking about, Lissa?' Joel grated. 'Simon Greaves? Then forget him,' he snapped. 'You're married to me, not him.'

The abrupt change from compassionate fellow hu-man being to arrogant male unnerved her, and she hurried down the stairs, turning towards the kitchen.

Warm, enticing aromas greeted her, but the wooden kitchen table was bare of all utensils. As she turned automatically to open drawers and collect cutlery Joel stopped her. 'It's all done,' he told her coolly, adding,

'I thought we'd dine in style tonight—in the dining room. You go through and sit down, and I'll bring the food.'

It was a novel experience for Lissa to be waited on by a man, but Joel did a superb job so calmly and efficiently that she must have betrayed her surprise, because he paused to smile at her and explained, 'I was in the army for a couple of years after leaving Oxford and if it taught me nothing else, it taught me to be self-sufficient.'

Lissa was surprised. She'd always thought that Joel had gone straight from university into his father's firm, and it was disturbing to realise how little she knew about him; and how guilty she was of having preconceived ideas about the type of man he was.

'Like you, as a teenager I was rebellious,' he further explained whilst they were eating. 'I wanted to travel...to see a little of the world before I settled down to the life my father wanted me to lead. I've always been more interested in the land than in industry, but as I was the eldest my father expected me to take over from him in the business. Later of course the situation resolved itself, but at twenty-two I couldn't see that far ahead and so I opted out—joined the army more in defiance of my father than anything else, but it's something I've never regretted. It...'

'Made a man of you?' quipped Lissa lightly, wanting to change the intimacy of their conversation, alarmed by the sensations and emotions he was arousing inside her. She didn't want to feel sympathy for him...she didn't want to feel anything. She wanted to hang on to her resentment and dislike. For some reason she needed to hang on to them. Why? she asked herself and knew the answer was because she felt it would be dangerous for her to get to know and like this man who was now her husband. Further than that she was not prepared to go.

'Not in the sense that I suspect you mean.' Joel's mouth twisted slightly and Lissa knew she had been successful in destroying his relaxed mood. 'More wine? You've barely touched yours. Don't you like it?'

The plain truth was that she was too tensed up to enjoy her meal at all, but dutifully she sipped the rich, ruby liquid, feeling it warm first her throat and then her stomach, relaxing over-taut nerves.

It was gone nine before they had finished their leisurely meal—or at least Joel had finished, she had done little more than toy with hers.

'Coffee?'

She shook her head tensely. 'No...no thanks. I'll take these things out to the kitchen.'

'I'll give you a hand.'

There was something disturbingly intimate about being in the ktichen with Joel, his easy, competent movements somehow pinpointing the uneasy tension of hers. When every last cup and plate had been cleared away he said easily, 'Why don't you go and check on the girls while I'm locking up? Oh and Lissa,' he added, less casually as he opened the door for her. 'Remember it's my room you're sleeping in tonight.'

Now was her time to tell him the truth, but Lissa knew that she couldn't. Trailing reluctantly upstairs she tried to convince herself that he might not notice her coldness; that it might not be as bad as she envisaged; that thousands upon thousands of women before her had endured the unwanted possession of the male sex. But Joel thought she was experienced and even worse eager for sex. Well he would soon learn the truth. All the fierce triumph she had felt at the thought of him being confronted with her innocence had gone, and a wild trembling seemed to seize hold of her limbs. She checked automatically on the two sleeping girls, leaving on the night-light in case one of them woke. The nursery was still relatively unfamiliar to them, and although on the surface they seemed to be accepting their parents' death, who knew what terrors their subconscious minds might harbour.

Knowing she could delay no longer Lissa turned in the direction of her own room, quickly gathering up her nightdress and robe. She daredn't linger here, because she wouldn't put it past Joel to come looking for her, and that was a humiliation she could not endure. She did not want to add cowardice to all her other faults.

Joel was already in the room, and he paused in the action of removing his shirt to look at her. The glow from a lamp illuminated the warm bronze of his skin. His chest was shadowed with a line of dark hair and Lissa felt her stomach plunge and twist crazily as though she were riding a switchback ride. No doubt most women would think she was crazy to fear Joel's possession so much. He was after all an extremely attractive man, and not just physically, she was forced to admit. He had a tender, gentle side to him that suggested that he would be a skilled and caring lover... A shudder washed over her, and watching it Joel frowned.

Lissa opened her mouth to tell him that there was no way she could go through with making love with him, but he anticipated her, shrugging off his shirt and coming across the room to take her hands in his. This close she could feel the heat coming off his body, smell the male scent of him, and she quivered nervously, her eyes huge and dark.

'Nervous? Me too,' he said softly.

Her surprise showed in her eyes and he added raspingly, 'Lissa, I *am* human too you know. I know quite well that you've married me for the sake of the girls and that reason alone; that right now I am not the man you want in your bed, but we could have a good life together...children of our own...'

'But...but what about love,' Lissa heard herself croak in an unsteady voice.

His hands dropped away from hers and he turned away from her. 'Can you honestly tell me that you've loved every man you've taken to your bed?' And as she heard the iron bitterness in his voice Lissa knew that her chance to tell him the truth was gone.

Looking at the situation from Joel's point of view it would seem all too logical that their relationship was a physical as well as legal one no doubt.

'Hell,' he swore briefly, 'I've forgotten something. Back in a minute.'

While he was gone Lissa dived into the bathroom, cleansing her face quickly and rushing into her night-dress. When she opened the bathroom door he still hadn't returned, and she scrambled into the huge dou-ble bed, firmly pulling the bedclothes up around her, tensing as the door opened.

Under his arm Joel was carrying an ice bucket and a bottle of champagne, two glasses in his hand. He raised his eyebrows queryingly as he put it down and a tiny ache began somewhere deep inside her. How would she be feeling right now, if things were differ-ent...if she loved Joel and he loved her... She could not deny his thoughtfulness and caring, and she could also sense the effort he was making to give their mar-riage some semblance of normality. Now she dreaded him knowing the truth for a different reason. She felt as though she were the one cheating him. But he had not married her for herself, she knew that. He had married her because she was the girls' aunt.

She heard the champagne cork pop and watched nervously as he filled the glasses. She had to sit up to take hers, and she could feel his eyes on her as she clutched the sheet to her body. The bubbles tickled her nose, making her catch her breath.

'Here's to us, Mrs Hargreaves,' Joel toasted softly. 'Shall we forget the past, Lissa, and have a new be-ginning?'

If only she could! If only she were really Joel's chosen bride, confident of his love... The thought jolted through her making her tremble. What was she *thinking?* It must be the champagne, she thought dizzily. She didn't want Joel to love her. Why should she?

He disappeared into the bathroom, and she listened to him moving about, every muscle tense, her body aching with dread. Memories from the past threatened to swamp over her, and when Joel finally emerged from the bathroom, she could only stare at him with unseeing eyes. He was wearing a towelling robe, his legs bare beneath the hem, she noticed, her glance skittering away and yet somehow drawn back to his body. She was twenty-three for God's sake, she derided herself mentally, not fifteen. But deep inside herself she was still only fifteen, locked for ever in the torment of a nightmare that featured this dark-haired man, who was now shedding his robe and getting into bed beside her.

'Lissa?' He tensed suddenly and for a moment Lissa thought he must have guessed the truth, but then he was frowning, throwing the bedclothes aside and pulling on his robe.

'I can hear one of the girls crying,' he told her tautly. 'Listen.'

# CHAPTER FIVE

IF ANYONE HAD ever told her that she would spend her wedding night comforting a distraught four-year-old she would never have believed them Lissa thought tiredly, glancing at her watch. Four o'clock in the morning and they had finally got Louise off to sleep.

'You go back to bed,' Joel told her. 'I'll sit with her now.'

It had taken both of them to calm the little girl out of her nightmare fears, but she had clung fiercely to them both once she was awake, refusing to let them go, only when Lissa had promised to stay with her, had she finally allowed Joel to go downstairs and make her a drink. Now she was sleeping at last, like Emma who had fortunately remained fast asleep throughout the whole thing.

As she crawled back into Joel's bed, Lissa reflected with niggling impatience that she ought to be feeling relieved that Louise's timely nightmare had occurred, but instead what she did feel was something almost approaching a sense of anti-climax. Surely she couldn't have *wanted* Joel to make love to her? Of course not... Then why this strange restless sensation that was gripping her, when in reality all she ought to be doing was dropping into an exhausted sleep?

Joel woke her at seven o'clock. A dark shadow covered his jaw and his hair was ruffled untidily.

'Sorry to wake you,' he apologised, 'but I've got to be at the factory at nine—a meeting that was arranged some time ago. I'll have a shower and get changed... If you could keep an eye on Louise, although I think she'll be okay now.'

'Has she had many nightmares like that?' Lissa asked him. He looked tired and drawn and she had a crazy impulse to touch him, to smooth the lines of tiredness away from his eyes.

'None quite as bad as that.' He turned towards the bathroom and Lissa slithered out of bed, tensing as he turned round unexpectedly and came over to her. Her nightdress was a long one and demure, but the bright February sunshine made the fine cotton almost transparent and the way Joel was looking at her made it impossible for her to move, even when he reached out and gently pulled her towards him.

'Good morning, Mrs Hargreaves,' he murmured against her ear, his breath tickling her skin, sending tiny shimmers of sensation coursing over it. 'That was some wedding night, wasn't it?'

She turned her head opening her mouth to respond, her words silenced by the warm pressure of Joel's lips caressing her own. Shivers of something that was not entirely fear raced through her. She made an inarticulate protest, surprised to find that Joel was holding her quite tightly, drawing her against his body, so that she was aware of the heavy thump of his heart and the warmth of his skin, and then she pulled away relieved when Joel released her.

'Perhaps you're right,' he muttered smiling at her. 'There isn't time now for me to make love to you as I want to. Surprised that I should desire you, Lissa?' he asked apparently reading her mind with ease.

'I thought you didn't like me…that you disapproved of me…' She made the admission slowly, still a little stunned to find that her mind clung obstinately to the memory of how his mouth had felt against hers.

He studied her quietly for a moment and then said slowly, 'Perhaps neither of us entered this marriage for the most altruistic of reasons, Lissa, but we *are* married, and I vote that as from now we put the past behind us, and make a completely fresh start.'

When seconds ticked by without her making any response, he released her almost abruptly, his eyes darkening, and his expression losing the elusive tenderness she had thought she glimpsed in it, and reverting to that she was more used to seeing—hard and unyielding, but Lissa was too stunned by her own thoughts and emotions to pay more than fleeting attention to Joel's tightlipped anger. Her heart was still thudding heavily with the shock of discovering how close she had come to agreeing with Joel's suggestion. Put the past behind them! She suppressed a half hysterical sound of pain in her throat. If only she could! But Joel didn't know what her past really was; and it was folly almost to the point of madness to allow herself to even think of responding to the half whimsical, half tender entreaty his words had seemed to hold. She must be going crazy, she thought over an hour later, still unable to banish Joel's image and his words from her brain. He made her feel vulnerable in a way that no other male had ever been able to do, and whilst Lissa acknowleged that much of this vulnerability sprang from the past; at least some of it was new. Shivering slightly she paced the kitchen floor. What was happening to her? Why after all these years of hating and resenting Joel was she now seeing another side to him; a side she had never imagined existed? Why…last night she had almost envied Louise because of his tenderness towards the little girl. She curled her fingers into the palms of her hands, swinging round abruptly and going upstairs. Emma was awake, but Louise was still asleep, worn out by the trauma of her nightmares.

Since they were now without a housekeeper she would at least have plenty to occupy her hands if not her mind, Lissa reflected grimly when she had washed and dressed Emma.

But keeping her hands busy did nothing to still the restless tension of her thoughts. She had been a fool to marry Joel…she couldn't have a normal marriage with him. Even at the thought of it odd tremors raced over suddenly hot flesh, her body trembling as though he were already touching it, caressing her… Emma gazed round-eyed at her as she suddenly clapped her hands over her ears and groaned out loud. What was happening to her? Why was she feeling like this? Why now after all these years was she suddenly experiencing this conflict within herself?

By lunchtime Louise was awake, and Lissa had just
settled both girls down to a light meal, when the
phone rang.

The sound of Joel's voice on the other end of the
line made the tiny hairs on her arm stand on end, his
curt, 'Lissa, is something wrong?' making her glad
that he could not see her pale face and betraying eyes.

'I'm just a bit tired that's all,' she told him coolly.

He asked about the girls and then told her that he
had to go up to London on business and would not
be back until the morning.

Having assured him that Louise seemed quite recovered, Lissa let him ring off. There was no reason
in the world why she should feel this sharp stab of
something very close to disappointment, no reason at
all and yet she did. It came to her then, as she walked
back to the girls that she had always enjoyed their
encounters in the past and that she had actually derived a certain savage pleasure in her confrontations
with Joel. Shaking her head over the complexity of
her own emotions she tried to dismiss him from her
thoughts.

By the time she had got the girls bathed and in bed,
Lissa felt extremely tired. She had telephoned the local paper during the afternoon to place an ad for a
cook-cum-housekeeper, and she had also spent some
time exploring the house.

Although much of the decor was not to her taste,
the house itself appealed strongly to her, and as she
wandered from room to room she found herself mentally refurbishing them, making plans for a future here

she was not sure she had. What would Joel do if she told him the truth?

If? Lissa grimaced inwardly. There was no if about it. She had to. She had come to that decision during the afternoon. Now that the fierce hunger for revenge which had eaten away at her had gone, she knew she had little alternative. Joel was not the monster she had always told herself he was. She had only to see him with the children to know that, and Lissa knew that much of the resentment and bitterness she had hoarded against him had had its roots in her feelings towards her father—*he* was the one who had rejected her, but because at fifteen she had been unable to cope with such ambivalent feelings towards her parents as love and resentment, she had focused her resentment on Joel. She sighed faintly. She was not telling herself anything she did not already know. Several years ago she had made herself re-live the traumatic years of her teens and had taught herself then to analyse what she had experienced, but she had never totally thrown off her hatred of Joel... Until now.

Too emotionally restless to settle she wandered tensely from room to room, pausing occasionally to study a portrait or an object without really seeing them. It was one thing to know and accept that much of her resentment of Joel was something she had transferred from her father's shoulders to his, but that did not explain away the sexual trauma she experienced whenever she was with someone else. Why should it always be Joel's image that rose up to taunt her when another man held her in his arms; why not her father's angry, forbidding features?

And why the overwhelming complex tangle of emotions she experienced whenever he was close to her? Both were questions she could not answer, any more than she could turn back time and control the tide of anger which had swept her into this marriage in the first place.

At last she settled in the sitting room, switching on the television but watching it without taking anything in. It was too early to go to bed yet—she would never sleep, and the evening stretched emptily ahead of her. The house felt different without Joel in it. What was the matter with her she chastised herself. Good heavens, how many evenings had she spent alone in her London flat without feeling the slightest desire for anyone else's company?

She curled up in one of the easy chairs, tucking her feet underneath her, gradually letting the tension ease out of her body. As soon as an opportunity presented itself to her, she must tell Joel the truth. If she didn't and he went through with his intention of making her his wife physically as well as legally he would discover some of it at least for himself anyway, and the childish desire for revenge which had carried her into their marriage now seemed childish and incredibly foolish. What good would it really serve either of them for him to discover the hard way that physically she was unable to respond to him, other than to prove how wrong his judgments of her were? The satisfaction she would gain would be nothing when set

against her embarrassment and mortification. It had
been very hard for her to accept that some vital element of her femininity had been destroyed, and she
couldn't bear to lie and watch the vagrant tenderness
she had thought she glimpsed in his eyes this morning, turning to bitter contempt. She had experienced
the angry and frustrated reactions of too many men
already for her to be in any doubt about Joel's.

And worse he would guess that she had deliberately
withheld the truth from him and why. She had seen
a different side of him these last few days; one she
had never guessed he possessed, and it caused a
strange yearning emotion inside her.

Her eyes closed and she let her thoughts drift, rang-
ing backwards in time and then forwards, gradually
relaxing into sleep.

'Lissa?'

She woke with a start, looking uncertainly towards
the door which Joel had just opened.

The unexpectedness of seeing him there disorientated her. She glanced at her watch, surprised to realise how long she had been asleep. It was gone twelve
o'clock.

'Joel!' she exclaimed in a sleepy, surprised voice.
'What are you doing back?'

She tried to move as she spoke, gasping in pain as
pins and needles attacked her legs. Her own fault for
falling asleep with them tucked up like that.

'Perhaps I couldn't bear to stay away.'

Joel's hands on her wrists, firmly folding her hands
in her lap before they moved to her legs, shocked her

into immobility. He spoke calmly enough, his voice so devoid of inflection that it was impossible for her to interpret whatever motive lay behind what he was saying. Was he being sarcastic, or simply making a light joke? She shivered, as his fingers touched her skin, rubbing the tingling sensation away.

'Are you all right?'

Now she could hear something in his voice, concern and something else she couldn't name, that made it rough and slightly husky. She could tell that he was frowning without looking up at him, and guessed that he was aware of her tension; of the way she tried to escape his touch.

'Fine,' she lied, giving him a brittle, tight smile. 'I think I'll go up…' She squirmed away from him, hoping he would move, but he kept his hands on either side of her on the chair arms.

'Something *is* wrong. What is it, Lissa?' He turned away from her abruptly, but she was too tense to get up. 'It's too late now for second thoughts; for wishing that I was Greaves.'

'I don't…' The denial was blurted out before she could retract it, and she felt a curious twist of emotion curl through her heart as he frowned down at her; a combination of fear and an excitement she could not analyse; a tiny thrill of apprehension.

'No? But you did shrink away from me,' he told her softly. 'Why, Lissa? Oh I know there's always been a degree of antagonism between us, but you're not naive, you know as well as I do that it's an antagonism sparked by mutual desire.' He looked

grimly at her, and continued before she could speak.
'Neither of us might be proud of desiring the other,
but I know if we're honest that neither of us could
deny it.'

He caught the small sound she choked back and
stared at her, watching the colour drain out of her
face.

'Lissa, for God's sake.' He sounded more angry
than concerned and Lissa flinched back from him as
he added, 'Let's stop the play-acting shall we? A
physical relationship between us was part and parcel
of the deal when you agreed to marry me. You knew
that...'

'Are you trying to tell me you married me solely
because you wanted to go to bed with me?' Lissa was
proud of the cool way she threw the taunt at him.

'Don't be ridiculous. You know damn well I didn't.
After all why the hell should I go to such lengths to
secure something other men—plenty of other men
have had for...' He caught her hand just before it
connected with his jaw, gripping her wrist so tightly
that it hurt. 'Cut out the injured innocent bit, Lissa...it
doesn't suit you.'

She was practically trembling with rage and yes
with pain too, hating him for what he was saying to
her; for revealing to her how he really viewed her. It
was intolerable, unbearable...and to think she had
contemplated telling him the truth! She could not endure to stay here a moment longer... The girls...all
the logical calm thinking she had done during the day

were forgotten… Nothing was more important than escaping from Joel and the agony he was causing her.

'Let me go.' She rubbed her aching wrists, as he released her, scrambling off the chair and moving on shaking legs towards the door.

'Lissa…'

'Don't touch me!' Her throat was so tight with pain she could barely speak, her voice a husky whisper of torment. 'Don't come anywhere near me! I'm leaving, now…this minute. I…' To her bitter humiliation tears clogged her throat, filling her eyes, and threatening to flood humiliatingly from her eyes. She felt so weak and alone…desperate for some haven in which to hide away from him, and yet knowing she had none.

'Lissa!' He ignored her demands, striding towards her, catching hold of her arm with strong fingers. Panic exploded through her in wave after wave of sheer terror. She was back at the party, fifteen again, only this time Joel wasn't just looking at her, he was touching her, hurting her physically as well as mentally. She gave a thin, high scream of pain, grateful for the deep heavy black void that opened up to receive her and grant her oblivion.

LISSA OPENED HER EYES reluctantly and stared round the shadowed bedroom. Where was she? Suddenly she remembered and she shuddered. This was Joel's room. No, *their* room, she corrected herself, bitterly. He must have brought her here after…after she'd fainted. She must get away… She must escape before he hurt her any more. She sat up groggily, swinging her feet to the floor.

'Lissa!

The peremptory command in his voice as Joel walked into the room froze her. He was carrying a tray with a cup of tea on it.

'Drink this.' He put the cup down on the bedside table nearest to her, 'And then you and I are going to talk.' He looked so grimly angry that Lissa started to tremble; her teeth chattering together as wave after wave of fear shuddered through her. She heard Joel swear and saw him come towards her, holding out her hands to ward him off. And then suddenly and un-nervingly she was crying…deep, wrenching sobs that hurt her chest and made her whole body shake.

'Shush…shush…it's all right…' Unbelievably being rocked in Joel's arm, with the warm pressure of his body against her own, created inside her an in-tense sensation of security and comfort. She wanted to cling to him Lissa realised numbly, to burrow against him and let the soft words he was murmuring soothe and relax her. But it was *Joel* who had pro-voked the emotional storm now racking her; Joel with his cruel jibing tongue who was responsible for her pain. It was also Joel who was easing it, she acknowl-edged hazily, Joel was making her feel cherished and cared for.

By the time the tearing sobs were under control she had recovered enough to want to pull away from him, deeply embarrassed and confused by her own behav-iour, but Joel wouldn't let her, subsiding on to the

side of the bed, and taking her with him, still holding
her in his arms.

'Now,' he said quietly, 'I want to know what all
that was about.'

Lissa managed a tight smile. 'Oh just another trick
in my repertoire,' she told him brittlely. 'Very effective isn't it?'

For a long moment he simply looked at her, and
then he said quietly, 'Extremely effective; so much
so that I find it impossible to believe it was fabricated.
And so no doubt you are going to tell me, was your
faint.' He watched the colour run up under her skin
and said sardonically, 'Exactly.

'I've seen fear before, Lissa, and I've seen panic,
and I know when they're genuine. What I don't know
is why *I* should invoke them so forcefully in you.'

Now there was no going back. She would have to
tell him, Lissa knew, and coupled with apprehension
and reluctance was also relief. She wanted to tell him;
she wanted to be rid of the emotional burden she was
carrying.

Lifting her head she answered simply, 'Because
you want us to be lovers,' and was rewarded by a
physical reaction every bit as violent in its own way
as her own had been. Dark colour burned up under
his skin, stretching it somehow until it was pulled
sharply over his cheek bones. His eyes glittered
darkly with a mixture of anger and something else
she couldn't put a name to, his fingers curling round
her wrist as he said grimly, 'You have a hell of a way
of putting a man down, Lissa. I won't ask what it is

that bars me from joining the ranks of those fortunate
enough to enjoy your favours—I dare not…'

'No…no…you don't understand,' Lissa interrupted
impetuously, determined now that she had committed
herself to honesty to go through with it. 'It isn't
you…at least, it is, but… Oh look, Joel, let me go
right back to the beginning.'

He released her wrist, and watched grimly as she
moved back from him, putting a distance between
them.

'I can't let you be my lover…or indeed any man
be my lover because…because I…find the thought of
sex… What I'm trying to tell you is that I'm…I'm
frigid,' she said flatly at last. 'I've never had sex with
anyone, Joel,' she told him forcing herself to look at
him and forestalling what she knew he must be going
to say by saying quickly, 'Yes, I know you must find
that hard to believe but it's true. That night, that party,
when I was fifteen…that was the first time…' She
swallowed, trying to concentrate on a piece of wallpaper safely taking her eyes away from Joel's and
allowing her to continue her story without having to
look at him and see how he was reacting.

'Nothing really happened…just a little very light
petting…'

'Your father told me you were wildly promiscuous,' Joel broke in curtly. 'Are you trying to tell
me…'

'My father and I didn't get on… I was extremely
rebellious…but never in that way. My parents disapproved of my crowd of friends. I'd been forbidden

to go out that night…but I disobeyed them—for the first and last time,' she added wryly. 'My father was an extremely strict man. Amanda knew how to get round him, but I didn't have the knack. You see,' she said with painful honesty, 'I was never what he wanted in a daughter, I wasn't blonde and small and cuddly like my mother and Amanda and… Oh well, no doubt much of it was my fault, because I never tried to conform to what he wanted me to do… You see I wanted him…both of them to love me for what I was…not as another Amanda, but you know how teenagers are, I couldn't articulate any of this to them. My father disapproved of teenagers anyway… Every time he read about teenage misdemeanours in the press he used to go on about it… I wasn't promiscuous at all… I suspect he confused you with what he no doubt described as my appalling behaviour; he did rather have a tendency for exaggeration. Of course the fact that I'd disobeyed him and then been found by him in the circumstances that I was… It was all quite innocent really, but he would never believe that…'

'I had no idea.' Joel was frowning now. 'He'd described you to my parents as extremely rebellious and wild. When he asked me to come with him and fetch you back from that party, I naturally assumed…'

'The worst!' Lissa supplied briefly. 'Yes…I can understand that.'

'So, given, that at fifteen you were innocent of the crimes attributed to you, I don't see…' He frowned and then said slowly, 'Lissa, are you trying to tell me that you're still a virgin?'

'I'm afraid so… Oh, not by choice,' she assured him grimly. 'Being virginal at fifteen is one thing, being in the same state at twenty-three is quite definitely another, but…' She got up off the bed, and paced the floor tensely, now that she was faced with telling him, at a loss to know how to.

'But *what*, Lissa?' It was plain that Joel was completely bemused, 'And don't try telling me that it is through lack of opportunity.'

'No, not that,' Lissa agreed drily, 'but because of what happened at that party I seem to have developed a mental block where sex is concerned. No matter how much I might think I want to make love when it comes to it I can't, because all I see is…'

'Your father's angry, disapproving face,' Joel guessed tersely, his mouth compressing grimly. 'Yes, I can understand that.'

Just for one cowardly moment Lissa was tempted to agree and let matters go at that. Her heart was thumping crazily with a mixture of adrenalin and reaction. She wanted to take the way out Joel was unknowingly offering her, but something, some stubborn quirk of pride would not let her, and so instead she shook her head.

'No?' Joel frowned. 'Then what? Tell me, Lissa. What?' he demanded getting up and taking hold of her. 'What?' he repeated, watching as she touched a tongue to dry, stiff lips.

'You,' she choked out at last, refusing to look at

him, her body tensing against his grip as she pulled instinctively away, fearing his reaction, dreading that if she did look at him she would see in his eyes the contempt that had haunted her dreams for so long. 'I see you,' she repeated instead in a low, tormented voice, 'and you look at me with such contempt and dislike that I...' She started to shake again, dimly aware of Joel cursing as he released her.

'Me? Lissa, look at me!' His hands gripping her face forced her to do as he wished. He was nearly as pale as she was herself but this was a different pallor, and Lissa shrank beneath the raw fury she could see glittering in his eyes until he said tersely, 'No, Lissa... Don't be frightened.'

'I shouldn't have told you.' She was mortified now by what she had revealed to him, unable to fully comprehend the reasons for the emotional outburst which she knew had been the release valve, allowing her to tell him the truth.

'But you have.' He looked at her in silence for several seconds, and then said abruptly, 'Is that why you agreed to marry me? As some sort of punishment... Or at least is that part of the reason?'

He was far too astute, Lissa thought hollowly. 'Initially,' she agreed, in an expressionless voice. She felt far too drained to endure any more emotions. 'But only because you had made me so very angry. Once my anger had cooled I wanted to retract, but then there were the girls to consider...I thought it would pay you back, you see,' she said simply, 'but of course once my temper had gone I realised how stu-

pid I was being… After all, it wasn't even your fault
that I…'

'No…it wasn't *my* fault at all,' Joel agreed harshly.
'No…*I* can't be blamed for condemning you out of
hand, can I, Lissa? After all, *I* wasn't fifteen, was I?
I was well into my twenties…and naturally it is perfectly understandable that I should have destroyed the
fragile illusions of someone little more than a
child…that I should have accepted someone else's
valuation of you without forming my own. No, of
course *I* can't be blamed. Like hell I can't,' he added
bitterly, turning away from her. 'Like hell.'

For a moment there was silence, while Lissa struggled to come to terms with Joel's savage reaction to
her disclosures. She had seen him exhibit tenderness
and concern for his nieces; and she had known there
was a gentler side to him, but she had never expected
this devastating reaction to her revelations; this rage
of anger directed against himself.

At last he said curtly, 'And so what now? Do you
want the marriage annulled? It could be.'

Did she? With a sudden, stifling leap of her heart
Lissa knew she did not, without quite knowing why.
All she could manage to say was a rather unsteady,
'Do you?'

'What does that mean?' Joel questioned. 'That you
wish to stay married to me perhaps, but in name only,
because of the girls?'

Gratefully Lissa seized on the opening he had given
her. 'Yes…' she agreed quickly. 'Yes…I couldn't
bear to lose them now. I feel that they need both of

us, Joel, just as you said but of course, now that you know that...that I...that...'

'That I can't make love to you,' he supplied harshly for her.

'Yes...yes,' Lissa agreed hurriedly, 'If because of that you want to be free...'

She found during the silence that followed that she was holding her breath, hoping that he would not say that he wanted to end their marriage she acknowledged inwardly.

'I owe you some recompense,' he said at last, 'and if marriage to me is what you want, Lissa...then that is what you shall have, but there is one thing I shall insist on.' He looked at her and then said coolly, 'We must continue to share this room. As much for the girls' sake as anything else. They've already been through far too much. You of all people will know how sensitive and quick children can be. They're used to their parents sleeping together and I believe that if we show any deviation from that pattern it could cause Louise more anxiety.'

Lissa nodded her head slowly. There was something in what Joel was saying, and what he asked was very little.

'What?' he queried when she assented. 'No demand for my solemn promise that I won't touch you?'

Lissa looked at him in surprise. 'But why should you want to?' she asked him, genuinely puzzled. 'You can hardly want me now. You're forgetting, Joel,' she reminded him wryly, 'I know *exactly* how off-putting men find my...my disability. I know you said you

wanted me, but that was when you thought I was
sexually experienced…able to respond to you…'

'Yes, so it was,' he agreed quietly, and just for a
second something intangible, a fleeting expression in
his eyes made a frisson of sensation run down her
spine. Before she could analyse it, it was gone, and
then Joel was saying curtly, 'Lissa, tell me have you
ever discussed any of this with anyone else…'

'No.' She looked at him in fresh surprise. 'Somehow I've never been able to.'

'I see.' He wasn't looking at her and Lissa was sure
she must have imagined the tiny thread of satisfaction
running through his voice because when he did look
at her, his face was carefully devoid of all expression.

'It's been a long day,' he said quietly. 'I think we
should both try to get some sleep.' He picked up the
now cold cup of tea he had made her earlier and said
calmly, 'I'll go down and make us both a nightcap
while you get ready for bed,' and Lissa knew that he
was telling her that he was giving her the privacy to
get undressed and into bed without him being there.
She was grateful to him for his understanding, she
thought tiredly as she slid between cool sheets a little
later, and yet as she closed her eyes and tried to court
sleep, the memory uppermost in her mind was of the
emotional and physical sensations she had experienced when Joel held her in his arms.

# CHAPTER SIX

'BUT YOU HAVEN'T KISSED Lissa "goodbye".'

They were having breakfast in the kitchen, the
scene a homely familiar one, Emma struggling with
her cereal in her high chair while Louise sat between
Joel and herself. Joel had an early meeting with one
of his tenant farmers and he had already finished his
breakfast. He had stood up to kiss Louise 'goodbye'—a formality she insisted on every morning, and
it was her shrill, piping complaint that drew Lissa's
attention away from Emma. Both of them were on
their guard for any signs of insecurity from Louise,
and over the top of her blonde head their eyes met in
mutual concern. Since the night she had admitted the
truth to him Lissa had found herself much more relaxed in Joel's company; much more able to appre-
ciate the side of him she had previously thought re-
served only for others. He was a compassionate caring
man, and a very strong one as well, she acknowledged. He had talked to her on several occasions
about her past, drawing her out in a way that afterwards had the power to amaze her. She had found
herself confiding things to him that she had never
dreamed of telling anyone, but conversely the closer

she felt drawn towards him the greater pains he seemed to take to preserve a distance between them. And somehow that hurt, even though it should not have done.

'Kiss Mummy,' Emma announced, spooning cereal liberally into and around her mouth. While Louise alternated in calling them Lissa and Joel and 'Mummy' and 'Daddy', Emma, too young to have any deeply lasting memory of her parents, had quickly transferred their titles to Lissa and Joel.

Both of them had agreed to let the girls call them whatever made them feel most comfortable, but it did something to her heart, Lissa admitted wryly, to hear Emma addressing her as 'Mummy'. She loved both girls with a fiercely protective maternalism that still half surprised her. They had entirely different person-alities; in Louise she detected certain of her own per-sonality traits, together with, quite surprisingly, some of Joel's, while Emma was completely Amanda's daughter.

Conscious of Louise's critically appraising scru-tiny, Lissa obediently lifted her face in the direction of Joel's as he bent towards her. His mouth touched her cheek, his lips cool and firm, and a tiny shiver ran through her. She started to pull away, but his hand curled round the back of her head, his thumb tilting her jaw. For one surprised second her eyes stared into his, noting that close they weren't flat, metallic gold at all, but warm and alive, glittering with topaz depths and then his mouth was on hers and instinctively her eyelashes fluttered down, her heartbeat surging into a faster tempo. Her body melted into soft pliancy with a swiftness that startled her, her lips enjoying the tactile sensation of Joel's moving against them. His grip on the back of her neck suddenly tightened and for a moment Lissa thought that he was actually going to kiss her properly, but then he released her stepping back, his mouth twisting in a derisive smile that reminded her of the old Joel she had resented so much.

'Daddy gone,' Emma exclaimed mournfully as the kitchen door closed behind him, and Lissa automatically directed her to finish up her breakfast, at the same time unable to stop her fingers from touching her still tremulous mouth, startled by the realisation that she had actually wanted Joel to kiss her. Why…why should Joel be able to arouse inside her a physical response that she was unable to give to anyone else?

It was probably because he knew the truth, she told herself and that because of that she was able to relax with him…knowing that she had nothing to fear; neither his anger nor his rejection. And after all he was an extremely attractive specimen of the male species she reminded herself wryly. She had grown so used to seeing Joel in his role as caring and concerned father-figure-cum-confessor that she was beginning to lose sight of the fact that he was also an extremely virile, sensual male. The thought was a disquieting one. At the moment Joel felt guilty enough about the past, and concerned enough for her and the girls for them to absorb all his spare time, but what would happen in the future when they were not such immediate concerns? When the girls were secure enough not to need so much attention? He was not a man she could ever envisage living like a monk... So he would take a mistress, a tiny voice told her coolly. What else could she expect? How could she object? How indeed? But more important why should she want to object? She didn't want Joel as her lover...did she?

That she should entertain even the slightest doubt rocked her into hurried action...anything to dispel such dangerous thoughts. Quickly she cleared away the breakfast things and got the girls buttoned into warm clothes so that she could take them for a walk.

Winterly had extensive gardens and Lissa took the girls outside for a walk most mornings. It was still only February, and although the weather was relatively mild there was definitely a chilly nip in the air.

They were out for almost an hour, returning with rosy cheeks and bright eyes, Emma now in Lissa's arms.

She had just put her down when the phone started to ring. Lissa picked up the receiver, delighted when she realised the woman on the other end of the line was calling in response to her ad for a new housekeeper. She lived locally, her caller told Lissa, and had been widowed eighteen months ago. In her late fifties she found herself with time on her hands and although she had had no previous working experience, she sounded so warm and pleasant that Lissa made an appointment to interview her.

With someone else to take over the more mundane household duties she would have more time to spend with the girls and some to spare to help Joel with his paper work. He had had a secretary who had come in a couple of days a week he had explained to her, but she had left the area when she married, and now he was relying on John's secretary at the factory complex, which was really an unsatisfactory arrangement. 'Mrs Hartwell already has more than enough to do,' he had told Lissa when they were discussing the matter, 'and once the new Managing Director is appointed, it would hardly be fair of me to appropriate his secretary's time for estate work.'

'Once we've got a new housekeeper I could help out here,' Lissa had offered, and she remembered now the way he had looked at her, thoughtfully almost as though he were trying to see into her mind.

'You already do more than enough,' he had told her rather abruptly. 'Just because you're my wife, Lissa, I don't expect you to work yourself into the ground.'

'But can't you see, I want to do it,' she had retorted. 'I want to help you as much as I can Joel...I need to be able to justify myself my role as your wife,' she had admitted, surprising herself by her honesty.

'Do you?' The expression in his eyes then had been one she couldn't interpret, but she had moved quickly away from him, alerted by some primitive instinct to do so, although quite what she had feared she had been at a loss to know. Certainly his mouth had curled into a distinctly cynical smile, and he had said in that quiet, silky, even voice of his which she had learned to recognise was one he used when he was particularly irritated, 'There's no need to run away, Lissa, I'm not going to pounce on you...'

Lissa had been immediately ashamed of her reaction. Not once in the three weeks since she had told him the truth had Joel given the slightest indication of wanting to touch her in any way. At first her relief in having told him the truth blotted out any other emotions but now...

Now what? she challenged herself as she made the girls' lunch. She was disappointed because Joel had kept to his word? Of course not. How ridiculous... How could she be?

She had arranged to see Mrs Fuller, the applicant for the housekeeper's post while the girls had their afternoon nap, and when she answered the door to her knock Lissa was agreeably pleased with what she saw.

Small and slightly plump, Mrs Fuller had an air of warmth about her that Lissa immediately liked. As she showed her over the house she explained the type of life they led, adding, 'Of course the girls will not be your concern, but they *are* part of the household and both Joel and myself want them to feel secure and happy here. I do believe in a certain amount of discipline, but if for instance you feel that you couldn't cope with muddy boots in the kitchen occasionally or toys in the hall, then this post won't be for you,' Lissa said firmly, feeling relieved when Mrs Fuller laughed warmly.

'Heavens, no, I think children make a home. I had three myself. They're all married now and living away from home. Both my girls live abroad—one in Australia the other in California, so unfortunately I don't get to see my grandchildren often enough, but I do know what it means to have young children about the place. Of course there'll be certain rooms that you won't want them to play in.'

'The drawing room, my husband's study and the formal dining room,' Lissa agreed.

They talked for a little while longer, and when Mrs Fuller eventually left having agreed to start work the following Monday Lissa was extremely pleased.

She told Joel about it over dinner, checking as she wondered if perhaps he would have preferred to interview Mrs Fuller himself.

'Good heavens, no,' he told her when she asked. 'That is entirely your province and if you say she's the right person for the job then I'm sure she is.'

He went on to tell her about the interviews he had been conducting to find a Managing Director to take over the running of the factory.

'I've managed to narrow it down to three,' he told her. 'I'm doing the final interviews tomorrow. I'll be glad when it's all sorted out.'

He looked tired Lissa realised, her frown deepening when she realised as well that he had lost a little weight. He had removed his suit jacket before he sat down for dinner and the fine silk of his shirt moved fluidly against his skin as he shifted in his seat. A strange, unfamiliar tension gripped her, her mouth suddenly dry, a pulse beating through her body with heavy forcefulness.

'Lissa?'

She realised that she was staring at him and dragged her gaze away, wondering if perhaps she was coming down with something. She felt so odd.

'Lissa, are you okay?' He stretched across the table, his fingers circling her wrist, his touch wholly clinical but it was like having a manacle of fire on her wrist. In shocked stupor Lissa found that she was looking at his mouth; remembering the cool strength of it against her own that morning. Something approaching faintness seemed to creep over her. She pulled away from him and tried to stand up, her legs refusing to support her properly.

'Lissa?'

Joel got up too, concerned for her, his eyes, as they always did when he was worried, darkening slightly. She knew so much about him now she thought hazily, shaking her head, and telling him that she was fine; little insignificant things she hadn't even known she knew until now...like the way the dark hairs grew against his skin...the way his eyes changed colour, betraying him despite the control he seemed to have over his features. She could even faithfully recall the way he moved, simply by closing her eyes and picturing him. She was familiar with the masculine contours of his torso—at least visually. He wore pyjama bottoms in bed—for her benefit, she was sure, and she hadn't realised until now how often she had silently studied the hard male lines of his body. Hot colour touched her skin, scorching it as her thoughts were scorching her mind.

'I'll go and make the coffee,' she said hurriedly.

They had fallen into the habit of continuing the conversation begun over the dinner table through coffee and often until quite late in the evening. Joel was interesting to listen to, and he made Lissa feel that he valued her opinions. She had never enjoyed anyone's company as much as she enjoyed his and it came to her as she busied herself in the kitchen that if he were to leave her life now, there would be an acutely painful void. But the fact that she found him good company and mentally stimulating did not account for her rapid pulse and accelerated breathing...neither did it account for the disturbing physical response she had just experienced. She wasn't totally naive; she had felt physical desire before even if it had only been fleetingly. But this was different...this was Joel. She couldn't desire Joel. Why not? an inner voice demanded to know. Why *shouldn't* she desire him? Because...because... Because what? the same voice jeered. Because you'd convinced yourself you hated him? Because you resented the fact that as a teenager he found you totally uninteresting until the night of that party.

Lissa bit down hard on her bottom lip, trying to quell her rebellious thoughts. It was true, she was forced to acknowledge with painful honesty, that on the very brief occasions on which she had seen Joel before that night—and they had been fleeting in the extreme—she had been instantly struck by the masculine aura he carried about him. Amanda had caught her staring at him once with rounded eyes and had teased her about it.

'For goodness sake don't go and develop a crush on Joel,' she had warned her. 'He eats little girls like you for breakfast.'

Unwilling to follow her thoughts any further, Lissa made the coffee and carried it through into the sitting room. Joel was reading a farming magazine which he put down to take the tray from her, asking briefly, 'Okay now?'

When Lissa nodded he added. 'I'm sorry I missed the girls' bedtime tonight. I'll be glad when I've got the responsibility for the factory off my hands. I've been neglecting my own work recently…and I don't intend to be just a figurehead in the girls' lives—someone they hear about but rarely see. As my own father was to me,' he added, surprising her with this information about his childhood.

'Oh yes,' he told her obviously reading her mind. 'Like you, I was very much second best as far as my father was concerned. He and I never hit it off the way he and John did, although my childhood was nothing like as traumatic as yours.'

'Mine was bad because I reacted too emotionally,' Lissa told him. 'I was too sensitive…too easily hurt and confused.' She got up to pick up the sweater she was knitting for Louise, and as she did so, stumbled against Joel's chair.

Instantly his hand shot out to steady her, his arm supporting her as she fell, so that somehow she ended up in his lap feeling both stupidly clumsy and flustered, but strangely enough with no desire to shrink away from him; with none of the tension she would have expected to feel.

'Lissa?'

She looked at him automatically, smiling herself when she saw the amusement lightening his eyes and curling his mouth. 'Do you suppose Louise is going to expect me to kiss you goodbye every morning?' he asked her in a lazy drawl.

The teasing amusement in his voice was familiar to her and she responded to it relaxing in the half circle of his arm, shrugging easily.

'Umm…well *I* suspect that she is,' he continued softly, 'and that being the case I definitely feel our technique could do with a little polishing.'

'I…' Whatever objection she had been about to make slid from her mind forever when Joel slid his fingers into her hair, their warmth spread across the back of her scalp, heating her skin, preventing her from moving; from avoiding the sensually slow downward movement of his head, as his lips feathered softly across her skin. First her temple, then the corner of her eye; the vulnerable hollow of her cheekbone where his breath against her ear, coupled with the slowly gentle movement of his fingers against her scalp, made her shiver with pleasure. With *pleasure!* Lissa acknowledged numbly, hearing him murmur her name and responding automatically to the sound of his voice so that she turned towards him, unwittingly facilitating the warm glide of his mouth against her own.

She had been kissed before; and had even enjoyed those kisses, before she discovered the truth about herself, but this somehow was different. For a start no one had ever kissed her with such gentle thoroughness; such innate tenderness and yet somehow at the same time conveying that there was a potential within that tenderness for something deeper and far more dangerous. There was nothing intimidating or frightening about the way Joel's mouth moved on hers, and yet her body was aware with a deep nerve-tingling frisson of awareness that if she were to signal that she desired it there could be much, much more.

And she *did* desire it, Lissa acknowledged inwardly... Unbelievably she was tempted to slide her arms round Joel's neck and hold him closer, to press her body against his and feel it harden with masculine desire.

She wanted him to make love to her! Immediately she tensed and he let her go. Instinctively she veiled her eyes from him, frightened of what he might see in them; that he might guess what she was feeling. And what? she asked herself. Take advantage of it? Feel sorry for her? She scarcely knew which she disliked the most. Somehow she managed to scramble off his knee, and outside the inner turmoil of her thoughts she was aware of the sound of her own voice, high and tense, gabbling inanities about the time, desperately trying to provide a smokescreen for her to hide behind.

She knew that Joel was studying her, watching her with unnerving narrow-eyed scrutiny. What was he thinking? Why had he kissed her? If it had just been a game then it had been a cruel one, and somehow unlike the man she knew him to be.

'Lissa, sometimes I'll have to kiss you,' he said quietly at last. 'It's expected occasionally of married couples, even in these enlightened times.'

That drew a shaky smile from her, and he smiled too. 'Surely it wasn't so bad?' There was a whimsical quality to his smile that relaxed her.

'No, of course not.' So that was it. Joel was just trying to accustom her to the social kisses they might have to exchange, but there had been a warm persuasiveness in the movement of his mouth against hers that had reminded her that he was a powerfully virile man and so she said awkwardly, 'Joel…what will you do…what will happen…? You can't live the rest of your life in celibacy,' she managed at last.

'Lissa, I've got so much on my mind at the moment that there just isn't room for sexual frustration,' he told her drily. 'When there is…' He shrugged and then said tight-lipped, 'Well let's just say I won't burden you with it.'

THE NEXT MORNING Louise didn't have to remind Joel to kiss her. He bent automatically and dropped a light caress on Lissa's cheek as he got up from the table, and she told herself that it couldn't possibly be disappointment that coursed through her at the lightness of that brief, preoccupied touch.

Joel was late coming home again. Louise pouted a little when she discovered that he wouldn't be there to read her bedtime story, but eventually settled down. In fact Lissa was delighted with the way both little girls had adapted to their new environment. Whenever Louise mentioned her parents Lissa made a point of talking to her about them, encouraging her to keep their memory alive without touching on the tragedy of their death. Louise seemed to have accepted the fact that they were gone from her life in the physical sense, although sometimes she betrayed a tendency to cling to either Joel or herself, Lissa acknowledged.

At eight o'clock Joel rang to say that he was on his way home. He sounded tired and yet good humoured. 'I've settled on someone for the Managing Directorship,' he told her. 'He starts next week.'

'Louise will be pleased,' Lissa told him. 'She was complaining tonight because you weren't here to read her story.'

Anyone listening to them would think them a long married couple, Lissa reflected when she replaced the receiver. But they were not married. Not in the real sense. What *would* Joel be like as a lover? Considerate, skilled, passionate…? Stop it she warned herself. Why was she continually exhibiting this desire to dance with danger…to flirt, even if it was only in the privacy of her own mind, with the idea of Joel as a lover?

Perhaps it was because the thought that he never

would be piqued her interest. But it wasn't pique alone that was responsible for the surge of physical awareness she felt whenever he was in the room.

She heard his car draw up as she was putting the final touches to their meal. He walked into the kitchen, surprising her with a brief kiss on her exposed nape, the way in which her bones turned to melting heat surprising her even more.

'Champagne,' he told her with a grin, showing her the bottle. 'I thought we'd celebrate the end of my career with Hargreaves International.'

Lissa laughed, catching his mood, banishing him from the kitchen while she finished what she was doing.

They had the champagne before dinner—and after it, and although Lissa demurred Joel insisted on her drinking some wine with her meal.

By the time she got up from the table she felt distinctly light-headed, but in such a relaxed carefree way that she couldn't refuse when Joel refilled her champagne glass. 'We've got to finish it,' he told her, 'otherwise it will go flat.'

The golden bubbles tickled her throat, sliding smoothly down it inducing a sensation of relaxed light-heartedness inside her. Even her blood seemed to be fizzing slightly. They talked, or at least Joel did, while she listened in a hazy cotton wool, otherworldly cloud of relaxation. Occasionally she had the impression that he was watching her…waiting for something…but she dismissed it as imagination. At ten o'clock she started yawning and when Joel suggested she go to bed she didn't demur.

'I'll clear these away,' he told her, indicating the empty glasses. 'Sure you can manage?' He grinned as she stood up and promptly wobbled slightly.

'If you're suggesting that I'm tipsy, then you're quite right,' she told him, 'and what's more it's all your fault.'

'Want me to carry you upstairs, or can you manage on your own two feet?' He said it teasingly, and yet when he looked at her Lissa felt the most unexpected surge of desire kick upwards along her nervous system. She giggled nervously to conceal it and shook her head.

Once upstairs, she showered languidly, studying the smooth slickness of her wet skin as she stepped out and reached for a towel. Her body was something she rarely looked at as a rule, but tonight she found herself studying it, aware of a certain sensuality to it that she had never noticed before. Fleetingly she wondered if Joel still found her desirable, trying to dismiss the thought as she towelled herself dry and then slipped on her cotton nightie, but unable to do so. She was like a child, excited by the thought of playing with fire, even while she knew that parental rule protected her from doing so she thought, angry with herself, trying to shake off the languorous indolence of her movements.

She had just climbed into bed when Joel came in.

'I've brought you a nightcap,' he told her, handing

her another glass. 'The last of the champagne. Drink it, it will help you sleep.'

The glass was three quarters full and Lissa sipped at it, watching him move about the bedroom. He took off his shirt and as though she were an observer to her own reactions she found herself monitoring her own physical response to him. His skin was faintly olive, tanned and sleek, his muscles hard without being over-developed. He disappeared into the bathroom, and Lissa heard the shower running.

She had just about finished her champagne when he came back and she watched him walk towards her.

'Finished?' As he got into bed beside her, he turned towards her and took her glass. She was still sitting up and as he turned away to put the glass on the tray his hand rested lightly on her shoulder preventing her from lying down. The bedside lamps were still on and as Lissa reached out to snap hers off, Joel reached across her, his arm a dark bar against the whiteness of her nightdress. For some reason Lissa seemed unable to take her eyes off it. Her light went out, Joel's arm moving against her body. Wonderingly she touched the olive skin of his forearm, completely absorbed in the sensation of his skin beneath her fingertips, warm and vital. She looked up at him, his face half in the shadow thrown by the other lamp. He leaned forward and his lips brushed hers. Curiously she was neither surprised nor apprehensive. It seemed as though some part of her mind had known that he was going to kiss her and directed her to turn into his kiss rather than away from it. His hand left the lamp and curled round her, turning her, but all her concentration was fixed on and fascinated by the slow movement of his mouth against her own and her own response to it. Easily, fluidly, she felt the natural reaction of her body to his proximity. Her mouth parted at the gentle insistence of his tongue, her senses half bewildered and totally confused by the delicately explorative way he ran it over her lips. She wanted more…more than this lightly arousing intimacy she realised inwardly, but that knowledge did not shock or frighten her. On the contrary, it seemed completely natural and right. So much so, that her hands lifted to Joel's neck, her lips parting yearningly for his kiss.

But he didn't kiss her. Instead he lay down, pulling her down on top of him, burying his face in her hair, tightening one arm round her waist while the thumb of his free hand, probed and stroked the vulnerable skin of her neck. Tiny frissons of pleasure shivered through her and while she knew Joel must be aware of them, she didn't feel ashamed or embarrassed, instead she arched closer to him, closing her eyes and abandoning herself to the shivering delight he was arousing.

'Lissa…Lissa, look at me.' His lips brushed lightly over her closed eyelids and dutifully she opened them, drowning in the deep gold pools of his. He kissed her cheek, lightly, trailing tantalising kisses to the corner of her mouth. Lissa gave a small tormented moan. She wanted him to kiss her properly. Almost as though he knew how she felt his mouth touched hers. But the contact was too light...to fleeting. He kissed her again just as lightly and Lissa could feel the blood drumming frantically in her veins. Her fingers curled protestingly into his shoulder, her lips clinging pleadingly to his when he kissed her again. Her small moan of protest when the pressure she craved for was removed was checked as his mouth returned to hers, this time satisfying the hunger inside her. Lissa gasped, reality melting like snow in the desert sun. Suddenly nothing was more important than that Joel kept on kissing her as he was doing right now. When he slid her nightdress straps off her shoulder she shuddered in reaction to his fingers against her skin but it wasn't a shudder of rejection. How had she never known until now how right it would be to feel his hand against her breast, slowly stroking its rounded shape. She made a sound beneath his kiss, suddenly hating the intrusion of her cotton nightdress for coming between his touch and her skin, and when he released her mouth she tugged ineffectually at the fabric protesting huskily, 'It's in the way. Take it off.'

The hot glitter in Joel's eyes made her tremble, but in anticipation not fear, eager for the moment when he slid her nightdress from her body and cupped her breasts in his hands. Her heart was racing so fast it was making her dizzy, through a champagne-induced cloud she gazed at Joel.

'Are you enjoying this, Lissa?' he asked huskily, 'Does it give you pleasure?'

Amazingly it did. She nodded her head slowly, watching the smile curl his mouth. 'So am I,' he told her softly. His mouth nuzzled her throat, finding and exploiting a thousand pleasure spots, his teeth nipping gently until she twisted and arched against him in heady abandon.

Beneath the slow caress of his hands her breasts swelled and ached, her nipples tight and hard, wanting something more than the lightly arousing brush of his thumb. When he bent his head and slowly dragged his tongue over the tightness of her nipple Lissa reacted instinctively, her finger-nails finding his spine and grating over the vertebrae until he shuddered. 'What is it you want, Lissa? This?' His mouth moved over her skin, sending shock waves of arousal shuddering through her when it reached her nipple. In the light from the lamp she could see their entwined bodies; his dark and lean, hers feminine, curved, pale apart from the rosy aureoles of her breasts. Her nudity which hitherto had always displeased her was now something she took pleasure in. Joel's hand cupped her other breast, his head bending towards it and desire kicked to life inside her, her body arching into his possession. She felt almost faint from the pressure of needing him so much. She muttered his name watching him slowly releasing the swollen tip of her breast, her fingers curling into his hair as the need to feel his mouth against her breast again overwhelmed her.

'Lissa...' There was a raw, primitive message of need in the way Joel said her name, the fierce demand of his mouth on hers, enflaming her senses further. She trembled against his body, flattening her palms

on his chest, confused by the harsh dragging cry that
came from his throat when she did so. Beneath her
hands she could feel the prickle of the dark hair that
grew on his chest and also the tightness of his nipples.
Were they as vulnerable to pleasure as her own?
Slowly she bent towards them, running her tongue
over their sharp outline as Joel had done with her.
She felt his chest muscles contract as he dragged air
into his lungs, his fingers curling into her hair.

'Oh God yes, Lissa. Yes…do that again.'

His abandonment excited her, the hoarse words of
praise and demand that came from his throat inciting
her to blindly follow his commands. There was pleasure to be found in touching as well as being touched
she was discovering, especially when Joel's response
to her left her in no doubts as to the way she aroused
him.

'I'm the one who's supposed to be doing the seducing,' he whispered in her ear. 'Not you.'

He was still wearing his pyjama trousers and as her
glance rested on them and then skittered away he released her rolling on to her side while he tugged them
off, quickly coming back to her. The heat and power
of the maleness of him against her skin was intensely
arousing and Lissa clung to him.

Now dimly, as though the information were of little
importance to her and somehow divorced from her
she realised that had it not been for the champagne
she had drunk she would not be here with Joel like
this; that she would never have been able to put her
fears and torturous self-doubts aside for long enough

to allow him to touch and arouse her as he had, but somehow this knowledge was only of minor import.

Slowly Joel caressed her body, his touch magically conveying to her that while he was the one who was in control, inciting and arousing the leaping pulses beating under her skin, he too was also held in thrall, paying homage to her femininity in the age old way of man; both master and slave to it.

In the shadowy half light she watched as his fingers described dizzying seductive patterns of delight against her skin; the curve of her hip, her thigh... She closed her eyes shuddering achingly, clinging to him, crying out his name.

His mouth brushed hers, calming, comforting as though he knew of the primaeval fear suddenly rushing through her body at the weight of his against it.

'Shush...relax...'

He was soothing her as he might have done Louise when she was in the grip of one of her nightmares Lissa realised but somehow it didn't matter, what did matter was that she clung to the reassuring calmness of his voice letting it strike at the deepest inner core of her. His mouth covered hers again and she clung to him letting the fierce need he was arousing inside her explode and drown out everything else. She was discovering within herself an intensely sensual streak that she now dimly perceived had perhaps always been there. Perhaps it was the very sensuality of her nature which had caused her to react so violently in the past. Her parents had been severely puritanical in their views; so much so that Lissa was beginning to see how her up-bringing must have been at war with much in her own nature.

'Are you enjoying this?'

Joel's question caught her off-guard. Before his near silence had added to the whole unreal aura that had enveloped her from the first moment he took her in his arms. Almost she had persuaded herself that she had strayed into some fantasy dream world from which she could simply wake up any time she wished, but now suddenly reality hit her. She *was* here…in Joel's arms, enjoying his lovemaking with an intensity that was sweeping away all her previous conceptions of herself.

As she looked into his eyes, seeing them clearly now, without the benefit of any champagne-induced fogging haze; seeing within them a fine mingling of compassion, tenderness, and something else… something so eternally masculine and elemental that her body responded automatically to it, curving into his, her husky 'Yes' was half lost against his skin as she pressed her lips to his throat confused by the maelstrom of emotions suddenly seething within her, knowing that it was not purely desire that was making her so femalely pliable in his arms.

His skin tasted salt against her tongue and while part of her acknowledged the pleasure of such tactile contact her mind laboured dully trying to understand by what tortuous tracks and byways she had come to where she was now…to loving him. The admission that she loved him slid so easily into her mind that she knew it must have been there some time. Instinct screamed at her that to love him would only bring her pain, but held within his arms it was impossible to listen to instinct or caution. She kissed him, tasting his skin, losing herself completely in the joy of absorbing all she could of him into her senses, feeling the suddenly accelerated thud of his heartbeat as his body responded to the touch of her hands and mouth.

Now when he touched her there was a hint of pagan savagery beneath his tenderness that drew a corresponding response from her; as though physically their bodies were communicating on a deeper more primitive level than their senses. There was nothing she wanted more than his ultimate and complete possession of her, in fact she wanted it so badly that she was the one to initiate it, moving arousingly against him, her hips writhing seductively against his in an age-old dance of seduction, which made it all the more bitterly devastating when suddenly, for no reason she could think of, behind her closed eyelids the old vision of him danced, bitter and contemptuous, freezing her body into rigid agony at the moment of his possession, destroying the golden bubble of pleasure that had enclosed her.

'Lissa!'

She shuddered under the harshly abrasive way he said her name. 'It's all right… Open your eyes.'

Unbelievably she was obeying him, opening her tightly closed eyes to look despairingly into his.

'See, it's all right. Look at me, Lissa. Look at me…' His heart was still thudding erratically, sweat glistening on his skin, but the topaz eyes were nothing like the ones that had haunted her darkness, the curve of his mouth; the way his skin clung tightly to his cheekbones making her realise that the portrait relayed to her by her mind's eye was actually a caricature of reality…and that the way he was looking at her, with desire, with need…but most of all with understanding bore not the slightest resemblance to the expression she had once thought she had seen.

The muscles of her throat started to relax, her small choked sob of distress, silenced by the gentle pressure of his mouth.

'I want you, Lissa. I want to make love to you…to feel your body hold mine like a silken sheath…' He was interspersing his words with hungry, drugging kisses and she could feel herself responding, mentally and physically. 'I need to be deep inside you.' He moved as he spoke and her body melted, heat radiating outwards from deep inside her as he thrust against her and then inside her, her resistance flooding away on a shuddering breath of pleasure.

If she had thought she had already tasted the heady wine of pleasure, it had been a mere sip compared to what she was now experiencing. Once the trauma of her self-imposed barriers had been overcome the brief pain of Joel's initial possession had been nothing; something fleetingly felt and then forgotten beneath the waves of sensation which had overwhelmed her.

It was like touching heaven; being immortal…escaping the bonds of human limitations, and to know that Joel had shared that pinnacle of human pleasure with her made it all the more precious.

As her body relaxed into lethargy she summoned enough energy to say drowsily, 'You got me drunk deliberately didn't you?'

''Not drunk,' Joel corrected her, 'merely pleasurably relaxed. Do you regret it?'

Lissa shook her head. 'No.' How could she regret it? How could any woman regret sharing the most mystic of all human experiences with the man she loved? But then of course Joel did not *know* that she loved him, and he certainly did not love her. So why, why had he made love to her? Not just on impulse but deliberately. She turned towards him, studying his face in the lamp light. He looked relaxed, younger...supinely male and satisfied. A tiny thrill of pleasure ran through her. It was frightening to realise how vulnerable she was; how easily the smallest thing about him could please her, even to the extent of knowing that it was making love to her that had brought that almost animal langour to his body.

'I don't regret it at all, Joel,' she told him honestly. 'But why? It wasn't just on impulse.'

· 'No,' he agreed. 'No it wasn't an impulse. Nor was it simply to satisfy my own desire for you. Oh yes,' he told her watching her, 'despite what you seem to have thought to the contrary; the fact that you were sexually inexperienced did not lessen my desire for you, Lissa, and I'm not going to pretend that what we just shared together was anything less than extremely pleasurable...nor that I'm not hoping that it's a plea-

sure we will share again, but after you'd told me
about your phobia it seemed to me that as I was the
focal point of your trauma, then I should be the one
to help you to overcome it. I thought if you could see
me, not as some disapproving intruder, but as a
man…a man very much aware of you as a beautiful
and desirable woman, and every bit as vulnerable as
you are yourself.' His thumb touched her cheekbone
as she turned towards him. 'Yes, you are beautiful
and desirable, Lissa,' he repeated softly. 'Didn't my
body tell you that?'

The memories conjured up by his words caused her
to tremble slightly with a tiny thrill of remembered
need.

'Yes,' she admitted huskily.

'It wasn't all entirely premeditated,' Joel added.
'The idea of getting you to relax via a few glasses of
champagne only occurred to me today. I'd noticed
that you didn't recoil quite as strongly from me when
I touched you, so I knew you were beginning to relax
with me.'

'But…but how did you know…that, that I'd be responsive to you?' Lissa asked him. Could he have
guessed what she had not? Could he have known that
she loved him? She hoped desperately that he did not.
What he had said to her had made it plain that he did
not love her; compassion and desire were not love.

'I didn't. It was a chance I had to take. For all I
knew you could have been completely turned off by
me physically, but I was hoping the champagne
would lower your inhibitions for long enough for me

to find out if that air of sensuality you have about you had any basis in reality. No matter what you might have been told, Lissa, one does not have to be wildly or passionately in love to enjoy a sexual relationship.'

'No, but surely love does add something,' she protested, remembering the surge of responsiveness she had felt when she realised that she loved him.

'A great deal,' he agreed, 'especially when we're talking about loving someone as opposed to being in love with them. You and I get on extremely well together Lissa...far better than I'd envisaged. It's my view that our marriage could be an extremely fulfilling and happy one—for both of us. Tonight was something of an experiment...an attempt on my part to make some reparation to you for the past. I felt I owed it to you to give you the freedom to overcome the past. I think I've succeeded, but now it's up to you to decide whether you wish to use that freedom in staying with me...as my wife...or whether you now feel you want to be free to form other relationships.'

Lissa knew that he was being completely fair and open with her but her heart ached for some whispered words of love...some absurd demand that she remain his and his alone, even if they were lies.

'Don't think about it now... Go to sleep.' As he switched off his lamp he asked teasingly, 'By the way, am I forgiven for my sins? Plying you with drink...seducing you?'

'I'll tell you in the morning,' Lissa responded drowsily. He wasn't going to have it all his own way.

# CHAPTER SEVEN

'LISSA!'

The shrill voice of her niece dragged Lissa from sleep. She opened her eyes tiredly to find Louise and Emma both next to her on the bed, still in their dressing gowns. Thin February sunlight streamed in through the windows, Joel's side of the bed empty. Her heart thudded in a mingling fear and delight. She shivered slightly wondering if last night had actually happened or if it had all been a dream, and then she glanced at her watch, stunned to discover that it was gone ten. Why hadn't Joel woken her? Her skin grew warm as she pictured him waking up and watching her sleeping…while she was so vulnerable. It was just as well it was Saturday and that Joel did not have to go over to the factory.

'Uncle Joel is making breakfast,' Louise told her importantly. 'He said we were to let you sleep.'

'Yes, I did, didn't I?' Joel agreed wryly, walking in carrying a tray and putting it down on her bedside table. The rich aroma of the freshly made coffee was mouth-watering. He had also made some toast and the tray was set with a crisp white cloth and a small vase with some snowdrops. Lissa touched their pale fragile petals gently with the tip of her finger, tears stinging her eyes as she did so. She bent her head so that Joel wouldn't see them, but he lifted her chin with warm fingers and their eyes met. The warmth and tenderness in his held her. For a moment the earth seemed to tilt on its axis, her heart lurching, knocking against her ribs, and then he bent his head and kissed her lingeringly. A tremendous surge of joy welled up inside her, a happiness so intense that she shook with it. Louise clamoured for attention, Joel released her and the moment of intimacy between them was gone, but Lissa thought she would never forget that even though he might not love her he had cared enough to make that special gesture…to let her know in the cold light of morning that he still remembered the night and that he wanted her to remember it too.

Her mood of light-heartedness lasted all through the day. In the afternoon they took the girls shopping. Louise needed new shoes and of course Emma had to have some too. Once on she refused to be parted from them, and they left the shop amidst smiles from the assistants.

Because Joel had missed so many bedtimes during the week, Lissa organised a family tea, allowing the girls to stay up beyond their normal bedtime. While they were eating Joel talked about his plans to improve the bloodstock carried on one of the estate farms. His suave air of sophistication could be misleading, Lissa reflected, remembering how awe-inspiring she had once found it. At heart he was very much a man who felt passionately about the land and everything connected with it. He was also extremely well read and interested in various aspects of the arts, especially music. All in all a complex, intelligent man with a hidden streak of sensitivity that would always endear him to the female sex. Fear brushed her heart leaving it thumping. Joel would always be attractive to other women. Had he loved her she had little doubt that he would remain faithful, but he didn't. What would happen if he ever met a woman that he did? How he would resent then his commitment to her... She couldn't bear it if that should happen. Stop it...stop it, she warned herself. She was crossing bridges she hadn't yet come to, dealing with problems before they arose.

They bathed the girls together, Louise clinging wetly to Lissa while she dried her, snuggling up to her and whispering, 'I love you, Lissa, do you love me...?'

Hugging her back, Lissa reassured her, suddenly aware that Joel was watching her.

'What is it?' she asked him, conscious of some slight withdrawal within him, some coolness that threatened her.

'Nothing.' He got up, picking Emma up. 'I'll put this one to bed, shall I?'

What had she done to make him withdraw from her like that? Lissa wondered. Had he perhaps thought looking at her of another woman...one whom he might love as he did not love her?

As they prepared for bed Joel said casually, 'You know we're going to have to start doing some socialising shortly. People have left us alone knowing about John and Amanda's deaths, but I've had a couple of invitations recently to dinner, drinks, that sort of thing.'

He didn't say any more, but nor did he make any attempt to touch her once they were in bed, and although Lissa tried to reassure herself that there could be any number of reasons for the coolness she sensed within him she was filled with fear, experiencing for the first time in her life the full vulnerability that comes with love.

On Monday morning Mrs Fuller arrived, and it was soon quite obvious that the girls were going to take to her. Lissa was in Joel's study going through the post for him when the phone rang. She picked up the receiver automatically, not recognising the cool feminine voice on the other end of the line, explaining that Joel was out.

'Oh, I see. You must be John's sister-in-law then, Lisa…'

'Lissa,' Lissa corrected, feeling an inexplicable tug of antagonism towards the unknown caller. 'And actually I'm now Joel's wife.'

'Oh yes, of course, I'd forgotten he'd got married.' The excuse was smoothly bland, but Lissa was not deceived. Her caller had known all right and apprehension started to trickle down her spine. 'Joel is an old friend of my husband's,' the other woman continued. 'I was ringing to invite him round for dinner, but of course both of you must come. We normally get together once a month or so, but obviously because of the tragedy…'

They eventually fixed a date, Lissa's caller introducing herself as Marisa Andrews before she rang off.

Lissa knew little of Joel's friends apart from odd remarks he had made, and although common sense told her it was ridiculous to feel that the other woman had deliberately set out to unnerve her, she still retained a distinct feeling that she had.

When Joel returned she told him about the phone call. He turned to look at the post, his back to her as he said, 'Marisa and Peter are old friends of mine. Peter and I were at university together. I was actually dating Marisa at the time and I introduced her to Peter.'

He didn't say anything else, but Lissa was conscious of an icy ache of depression that stayed with her all evening. When they eventually went to bed she deliberately turned her back to Joel, keeping well to her own side of the mattress. She thought she felt him touch her hair but she refused to turn round, and eventually the mattress shifted as he turned out his lamp. It was hours before she managed to fall asleep her mind churning sickly. Perhaps she was making a mountain out of a molehill…after all just because Joel had once dated this Marisa, it didn't mean she was the love of his life. Try to keep a sense of proportion, she told herself, but the fear would not go away and neither would the feeling that Joel had cooled towards her. He was still pleasant, but there was no warmth, no hint of teasing intimacy in the occasional duty kisses he gave her when he went out, and by Friday, Lissa was dreading the coming ordeal of Saturday's dinner party.

On impulse on Friday afternoon she asked Mrs Fuller if she would keep an eye on the girls, explaining that she wanted to buy a new dress. The housekeeper had already promised to look after them on the Saturday evening and Lissa had no qualms about leaving her with them. They enjoyed her company as much as she enjoyed theirs.

She had already been through her wardrobe and had found nothing there that would give her the confidence she felt she so badly needed, and so she decided she would go up to London. She arrived just after two and headed straight for Knightsbridge, determined to find herself a dress that would show the as yet unknown Marisa Andrews that she was no insignificant dreary little mouse. Joel had left the house that morning after breakfast saying that he had some business to conduct and not to expect him back until early evening. He hadn't said exactly where he was going and Lissa had found his unusual reticence chilling.

Trying to concentrate on the task in hand she hurried into Harvey Nicholls. Two hours later she emerged feeling light-headed with success and slightly guilty over the amount of money she had spent.

Her dress was very plain, long sleeved and high necked in fine wool crepe, fitting snugly over her waist and hips and then flaring out into a slightly bias cut skirt, but the simplicity of the design was more than compensated for in the rich dense blue colour of the fabric. It was a dress cut by a master hand for a woman who enjoyed being a woman and in it Lissa felt confidently sure of her femininity and appeal.

She had been lucky enough to get shoes to go with it, black suede with blue heels and satin ribbons, a touch of frivolity to offset the plainness of the dress.

She had just emerged into the street when she felt someone touch her shoulder. Swinging round, she saw Simon Greaves.

'Good heavens…what a coincidence!'

'I've just been to see a potential client,' he told her. 'I couldn't believe it when I saw you. I thought you were immured in the depths of the country.'

'I came up to do some shopping.' It was hard to believe that she once thought herself attracted to him. Compared with Joel he seemed lacklustre somehow.

'Enjoying marriage, are you?' There was a nasty little bite to the words, and Lissa was faintly surprised by it, but when he suggested they chat over a cup of coffee, she could think of no reason for refusing without being impolite and so she allowed him to guide her towards a small coffee house.

They were given a table in the window and once they had been served Simon started to ask her again how she had settled down in the country. He looked disbelieving when she said she was enjoying it, telling her, 'I got the distinct impression that you were being rather railroaded into this marriage. You know, Lissa, I miss you,' he added, covering her hand with his

own. Since she could not snatch it away without causing a fuss, Lissa let it lie there, feeling her irritation
towards him growing. 'Come back to my place this
afternoon,' he cajoled. 'We can talk there.' The way
he looked at her warned Lissa that talk wasn't all he
had in mind and she felt instantly angry. Did he really
think she was the sort of person who would contem-
plate breaking her marriage vows for something as
shallow as a brief sexual fling? As she fought down
her anger, she felt a prickle of awareness run down
her spine. Someone was staring at her. She lifted her
head and looked through the window. There was no
one there. Shaking it, she told herself that she would
have to stop being so over-imaginative and then
turned to tell Simon in no uncertain terms that she
was not interested in what he was proposing. They
parted less than amicably. A cold, frigid bitch, he had
called her. Once she would have believed him, but
now, thanks to Joel she knew better. Joel! Her heartbeat quickened as she thought about him, and suddenly she couldn't wait to get home. If only she knew
what was making him so cool towards her. She froze
almost in her tracks, other shoppers bumping into her.
Dear God, what if Joel *had* guessed the truth. What
if he suspected that she loved him and he was keeping
her at a distance because he did not want any deep
emotional involvement with her? She bit her lip in
sudden anguish. Was that it? Had she stumbled on
the truth? If so, what was she to do? She could only
play the game by Joel's rules, she decided as she
made her way home. She would have to be as cool

to him as he was to her so that he would not be
burdened with an emotional commitment he obviously did not want. Unwanted love could be a burden
and an embarrassment she acknowledged. Perhaps
Joel feared that she would demand more of him than
he could give and so had decided to hold himself
aloof from her as a warning. She thought about the
dress she had just bought with the express intention
of showing herself off to her best advantage, and
swallowed hard. She would have to pretend it was
one she had had for some time. Pride stiffened her
determination. From now on she would do nothing...nothing that would betray how she felt. She
would be as cool and distant as Joel.

Luckily he was not in when she got back and she
was able to take her purchases upstairs and put them
away. He came in while she was watching the news
on television, looking sombrely formal and almost
chillingly forbidding. The expression on his face was
close to the one of her nightmares, and her heart
quailed as she looked at him.

'Busy day?'

'Yes... And you?'

Were they really reduced to this...to these banali-
ties, she wondered miserably, contrasting them with
the discussions and conversations they had shared
with such enthusiasm not so very long ago.

'No...not really.' She wasn't going to tell him
about her trip to London. He would want to know
why she had gone, and that was something she wasn't
going to tell him now.

She looked across at him, dismayed by the coldness in his eyes, conscious of a leashed tension about his movements. Was it purely because of her, or was it something to do with the fact that tomorrow they were dining with his old girl friend?

'I'm going out.'

The harsh anger in his voice cut coldly through her frail defences, chilling her, and she shivered.

'When will you be back?'

'I don't know.' The curt dismissal in his voice hurt.

'What about dinner?'

'If I'm not here then start without me,' he told her derisively, striding towards the door, slamming it on his way out. She listened to his footsteps dying away and then the sound of his car engine firing, standing tensely where he had left her until that too faded. She then went into the kitchen pinning a bright smile to her face as she greeted the girls and Mrs Fuller.

Louise wanted to know where Joel had gone.

'He had to go and see someone about business,' she told the little girl, wondering as she did so, rather bleakly, how many times in the months and years to come she was going to repeat that phrase.

The physical consummation of their marriage, the tenderness Joel had shown her then, which should have boded so well for their marriage, seemed only to have widened the gap between them.

Feeling thoroughly depressed, Lissa went upstairs into her bedroom and opened her wardrobe door, staring miserably at the blue dress she had bought with such fervent determination to draw Joel's attention to her.

Joel did return in time for dinner but he was withdrawn, curt to the point of aggressiveness whenever she talked to him so that gradually her questions ceased and a tense silence filled the room.

She was not surprised, rather relieved in fact, when after dinner Joel announced that he had work to do and disappeared in the direction of his study.

Lissa went to bed early but it was gone one when Joel came up, walking into the bedroom so quietly, not switching on any of the lights, so that she was forced to the conclusion that he would prefer her to be asleep. Her heart ached with love and despair.

Tomorrow was another day, and somehow she must find the courage to face it—and Marisa Andrews.

# CHAPTER EIGHT

NO ONE COULD ever have dressed for a dinner party with less enthusiasm, Lissa thought miserably as she brushed her hair. Joel was in their bathroom; she could hear him splashing about under the shower. Disturbing mental images of the lithe maleness of him tormented her, making her hands shake so much that she had to put down the brush. Her body now awakened to the pleasure of Joel's lovemaking seemed to crave it with all the single minded intensity of an addict for his favourite drug. Whenever he was in the same room with her she ached with a tension that had nothing to do with tiredness or over-stretched nerves. It was humiliating that she should feel like this. How could she love and want him to this extent, especially when she knew that he cared little or nothing for her?

He came out of the bathroom while she was zipping up her dress. Out of the corner of her eye Lissa studied him, tiny shivers of awareness feathering down her spine as he shrugged off his robe and started getting dressed. Unlike her he seemed totally unself-conscious about his nudity; totally unaware of the dry-mouthed anguish with which she fought not to look at him because to look was to want to touch and to go on touching...

Her zipper stuck and she made a small impatient sound. Joel looked up and frowned, immediately perceiving what had happened.

'Here let me.' His voice was as cool as the touch of his fingers against her over-heated skin. She could smell the clean male scent of him and she wanted nothing more than to turn round and be taken into his arms. The intensity of her own emotions overwhelmed her, making her tense her body against any such betrayal.

'Relax.' The cool bite in Joel's voice chilled her. 'I'm not about to rape you, if that's what's worrying you.'

Painful colour stung her skin as she caught the cynically bitter undertones to his voice. 'I didn't think you were.'

Her zip came free and slid smoothly upwards. Joel stepped away from her, turning his back on her as he continued dressing. He looked devastatingly masculine in the formality of his evening clothes, Lissa acknowledged miserably, watching covertly as he inserted gold links into his shirt cuffs, deftly snapping them closed.

'Ready?'

His glance swept over her, dismissing her without comment, his indifference towards her so painful that her face felt stiff from the effort of trying to conceal her feelings from him.

They went downstairs together, Joel's attitude towards her punctiliously correct as he handed her into the car.

As he started the engine he inserted a cassette into the tape deck, turning up the sound just loudly enough to make conversation difficult, effectively shutting her off from him, Lissa thought. He couldn't have made it more plain if he had spelled it out for her, how uninterested in her he really was.

It took just under an hour for them to reach the Andrews' house—a rather solid Victorian red-brick building on the outskirts of a small village. The gateposts and short drive were illuminated clearly enough for Lissa to have a brief glimpse of the edge of an immaculate lawn that somehow matched the mental picture she had already built up of Marisa Andrews— cool, immaculate, perfectly groomed.

Joel stopped the car and released his seat belt, Lissa doing the same. She was out of the car before he could help her, and he gave a rather grim smile as he waited for her to precede him up the shallow flight of stone steps.

The door was opened before they rang. 'Joel, darling, I thought I recognised your car.'

Lissa recognised the smoothly feline feminine voice instantly. She could feel the tiny hairs on the surface of her skin prickling with atavistic dislike. 'Do come in, both of you.'

As Lissa walked into the hall ahead of Joel she had ample opportunity to study their hostess, as Joel bent to kiss her cheek. Small, much smaller than herself, ash blonde hair cut to emphasise the delicacy of her features; she was everything that she herself was not Lissa recognised on a downward plunge of her heart.

Although she suspected that her hostess must be somewhere in her early thirties, she could easily have passed for a woman of twenty-seven or -eight. Although she tried not to, Lissa couldn't help but be aware of the way Marisa's fingers clung to Joel's shoulder, as she prolonged his greeting kiss, neither could she miss the look of cold malevolence which her hostess directed towards *her* as she cooed with soft sweetness. 'Joel darling, you're neglecting your new wife. Do please introduce her to me.'

Grimly Lissa listened to Joel's introductions, hating the tinklingly false laugh Marisa gave when she interrupted gaily, 'Oh Joel, no need to be quite so formal. Joel and I have known one another for years,' she told Lissa, directing a coquettish glance towards Joel. 'You know darling, you've grown into such an impossibly handsome man, that I really think perhaps I should have married *you* and not Peter. But then handsome men always make difficult husbands, don't they, Lissa? One always has to be on one's guard in case one loses them to someone else, wouldn't you agree, Lissa? Far better I always think to be a handsome man's mistress than his wife. So much more fun.'

Lissa managed a cool smile, knowing quite well that Marisa was trying her best to make her feel uncomfortable and outside the charmed circle she had so plainly drawn around Joel and herself.

'Where's Peter?' Joel enquired easily. 'I haven't seen him for ages.'

'Oh, he's in the drawing room.' Marisa pulled a

face. 'He's watching some stuffy programme on high finance. It should be over soon. My husband's a stockbroker,' she explained to Lissa, 'and sometimes I think he cares more about his stocks and shares than he does about me.'

'Impossible,' Joel replied smiling at her. 'Or at least if he does, then he's a fool.'

Lissa could feel the anger inside her, heating to a white-hot glow as she observed this interchange. Her nails were pressing so hard into the palms of her hands that they hurt.

The proprietorially flirtatious manner Marisa had adopted towards Joel set the tone for the whole evening, and Lissa had to grit her teeth and pretend not to notice the number of times her hostess excluded her from the conversation by referring to events which had happened in the past. She also had to pretend not to notice how often Marisa managed to touch Joel, or to draw his attention to her. To counteract her hostess's rudeness, Lissa directed her attention towards Peter Andrews, who despite his rather solid appearance had a keen, rather dry wit, which he exercised to their mutual enjoyment.

'Old Joel married,' Peter murmured jovially when they had reached the coffee stage. He directed a brief grin towards his friend and added, 'I was beginning to think I'd never see the day.'

'Oh come on, darling, be practical,' Marisa interrupted. 'Naturally Joel had to marry. After all he has those children to think of now...'

As she waited for Joel to at least make a token

attempt to deny Marisa's insinuation Lissa could feel
her face burning with humiliation and resentment.
How dare he subject her to Marisa's bitchiness? How
dare he bring her here to be insulted and tormented
by the sight of Marisa continually making it plain
how much she wanted him?

Peter gave an embarrassed cough and glanced
rather uncertainly towards Lissa.

Pride came to her rescue. With a brittle smile she
said tightly, 'That's right, Marisa. The children are
Joel's responsibility and as I've discovered, he's a
man who takes his responsibilities extremely seriously, but of course, taking our marriage seriously
doesn't preclude either of us from...' she managed a
tiny, expressive shrug, 'shall we say making other
friendships outside that marriage.'

There was a definite silence when she had finished.
Without looking at either Joel or Marisa she picked
up her coffee cup and made a pretence of drinking.
Let Marisa make what she liked of that, she thought
viciously.

'Goodness. How very...civilised of you,' was Marisa's eventual comment. She turned to Joel. 'Darling
I must say that had you married me, I'm afraid I
wouldn't have been anything like as practical, and
how you must have changed.' She directed Lissa a
smile of sweet malice. 'You perhaps won't believe
this, but I remember Joel as being quite outrageously
possessive and jealous.'

'Yes, I'm sure,' Lissa agreed with commendable
control, and an acidly sweet smile of her own, 'but

that was a long time ago, wasn't it? I think everyone feels things more intensely in their late teens and early twenties. I know I did.'

The evening dragged on interminably. Marisa insisted on taking Joel into her own private sitting room to show him some prints she had recently bought, and to judge by the willingness with which Joel went with her, she had been right to suspect that Joel still cared for her. Why had Marisa married Peter when it was so obvious that she preferred Joel, Lissa wondered miserably. Had she perhaps married Peter on some impulsive whim only to discover that it was Joel she really wanted?

'You mustn't mind Marisa,' Peter told her, breaking in on her thoughts. 'I'm afraid she's grown rather used to thinking of Joel as her exclusive property.'

'No, of course not,' Lissa agreed, feeling rather sorry for him. 'I realise that you're all very old friends.'

'Yes...Joel was dating Marisa when he introduced her to me,' Peter agreed, confirming what Joel himself had told her. 'Of course, he wasn't in a position to get married then. His father was extremely strict with him—kept him on a very tight rein financially.'

Lissa bit her lip. Was that the reason Marisa had married Peter in preference to Joel? Because Peter had been the better-off financially. Lissa was under no illusions about the other woman. Marisa was a woman who wanted the very best that life had to offer. Her marriage to Peter had given her financial security, but now she wanted more...she wanted Joel...

And Joel quite plainly wanted her, Lissa reflected sickly seconds later as they both walked into the room. There was still a faint smear of lipstick on Joel's mouth, and she felt the sickness boil into fierce hatred as she averted her eyes from Marisa's cat-like expression of complacency.

It was gone one in the morning when they eventually left. The angry surge of adrenalin which had kept Lissa going throughout the evening evaporated the moment she got into the car, leaving her unbelievably exhausted and more miserably unhappy than she could ever remember being in her life.

They had driven half a dozen miles or so when the tape finally stopped. As Lissa reached out to turn it over, Joel stopped her, his eyes meeting hers briefly for a moment, before he bit out, 'And just what the hell were you trying to do to Marisa?'

What was *she* trying to do to *her!* Lissa took a deep breath and tried to steady herself, her voice when she eventually managed to speak sounded unfamiliar, but reassuringly steady. 'Only the most stupid or appallingly cruel man would confront his wife with his mistress in such intimate conditions,' she told him huskily. 'If I was rude to Marisa, then I was only responding to her verbal attacks on me.'

For a moment it seemed to Lissa that he checked and would have said something, but then he paused and at last said coolly, 'In self-defence? Is that all it was? There were one or two moments when I thought I detected more than a hint of jealousy.'

His astuteness infuriated her. 'Me, jealous of your

relationship with Marisa? Why did she marry Peter and not you in the first place, Joel? Was it because he promised to be the better husband from a material point of view?'

He stopped the car with a jerk that threw her forward in her seat belt with such force that her head almost bumped into the windscreen. The jolt winded and shocked her, but Joel made no allowances for that, his hands gripping her shoulders as he swung her round to face him, his eyes glittering with a savagery that made her draw in her breath. He did love Marisa. He would never have reacted like this otherwise. Pain…awful and all-consuming filled her until there was no room for anything else, not even the ability to be alarmed by the quality of his anger.

She let what he was saying wash over her, and then when he had finished said numbly, 'You've still got her lipstick on your mouth…'

She watched in anguish as he raised his hand and rubbed it off.

'Even if you didn't care about humiliating me, Joel,' she said tiredly as he re-started the engine, 'I should have thought you might have spared some consideration for Peter. After all he is supposed to be your friend.'

'Peter knew what he was getting into when he married Marisa,' Joel informed her harshly.

After that neither of them spoke until they reached Winterly. Lissa got out of the car quickly and went straight upstairs to the girls' room. Mrs Fuller had promised to listen out for them, but they were both

fast asleep. Emma was sucking her thumb, Lissa released it from her mouth, and bent down to kiss both
girls, tears stinging her eyes. Joel had married her for
their sake; and she must always bear that in mind.
The tender, caring lover she thought she remembered
had just been an illusion. Now she had no idea why
Joel had made love to her. Once she had thought she
knew, but after tonight... She shuddered, suddenly
picturing him with Marisa...the sickness grew inside
her and she dashed into the girls' bathroom. Joel
walked in just as she was wiping her face, frowning
quickly.

'Something wrong?'

'I must have eaten something that disagreed with
me,' Lissa told him shakily, snapping off the light. 'I
think I'll go to bed now, Joel. I'm tired.'

'Of me? Is that what that little speech to Marisa
about marriage was all about?'

He followed her into their room and tugged savagely at his shirt buttons, stopping suddenly to frown
and walk over to his tallboy. He opened a drawer and
took out a long flat gift-wrapped package, which he
tossed casually over to her. 'I nearly forgot, today's
your birthday, isn't it?'

Lissa could have wept. It was, and she herself had
almost forgotten about it. She would rather have had
no present at all from Joel than one thrown at her in
this careless manner which made it plain that it was
no more than a duty gift.

'Aren't you going to open it?'

She did so reluctantly with fingers that trembled,

unable to suppress a small gasp of surprise when she opened the slim box and discovered the pearl choker inside.

'I...' She didn't know what to say to him. Tears misted her vision, swimming in front of her eyes. She touched the pearls gently, and wished that he was giving her this gift with love and caring.

'They're beautiful.'

'I bought them because the texture and sheen reminded me of your skin.'

Her eyes opened wider, her head lifting until her glance met his, the visions conjured up in her mind by his quiet words making her go hot with need. If she closed her eyes she could almost imagine he was touching her, caressing her with the slow intensity she remembered so vividly, learning the contours of her body, absorbing her into himself as though he never wanted to be apart from her.

'I...'

'I went up to London to get them the other day,' he continued quietly, but now there was a new note to his voice, a grim bitterness that caught her attention. She frowned and he laughed harshly. 'Yes, that's right...the day you also decided to visit the city. Why did you go there, Lissa? Or can I guess? Was the temptation to see Greaves too much to resist? Did you want to see what effect you would have on him now that you're free to take him as your lover? Did you, Lissa? Did you let him take you back to his flat and make love to you?'

Lissa could only stare at him. Joel had seen her

with Simon! She remembered now that she had felt as though someone had been watching her when they were sitting in the café. The words of explanation and denial trembled on the tip of her tongue, and then she remembered Marisa.

'Is that why you made it so obvious tonight that Marisa is your mistress, Joel?' she countered with commendable coolness. 'Because you saw me with Simon?'

'So you don't deny it?'

He was watching her with menacing intensity, the glittering rage so clearly discernible in his eyes igniting a strange mixture of misery and exhilaration inside her which spurred her on to ignore the warning signs.

'Why should I? Do you deny that Marisa is your mistress? If *you* are free to enjoy a sexual relationship with someone else, then why should I not be?'

'If it's sex you want, then I can satisfy that need for you right here and now.'

Too late she realised her mistake. Lissa backed away hastily, the box containing her pearls clattering on to the carpet. Common sense told her to face Joel and tell him quite simply that it was all a stupid mistake, and that far from encouraging Simon to make sexual advances towards her, she had been telling him quite categorically that she didn't want him, but something deeper than common sense took hold of her. She turned to run, motivated purely by blind, unthinking instinct. Joel caught her before she reached the door, swinging her round and into his

arms, tightening them round her until she could feel
the buttons of his shirt pressing into her. Even to
breathe hurt, and although she twisted desperately
against him she couldn't break free. One hand tangled
in her hair, tugging painfully on the roots forcing her
mouth to accept the bruising pressure of his. He
kissed her with a sexual savagery that shocked her,
and yet beneath her fear and anger ran an undeniable
thread of liquid pleasure; a fierce need to match fire
with fire and to respond to him with all the aching
need that was building up inside her. It was hard to
fight against herself and him, and even while she told
herself that this was not right; that any intimacy between them while he was in this savagely punishing
mood could only lead to further unhappiness for her,
she could feel her will to resist slipping away from
her. It was no use telling herself that he was simply
using her as a vent for his frustrations and anger…that
afterwards she would only feel renewed self-contempt
and loathing…that by responding to him she was en-
dangering her own self-respect. Her mouth softened
under his, her heart thudding with delirious release as
he recognised her surrender and took swift advantage
of it, his tongue impatiently seeking access to her
mouth, and when granted it, using her weakness ruthlessly against her. His fingers found her zipper and
slid it down. Lissa was dimly conscious of his hands
against her skin, smoothing up over her back, making
her shiver first with pleasure and then with need as
he pushed her dress away from her body. She was
touching him too, sliding her hands inside his shirt,

re-discovering the contours of his body. His mouth left hers, burning hotly against her skin as he tilted her head back, devastating her senses as he slowly ravaged the taut column of her throat.

'Is this what you want, Lissa?' His fingers sought the clasp of her bra, freeing her breasts to his knowing touch. She managed a strangled protest that died away into a whimpering admission of pleasure as his lips followed his hands, the movement of his tongue roughly erotic as it brushed the sensitive peaks of her breasts. Her fingers bit protestingly into his shoulders, a fierce surge of pride and anger that he could do this to her making her fight against the sexual coercion he was using so cold bloodedly. He made a harsh sound of pain but far from releasing her pushed her down on to the bed, following her there. Momentarily her hands were free, and Lissa used them to fend him off, anger turning swiftly to fear when her nail accidentally caught his shoulder, tearing his flesh. Joel swore, swiftly imprisoning both her hands, pinning them above her head. A wild reckless sexual excitement thundered through her as she saw his expression and read in his eyes the same fierce hunger that was in her own. Joel wanted her! It was savagely satisfying to know that even though he loved Marisa she could make him want *her*. She wanted to taunt him with her knowledge to humiliate and denigrate him as he had done her. He moved against her, expelling a deep breath, and she caught sight of the thin thread of blood against his skin where she had scratched him. His glance followed hers. Their eyes meshed, his burning dark metallic gold, hers a dark bright, defiant hazel. She could feel the hard muscles of his thighs against her body…she knew that he wanted her… This should have been her moment of triumph, her chance to show him that he was not invincible. He moved slightly and her eyes were drawn back to his shoulder. Almost absently she touched his skin with her tongue, feeling him flinch and tense. His blood tasted slightly rusty, the knowledge that she had caused it to flow turning her bitterness to guilt. What if at this moment he did want her? Wasn't he only really using her as an escape valve because he couldn't have the woman he really loved? The fight went out of her, leaving her empty…drained. She felt Joel's grasp of her wrists slacken and prepared to move away from him. His hand cupped her face and she turned to look at him, dreading the words of contempt she was sure she was going to hear. As she looked into his eyes the expression glittering back at her there was one she didn't recognise. His skin seemed to be drawn too tightly over his bones, a dark flush staining it.

'Lissa.' He said her name in a thickly unfamiliar voice. 'Do that again,' he commanded, moving so that her mouth was pressed against his shoulder. A deep shudder ran right through him as she automatically complied, touching his skin with her tongue with nervous delicacy, stunned that such a brief physical contact should apparently have so much power to move him. His hand found her breast, his thumb rubbing urgently against her swollen nipple. Lissa forgot that he didn't love her, silencing her moan of anguished desire against the warm flesh of his throat. She felt his body surge against her own and recklessly arched up against him prolonging the tingling contact. Joel bent his head, his mouth fiercely claiming the aroused peak of her breast, his fingers caressing its twin.

Lissa arched and writhed beneath him, her nails raking helplessly against his skin, desire exploding tumultuously inside her as Joel continued to arouse spirals of unbearable delight inside her, tiny darts of fire running shuddering through her body from its point of contact with the fierce heat of his mouth.

'You're my wife, Lissa.' He said it thickly, against her skin, whether as a reminder that he had every right to make love to her if he chose, or as an explanation for the fact that he was doing so, she didn't know. She ought to stop him, to remind him that he didn't love her, but her treacherous body ached too much for the sweet agony of consummation. When he removed the rest of their clothing she didn't stop him, simply watching him silently. Shadows made a subtle play of shading against his skin, one moment soft gold the next bronze. She ached to touch him Lissa acknowledged, watching him as he bent over her, removing her underclothes.

A slight shiver ran through her as his hand brushed her hip.

'Cold?'

She shook her head as his hand curled round the spot he had just touched. He was kneeling beside her, and when she first felt the light brush of his tongue where his hand had rested she thought she must be imagining it. Her head lifted and swivelled round and she gasped as she felt the brief caress again. Her skin quivered responsively where he had touched it, darting quick-silver thrills of pleasure running from nerve ending to nerve ending. She could hardly believe it when Joel bent his head and slowly started to drag his tongue over the slight swell of her stomach. She jerked away from him in helpless torment, but he imprisoned her against the bed, his hands holding the narrow bones of her hips, while his tongue left quivering trails of moist destruction over her skin.

Lissa was completely powerless to stop him, and after a while she no longer wanted to try, held thrall to the swift, leaping fires of pleasure that burned inside her. At first she twisted helplessly from side to side as much in an attempt to escape the devastation of her senses as to avoid Joel's skilfully delicate touch, but all her struggles seemed to do was to give him access to areas of her skin that seemed even more responsive to him than the others had been.

'Joel what are you dong?' she managed to demand huskily at one point, tensing agonisingly as his tongue described a slow circle round her navel and then dipped tormentingly to explore its slight indentation. 'Just trying to keep you warm,' he replied suavely, 'you are getting warm aren't you, Lissa?' he tormented softly.

Warm? She was burning up, her skin on fire.

By the time Joel's slow devastation of her body had reached her breasts she was shivering helplessly, aching for the full consummation of his possession. He kissed the tender fullness of their curves with mind-destroying slowness until Lissa couldn't hold back the fevered protest that left her lips. Once that final wall in her defences had been breached she couldn't keep silent her agonised pleas for him to end her torment, shattering the thick silence of the night, until Joel reached up and silenced her by pressing his finger against her mouth. Her lips parted, her tongue running frantically over the tips of his fingers, until driven half mad by the slow drift of his mouth against her breast she sucked feverishly on his fingers.

Dimly she was aware of Joel groaning, of him shifting his weight so that his body lay between her thighs, his lips exploring her throat, in between muttering hoarse words of praise and enticement against her skin. He withdrew his fingers from her mouth, brushing the outline of her lips with his thumb, lifting his head to look deeply into her eyes, his hands moving slowly down over her body, lifting it into his own.

Lissa shivered, trembling with aching desire. 'Tell me you want me more than you wanted him,' Joel demanded softly, watching her.

For a moment Lissa's mind was completely blank, and then when she realised the truth she could have wept with anguish. Joel had done this to her, aroused her to a pitch where her need for him was a throbbing ache that threatened to consume her, simply because his pride demanded that she want him more than she wanted Simon. If only he knew!

'Tell me!'

His face blurred for a moment as she blinked away tears. 'I want you more than I want Simon, Joel,' she said shakily at last. 'Much more.'

It was after all no less than the truth, and what he had done to her diminished him as much as it did her. Her body which had ached and hungered for his possession felt curiously drained of all feeling as he moved slowly and skilfully within her, rather like an overwound toy that was now broken, Lissa thought hazily, conscious of an overwhelming desire to break down and cry. Where she had ached for physical fulfilment now she ached for an emotional commitment to match her own. She heard Joel swear and then withdraw from her, but she was feeling too numb and lacerated to react.

'Lissa...what's wrong?' There was a raw uncertainty in Joel's voice that made her want to reach out and comfort him, but something stopped her. Joel didn't want *her*, he wanted Marisa. She felt her heart harden and shrink into a block of ice.

'Lissa!'

The tone of his voice demanded a response, but all she could manage was a flat, 'Using substitutes doesn't seem to work, does it, Joel?' before she slid down into a yawning black void of nothingness.

# CHAPTER NINE

SHE WAS VIOLENTLY ILL when she woke up in the morning—a sure sign that she must have eaten something that disagreed with her, Lissa thought as she washed and dressed.

Joel was up already, and mentally thanking God that she did not have to face him she made her way downstairs. They could not go on the way they were, last night had shown her that. What had happened to the compassionate tender man she had briefly known? She went into the kitchen, grimacing when she caught the smell of bacon and eggs.

Mrs Fuller looked at her in concern.

'Are you all right?'

'Just a little queasy,' Lissa explained. 'Something I ate, I expect.'

The housekeeper grinned at her. 'If you say so.'

It was several seconds before the import of her teasing remark sank into Lissa's consciousness. When it did, she went pale and sat down heavily on one of the chairs, staring blankly at the wall. Dear God, she hadn't thought of that! What if she should be pregnant?

Impossible! Hardly, an inner voice taunted her—in

fact it was all too probable. She had simply never thought about using any form of birth control. It had never been necessary. While she was trying to come to terms with her shock, Joel and the girls walked in. All three of them looked healthily windblown, their cheeks glowing, Emma on Joel's shoulder, while Louise clung to his hand.

'Joel said we were to let you rest,' Louise announced, releasing Joel to run over to Lissa, clambering on to her knee and cuddling into her. She was discovering in her elder niece a very deep need to exhibit her affections physically, and Lissa responded to her unspoken plea for reassurance, hugging and kissing her.

'We went for a walk,' Emma announced as Joel placed her in her high chair.

Mrs Fuller served them breakfast, and Lissa felt relieved when she was simply given two slices of dried toast. Joel raised his eyebrows.

'I'm not hungry,' Lissa told him hastily, avoiding his eyes, and grateful for the housekeeper when she kept silent, merely exchanging a thoughtful glance with her over Joel's downbent head. She had dreaded facing him this morning after the way she was sure she must have betrayed herself to him last night, but now she had something even more worrying on her mind. What on earth would she do if she was pregnant?

Stop thinking about it, she cautioned herself, it's probably nothing…too much rich food last night. She ought to have been reassured, but somehow she was not.

When he looked at her again there was a strange bitter tension in his eyes, a tightness to his mouth that took her back to that night almost ten years ago. Unknowingly she flinched, pushing her plate away, shivering slightly, aware of Joel getting up and coming towards her, and almost cringing away from him as he did so. How could she bear to have him touch her now when she knew that every time he did, it was another woman he had in his heart.

The phone rang shrilly, the sound harsh and challenging. Joel frowned, glanced at her, and then walked across the kitchen to pick up the receiver. Once he had moved away from her Lissa was conscious of an easing of the constriction in her muscles. Louise and Emma were both far too young yet to be aware of the strained atmosphere between the adults, but Mrs Fuller must have noticed it. If only she had known about Marisa before she agreed to marry Joel! Even loving him as she now admitted she did, she would not have done so. While she had thought there was no other woman in his life she had hoped, ridiculously no doubt, that somehow a miracle would occur and Joel would eventually turn to her with more than mere physical desire and compassion.

Compassion! She checked a bitter little laugh. There had been precious little of that between them these last few days. In fact if she hadn't seen that other side of him she would never have believed it existed.

'Lissa.'

She turned at the sound of Joel's voice, abrupt and grim. 'It's for you,' he told her, holding out the receiver. 'Guess.'

Simon? Ringing her, but why, Lissa wondered, automatically getting up and walking over to the phone.

Joel moved away the moment she reached him. He looked angry, she noticed, his mouth compressed. A spurt of defiant anger welled up inside her. If it was permissible for him to have his affair with Marisa then what right had he to look so annoyed simply because another man telephoned her.

She turned her back on him, holding the receiver close to her ear.

'Lissa, is that you?'

'Yes, Simon.'

'Look, I'm just ringing to apologise for the other day. I know I was out of line.'

Lissa listened absently to his apologies, conscious all the time of Joel's presence in the room.

'How about lunch one day just to show that I'm forgiven,' Simon suggested.

'Lunch?' Lissa turned round and met the coldly condemning look in Joel's eyes. She took a deep breath. 'Yes, why not,' she agreed gaily. 'I'll give you a ring, shall I?'

They chatted for several more minutes, although when she eventually replaced the receiver, she couldn't have said what they talked about. A feeling of almost frightening exhilaration had lifted her out of her previous misery, and she knew it came from knowing that at least if she did not have the power to move Joel to love, she could move him to anger. She was flirting with danger, she warned herself as she sat down again, avoiding Joel's eyes, but why not? Joel didn't want her himself...so why should he get angry because he thought someone else did.

She already knew the answer to that question, Lissa reminded herself.

Joel had made it plain enough when they married that he expected and intended to have her fidelity. But then she had expected something in return from him. Not love perhaps, but loyalty at least...an attempt to preserve the fiction that they had married because in part he cared for her. She had not expected to have his mistress flaunted openly in front of her without any show of concern about how she might feel.

She had half expected Joel to tackle her about Simon's phone call, but in the event he said nothing, and somehow that was worse.

As the days passed Lissa had the distinctly unpleasant sensation of something hanging ominously over her, a sensation too uncomfortably reminiscent of her childhood for her to bear it easily. She was also still suffering from nausea, and an acute nervous tension, which she knew she was communicating to Louise. The little girl had become clinging and petulant, and while Lissa fully understood and sympathised with her insecurity, the constant succession of broken nights they were enduring with Louise's recurrent nightmares were beginning to take their toll on her. Joel was so cold and distant towards her that she could hardly believe that they had ever really been lovers. He spent far more time away from the house, often going out in the evening and returning late. Lissa never questioned him as to where he had been, her stubborn pride refusing to allow her to let him see how much he was hurting her.

One week went by and then another. She had lost weight and there were dark circles under her eyes. Mrs Fuller who could not have failed to notice the atmosphere that existed between Joel and herself, and his constant absences, said nothing, but Lissa was acutely aware of her silent sympathy. It struck her that being a local Mrs Fuller might be quite aware of Joel's relationship with Marisa, and that too stung her pride.

She had intended to start Louise at playschool, but she herself felt far too lethargic to do anything about it. The last week in March, the temperature suddenly dropped several degrees, and Joel, for once appearing for dinner remarked that he felt they could expect snow. He frowned slightly as he said it, and Lissa guessed he was thinking of the safety of the stock.

Lissa had never realised until these last few weeks how lonely and cold a double bed could be when it was shared with a man one loved who felt nothing but indifference tinged with anger in return.

'Are you...are you planning on going out again tonight?' She wished she hadn't voiced the impulsive question when he frowned. For a moment she thought he didn't intend to reply and then he said suavely, 'Why, had you got something planned yourself?'

His blatant indifference and coldness towards her defeated her. She wanted to talk to him, to plead with him to discuss the state of their marriage and what future if any he envisaged for them. The sudden change in his attitude towards her was still something she hadn't really come to terms with. There were days when she felt completely muddled, unable to understand why he had changed from the tender considerate lover to whom she had given her heart and body to this cold, withdrawn man he was now. Maybe it was because he felt guilty about making love to her, seeing it as a betrayal of his love for Marisa? Maybe it was as she had originally thought, that he feared she would read into his lovemaking a greater emotional commitment than he was prepared to give her. Either way there was only one way she would learn the truth and that was for him to tell her, but he continually blocked all her attempts to talk seriously to him on any subject other than the children. What hurt almost more than all the rest put together was that to the girls he was still the same loving, compassionate person he had been right from the very start, underlining for her, if she had needed that doing…that it was *her* and *her* alone that brought out the cold distance in him she was now experiencing.

Lissa went to bed early while Joel was still out. She heard him come in and move about the bedroom, preparing for bed. Lying beneath the bedclothes she trembled with aching tension longing for him to turn to her and take her in his arms, but knew even as she did so that she was longing for the impossible. She closed her eyes, squeezing back weak tears. Sooner or later she would have to tell him of her suspicions that she was carrying his child. What would his reaction be? It was impossible to doubt his love for Louise and Emma, and in other circumstances, had she been Marisa for instance, she had little doubt that the news would have overjoyed him. But she was not Marisa, and the fact that she was to have his child would create another tie between them…a tie she was sure he would not want. She bit down hard on her bottom lip. If she *was* pregnant there was nothing she wanted more than to have his child…but how could she bring it into the world knowing how Joel felt about her?

The first thing Lissa noticed when she woke up was the pure clarity of the light streaming in through the curtains. As she sat up and glanced curiously towards the window, Joel walked in from the bathroom. His hair clung damply to his scalp, moisture beading his bare chest. He had wrapped a towel round his hips and Lissa felt the beginnings of reactionary sensations erupt inside her. It was a physical effort to drag her gaze away from him. Her heart was thudding heavily, her mouth dry.

'I see it snowed during the night,' Joel commented, flicking back a curtain, his comment explaining the unfamiliar brightness. 'Only a couple of inches by the looks of it, but there's more on the way. We'll need to make arrangements for feeding the stock in case it gets worse.'

Over breakfast, Louise's excitement about the

snowfall successfully covered the empty silence between them, Mrs Fuller coming and going with toast and coffee. Lissa noticed the dry crackers on her own plate and the weak cup of tea. Thankfully most mornings Joel had left their bedroom before she actually got up, and so far had not noticed her brief bouts of nausea. She couldn't go on ignoring her symptoms any longer, though, she admitted, deftly preventing Emma from overturning her cereal bowl. She would have to make an appointment to see the doctor.

Once that mental decision had been made it was easier to ring the local surgery and make an appointment, which she did as soon as Joel had left the house. She couldn't go on for much longer with the present situation, and nor could she tell Joel of her suspicions without making any attempt to have them confirmed.

Mrs Fuller had gone out to do some shopping, taking both girls with her, and when the receptionist offered her an almost immediate appointment, Lissa took it.

As she stepped outside it started to snow again, small flurries at first, increasing in density so that by the time she had reached the main road it was snowing quite heavily. Fortunately there was very little traffic on the road, but when she skidded slightly on one sharp bend Lissa began to wish someone else was driving. Living in London had blinded her to the dangers of adverse weather conditions, and her stomach muscles tensed protestingly as she switched her windscreen wipers on to fast in order to clear her window.

The doctor's surgery was in the nearest town, in the opposite direction from the small village where Mrs Fuller had taken the girls, and the road to it was a narrow, little used one.

It was nearly an hour before Lissa reached the small market town. She found an empty space in the surgery car park, and hurried on jelly-like legs towards the building.

She wasn't kept waiting very long. The partner she saw was new to her, a pleasant, quietly spoken woman in her mid-forties, who briskly confirmed her own suspicions. 'We shan't know for definite of course, until we get the results back,' she added, 'but from what you've told me there seems little doubt that you are pregnant.'

She went on to discuss pregnancy in general with Lissa and advised her to ring her in a couple of days when they should have obtained the results of her test.

Although she had been in the surgery less than half an hour it had been long enough for the roof and bonnet of her car to become covered in snow, as were her tyre tracks. Huddling deeper into her jacket Lissa unlocked her door and climbed in, trying not to dread too much the drive back home.

A cold, biting wind had sprung up while she was inside, whirling the heavily falling snow into a blinding storm. Crawling along in a low gear Lissa prayed that she would reach home safely. Several times she skidded but on each occasion she managed to control the car before any damage was done. When at last she was on the familiar half mile or so of road that led to Winterly's gates relief poured over her, relaxing her tense muscles. She was just about to turn into the entrance when a Land-Rover turned the corner beyond the gate, heading towards her from the opposite direction. She braked instinctively, gasping with shock as she felt her car start to slide towards the stone wall that encircled the park, knowing that she was helpless to prevent the collision.

Her seat belt pulled tightly against her body as her front wheels dropped into the ditch, the bonnet of her car screeching horribly against the stones. Part of her was conscious of doors slamming and footsteps coming towards her, but until her door was wrenched open and Joel bent down and across her, releasing her seat belt mechanism, she hadn't realised he was in the Land-Rover.

'What the hell did you brake for?' he demanded grittily, almost pulling her bodily out of the car. 'We'd seen you coming and we were waiting for you to turn into the drive. Didn't it strike you that the Land-Rover is far easier to control in weather conditions like these?'

'I didn't think...I just reacted instinctively,' Lissa admitted huskily. Now that the initial shock of the impact had worn off she was beginning to feel distinctly odd...only too glad of the hardness of Joel's chest behind her, as he half carried and half dragged her away from her car.

'Where the hell have you been, anyway?'

Conscious of the fact that Joel's companion—one of the tenant farmers—was watching them, Lissa shook her head, closing her eyes on a sudden wave of sickness. She must have gone completely limp in Joel's grasp because instantly his arms tightened round her, and she heard him swearing under his breath as he swung her up off the ground and carried her towards the Land-Rover.

'I'll take my wife up to the house,' she heard him saying to his companion. 'You see if you can get her car out of the way. Left there it will only cause a hazard.'

Dimly, like someone in a dream, Lissa was conscious of Joel shouldering open the Land-Rover door and depositing her on the hard seat, before taking his place next to her. The engine started, its roar filling her senses like the sound of waves pounding on to surf, and then they were jolting down the drive towards the house, each jolt making her shudder and clench her stomach muscles against an increasing need to be sick.

The moment Joel stopped the Land-Rover she scrambled out, making for the downstairs cloakroom.

'You'd better call the doctor,' she heard Joel speaking behind her, his voice curt, angry almost. 'Lissa's just had an accident in her car. I'll take her upstairs and get her in bed.'

She wanted to protest that she was neither deaf nor dumb and moreover, perfectly capable of putting herself to bed, but the bout of nausea had left her too weak to do more than moan a miserable protest, as Joel picked her up and strode towards the stairs.

In their room he placed her on the bed, and stood

frowning over her for a few seconds before asking tersely, 'Are you hurt at all? Did you bang your head…'

'I'm fine, Joel,' she told him weakly, 'it's just the shock…' Instinctively her hand went to her stomach, and lay tensely there, but Joel missed the betraying gesture, his eyes on the scene beyond the window.

'What on earth possessed you to take the car out in the first place? Where the hell had you been?' He broke off as Mrs Fuller tapped on the door and came in with a tray of tea.

'I've rung the doctor and he should be out soon.'

A numbing lethargy was creeping over Lissa. All she wanted to do was to close her eyes and go to sleep, but Joel wouldn't let her. He kept on talking to her, demanding to know where she had been. If only he would go away Lissa thought weakly, refusing to answer.

'Lissa, you mustn't go to sleep.' His voice was painfully harsh, ringing dauntingly in her ears. 'You might be suffering from some slight concussion… Open your eyes…'

Wearily she did as he instructed. He looked quite pale, she noted with detached curiosity. He also looked extremely angry. It gave her a certain amount of quiet satisfaction to realise that she had escaped somewhere where neither of these emotions could touch her. Indeed she felt extraordinarily detached herself…quite strangely so. She must close her eyes…

'Lissa!' The sound of her name exploding beside

her with angry vehemence forced her to open them again. Joel's head jerked up and he stared at the window, getting up to go and look out.

'The doctor's arrived, thank God.'

His fervency hurt her, betraying how anxious he was to escape from her presence.

Her door opened and Mrs Fuller came in. Lissa smiled weakly at the doctor. The older woman raised her eyebrows. 'Well now…what's all this?' she demanded briskly.

'I had a slight bump in my car,' Lissa began to explain, but Joel over-ruled her, telling Dr Soames what had happened in terse, bitten-out sentences.

'She was very sick almost immediately afterwards. I was concerned that there might be some degree of concussion.'

'Umm…I don't think so,' Dr Soames pronounced, examining Lissa's forehead. 'She doesn't seem to have bumped her head at all. More likely to be the nausea was caused by her pregnancy.' She frowned a little and said to Lissa. 'I suggest you spend the rest of today in bed. In my view it's too early yet for your accident to bring on a miscarriage, but we won't take any chances. Any other bumps or bruises?'

Lissa shook her head, unable to look at Joel. He had gone to stand by the window when Dr Soames came in and he was still standing there with his back towards her, the intense rigidity of his spine making her heart sink. This wasn't how she had planned to tell him that she might be carrying his child.

# CHAPTER TEN

'WHY? Why the hell didn't you *tell* me?'

They were alone, Dr Soames having left, and Mrs Fuller having tactfully shepherded both girls downstairs. Joel swung round to stare at her. Her head was aching muzzily, and Lissa reflected wryly that fate seemed determined to work against her. How on earth was she to marshal her arguments against Joel when her brain refused to work properly.

'I wasn't sure myself. That's why I went to see Dr Soames this morning. I knew it was something we'd have to talk about but I wanted…I wanted to be sure of my facts before we did…'

'Sure of your facts…' How brittle and angry Joel's voice sounded. He swung round and she saw his face, confused by the grimness of his voice and the pallor of his skin. No doubt it had come as a shock to him to discover that she was carrying his child especially when…she bit her inner lip painfully to stop the weak tears from forming and forced herself to face the truth. How could Joel want her to carry his child when in reality he loved Marisa?

'Well it seems now that there's precious little doubt.'

She didn't blame him for being angry, but it wasn't entirely her fault, she reminded herself, trying not to remember the sensation of his hands on her skin…his mouth against hers, his heart thudding out its primitive intoxicating message against her body.

'Do you want to abort it?'

Lissa couldn't hide the flash of shocked pain in her eyes, but managed to whisper croakily, 'Do you?' She ought to have been prepared for this, but somehow she had not. It was, after all, the neatest, tidiest solution, but it was not one she could ever agree to. Even if Joel rejected her she still intended to go ahead with her pregnancy.

'No.' His voice was harsh, his head averted so that she couldn't see his expression.

'Neither do I,' she admitted huskily.

'You realise what you're committing yourself to, do you, Lissa?' he demanded, still without looking at her, 'and I don't just mean motherhood. I want to make it quite clear now that there is no way I would ever allow anyone else to take my place in my child's life. I won't divorce you so that you can go to Greaves,' he told her levelly, facing her for the first time.

At first Lissa was too shocked to respond.

'But…'

'Don't bother to deny it, Lissa. I saw the two of you together in London—remember?'

She bit her lip. It was tempting to allow Joel to go on believing that she was in love with Simon, for the sake of her pride if nothing else, but if she did… She thought about the child she was carrying…Joel's child…life would be difficult enough for it as it was with a father who merely tolerated instead of loving its mother. It was better to tell the truth.

'That was a chance meeting, Joel,' she told him quietly. 'I bumped into him in the street the day I went to buy a new dress for the dinner party. I didn't tell you at the time because…' She laced her fingers together and stared down at them as fiercely as though they were something she had never seen before, concentrating on them so that she would not have to look at Joel.

'Because…?' he prompted, his voice steel soft.

Suddenly she felt totally exhausted, her hands relaxed, her body slumping into the mattress. 'Do you really need to ask,' she said tiredly. 'Please let's not play games now, Joel…'

He was at her side in a second, his fingers cool against her unexpectedly hot forehead, his eyes, in the brief second she allowed hers to meet them, deeply concerned…so concerned that she felt she must be hallucinating.

It was pointless feeling pain because he had not denied his involvement with Marisa, what had she in all honesty expected?

'No games,' he promised quietly, 'but we must talk, Lissa. I must admit that this was not entirely the outcome I…hoped for when…'

'When you made love to me,' Lissa supplied tiredly. 'No…I think I understand what motivated you, Joel.'

A shadow darkened his eyes, and she thought for a moment that he looked almost haunted...a trick of the light of course.

'And understanding that...'

She cut him off before he could go on to tell her as he undoubtedly would that his own feelings had never been involved on more than a merely concerned level. 'It makes no difference, Joel,' she told him curtly, turning her face away from his so that he couldn't see the anguish in her eyes. 'I *am* carrying your child, and we are both agreed that the pregnancy should not be terminated. You don't want us to divorce...'

'Do you?' He shot the question at her with explosive force, her head automatically turning so that she could look at him. She had seldom seen him look as he was doing now—as though he were fighting to control his anger.

'I believe that for the sake of the children—the girls as well as our own child—we should stay together but...' She bit her lip wondering if she dare tell him that she did not know how long she would be able to go on as they were now without completely breaking down. Every time he went out without telling her where he was going—every night he came home late she imagined him with Marisa. Jealousy was a bitter corrosive emotion and one she would far rather not have suffered from.

'But?' Joel prompted harshly. His eyes glittered almost blackly beneath thick spiky lashes. He seemed to have aged somehow, and as he walked towards the window Lissa recognised an inner tension in his movements that tore at her heart.

'When we were first married,' Lissa began carefully, picking her words with forethought, too aware of the delicacy of the ground she was now venturing on to speak completely openly, 'we managed to get on reasonably well, before…'

'Before I made love to you?' Joel interrupted harshly, his face oddly drawn. 'Is that what you were going to say?'

It wasn't, but it would suffice. She had meant before she realised the truth about Marisa, but didn't want to say so. Her pride would not allow her to reveal to Joel how she felt about him, or how jealous she was of Marisa.

'Well if that is all that's worrying you, don't let it. From now on our relationship will be as sexless as that of brother and sister if that is what you want?'

For a moment Lissa almost hated him. What on earth did he expect her to do? Beg for his lovemaking? When she knew he loved someone else?

She turned her face away from him and said quietly, 'I don't think I need to answer that question, do I, Joel?'

She heard the door slam as he went out and only when she was quite sure he was gone did she release a shuddering breath of tension.

IN THE DAYS THAT FOLLOWED while it couldn't be said that there was a complete return to the easy fa-

miliarity that had developed between them in the
early days of their marriage, Lissa was conscious that
Joel was making an effort to put their relationship
back on a more relaxed footing.

Her pregnancy test had been confirmed as positive
and it was Joel who insisted on driving her to the
surgery and waiting with her until Dr Soames had
seen her.

The doctor was reassuringly matter of fact. 'I don't
envisage that you'll have any problems. The sickness
should start to wear off after the third month.' She
went on to discuss various aspects of pregnancy inviting Lissa to ask her as many questions as she cared
to. The birth would take place in the small local hospital which had its own maternity wing. 'You'll see
round that later,' Dr Soames told Lissa as she ushered
her towards the door. 'Don't forget, any problems...give me a ring.'

'I'd thought about taking you out to lunch—by way
of a small celebration,' Joel commented when Lissa
gave him the news, 'but somehow I didn't think it
would be what you wanted.'

Remembering how acutely nauseous she seemed to
be almost every time she ate, Lissa agreed, surprised
by the sudden withdrawal of his hand from her arm,
and the shuttered withdrawn expression on his face
throughout the drive back to Winterly.

It had been decided that the girls were too young
as yet to be told of her pregnancy at this early stage—
plenty of time for that later, Lissa suggested, wondering if now was a good opportunity to ask Joel

about redecorating the nursery, but he forestalled her by saying as he parked the car, 'I've been thinking that now you might want your own bedroom.'

He said it abruptly, and Lissa was conscious of a fierce stab of pain. No one knew better than she the loneliness of a double bed when both parties kept strictly to their own side, but to be banished to another room. She felt helplessly bereft, and said unsteadily, 'Don't you think it might seem rather odd…? Mrs Fuller…'

Joel shrugged. 'It's your decision Lissa, I was only thinking of you.'

She took a deep breath and without looking at him said quietly, 'Then I would prefer to continue as we are,' and before he could say anything she hurried past him and into the house, glad of the noisy attentions of the girls which put a stop to any further intimate conversation.

March died into April and April into May. Louisa had started playschool two mornings a week and Lissa drove her there. She had got to know a couple of the other mothers by sight and life seemed to have settled down into an uneventful routine. Joel was punctilious about returning home for dinner, and about spending most of the evening with her, but Lissa was finding herself increasingly tired at night, only too happy to go to bed early. What Joel did once she had, she daredn't even think about. If he went to Marisa, then she didn't want to know. She knew she was behaving like a coward, but she couldn't help it. To live with Joel as his wife knowing he didn't really love her was agony it was true, but to live without him…that would be sheer hell.

On the mornings she took Louise to playschool, Lissa normally also did whatever shopping was needed and then picked up the little girl in time to take her home for lunch. This particular Tuesday they were running a little late, as she had got involved in conversation with another mother.

As she walked into the house Lissa heard the telephone ringing, its sharp sound cut off as Mrs Fuller obviously answered it. As Lissa opened the kitchen door she heard Mrs Fuller saying, 'Mrs… Oh I'm afraid she's out at the moment.' She caught sight of Lissa and then corrected herself, 'No…she's just walked in.'

'Who is it?' Lissa mouthed as she took the receiver.

'A Mrs Andrews.'

The shock was so great that Lissa almost dropped the receiver. Since the night of the dinner party she had had no contact at all with Marisa. A cold finger of dread touched her heart. Had Joel told Marisa that she was pregnant? It was something she hadn't been able to bring herself to ask him.

Forcing herself to appear calm, she smiled into the receiver. 'Marisa?'

'Ah, Lissa. Good. Is Joel there?'

Lissa's fear grew. 'No, I'm afraid he's not.'

'Oh dear. I need to speak to him rather urgently. I've left Peter… It's been on the cards for quite some time of course. I should never have married him…*never*. But then one does such foolish things when one is young… Joel has always understood.'

A feeling of sick dismay was spreading through Lissa's body. Marisa had left Peter…and she was making it clear that she now wanted Joel… Shivering with reaction and sick misery, Lissa managed to say that she would pass her message on to Joel when he came in. The soft satisfaction purring through Marisa's voice tormented her, even when she had replaced the receiver.

'Lissa, are you all right?' Mrs Fuller's voice cut through her pain.

She managed to shake off the terrible feeling of pain consuming her, long enough to smile and fib, 'Yes…yes…fine… Just a little bit tired, I think I'll go upstairs and lie down for a while. If Joel comes in could you ask him to ring Mrs Andrews. She wants to speak to him.'

Sleep was impossible, her thoughts a plunging chaos of pain and misery. She had little doubt in her heart that Joel would want to go to Marisa. How could he not do? But he was tied to her. She would have to let him go. How could she keep him married to her when she knew he loved and wanted someone else? While Marisa had been married their relationship might have stood some chance, but now… How could she face herself when she knew that she was the only thing standing between Joel and happiness?

But she was having his child. Her hand cupped her gently curved stomach protectively and deep shudders of anguish racked through her.

She heard Joel's car drive up and forced herself into the bathroom to wash the tear stains off her skin and make herself look presentable. Sooner or later she would have to face Joel, and it might just as well be sooner.

When she went downstairs the study door was open. Joel was standing behind his desk, just replacing his telephone receiver.

'Did you get the message from Marisa?'

How empty and toneless her voice sounded, completely in contrast with the wild fever of emotions inside her.

'Yes, I've just rung her. I'm going to see her this afternoon.' He was frowning, and in the midst of her own anguish Lissa could still feel pain for him. How much he must be regretting now that he had ever married her...ever made love to her.

'Mrs Fuller said you weren't feeling well?'

'Just a little tired.' She smiled, hoping he wouldn't notice how plastic a gesture it was. Her face felt as stiff as a mask, her skin drawn too tightly over her bones.

She spent the afternoon with the girls. Emma was growing up quickly and both of them now called her 'Mummy' quite naturally. How would they react to another upheaval in their lives? How would she feel if Joel took them away from her? Tears stung her eyes, and she blinked them away, but not before Louise's sharp eyes had spotted them. 'You're crying,' she accused, and watching the apprehension dawn in the childishly rounded eyes, Lissa sought to reassure her. 'No, I've just got something in my eye,' she fibbed, distracting her attention, but reaching for one of their colourful nursery books and offering to read to them.

It was Mrs Fuller's evening off, and suspecting that it would be some time before Joel returned—after all he and Marisa would have a good deal to talk about—Lissa ate with the girls.

Once they were in bed she wandered restlessly round the sitting room switching on the television but too tense to really watch it.

It was just gone eight when Joel walked in. He looked tired...almost to the point of exhaustion, she thought as he sank down into a chair.

When she asked him what he wanted to eat he shook his head. 'I ate with Marisa.' He was curt and withdrawn, and although she longed to reach out to him...to help him, Lissa admitted with a surge of bitterness that comfort from her was not what he wanted.

His silent, withdrawn mood lasted for several days and then one night just as Lissa was preparing for bed, he walked into their room and said abruptly, 'Lissa, I have to talk to you.'

This was it! The moment she had been dreading ever since Marisa told her she had left her husband. If she was any sort of woman at all Lissa thought bitterly, she herself would have already faced Joel and had the pride to tell him that she was leaving, but she had just not been able to do it.

She had already showered and was in her night-dress, and at the cold shiver of apprehension that ran through her body Joel frowned, reaching for his own robe which he handed to her, with a curt, 'You're cold, put this on.'

The scent of him clung to the fine silk, making her shiver more.

She hadn't missed the way he had recoiled from her when their hands had accidentally made contact.

'Lissa, we can't go on as we are doing at present.' He had his back to her, and she was bitterly conscious of the tension inside him. One half of her, because she loved him, sympathised with the agony he was going through the other half, again because she loved him urged her to cover her ears, to shut out whatever painful truths he was now going to tell her.

'It isn't fair on you and it isn't fair on the girls...' His words made her mouth tighten bitterly. Whatever she had thought of him she had never considered him the sort of man who would make excuses...avoid the truth. What he should be saying was that he could no longer endure living with her and not with Marisa, but she didn't interrupt him.

'I know we said we'd make a fresh start—but then I didn't realise...' He turned towards her and the white torment of his face shocked her. Instinctively she stepped towards him intent only on comforting him, immediately falling back as she saw the shutters come down, blocking her out, warning her against going to him.

'Well that doesn't matter...what I'm trying to say to you is that for all our sakes, I've decided it would be best if we lived apart. I want you and the girls to stay here. I'll move out…and of course I'll continue to see the girls…and…and our child…'

'Just as long as you don't have to see me as well,' Lissa managed huskily, turning away from him so that he wouldn't see her tears.

'For God's sake don't make this harder for me than it already is!' She could feel the anguish within him, see it as his body literally shook with tension. His face was white and drawn, his eyes glittering febrilely.

What could she say? How could she plead with him to stay when she knew that he didn't love her.

'I know this whole situation is my fault,' he said bitterly. 'I'm the one who carries all the blame. I forced you into marriage with me. I was arrogant and stupid enough then to think I could make it work. I was even arrogant enough to believe that I could—' He broke off and stared into space for several seconds before demanding huskily, 'Just tell me one thing Lissa, that first time I made love to you…I…'

'You were acting on purely humane grounds?' Lissa supplied for him emotionlessly. 'You were trying to make me feel like a woman and not a child because you felt you had some sort of responsibility towards me? Yes, Joel I realise all that.'

For a moment there was silence and then he asked jerkily, as though unable to suppress the question, 'And did I Lissa…did I make you feel like a woman?'

She could see that he was suffering and all her love for him welled up inside her. 'Yes,' she admitted softly. 'Yes, Joel you did.'

She moved towards him again and he stepped back awkwardly, the first movement she had ever seen him make that wasn't completely coordinated. 'For God's sake don't touch me.' The harsh demand splintered her self-control, wiping her face clean of the mask of calmness she had assumed; pain registering in her eyes, her fingers curling closed as she cringed back from him and stumbled towards the door.

'Lissa. No…no…!' Joel reached the door before her, his arm barring her flight. 'I'm sorry…' He leaned against the door and dropped his head into his hands. 'I didn't mean…don't look at me like that. I'm sorry… It's all my fault, but I genuinely did think we could make it work. I knew when I married you that you didn't love me, but I felt sure there was some spark of desire…something we could build on, and then when I discovered the truth… It was arrogant and unforgivable of me to believe that because I was your first lover I could use that to tie you to me. Look…' He straightened up and looked at her. 'I can't take any more right now. These last weeks…living with you, sleeping next to you at night…' A slow shudder tore through his body. 'I just can't do it any more. If I stay there's no way I'm going to be able to stop myself from making love to you…no way at all.'

Lissa stared at him unable to believe her ears. *Joel* was saying he wanted *her?* But he loved Marisa, an inner voice warned her. She ignored it, filled with sudden feminine power, moving towards him until she was close enough to touch him, placing her palms against his chest, feeling the uneven drum-beat of his heart.

'Lissa.' He groaned her name, burying his face in her hair, his arms coming round her, imprisoning her against his body. His mouth found her throat and explored the satin soft skin roughly, passion bringing a hectic throb to his pulse. He raised his head reluctantly and looked at her, his eyes glittering fiercely. 'I want you, Lissa,' he told her rawly, 'and if you don't stop me now... If you don't send me away, there's no way I'm going to be able to stop myself from touching you. For years I've wanted you...alternated between desire and dislike for you. Did you know that?'

Lissa shook her head, quivering as his mouth feathered across her cheek and touched the corner of her own.

'We hardly ever saw one another,' she managed to croak, unable to believe what she was hearing.

Joel laughed harshly. 'Because I took great care that we should not. It appalled me that I should be attracted to you, especially knowing what I did about you. Me...a man going on twenty-three had fallen head over heels in love with a promiscuous child of fifteen.'

'What?' Lissa pulled away from him to look at him. 'But, Joel.'

'Ridiculous I know, and I soon managed to convince myself that I was imagining it. I pushed you out of my mind...told myself I was suffering from some sort of delayed adolescent crush, but when John and Amanda died and I was faced with the prospect of seeing you marry someone else I knew I couldn't let it happen. I wanted you for myself, and so I used the threat of taking the children away from you...'

She was quivering with a strange sensation of everything being totally unreal. Joel in love with her? She couldn't believe it...and besides...

'But Marisa,' she managed to demand. "What about Marisa?'

He frowned down at her. "What about her?'

'I thought...you...she...I thought you were lovers,' Lissa told him quietly, 'I also thought tonight you were trying to tell me you wanted to leave me so that you could be with her.'

His stunned incredulity might have been almost funny in other circumstances, but when Lissa thought of the agony she had put herself through believing him in love with the other woman she felt closer to tears than laughter.

'Marisa is the wife of a friend of mine and that's all,' he told her firmly. 'Okay, once I went out with her, and I agree she might sometimes have given the impression that there was more between us than there genuinely was, but that's all there is to it.'

'But you went to see her...'

'To help her sort out somewhere to live and give her some financial advice. I also suggested that she think again about leaving Peter.'

'But all those evenings when you went out...'

'I drove around in the car because it was the only thing I could think of to do to keep my hands off you.

Lissa, after I'd made love to you it suddenly struck me how selfish I'd been. You said I'd acted humanely. Well maybe you see it that way, I don't. I wanted to free you from the trauma of the past yes, but do you honestly think for one moment that if I hadn't loved you as much as I do that I would have done that by making love to you? Couldn't you tell when I touched you how I felt about you?' His hands cupped her face, his expression so tender, so revealing that her heart seemed to stop beating. 'I had to leave you alone after that night. I had to give you at least a chance to re-assess our relationship without the additional pressure of any sexual demands from me. I had to give you the opportunity to do at least some of the experimenting you never had the opportunity to do as a teenager. When I saw you with Greaves I feared the worst…and then when you didn't tell me you'd seen him.'

'It wasn't my meeting with Simon I was trying to hide from you,' Lissa admitted with a rueful smile, 'it was the fact that I'd gone especially to London to buy a new dress, purely because I wanted you to admire me in it. When I thought that Marisa was your mistress—the true love of your life, I couldn't bear to admit the truth to you in case you guessed…' She broke off, and Joel prodded softly.

'In case I guessed what?'

'That I love you.'

He studied her face silently for so long that she began to think she had imagined it all…that he didn't love her at all…that it was all a cruel trick but then he bent his head, his mouth gentle on hers, and then less gentle as he felt her response.

'I couldn't believe it when I found out you were carrying my child,' he told her huskily when he released her. 'I thought you must hate me because of it…because it would prevent you leaving me for Simon.'

'And I thought you would hate me because it would prevent you from going to Marisa,' Lissa admitted. 'You were so different from the ogre I'd always imagined you to be,' she told him dreamily. 'So tender and caring that how could I avoid falling in love with you? Then you changed, and reverted to the man I'd always thought you were. I thought it was your way of telling me that you did not want any emotional commitment from me. I thought you'd guessed how I felt about you, and that your coldness towards me was because you didn't want to encourage my feelings.'

'Whereas in reality it was directed at myself. The fact that I'd made love to you, quite deliberately…in the hope of making you want me physically and then emotionally, destroyed all the previously conceived notions I held about myself. In any other man I would have ruthlessly condemned what I had done.'

'You mean seducing me with champagne and kisses,' Lissa laughed softly and gave him a coquettish smile. 'Oh I don't know…' Happiness bubbled up inside her. 'I rather enjoyed it!'

'Oh did you indeed?'

There was nothing in the soft way he murmured

the words to cause her heart to jolt into an accelerated beat, but Lissa wasn't really listening to what he was saying, she was too busy looking into his eyes and reading the very private and explicit message they were holding for her.

Joel glanced at his watch and then smiled teasingly at her. 'It's just gone nine. Too early to go to bed, do you suppose?'

'Oh definitely!'

'Umm. Well then I shall just have to insist that we finish our fascinating discussion in the privacy of our own room. What do you say to that?'

'I say that it sounds like an extremely good idea,' Lissa confirmed innocently, teasing amusement gleaming in her eyes.

As he slipped his arm round her and propelled her towards the stairs she paused, watching the quick frown touch his forehead.

'Something wrong?'

''Nothing at all,' she assured him. 'I was just wondering if we had a bottle of champagne anywhere.'

# The Six-Month Marriage

# CHAPTER ONE

'SAPPHIRE, YOU HAVEN'T heard a word I've said. What's wrong?' Alan asked her.

The densely blue, dark lashed eyes that were the reason for Sapphire's unusual name turned in his direction, her brief smile not totally hiding the concern in their dark blue depths.

'I've had a letter from home this morning, and apparently my father isn't well.'

'Home?' Alan gave her a strange look. 'Funny, that's the first time I've heard you call it that in the four years that you've worked for me. Before it's always been Grassingham.'

Frowning slightly, Sapphire left her desk, pacing restlessly. It was true that in the four years she had worked in London she had tried to wipe her memory clean of as much of the past as she could, and that included any foolishly sentimental references to the border village where she had grown up as 'home', but in times of crisis, mental conditioning, no matter how thorough, was often forgotten. Her father confined to bed and likely to remain a semi-invalid for the rest of his life!

Unconsciously she stopped pacing and stared

through the large window of her office, but instead
of seeing the vista of office blocks and busy London
streets all she could see was her childhood home; the
farm which had belonged to many generations of
Bells and which had been handed down from father
to son from the time of Elizabeth the First. But of
course *her* father had no son to carry on farming the
land he loved, that was why… Sapphire gnawed
worriedly at her bottom lip. In the Borders people
adapted to social changes very slowly. Those who
lived there had a deeply ingrained suspicion of 'new
ideas', but had she wanted to do so, she knew that
her father would have encouraged her to undertake
the agricultural degree needed to successfully run a
farm the size of Flaws. However, although she had
grown up on the farm she had had no desire to take
over from her father.

Flaws valley was one of the most fertile in the
area, and should her father decide to sell, there
would be no shortage of buyers. But how *could* he
sell? It would break his heart. After her mother had
left him he had devoted himself exclusively to the
farm and to her. Her mother. Sapphire sighed. She
could barely remember her now, although she knew
that she looked very much like her.

It was from her American mother that she had
inherited her wheat blonde hair and long lithe body,
both of which were viewed with a touch of scorn in
the Borders.

'She's the looks and temperament of a race horse,'
one neighbour had once commented scornfully to her

father, 'but what you need for these valleys is a sturdy pony.'

Acutely sensitive, Sapphire had grown up knowing that the valley disapproved of her mother. She had been flighty; she had been foreign; but worst of all she had been beautiful with no other purpose in life but to *be* beautiful. Although she had been fiercely partisan on her father's behalf as a child— after all she too had shared his sense of rejection, for when her mother left with her lover there had been no question of taking a four-year-old child with her—older now herself Sapphire could understand how the valley had stifled and finally broken a woman like her mother, until there had been nothing left for her other than flight.

A farmer's hours were long hours, and her mother had craved parties and entertainment, whereas all her father wanted to do in the evenings was to relax. Her mother was dead now, killed in a car accident in California, and she... Despite the warmth of her centrally heated office Sapphire shivered. She knew she had never been wholly accepted by her peers in the valley and that was why she had responded so hungrily to whatever scraps of attention she had been given. A bitter smile curved her mouth and she looked up to find Alan watching her worriedly.

Dear Alan. Their relationship was such a comfortable one. She enjoyed working for him, and after the emotional minefields she had left behind her when she left the valley, his calm affection made her feel secure and relaxed. Their friends looked on them as an established couple although as yet they weren't lovers, which suited Sapphire very well. She wasn't sure if she was strong enough yet to involve herself too intimately with another human being. As she knew all too well, intimacy brought both pleasure and pain and her fear of that pain was still stronger than her need of its pleasure. Divorce was like that, so other people who had been through the same thing told her. Along with the self-doubts and anguish ran a deep current of inner dread of commitment.

'Alan, I'm afraid I'm going to have to ask for time off so that I can go and see my father.'

'Of course. If we weren't so busy, I'd drive you up there myself. How long do you think you'll need? We've got quite a lot to get through before the end of the month and we're away for all of March.'

Alan's small import business had been very successful the previous year and he was rewarding himself and Sapphire with a month's holiday cruising round the Caribbean; an idyll which Sapphire sensed would culminate in them becoming lovers. Without saying so outright Alan had intimated that he wanted to marry her. Her father seemed to have sensed it too because in his last letter to her he had teased her about the 'intentions' of this man she wrote about so often. She had written back, saying that they were 'strictly honourable'.

'Don't worry too much.' Alan comforted, misunderstanding the reason for her brief frown. 'If your father's well enough to write...'

'He isn't.' Sapphire cut in, her frown deepening.

'Then who was the letter from?'

'Blake.' Sapphire told him brittly.

When Alan's eyebrows rose, she added defensively, 'He and my father are very close. His land runs next to Flaws Farm, and his family have been there nearly as long as ours. In fact the first Sefton to settle there was a border reiver—a supporter of Mary Queen of Scots, who according to local rumour managed to charm Elizabeth enough to be pardoned.'

'Do you still think about him?'

For a moment the quiet question threw her. She knew quite well who the 'him' Alan referred to was, and her face paled slightly under her skilful application of makeup. 'Blake?' she asked lightly, adopting the casual tone she always used when anyone asked her about her ex-husband. 'We were married when I was eighteen and we parted six months later. I don't think about him any more than I have to, Alan. He was twenty-six when we were married, and unlike me he knew exactly what he was doing.'

'I hardly recognise you when you talk about him,' Alan murmured coming across to touch her comfortingly. 'Your voice goes so cold...'

'Perhaps because when I talk about Blake that's how I feel; terribly cold, and very, very old. Our marriage was a complete disaster. Blake was unfaithful to me right from the start. The only reason he married me was because he wanted Flaws' land, but I was too besotted—too adolescently infatuated with him to see that. I thought he loved me, and discovering that he didn't...'

She shuddered, unable to go any further; unable to explain even now the terrible sense of disillusionment and betrayal she had experienced when she discovered the truth about her marriage. It was four years since she had last seen her father, she reminded herself, mainly because she had refused to go home and risk meeting Blake, and her father had been too busy with the farm to come to London to see her. And now this morning she had received Blake's letter, telling her about the pneumonia that had confined her father to bed.

A terrible ache spread through her body. It hurt to know that her father had been so ill and she had not known. He had not written or phoned to tell her. No, that had been left up to Blake, with the curt p.s. to his letter that he thought she should come home. 'Although he doesn't say so, I know your father wants to see you,' he had written in the decisive, black script that was so familiar to her—familiar because of that other time she had seen it; the day she had discovered the love letter he had written to one of his other women. The tight ball of pain inside her chest expanded and threatened to explode, but she willed it not to. She had already endured all that; she wasn't going to allow it to return. There was a limit to the extent of mental agony anyone could be expected to suffer, and she had surely suffered more than her share, learning in the space of six months that the husband she worshipped had married her simply because he wanted her father's land, and that he had not even respected their marriage vows for a week of that marriage. While he left her untouched save for the brief kiss he gave her each morning as he left the farm, he had been making love to other women; women to whom he wrote intensely passionate love letters—love letters that had made her ache with longing; with pain; with jealousy. Even now she could still taste the bitterness of that anguished agony. She had gone straight from discovering the letters to her father, complaining that she did not believe that Blake loved her. Not even to him could she confide what she had found, and when he questioned her, she had simply told him of Blake's preoccupation; of his darkly sombre moods, of the little time he spent with her. 'I don't know why he married me,' she had cried despairingly, and her father taking pity on her had explained how worried he had been about the future of the farm once he was gone, and how he and Blake had agreed on their marriage, which was more the marriage of two parcels of land than two human beings.

She hadn't told her father about discovering Blake's infidelities, and for the first time in her life she had truly appreciated how her mother must have felt. From that to making the decision to leave Flaws valley had been a very short step. Blake had been away at the time buying a new ram and she vividly remembered, tiptoeing downstairs with her suitcase and out through the large flagged kitchen, leaving a note for him on the table. In it she had said simply that she no longer wanted to be married to him. Her pride wouldn't let her write anything else, and certainly nothing about Miranda Scott who had been one of Blake's regular girlfriends before he started dating her. She had bumped into Miranda in the library and the other girl had eyed her tauntingly as she told her about the night she had spent with Blake the previous week. Blake had told her that he was buying fresh stock and that he would have to stay in the Cotswolds overnight.

She had asked if she could go with him, thinking that away from the farm she might find it easier to talk to him about her unhappiness with their marriage. In the months leading up to it she had been thrilled by the way he kissed and caressed her and had looked forward eagerly to their wedding night, but she had spent it alone as she had all the nights that followed, and that had been one of the most galling things of all, the fact that her husband didn't find her attractive enough to want to make love to her.

But he found Miranda attractive—so attractive that he had taken her to the Cotswolds with him.

At first when she reached London she had used an assumed name, terrified that Blake would try to find her, and terrified that if he did, she wouldn't have the pride or strength of will to refuse to go back to him. Not that she was under any illusions any more that he wanted her. No, he wanted her father's land!

Those first six months in London had been bitterly lonely. She had drawn all her money out of her bank account before leaving the valley and there had been enough to support her for the first three months while she took a secretarial course. Her first job she had hated, but then she had found her present job with Alan. She had also enough confidence by then to find herself a solicitor. She could have had her marriage annulled—after all it had never been consummated—but she hadn't wanted anyone to know the humiliating truth—that her husband hadn't found her attractive enough to want to consummate it—so instead she had patiently waited out the statutory time before suing for divorce. She had half expected, even then, some reaction from Blake but there had been none and their divorce had become final just five months ago.

Sapphire had been in London seven months before she wrote to her father. Before leaving the valley she had posted a letter to him telling him she was leaving Blake, and saying that nothing would make her come back.

With hindsight she could see how worried her father must have been when he didn't hear from her, but at the time she had been so concerned with protecting herself both from Blake and from her own treacherous emotions that she hadn't been able to think past them.

''Do you plan to drive North, or will you go by train?'

Jerked out of her reverie by Alan's voice Sapphire forced herself to concentrate. 'I'll drive,' she told him. 'There isn't a direct train service and driving will save time.'

'Then you'd better take my car,' Alan told her calmly, 'I wouldn't feel happy about you driving so far in yours.'

It was true that her battered VW had seen better times, and Sapphire felt the same warm glow she always experienced when Alan was so thoughtful. Being married to him would be like being wrapped in insulating fibre; protected. Protected from what? From her past? From her foolish adolescent craving for the love of a man who was simply using her? That's all over now, Sapphire told herself sharply. Blake means nothing to me now. Nothing at all.

'Look, why don't you go home now and get yourself organised,' Alan suggested. 'You're too strung up to be much use here, and you'll need an early start in the morning. Here are my car keys.' He frowned. 'No, I'll go and fill the tank up first. That should be enough to get you all the way there. And when you arrive, 'phone me won't you? I wish there was some way I could come with you.'

'Dear Alan.' Sapphire rested her head against his shoulder—a rare expression of physical affection for her. 'You're so good to me.'

'Because you're worth being good to,' Alan retorted gruffly. Expressions of emotions always embarrassed him, and as she withdrew from him Sapphire wondered why she should remember so clearly the sensual seduction of the words Blake had written; words which still had the power to move her even now, and yet Blake too was a man of few words, but then unlike Alan, Blake's words were always pithy and to the point. Blake deplored waste of any kind; a true Sefton; and yet there was something about him that had always attracted and yet frightened her. He had spent several years in the army after leaving university. Perhaps that was where he had developed that hard veneer that was so difficult to get past. Sapphire knew that he had been posted to Northern Ireland, and yet his experiences there were something he never did discuss—not even with her father. When she had commented on it once, her father had simply said, 'There are some things a man can't endure to remember, and so for the sake of his sanity he forgets them. War is one of them.'

AN HOUR LATER, gripping the cord of the telephone receiver as she waited for someone to answer the 'phone, she felt her stomach muscles contract with tension. According to Blake's letter her father didn't know he had written, so she must try to pretend that she knew nothing of his illness. The ringing seemed to last for ever, and for one dreadful moment Sapphire pictured her father lying in bed, listening to the demanding sound, too ill to do anything about it, but then the receiver was lifted, the ringing abruptly cut off. Relief made her voice hesitantly husky, 'Dad, it's Sapphire.'

The cool male voice, edged with taunting mockery, wasn't her father's, and the tiny hairs on her arm stood up in prehensile alarm as she recognised it.

'Blake?'

'How very flattering that you should recognise my voice so quickly after all this time.'

'They say people always remember anything connected with acute trauma,' Sapphire snapped sharply. 'Blake, I've got your letter. My father, how is he?'

'Why don't you come home and see for yourself, or are you still running scared?'

'What of? You? Of course I'm coming h...back, but I can hardly arrive without warning Dad to expect me.'

'Very thoughtful. Giving him time to kill the fatted calf is that it? I take it you're coming alone,' he added, before she could respond. 'Flaws Farm only has three bedrooms remember; your father's in one, his housekeeper's in the other, and I'm sure I don't need to tell you how the valley will feel about one of its daughters openly co-habiting with a man she isn't married to—to say nothing of your father's feelings.'

Gritting her teeth Sapphire responded. 'I'm coming alone, but only because Alan couldn't make it. Now may I please speak to my father?'

It was only when Blake put the receiver down that she realized she hadn't asked him what he was doing at Flaws Farm. He had sounded very much at home, and she bit worriedly at her bottom lip. She had forgotten how freely Blake was used to coming and

going in her old home, and if she was forced to endure the constant sight of him how would it affect
the calm control she had sheltered behind for so
long?

It won't affect it at all, she told herself angrily.
Why should it? Blake had effectively killed whatever
feelings she had had for him—and they had only
been infatuation—a very deep and intense infatuation agreed, but infatuation nevertheless...

Five minutes later she was speaking to her father,
unable to stop the weak tears rolling down her face.
Normally they only rang one another at Christmas
and birthdays, and it shocked her to hear the hesi-
tancy in his voice.

'Blake tells me you intend paying us a visit?'

'If you've got room for me. I hear you've got a
housekeeper?' Sapphire responded drily.

'Yes, Mary Henderson. You probably remember
her from the old days. She used to nurse at the local
hospital. She was widowed a couple of years ago,
and her husband left a lot of debts, so she had to sell
her house and look for a job. Blake recommended
her to me. This is still your home Sapphire,' he
added in a different voice. 'There's always a room
for you here.'

Without saying it he was making her aware of all
the times she should have gone home and hadn't,
because she hadn't been able to conquer her weakness; her fear of meeting Blake, and discovering that
she wasn't as strong as she had believed. What was
she really frightened of though? Blake seducing her?

Hardly likely—after all he hadn't wanted her when they were married, so why should he want her now?

'Expect me late tomorrow evening,' Sapphire told him. 'Alan's lending me his car, because he doesn't think my old VW is reliable enough.' For some reason Sapphire found the silence that followed oddly disconcerting.

'You'd better use the top road,' her father said at last. 'They've been doing some roadworks on the other one and there've been traffic jams all week just this side of Hawick.'

Mentally revising her plans, Sapphire said her goodbyes. She had planned to drive up the M6 to Carlisle and then take the A7 through Hawick and Jedburgh, rather than using the 'top road' which was shorter but which meant driving along the narrow winding road which crossed and re-crossed the Cheviots.

That night, too wide-awake to sleep, she acknowledged that hearing Blake's voice had disturbed her—dangerously so. The sound of it brought back memories she had struggled to suppress; herself at fourteen watching with shy adulation while Blake worked. Fresh from university he had seemed like a god from Olympus to her and she had dogged his footsteps, hanging on to his every word. Was it then that he had decided to marry her? It was certainly then that he had started to put into practice the modern farming techniques he had learned partially at university and partially during his working holidays in New Zealand into force. Perhaps it was also then that he had first cast covetous eyes on Flaws Farm and mentally calculated the benefits to himself of owning its rich acres in addition to his own. She would never know, but certainly he had been kind and patient with her, carefully answering all her shy questions, tactfully ignoring her blushes and coltish clumsiness. She remembered practically falling off her pony one day straight into his arms, and how she had felt when they closed round her, the steady beat of his heart thumping into her thin chest. From that day on she had started to weave the fantasies about him that had taken her blissfully into their marriage.

At eighteen she had known very little of the world—had only travelled as far as Edinburgh and Newcastle and had certainly not got the sophistication to match Blake. He had left the valley when she was fifteen to join the army and had returned two years later the same and yet different; harder, even more sure of himself and possessed of a dangerous tension that sent frissons of awareness coursing over her skin whenever he looked at her.

The Christmas she was seventeen he had kissed her properly for the first time in the large living room of Sefton House—the large rambling building his great-grandfather had built when a fire had gutted the old farmhouse. There had been a crowd of people there attending a Boxing Day party and someone had produced a sprig of mistletoe. Even now she could vividly remember the mixture of anticipation and dread with which she had awaited Blake's kiss. She had known he *would* kiss her. He had kissed all the other girls, but the kiss he gave her was different, or so she had told herself at the time. Her first 'grown-up' kiss; the first time she had experienced the potency of sexual desire. His mouth had been firm and warm, his lips teasing hers, his tongue probing them apart.

Restlessly, Sapphire sat up in bed, punching her pillow. She must get some sleep if she was going to be fresh for her drive tomorrow. No doubt if Blake were to kiss her now she would discover that his kisses were nothing like as arousing as she remembered. She had been an impressionable seventeen-year-old to his twenty-five already halfway to worshipping him, and during the brief spring days he had cashed in on that adoration, until by summer he filled her every thought. He had proposed to her one hot summer's day beside the stream that divided Sefton and Bell land. Blake had wanted to swim, she remembered, in the deep pool formed by the waterfall that cascaded into it. She had objected that she hadn't brought her suit and Blake had laughed at her, saying that neither had he. She had trembled as revealingly as a stalk of wheat before the reaper, not troubling to hide her reaction. He had pulled her to him, kissing her; caressing her with what she had naively taken to be barely restrained passion. God how ridiculous she must have seemed. Blake's actions couldn't have been more calculated had they been programmed by computer, and whatever passion there had been had been for her father's lands and nothing else.

'DAMN BLAKE, this is all his fault,' Sapphire muttered direfully the next morning, as she ate a hurriedly prepared breakfast. Ten o'clock already, and
she had hoped to leave at eight, but she hadn't been
able to get to sleep until the early hours and then
when she had done she had slept restlessly, dreaming
of Blake, and of herself as they had been. Now this
morning there was a strange ache in the region of
her heart. She couldn't mourn a love she had never
had, she reminded herself as she had done so often
during those first agonising months in London, and
Blake had never loved her. It had been hard to accept
that, but best in the long run. She had once suffered
from the delusion that Blake loved her and the pen-
alty she had paid for that folly had warned her
against the folly of doing so again.

It was eleven o'clock before she finally managed
to leave. The day was crisp and cold, a weak sun
breaking through the clouds. February had always
been one of her least favourite months—Christmas
long forgotten and Spring still so far away, and she
was looking forward to her holiday. There was
something faintly decadent about going to the Caribbean in March.

A John Williams tape kept her company until she
was clear of the City. Blake had had very catholic
tastes in music and in books, but it was only since
coming to London that her own tastes had developed. Music was a key that unlocked human emotions she thought as she slowed down to turn the
tape over. Alan's BMW was his pride and joy, and

although she appreciated his thoughtfulness in lending it to her, she was slightly apprehensive with it.

She had planned to stop for lunch somewhere round Manchester, but oversleeping had altered her schedule, and she glanced at her watch as she travelled north and decided instead to press on to Carlisle and stop there.

She found a pleasant looking pub a few miles off the motorway and pulled up into the car park, easing her tired body out of the car. As she walked in the bar she felt the sudden silence descending on the room, and suppressed a wry grimace. She had forgotten how very conservative northern men were. Even now very few women up here entered pubs alone, but she shrugged aside the sudden feeling of uncertainty and instead headed for the bar, breathing in the appetising smell of cooking food.

The menu when she asked for it proved to be surprisingly varied. She ordered lasagne and retreated to a small corner table to wait for it to be served. While she waited she studied the people around her; mostly groups of men, standing by the bar while their womenfolk sat round the tables. So much for women's lib, she thought drily, watching them. If she had stayed at home she could well have been one of these women. And yet they seemed quite happy; they were fashionably dressed and from the snatches of conversation she caught even the married ones seemed to have jobs, which to judge from their comments they enjoyed.

A chirpy barmaid brought the lasagne and the cof-

fee she had ordered. The pasta was mouth-
wateringly delicious. She hadn't realised how hungry she had been, Sapphire reflected as she drank
her coffee, reluctant to leave the warmth of the pub
for the raw cold of the February night outside, but
she was already late. At last, reluctantly, she got up
and made her way to the car, unaware of the way
several pairs of male eyes followed her tall, lithe
body. She had dressed comfortably for the journey,
copper coloured cords toning with a coffee and copper sweater, flat-heeled ankle boots in soft suede
completing her outfit. She had always worn her hair
long, but in London she had found a hairdresser who
cared about the condition of his clients' hair and now
hers shone with health, curving sleekly down on to
her shoulders.

The BMW started first time, its powerful lights
picking out the faint wisps of mist drifting down
from the hills. Living in London insulated one from
the elements, Sapphire thought, shivering as she
drove out of the car park, and switched the car heater
on to boost. She had to concentrate carefully on the
road so that she didn't miss the turning which would
take her on to the 'top road' and she exhaled faintly
with relief when she found it. The mist had grown
thicker, condensation making it necessary for her to
switch on the windscreen wipers, the BMW's engine
started to whine slightly as the road climbed. She
had forgotten how quickly this road rose; the Cheviots were gentle hills compared with some, but they
still rose to quite a height. It was an eerie sensation

being completely alone on this empty stretch of road, her lights the only ones to illuminate the darkness of the bare hills. Here and there her headlights picked out patches of snow and then visibility would be obscured by the mist that seemed to waft nebulously around her.

Despite the heater she felt quite cold. Nerves, she told herself staunchly, automatically checking her speed as the mist started to thicken. Now she noticed with dismay the patches of mist were longer, and much, much, denser. In fact they weren't mist at all, but honest-to-God fog. It was freezing as well. She had thought it might be several miles back when she felt so cold, but now she felt the BMW's front wheels slide slightly, and tried not to panic. The BMW had automatic transmission, but there was a lower gear and she dropped into it, biting her lip as she crawled down a steep hill.

Nine o'clock! Her father would be wondering where on earth she was. Why hadn't she rung him from the pub and told him she was likely to be late? It was useless now chastising herself for not antici-pating adverse weather conditions. One of the first things she had learned as a child was not to trust the Border weather, but she had lived in London for so long that she had forgotten. She tensed as the BMW slid sickeningly round a sharp bend, blessing the fact that she had the road to herself. She ought never to have come this way. The traffic jams in Hawick would have been much preferable to this.

How many miles had she come? It felt like hun-

dreds, but it was probably barely ten, and it was at
least thirty to Flaws valley. She hadn't reached the
highest part of the road yet either.

Trying not to panic Sapphire concentrated on the
road, watching the thick grey film in front of her
until her eyes ached. The road had no central mark-
ings; no cat's eyes, and on several occasions she felt
the change in camber, warning her that she was veer-
ing too much to one side or the other.

It was a terrible, nightmare drive, and when the
road finally peaked, and she was out above the fog,
she trembled with relief. Snow still lined the road,
this high up, and the tarmac surface shone dull grey
with frost. She was over halfway there now.

Gradually the road started to drop down until she
was back into the fog. In her relief to be over the
top she had forgotten the sharpness of the bends on
the downward road. Several times she felt the BMW
slide as she cornered, and each time she prayed she
wouldn't panic, refusing to give in to the temptation
to brake, trying to steer the car into and then out of
the skid.

When she eventually saw the sign for Flaws
Valley she could hardly believe her own eyes! Ela-
tion made her weak with relief as her senses relayed
to her the familiarity of the straight road through the
village. Everything was in darkness. People in Flaws
village kept early hours. Most of them worked on
the land and there was nothing in the village to keep
them out late at night. And yet as she remembered
it she had never suffered from boredom as a teena-

ger; there had always been plenty to do. Harvest Festivals; Christmas parties and pantomime; summer haymaking; barbecues. Lost in her thoughts she turned instinctively into the road that ran past Blake's farm and then on to her father's. A wall loomed up in front of her with shocking suddenness, emerging from the mist, making her brake instinctively. She felt the car skid almost immediately, wrenching the wheel round in a desperate effort to avoid the wall. She felt the sudden lurch as the car left the road and came to rest with its front wheels in the ditch. Her head hit the windscreen, the pull of her seatbelt winding her. The shock of her accident robbed her of the ability to do anything but grasp the wheel and shiver. The front of the car had hit the wall. She had heard the dull screech of metal against stone.

She must get out of the car. Shakily she switched off the ignition and freed herself from her seatbelt. Her forehead felt cold and damp. She touched it, staring foolishly at the sticky red blood staining her fingers as she pulled them away. She had cut herself, but she could move, albeit very shakily. The car door opened easily and she stepped out on to the road, shuddering with shock and cold as the freezing air hit her. What next? She was approximately five miles from home and two from the village. Blake's house was half a mile up the road, but she couldn't go there. The village was her best bet. Shakily she started out, only to tense as she heard the sound of another vehicle travelling down the road. From the

sound of it, it was being driven with far more assurance than she had possessed. Its driver seemed to
know no fear of the fog or the ice. Instinctively Sapphire stepped back off the road, wincing slightly as
she realised she must have twisted her ankle against
the pedals. Bright headlights pierced the fog, and she
recognised the unmistakeable shape of a Land
Rover. It stopped abruptly by the BMW and the engine was cut. The driver's door jerked open and a
man jumped out. Tall and lean, his long legs were
encased in worn jeans, a thick navy jumper covering
the top half of his body. He walked towards the
BMW and then stopped, lifting his head, listening as
though he sensed something.

'Sapphire?'

Her heart thumping, her body tense Sapphire
waited. She had known him immediately, and was
shaken by her childish desire to keep silent; to run
from him.

''Sapphire?' He called her name again and then
cursed under his breath.

She was being stupid, Sapphire told herself, and
added to that she was beginning to feel distinctly
odd. Blake's shadowy figure seemed to shift in patterns of mist, the sound of her own heartbeats one
moment loud the next very faint.

'Blake...over here.' How weak her voice sounded
but he heard it. He came towards her with the cer-
tainty of a man who knows his way blindfolded. As
he got closer Sapphire could see the droplets of
moisture clinging to his dark hair. His face was

tanned, his eyes the same disturbing gold she remembered so vividly. He was so close to her now that she could feel his breath against her skin.

'So you decided to come after all.' He voice was the same; that slight mocking drawl which had once so fascinated her was still there. 'I began to think you'd chickened out... What's the boyfriend going to say when he knows you've ruined his car?'

Not one word of concern for her. Not one solicitous phrase; not one comforting touch...nothing. She knew she had to say something, but all she could manage was a pitiful sound like a weak kitten, her senses acutely attuned to everything about him. She could feel the leashed energy emanating from his body; smell the clean cold scent of his skin. She shivered feeling reality recede and darkness wash over her. As she slid forward she felt Blake's arms catch and then lift her.

'Well, well,' he murmured laconically. 'Here you are back in my arms. The last place you swore you'd ever be again. Remember?'

She tried to tell him that she had never been properly in his arms; that she had never known them as those of a lover, but it was too much effort. It was simpler by far to close her eyes and absorb the delicious warmth emanating from his body, letting her senses desert her.

# CHAPTER TWO

'COME ON SAPPHIRE, the shock can't have been that great.' The coolly mocking words broke against her senses like tiny darts of ice as she started to come round. She was sitting in a chair in the kitchen of Sefton House, and that chair was drawn up to the warmth of the open fire. The flames should have comforted her, but they weren't powerful enough to penetrate the chill of Blake's contempt. 'Flaws Valley females don't go round fainting at the first hint of adversity,' he taunted, watching her with a cynical smile. 'That's a London trick you've learned. Or was your faint simply a way of avoiding the unpalatable fact of our meeting?'

She had forgotten this side of him; this dangerous cynical side that could maim and destroy.

'I knew when I came up here that we were bound to meet, Blake.' She was proud of her composure, of the way she was able to meet the golden eyes. 'My faint was caused simply by shock—I hadn't expected the weather to be so bad.' She glanced round the kitchen, meticulously avoiding looking directly at him. She lifted her hand to touch her aching temple, relieved to discover the cut had healed. 'Don't worry,' Blake tormented, 'it's only a scratch!'

She had either forgotten or never fully realised, the intensity of the masculine aura he carried around him. It seemed to fill the large kitchen, dominantly. Droplets of moisture clung to the thick wool of his sweater, his hair thick and dark where it met the collar. His face and hands were tanned, his face leaner than she remembered, the proud hard-boned Celtic features clearly discernible.

The gold eyes flickered and Sapphire tensed, realising that she had been staring. 'What's the matter?' Blake taunted, 'Having second thoughts? Wishing you hadn't run out on me?'

'No.' Her denial came too quickly; too fervently; and she tensed beneath the anger she saw simmering in his eyes. The kitchen was immaculately clean; Blake had always been a tidy man but Sapphire sensed a woman's presence in the room.

'Do you live here alone?'

She cursed herself for asking the impulsive question when she saw his dark eyebrows lift.

'Now why should that interest you? As a matter of fact I do,' he added carelessly, 'although sometimes Molly stays over if it's been a particularly long day.'

'Molly?' She hoped her voice sounded disinterested, but she daren't take the risk of looking at Blake. What was the matter with her? She had been the one to leave Blake; she had been the one to sue for a divorce, so why should she feel so distressed now on learning that there might possibly be someone else in his life? After all he had never loved her.

Never made any pretence of loving her. But she had loved him…so much that she could still feel the echoes of that old pain, but echoes were all they were. She no longer loved Blake, she had put all that behind her when she left the valley.

'Molly Jessop,' Blake elucidated laconically, 'You probably remember her as Molly Sutcliffe. She married Will Jessop, but he was killed in a car accident just after you left. Molly looks after the house for me; she also helps out with the office work.'

Molly Sutcliffe. Oh yes, Sapphire remembered her. Molly had been one of Blake's girlfriends in the old days. Five years older than Sapphire, and far, far more worldly. She had to grit her teeth to stop herself from making any comment. It was no business of hers what Blake did with his life. As she had already told him she had known they would have to meet during her stay, but not like this, in the enforced intimacy of the kitchen of what had once been their home. Not that she had ever been allowed to spend much time in here. The kitchen had been the province of Blake's aunt, a formidable woman who had made Sapphire feel awkward and clumsy every time she set foot in it.

'What happened to your aunt?' she questioned him, trying not to remember all the small humiliations she had endured here in this room, but it was too late. They all came flooding back, like the morning she had insisted on getting up early to make Blake's breakfast. She had burned the bacon and broken the eggs while his aunt stood by in grim silence. Blake had pushed his plate away with his food only half eaten. She was barely aware of her faint sigh. The ridiculous thing had been that she had been and still was quite a good cook. Her father's housekeeper had taught her, but being watched by Aunt Sarah had made her too nervous to concentrate on what she was doing; that and the fact that she had been trying too hard; had been far too eager to please Blake. So much so that in the end her eagerness had been her downfall.

'Nothing. She's living in the South of England with a cousin. I'll tell her you've been enquiring about her next time I write,' Blake mocked, glancing at the heavy watch strapped to his wrist. 'Look I'd better ring your father and tell him you're okay. I'll run you over there in the morning and then see what we can do about your car.'

'No! No, I'd rather go tonight. My father's a sick man Blake,' she told him. 'I'm very anxious to see him.'

'You don't have to tell me how ill he is,' Blake told her explosively, 'I'm the one who told *you*— remember? Don't expect me to believe that you're really concerned about him Sapphire. Not when you haven't been to see him in four years.'

'There were reasons for that.' Her throat was a tight band of pain, past which she managed to whisper her protest.

'Oh yes, like you didn't want to leave your lover?' His lips drew back in a facsimile of a smile, the vulpine grin of a marauding wolf. 'What's the matter

Sapphire? Did you hope to keep your little affair a secret?'

'Affair?' Sapphire sat bolt upright in her chair.

'Yes…with your boss…the man you're planning to marry, according to your father. What took you so long?'

'It's only five months since I got the divorce,' Sapphire reminded him stiffly.

'But you could have got an annulment—much, much faster… Why didn't you? Or was it that by the time you realised that you could, that the grounds no longer existed?'

It took a physical effort not to get up and face him with the truth, but somehow she managed it.

'My relationship with Alan is no concern of yours Blake,' she told him coolly. 'I'm sorry I've put you to all this trouble, but I'd like to get to Flaws as soon as possible.'

'Meaning you'd like to get away from me as soon as possible,' Blake drawled. 'Well my dear that may not be as easy as you think. In fact I suspect that when I ring your father now and tell him you're here, he'll suggest you stay the night.'

'Stay the night? Here with you, when the farm's only five miles up the road, don't be ridiculous.'

She glared at him, her eyes flashing angrily.

'You know it's probably just as well that you and I have had this opportunity to talk Sapphire. Your father's perked up a lot since you told him you were coming back. He hopes you and I will bury our differences and get back together.'

Stunned, Sapphire could only stare at him. 'You must be mad,' she stammered at last. 'We're divorced…my father…'

'Your father is a very sick man, still as concerned about the future of his family's land as he was…'

'When you married me so that you could inherit it,' Sapphire broke in. 'You took advantage of my naiveté once Blake, but I'm not a seventeen-year-old adolescent in the grips of her first crush now. We're divorced and that's the way we're going to stay.'

'Even if that means precipitating your father's death?'

She went white with the cruelty of his words. 'His death, but…'

'Make no mistake about it, your father's a very sick man Sapphire. Very sick indeed, and worse, he's a man with no will left to struggle. You know that he's always wanted to see the two farms united. That was why he wanted us to get married in the first place.'

'If he's so keen for you to have the land, why doesn't he simply give it to you?' Sapphire asked him angrily.

'Because he wants to think some day that a child of ours—carrying his blood as well as mine—will inherit Bell land.'

'Oh so it isn't just marriage you want from me,' Sapphire stormed, 'it's a child as well? I wonder that you dare suggest such a thing when…'

'When?' Blake prodded softly when she stopped abruptly. 'When you couldn't bring yourself to touch me when we were married,' she had been about to say, but the pain of that time still hurt too much for her to be able to talk about it.

'When you know that I'm planning to marry someone else,' she told him coolly. 'Blake, I don't believe a word of what you've just said. My father must know that there isn't a chance of you and I getting together again. For one thing, there's simply nothing that such a relationship could offer me.'

'No.' His eyes fell to her breasts, and although Sapphire knew that the bulky wool of her jumper concealed them, she was acutely aware of a peculiar tension invading her body, making her face hot and her muscles ache.

'I would have said that being able to give your father a considerable amount of peace of mind would be a powerful incentive—to most daughters, but then you aren't like most daughters are you Sapphire?' he asked savagely. 'Or like most women for that matter. You don't care who you hurt or how much as long as you get what you want. Look, I don't want to be re-married to you any more than you want it, but I doubt it would be for very long.'

He watched her pale, and sway, with merciless eyes. 'Your father knows already how little time he's got, and whether you want to admit it or not he's very concerned about the future of his land—land which has been in his family as long as this farm has been in mine. Would it hurt either of us so much to do what he wants—to re-marry and stay together until...'

'Until he dies?' She hurled the words at him, shaking with pain and anger. 'And for how long do you estimate we should have to play out this charade Blake? You must know, you certainly seem to know everything else.'

'I was the closest thing to family he has left,' Blake told her simply, 'Naturally his doctor...' he broke off, studying the quarry tile floor and then raised his head and it seemed to Sapphire that she had been wrong in her original estimation that he hadn't changed. Now he looked older, harder, and she knew with an undeniable intuition that no matter what lies he might tell her about everything else, Blake did genuinely care for her father. Despair welled up inside her. Her father dying... Remorse gripped her insides, her throat tense and sore. She badly wanted to cry, but she couldn't let Blake see her break down.

'Six months or so Sapphire,' he said quietly at last. 'Not a lot to ask you to give up surely? And you have my word that afterwards...that we can part quickly and amicably. This time our marriage will be dissolved.'

'And the farm...my father's land?'

'I'd like to buy it from you—at the going rate of course, unless your London lover wants to try his hand at farming?'

Just for a moment Sapphire taxed her imagination trying to picture Alan leading Blake's life. Alan would hate it, and she couldn't keep on the farm and work it herself. Even so, all her instincts warned her against agreeing to Blake's suggestion.

'It's a ridiculous idea, Blake,' she told him at last, taking a deep breath.

'You mean you're too selfish to acknowledge its merits,' he countered. 'I thought you might have grown up Sapphire; might have come to realise that there are other things in life apart from the gratification of your own wants, but obviously I was wrong. Come on,' he finished curtly, 'I'll take you to Flaws.'

He strode across the kitchen, thrusting open the door without waiting to see if she was following him. Wincing as she got up from the ache in her ankle, Sapphire hobbled to the door. Cold air rushed in to embrace her in its frosty grip. Across the cobbled yard she could make out the bulky shape of the Land Rover. Blake opened the door and started up the engine. He must be able to see that she was having difficulty walking, Sapphire fumed as she was caught in the beam of the headlights, but he made no effort to help her.

It was only when she reached the Land Rover that he finally got out, walking round to the passenger side to open the door for her. When his hands suddenly gripped her waist she froze, her whole body tensing in rejection, her stiff, 'don't touch me,' making him tense in return. She could feel it in the grip of his fingers, digging through the wool of her jumper to burn into her skin. 'What the hell...' For a moment he seemed about to withdraw and then he spun her round, the proximity of his body forcing her back against the cold metal of the Land Rover. 'What is it you're so afraid of Sapphire,' he mocked, his gold eyes searching her too pale face. 'Not me, surely.' His eyes narrowed. 'As I remember it I barely touched you. So it must be yourself.'

'I'm not frightened of anything Blake,' she managed to reply coolly, still holding herself rigid within the grip of his hands. The warmth of his breath lifted her hair, and she was so acutely aware of him that it was a physical agony. Why, oh why had she come back? She had thought herself strong enough to cope, but she wasn't. Blake still had the power to upset and disturb her. He made her feel just as awkward and insecure as he had done when she was seventeen. 'I just don't want you touching me.'

'Frightened I might make you forget all about your London lover?' The soft goading tone of his voice was too much for her. Drawing in her breath on a sharp gasp she said coldly. 'That would be impossible.' She turned away as she spoke, leaning into the Land Rover. Blake's fingers continued to dig into her waist and then he was lifting her, almost throwing her into the seat with a force that jolted the breath from her body and made her aware of her aching bruises.

He didn't speak until he was in the Land Rover beside her, his eyes fixed on the fog-shrouded lane as he said softly, 'Don't challenge me Sapphire—not unless you want me to accept your challenge. You've come back from London with some fine

haughty airs, no doubt meant to keep country bump-
kins like myself in their place but it wouldn't take
much for me to forget mine Sapphire. There's one
hell of a lot of anger inside me towards you, and
believe me it would give me great pleasure to give
it release.'

Why should Blake be angry? Resentment burned
through Sapphire as they drove towards Flaws Farm.
She was the one who should be that; and not just
angry but bitter too. Blake had never wanted her; he
had callously used her adolescent adoration of him,
had ruthlessly exploited her feelings, and now he
was saying he was angry. He could say what he
liked, but there was no way she was going to agree
to his outrageous suggestion that they re-marry. Did
he think she was totally without intelligence? She
knew what he wanted well enough—the same thing
he had always wanted. Her father's land. The Seftons
and the Bells hadn't always been friendly to one another, and the border reiver had spawned a race of
men who all possessed his reckless touch of acquis-
itiveness. There had been several Seftons who had
cast covetous eyes on Flaws farm and thought to
make it theirs, but so far none had ever succeeded.

Now she was being foolish, Sapphire chided herself. Blake was no border reiver, for all that he had
inherited his wild ancestors' darkly Celtic looks, and
it was true that her father admired and respected him,
but surely not to the extent of wanting her, his
daughter, to put herself within his power once more?

Sapphire darted a glance at Blake. He was concentrating on his driving, his profile faintly hawkish, his hands assured and knowing as he turned the wheel. There was nothing indecisive or unsure about Blake, she acknowledged. That was what she had admired so much in him as a teenager, and even now, watching him she was conscious of a faint frisson of awareness, a purely feminine acknowledgement of his masculinity. Stop it, she warned herself as they turned into Flaws Farm Lane. Stop thinking about him.

When the Land Rover stopped, she glanced uncomfortably at him. 'Are you coming in with me?'

'Do you really want me to?' he asked mockingly, before shaking his head. 'No, unlike you Sapphire, I'm not hard enough to raise hopes in your father's heart that I can't fulfil. Your father means a lot to me,' he added, startling her with his admission. 'I've always admired him, even patterned myself on him as a youngster I suppose—my own grandfather was too cold and distant—he never ceased mourning my father. I'd give a lot to see your father happy.'

'And even more to make sure that you get Flaws land,' Sapphire threw at him bitterly, 'even to the extent of marrying me. I fell for it once Blake, I'm not going to fall for it again.'

It was only as she struggled across the yard that she remembered about her luggage, still in Alan's car. It was too late to turn around and call Blake back now, he was already reversing out of the yard. Sighing, Sapphire found the familiar back door and unlatched it. The kitchen was much as she remembered it. Her father used to employ a housekeeper to look after the house, but she had retired just after Sapphire's marriage. For a while he had managed with daily help from the village, but now it seemed he was employing someone else.

The door to the hall opened as Sapphire stepped into the kitchen and a woman entered the room. For a second they stared at one another and then the woman smiled tentatively, offering her hand. 'Mary,' she introduced herself, 'and you must be Sapphire. Your father's been worrying about you.'

There was just enough reproof in the calm, softly burred voice for Sapphire to flush and feel at a disadvantage. Mary was somewhere in her late thirties, plumpish with smooth brown hair and warm eyes. The sort of calm, serene, capable woman she had always envied.

'I'm sorry about that.' Quickly she explained how she had been delayed, warmed by the quick sympathy in the hazel eyes.

'May I see my father?' Sapphire asked tentatively. She had been nerving herself for this moment ever since Blake had told her the seriousness of her father's condition, and her palms were damp and sticky as she followed Mary up the familiar stairs. Her father's bedroom had windows that looked out over the hills, but tonight the curtains were drawn to obscure the view.

'It's all right Mary, you can switch the lamp on,' her father's familiar voice growled as Sapphire stood awkwardly by the door in the half light. 'I am awake.'

'Sapphire's here,' Mary told him, snapping on the bedside light. Perhaps it was the warm glow from the lamp but her father didn't look as ill as she had anticipated. Her legs felt shaky as she approached his bed, regret, guilt, and a dozen other emotions clamouring for expression. In the end all she could manage was a choked 'Dad,' and then she was in her father's arms, hugging him tightly, trying not to give way to tears.

'Well now, and how's my lass? Let me have a look at you.' As he held her slightly away from him, studying her features, Sapphire studied his. Her father had always had a tall, spare frame, but now he was gaunt, almost painfully thin, the weathered tanned face she remembered frighteningly pale—a sick-room pallor Sapphire acknowledged.

'Dad, if only I'd known…'

'Stop tormenting yourself, I wouldn't let Blake tell you. You're far too thin,' he scolded. 'Mary will have to feed you up while you're here. Borders' men don't like their women skinny.'

'But London men do,' Sapphire responded, withdrawing from him a little, sensing danger.

'You're later than we expected.'

'Umm, I had a slight accident.' Quickly she explained.

'You should have stayed overnight with Blake.'

'I'm sure neither Blake nor I would have felt comfortable if I had Dad,' she said quietly. 'We're divorced now.'

'More's the pity.' He frowned, the happiness fading from his eyes. 'You should never have left him lass, but then you were so young, and young things take things so seriously.'

If anyone had asked her only days ago if her father had accepted her divorce Sapphire would have had no hesitation in saying 'yes' but now, suddenly, she knew he had not. She looked away from the bed, blinking back tears she wasn't sure were for her father or herself. As she did so she saw Mary glance sympathetically at her.

'I'll run you a bath,' she offered, 'You must be exhausted.'

'Yes, you go along to bed,' her father agreed. 'We'll talk in the morning.' He closed his eyes, his face almost waxen with exhaustion and fear pierced her. Her father was going to die. Until now she hadn't truly accepted it, but suddenly seeing him, seeing his frailty she did. 'Dad, who's looking after the farm?' she asked him trying to force back the painful knowledge.

'Why Blake of course.' He looked surprised that she needed to ask. 'And a fine job he's doing of it too.'

Mary's hand on her arm drew her away from the bed. On the landing Sapphire turned to the older woman, unable to hold back her tears any longer. 'Why?'' she asked bitterly. 'Why did no-one tell me? Get in touch with me, I'd no idea...'

Shaking her head Mary gestured downstairs, not speaking until Sapphire had followed her down and they were back in the kitchen. 'Blake said not to,' she said quietly, 'he thought it best. At least at first.'

Blake had thought... Blake had said... Bitterness welled up inside her coupled with a fierce jealousy as she acknowledged something she had always kept hidden even from herself. Her father would have preferred a son...a male to continue the family line and although he loved her, it was to Blake that he had always confided his innermost thoughts, Blake who he thought of as a son...Blake who he turned to when he needed someone to lean on and not her.

'There, sit down and cry it all out,' Mary said gently. 'It must have come as a shock to you.'

'Is it true that...that my father...' Sapphire couldn't go on. Tears were streaming down her face and she dug in her jeans pocket for a handkerchief. 'He's been a very sick man,' Mary said compassionately, her eyes sliding away from Sapphire's. 'His heart isn't too strong and this bout of pneumonia, but having you home has given him a real fillip.'

'I never knew how he felt about the divorce until tonight.' Sapphire almost whispered the words, saying them more to herself than Mary, but the other woman caught them and smiled sympathetically. 'Blake means a lot to him,' she agreed, 'he thought that your marriage protected both you and Flaws land.'

'He worries a lot about the land doesn't he?' Sapphire's voice was unconsciously bitter.

'And about you,' Mary told her. 'The land is like a sacred trust to him and he has a strong sense of duty and responsibility towards it.'

'Strong enough to want to see Blake and me back together again?' Sapphire asked bleakly.

Mary said nothing, but the way her eyes refused to meet Sapphire's told her what she wanted to know.

'You obviously know my father very well,' she said quietly at last. 'He confides in you far more than he ever confided in me.'

'I'm a trained nurse,' Mary told her, 'and that is how I first came to know your father. When he was first ill he needed a full-time nurse. Dr Forrest recommended me, and your father asked me to stay on as his housekeeper-cum-nurse. The relationship between patient and nurse is one of trust. It has to be. I can't deny that your father, like many people of his generation, doesn't wholly approve of divorce, and he does feel that the land would be properly cared for by Blake, and...'

'And that if Blake and I had a son that son would inherit Flaws Farm and would also be half Bell.'

Sapphire sighed, suddenly feeling intensely tired. Too much had happened too soon, and she couldn't take it all in.

'There was a phone call for you,' Mary added, 'an Alan. I said you'd ring back in the morning.'

Alan! Sapphire started guiltily. She had almost forgotten about him, and even more unforgivably she had forgotten about his car. The BMW was Alan's pride and joy and he wouldn't be too pleased to hear about her accident.

Tomorrow, she thought wearily as she climbed into bed. Tomorrow she would think about what had happened. Somehow she would have to convince her father that there was no chance of her and Blake getting together again. Selfish, Blake had called her. Was she? Her father had very little time left to live…six months or so…if she re-married Blake she would be giving her father a gift of happiness and peace of mind which surely meant more than her own pride and freedom? She wasn't seventeen any more, held in thrall by her adoration of Blake. She could handle him now as she hadn't been able to do then. A six-month marriage which would be quickly annulled—six months out of her life as payment for her father's peace of mind. What ought she to do?

and Blake were parted for good. Even now she could still remember that agony of those first months in London, of having to come to terms with the truth about her marriage; about Blake's feelings for her. He had tolerated her because he wanted the farm. He had never loved her, never desired her and knowing that she had not seen these truths had diminished her self-esteem to such an extent that she had felt somehow as though everyone who saw her or spoke to her, must share Blake's opinion of her. The only way she could escape had been to shut herself off mentally from the rest of the world. There had been days when she felt like dying; days when she would have given anything simply not to wake up in the morning. But all that was past now, she reminded herself. She had overcome the trauma of Blake's rejection; had put the past and all that it held, safely behind her. But she couldn't forget it, she acknowledged. She still occasionally had those terrible dreams when she was forced to witness Blake making love to Miranda, when she had to endure the sound of their mocking laughter. How she had hated herself; *everything* about herself, from her height to the colour of her hair, torturing herself by imagining how many times Blake must have looked at her and put Miranda in her place. The only thing that surprised her was that Blake hadn't married. Those love letters she had found had obviously been meant for Miranda.

No-one, not even Alan knew how totally Blake had rejected her; physically, mentally and emotionally. And facing up to that knowledge had driven her almost to the point where she lost her sanity. But she had emerged from it all a stronger person. Being forced to come face to face with the truth had made her re-evaluate herself completely. No man would ever hurt her now as Blake had done. She allowed no-one to come close enough to her to do so.

If Alan did propose to her she would probably accept him. She wanted a family; she and Alan got on well. She would never feel for him what she had once felt for Blake, but then he would never look at her body, imagining it was another woman's, he would never lie to her, or look at her with contempt. Blake was an arrogant bastard, she thought bitterly as she stood at the top of the stairs, poised to enter her father's room. After what he'd done to her, she didn't know how he had the nerve to suggest what he had.

'Sapphire.' Her father greeted her happily, from his chair by the window. The cold March sunshine picked out with cruel clarity the signs of wasting on his face, and Sapphire was overwhelmed with a rush of emotion.

'Dad.' She went over to him, hugging him briefly and then turning away before he could see her tears.

'What's this?' Her eye was caught by the heavy, leather bound book on his lap. 'Don't tell me you're actually reading something, other than a farming magazine,' she teased. Never once during her childhood could she remember seeing her father reading. He had always been an active, physical man more at home in his fields than in the house. It saddened her unbearably to see him like this. Why...why? she cried bitterly inside.

'It's the family Bible.' His smile was as she had always remembered it. 'I haven't looked at it since your mother wrote your name inside.'

After her, her mother had not been able to have any more children. Had she too, like Sapphire, sensed how much her father felt the lack of a male heir? Had that in part contributed to the break-up of their marriage? Questions she would never know the answer to now, Sapphire thought dully, watching her father open the Bible.

His hand trembled slightly as he touched the old paper. 'This Bible goes back as far as 1823, and it lists the birth of every Bell since.' He gave a faint sigh and closed it. 'I had hoped I might see the name of your's and Blake's child added to that list, but now...' He turned away dejectedly.

The words Sapphire had intended to say died unspoken. A tight knot of pain closed her throat. She reached out her hand touching her father's shoulder, 'Dad...' He turned to look at her, and as though the words were coming from another person, she heard herself saying shakily, 'Blake and I are going to try again. I...we...we talked about it last night.' She looked out of the window without seeing the view. Could her father honestly believe that what she was saying was true? Perhaps not, but he would accept it *as* the truth because he wanted to believe it so desperately; just as she had once desperately wanted to believe that Blake loved her.

'You mean the two of you plan to re-marry?'

'We may…' What on earth had she got herself into? Panic clawed at her. She *couldn't* marry Blake again. But she had just told her father that she might.

'I suppose if we do it will make the local tongues wag.'

'Not necessarily. I don't think Blake's ever told anyone that you're divorced. Most people think you're still just separated.'

*Why* hadn't Blake told them? Could it be that he was using her father's illness as a lever to force her to fall in with his plans? He would buy the land from her, he had told her, but as her husband he wouldn't need to buy it, and being married to her need not stop him from finding love elsewhere. It hadn't stopped him before.

She *must* tell her father that she had changed her mind, she thought frantically, she must tell him now, before this thing went any further. Even now she couldn't believe that he was dying. He looked ill yes, but… But hadn't she learned the futility of self-deception yet?

'Dad…'

'Isn't that the Land Rover?' he asked interrupting her. 'Blake must have arrived.'

'Dad, I…'

Both of them turned at the sound of firm footsteps on the stairs, Sapphire unconsciously blending into the shadows of the room as the door was thrust open and Blake strode in. Strangely his eyes met hers almost immediately, as though he had known by instinct where she was.

'Blake, Sapphire's just told me the good news.' If she hadn't known better she might almost have believed the look the two men exchanged was one of complicity, but even as the thought formed it was gone as her father turned his head and the harsh light through the window made her acutely conscious of his illness.

'Has she now.' For a man who spent so much of his life outdoors Blake moved exceptionally gracefully, and far too swiftly. She had no opportunity to avoid him as he walked towards her, lean brown fingers curling round her upper arm. 'And do you approve?'

'Need you ask?'

'Not really.'

'I'm sure you two have lots to discuss.' Sapphire snapped out the words bitterly, resenting their male unanimity. 'I must go and telephone Alan. He doesn't know about his car yet.'

'Or about us,' Blake reminded her, and while the look in his eyes might have been mistaken for one of possessive hunger Sapphire knew it was for her father's land rather than for her.

Outside the room she paused on the landing feeling acutely sick. Why had she said what she had to her father? Heaven only knew, she didn't want to be married to Blake again, no matter how temporarily. And yet her father had been pleased; pleased and relieved and surely for six months... Gnawing on her bottom lip she walked down to the kitchen and picked up the 'phone. Alan answered almost straight away.

'Where've you been?' he demanded. 'I expected you to ring hours ago.'

'I overslept I'm afraid. Alan, I had an accident last night and damaged your car.' She waited for his anxious spate of questions to finish before explaining what had happened. 'Don't let them touch the car—these country garages, God alone knows what sort of damage they might do. I'll come up and sort it out myself.'

'Alan no…' Sapphire started to say, but it was too late. 'Look I've got to go,' he told her before she could continue. 'I've got an appointment. I'll be up as soon as I can—possibly in three or four days.'

'Everything okay?' Mary nodded to the kettle. 'Fancy a drink? I normally take one up to your dad about now.'

'No…no thanks, I think I'll go out for a walk.'

'Well, don't go too far,' Mary cautioned her. 'The temperature's dropping and we might well have snow. Snow in March isn't uncommon up here,' she reminded Sapphire dryly when she raised her eyebrows. 'Many a farmer's lost a crop of newborn lambs to the weather. *You* should know that.'

She needed time to think, Sapphire acknowledged as she walked into the cobbled yard and through into the field beyond; time to come to terms with what she herself had set in motion. She couldn't back out now; that much was plain. How could she have been so stupid as to allow Blake to manoeuvre her into this situation?

But it hadn't been Blake's logical, reasoned arguments that had won her over, it had been her father's pain. Guilt was a terrible burden to carry. She shivered suddenly, conscious that her jumper was no real protection against the bitter east wind, but she wasn't ready to go back to the farm yet. Going back meant facing Blake; and that was something she wasn't ready for yet. But she couldn't avoid him forever, and it was getting colder. Reluctantly she turned and re-traced her steps but when the farm came in sight and she saw that the Land Rover was still there, instead of heading for the house she walked towards the large attached barn.

In the days when Flaws Farm had possessed a small dairy herd this barn had housed them but now it was empty apart from the farmyard hens whose eggs were purely for domestic use. She had kept her pony, Baron, in here and had spent many hours grooming him, preparing him for local agricultural shows. They had even won a couple of prizes. Sighing faintly she wandered deeper into the barn stopping beside the ladder into the hayloft. As a teenager she had retreated up there to read and daydream. The sound of familiar footsteps made her body tense. Even without turning round to look she knew who it was.

'Something told me you might be in here.' Blake's voice was mocking. 'You always did use it as a bolt-hole.'

She turned round, trying to blank all emotion out of her features, while Blake studied her with a slow, insolent appraisal that set her teeth on edge. Inwardly shaking with nerves she refused to let him see how much his presence disturbed her. 'Finished?' she asked sourly. 'What exactly were you doing Blake?'

'Just wondering why you choose to wear such masculine clothes.' It was a blatantly challenging statement when coupled with his open study of her, and to her resentment she knew she had already been betrayed into a response to it, even if it was only in the increased stiffening of her muscles.

'These happen to be the only clothes I had this morning. No doubt you like your women dulcet and feminine, compliant and obedient, but I'm not like that Blake. Not any more.'

'No, you're not are you?' There was just a suspicion of laughter trailing in his voice, enough to make her stare back at him aggressively and refuse to give way as he came towards her. 'I also like them aroused and responsive—just as you are at the moment.'

The explosive denial trembling on her lips died as he reached forward, his thumb stroking along her throat to rest on the point where her pulse thudded betrayingly. 'Anger is a form of arousal isn't it?' he mocked lightly. 'And you *are* angry with me, aren't you Sapphire?'

'Not as much as I am with myself,' she told him curtly, drawing away. She wasn't going to give

Blake any advantages this time. 'What I said to you last night still holds good, I don't want to marry you.'

'But you told your father that you did.'

'No. I told him that I *was* doing. I didn't mean to, but before I could retract you arrived.'

'And now?' He asked the question softly, watching her with eyes that gave nothing of his own feelings away.

'I'll have to go through with it—you know that. You saw how he reacted. Dear God, even now I can't believe that I'm going to lose him.' She paced distractedly, too strung up to give way to tears and yet needing to release some of her nervous energy.

'And what about the boyfriend—have you told *him*?'

'Alan? No…not yet, but he's coming up for his car soon, I'll tell him then.'

'How soon is soon?' Blake asked idly. 'Because in three days' time we'll be married.'

Three days! She looked up at him not even attempting to hide her shock. 'So soon?'

Blake shrugged his shoulders and against her will Sapphire found herself comparing the masculine breadth of them to Alan's. Even dressed in faded jeans and an old woollen checked shirt Blake possessed a lithe masculine sensuality that Alan would never have, for all his expensive tailoring Alan believed that appearances were important and Sapphire wouldn't have denied it, but Blake was one of those men who could afford to break life's rules. Angrily she pushed the thought away.

'Why wait?' Blake asked laconically. 'The sooner it's done the happier your father will be.'

'He told me that most people up here don't even know that we're divorced.' Her voice gave away her anger.

'Most people? No-one knows,' Blake corrected, blandly.

'Not even Miranda?'

His eyebrows rose, and Sapphire felt her face flush. What on earth had possessed her to bring Miranda's name up? She had no interest in Blake's love life—it was his own affair.

'Why mention Miranda in particular?' Blake mocked.

'Perhaps because it's the sort of thing a man would tell his mistress,' Sapphire came back curtly. 'After all you told her that our marriage...wasn't consummated.'

'How do you know that?' His voice had sharpened, hardened almost, but he had turned slightly away so that Sapphire couldn't see his expression, but she had definitely caught him off guard. Good, she thought, watching him. Obviously he didn't know what Miranda had said to her.

'Because she told me.' She shrugged disdainfully as he turned round and stared at her with cold hard, golden eyes. 'It was at the same time as she told me about the weekend the two of you spent in the Cotswolds actually.' Giving him a cold smile she marched past, heading for the barn door. It would do him good to realise that she wasn't as naive as he had always believed, but just as she drew level with the door his arm snaked out, his fingers curling painfully round her wrist.

'And that, of course, was why you left me?'

'It was *one* of the reasons—there were others.' It was her turn to shrug dismissively. 'But none of that matters now, I merely asked about Miranda so that I could be prepared for any situation that might arise.'

'She doesn't know we're divorced,' Blake told her. 'After my experiences with you I decided I preferred the life of a bachelor.'

'And having a wife tucked away in the background made it all a lot simpler. Yes I can see that. Let me go Blake, I want to go back to the house.'

'Isn't there something you've forgotten?'

She frowned, glancing uncertainly at him.

'Loving partners normally part with a kiss,' he told her mockingly.

'Maybe *they* do, but there's nothing "loving" about our relationship,' Sapphire snapped. 'You didn't want to kiss me four years ago Blake, I can hardly see why you would want to now.'

'No? Perhaps I want to see how much your London lover has taught you.' His head bent towards her and Sapphire immediately tensed trying to pull away, but Blake was still gripping her wrist. His free arm fastened round her, his hand on the small of her back forcing her against him.

A mixture of sensations raced through her as the heat of his body imposed itself against her; anger; tension, but most of all a resurgence of a familiar vulnerability she thought she had long ago overcome. The knowledge that she hadn't, blinded her to everything else. She trembled against Blake, closing her eyes to blot out his mocking smile trying to convince herself that she was wrong; that the panic storming through her came from anger and not from fear.

But what was it she feared? Not Blake. No, herself, she admitted sensing the downward descent of his mouth, and twisting away to avoid it. Not Blake, but herself, her vulnerability towards him; her...

His mouth brushed hers and she tensed. 'Is that *all* you've learned? Not very good,' Blake drawled, as his mouth moved from her lips to her ear. His tongue tip explored the delicate shaping of her ear and panic exploded inside her. She mustn't let him do this to her, she... Another moment and he would be kissing her again and this time... No she wouldn't let him see that he could evoke a response from her...a response that was really surely nothing more than a conditioned echo of the old feeling she had had for him?

His mouth was feathering across her skin towards her lips. Taking her courage in both hands, Sapphire turned to meet it, willing herself to relax. She had dated several men in London before settling for Alan, and surely she had learned enough technique from them to show Blake that she wasn't a frightened seventeen-year-old any more.

Forcing herself to ignore the screaming protest of her nerves Sapphire opened her mouth inviting his deeper invasion, teasing him with the tip of her tongue. She actually felt the sudden tension in his muscles, the quickly controlled start of surprise, but her brief advantage was lost as Blake's arms tightened around her, his mouth taking what she had so recklessly offered, his lips harshly possessive against hers.

If only he had kissed her like this when she was seventeen. The thought surfaced through a whirling jet-stream of jumbled emotions, fiercely clamped down as soon as she acknowledged it, and pushed Blake away.

He let her go, watching her with unblinking gold eyes. Almost as though he willed her to do it, Sapphire ran her tongue over the swollen contours of her mouth. 'Well, well… That was quite something.'

His mouth was wry where she had expected it to be triumphant, because she couldn't deny to herself that there had been a moment in his arms when she had forgotten everything that lay between them and she had responded to him in a way she had never responded to any other man, but if anything he looked angry.

'He's obviously taught you well.' The comment bordered on the harshly accusatory and coming from anyone else Sapphire would have instantly taken exception to it, but sensing that for some reason she had got under his skin she responded lightly. 'And very extensively, I'm not seventeen any more Blake.'

'No, you're not are you,' he agreed, 'so don't expect me to handle you with kid gloves will you?'

'I don't expect you to "handle" me at all Blake— that's part of our agreement—remember?'

'Oh I think I'll be able to, now, but will you?'

He turned on his heel and left before she could speak, and although Sapphire told herself it was relief that made her shake so much that she had to lean against the stairs, in reality she knew that her emotions were far more complex than that.

What had she let herself in for agreeing to remarry Blake? She had always known he must despise her, but the anger she had just seen, so savage and bitter, that was something she hadn't guessed at. He must want Flaws Farm very badly, she thought bleakly as she made her way on shaky legs back to the house.

'Blake gone?' her father asked, when she walked into his room. Already he looked much better, and Sapphire realised with an aching pang how much her marriage to Blake meant to him.

'Yes.' She couldn't inject any enthusiasm into her voice. 'Never mind.' Her father obviously mistook the reason for her listlessness. 'You'll be seeing him tonight. He's taking you out to celebrate—at least that's what he said to me.'

To celebrate! Sapphire grimaced, inwardly resenting the fact that Blake hadn't said anything to her about going out. Had he done so, she would have refused.

'I can't tell you how much it means to me that the pair of you are getting back together again,' her father said quietly. 'He's a fine man Sapphire. A good strong man, the sort of man you need.'

She made her escape from the room without giving any response, half-blinded by the weak tears threatening to obscure her vision. In her own room she opened the suitcase Blake must have brought up. Even to think of him walking into her room made prickles of antagonism run down her spine. How on earth was she going to live with him for six months when she hated him so much?

She hadn't brought much with her, certainly nothing she could go out in to 'celebrate'—and nothing she could wear to get married in. Fresh tears blurred her eyes as she remembered the dress she had worn the first time they were married. Stupid sentimentality, she derided herself; their wedding had just been another part of Blake's elaborate charade, just like the half-reverent, almost worshipping kiss he had given her just outside the church doors. Sighing, Sapphire hung up her clothes. She would wear the plain black wool dress she had brought; it was a perfect foil for her colouring and a perfect accompaniment for her mood; Alan had always liked her in it.

Alan! She hadn't told him yet about Blake. She gnawed on her lip uncertain as to whether to ring him, or wait until he came up. She was sure he would understand; Alan was always logical and reasonable. For the first time it struck her just what she had committed herself to. She would have to give up her job; her flat; her London life; everything she had fought so hard for when she left Blake. But surely it was a small price to pay for her father's peace of mind? But say Alan did not accept her decision. She would not only have lost her job, she would have lost a good friend and potential lover as well. She couldn't understand why the knowledge should cause her so little pain. Perhaps the agony of meeting Blake again; of being forced to remember how much he had hurt her had anaesthetised her against other, lesser hurts. Sighing she finished unpacking and went downstairs. One thing she did remember about farm life was that there was always work to be done and work, as she had learned in London, was a very effective panacea.

'I'm just going down to the village to do some shopping and pick up your father's prescription,' Mary told her when Sapphire asked if there was anything she could do. 'Want to come with me?'

'No, I'll stay here if you don't mind.' Sapphire frowned. 'I would have thought the doctor would call every day, in view of Dad's illness.'

Mary eyed her sympathetically. 'There's really no point now,' she said gently. 'Are you sure you won't come with me?'

'No...no thanks.'

'Well I'll be on my way then. I want to call at the

butchers, your father loves shepherd's pie and I thought I'd make one for him tonight.'

How could Mary be so matter of fact, Sapphire wondered, watching the other woman driving away, but then as a nurse she would be used to death; she would have learned to accept the inevitable. As *she* had not, Sapphire acknowledged, but then she had had so little time to come to terms with the reality of her father's condition. Blake had broken the news to her almost brutally. The way he did everything. Unable to settle to anything she went up to her father's room, but he was asleep. Not wanting to disturb his rest she left again. What on earth could she do with herself? Perhaps she ought to have gone with Mary. She wandered aimlessly into the yard, bending to pet the sheepdog that suddenly emerged from the field. Tam, the shepherd followed close behind, a smile splitting his weather-seamed face as he recognised her. Tam had been her father's shepherd for as long as she could remember. He had seemed old to her when she was a child, and she wondered how old he was. He was one of a dying breed; a man who preferred the solitude of the hills, spending most of the summer in his small cottage watching over his flocks. The rich acres of farmland in the valley were given over to crops now, but her father still maintained his flock of sheep on his hill pastures.

'Weather's going to turn bad,' Tam told her laconically, 'Ought to get the sheep down off the hills, especially the ewes. Suppose I'd better get over to

Sefton and see Blake,' he added morosely, whistling to his dog.

Watching them go Sapphire realised the extent of Blake's influence on Flaws Farm. No wonder he didn't want to lose the land. He probably looked on it as his own already. She had wanted to protest to Tam that her father was the one to ask about the sheep, but instinctively she had known that Tam wouldn't have understood. What she considered to be Blake's interference would be taken as good neighbourliness by the old shepherd.

As she walked back into the kitchen the 'phone was ringing, and she answered it automatically.

'Sapphire, is that you?'

'Yes, Blake.'

'I forgot to mention it this morning, but I'll be round about seven-thirty tonight to take you out to dinner, and before you say anything, I didn't plan it. It was your father who mentioned it; he seemed to think some sort of celebration was in order, and I think he's probably right. If we're seen dining together, it won't come as too much of a surprise to people when they know we're back together.'

'Surprise? Don't you mean shock?' Sapphire gritted into the receiver. 'Especially where your female friends are concerned Blake.'

'If I didn't know better I might almost believe that you're jealous.'

'Funny,' Sapphire snapped back. 'I never realised you had such a powerful imagination. I must go now Blake,' she lied, 'Dad's calling me.'

'See you tonight.'

She hung up quickly leaving her staring at the black receiver. How could her life have changed so radically and so fast. One moment she had been looking forward to her holiday with Alan; to their relationship perhaps deepening from friendship into marriage, convinced that she had laid the ghosts in her past, and now, so swiftly that she could scarcely comprehend even now how it had happened, her life had somehow become entangled with Blake's again, but this time she was older and wiser. She had been burned once—so badly that there was no way she was ever going to approach the fire again.

But fire has a way of luring its victims, she acknowledged, bitterly, just like love.

# CHAPTER FOUR

SHE WAS READY when Blake arrived. He gave her black-clad body a cursory examination as he stepped into the kitchen and then drawled, 'Mourning, Sapphire?'

'It was the only dress I had with me.'

Again those golden eyes studied her body, but this time there was no mocking warmth to light their amber depths as Blake said coolly, 'You should have told me, I've still got a wardrobe-full of your things up at the house, and by the looks of you you could still get into them.'

He made it sound more of an insult than a compliment, and Sapphire turned away so that he wouldn't see the quick flush of colour warming her skin. Why was it that Blake seemed to possess this ability to put her in the wrong, even when she wasn't?

'If you're ready I think we'd better be on our way. I've booked our table for eight.' He glanced at his watch, the brief glimpse she had of his dark sinewy wrist doing strange things to Sapphire's stomach. She recognised the sensation immediately, and it gave her a sickening jolt. She had thought she was long past the stage of experiencing sexual appreciation of something as mundane as a male arm. As a teenager, the merest glimpse of Blake in the distance had been enough to start her stomach churning with excitement but that was all behind her now. Shrugging aside her feelings as an echo of the past she picked up her coat and followed Blake to the door.

To her surprise he hadn't brought the Land Rover but was driving a sleek black BMW. Some of her surprise must have communicated itself to Blake because he glanced at her sardonically, his eyebrows raised as he waited for her to join him, opening the door for her as she reached the car. But then he always had had that air of masculine sophistication, a rare commodity in the Borders where most of the boys she had grown up with thought only of their land and their stock. But she had lived in London for long enough not to be overawed by Blake any longer, surely? Alan was always meticulous about handing her into his car, but his fingers beneath her elbow didn't provoke the same jolting, lightning bolt of sensation that Blake's did, her senses told her treacherously.

Ridiculous to feel so affected by such casual contact—no doubt she was over-reacting. She had had to guard herself against thinking about Blake for so long that she was almost hyper-sensitive to him. Yes, that must be the explanation Sapphire decided as Blake set the car in motion. Of course she was wound-up and tense, who wouldn't be after learning that their father was close to death and that the one

thing he wanted in life was the one thing she least
desired. Marriage to Blake! She glanced covertly at
his profile. He was concentrating on the road, his lips
set in a hard line. Reaction suddenly shivered
through her. What had she committed herself to? Despite the warmth from the car's heaters she felt
chilled, and yet her face seemed to be burning. She
*couldn't* go through with it. Her father would understand. She must talk to Blake, she...

'If you're having second thoughts, forget them,
I'm not letting you back out now Sapphire.' The
coldly harsh words cut through her anguished
thoughts like a whiplash. How had he known what
she was thinking? He was right about one thing
though, it was too late to back out now. Her father
wanted their reconciliation too desperately.

'Where are we going?' She asked the question
more to dispel the tense atmosphere inside the car
than because she really wanted to know.

'Haroldgate,' Blake told her briefly.

She only just managed to catch back her protest.
Haroldgate was a small village nestling in one of the
valleys and as far as she knew it possessed only one
restaurant. Blake had taken her there the evening he
had proposed to her. She had been so thrilled by his
invitation. 'The Barn' at Haroldgate was the most
sophisticated eating place in the area and she had
never been before. She could vividly recall how im-
pressed she had been by her surroundings, and how
tense. Shaking herself mentally she tried to appear
unconcerned. 'The Barn' might have seemed the

very zenith of sophistication to an awkward seven-teen-year-old who had never been anywhere, but it could hardly compare with some of the restaurants Alan had taken her to. Alan was something of a gourmet and discovering new eating places was one of his hobbies. He also liked to be seen in the right places, unlike Blake who had little concern for appearances or being seen to do the 'right thing', Sapphire acknowledged. Neither did Blake make a sacred ritual out of eating as Alan did. Frowning Sapphire tried to dispel the vague feeling that somehow she was being disloyal to Alan by comparing him with Blake. They were two completely different men who could not be compared, and of the two...

'We're here.'

The curt comment broke across her thoughts. Blake stopped the car and in the darkness Sapphire felt him studying her. Her muscles tensed automatically and defensively, although she couldn't have said why.

'I won't have you thinking about him while you're with me,' he told her tersely. 'I won't have it Sapphire, do you understand?'

She was far too taken aback by the tone of his voice to make any immediate comment. How had Blake known she was thinking about Alan? And why should he object? His attitude fanned the embers of resentment that had been burning in her all day.

'You don't own my thoughts Blake,' she told him mockingly, 'and if I choose to think about the man I love that's my affair. You can't stop me.'

'You think not?'

The headlights from another car turning into the carpark illuminated the interior of the BMW briefly and Sapphire was struck by the white tension of Blake's face. Did getting her father's land mean so very much to him? Fear feathered lightly along her spine.

'Don't push me too hard Sapphire,' he warned, as he unfastened his seat belt. 'I *am* only human.'

'You could have fooled me.' She muttered the words flippantly beneath her breath, but he caught them, leaning across to grasp her forearms while she was still fastened into her seat.

'Could I? Then perhaps this will convince you just how human I can be, and not to rely too heavily on your own judgment.' The words carried a thread of bitterness Sapphire couldn't decipher but there was nothing cryptic about the pressure of Blake's mouth against her own, hard and determined as his hands pressed her back into her seat.

It was a kiss of anger and bitterness, even she could recognise that, and yet it called out to something deep inside her; some shadowing of pain she hadn't known still existed and which suddenly became a fierce ache, leaping to meet and respond to the anger she could feel inside Blake.

The result was a devastation of her senses; a complete reversal of everything she had ever thought about herself and her own sexuality; her physical response to Blake so intense and overwhelming that it succeeded in blocking everything else out.

Without her being aware of how it had happened her arms were round his neck, her fingers stroking the thick softness of his hair, and yet it was pain she wanted him to feel—not pleasure, and it was anger she wanted to show him as she returned the fierce intensity of his kiss, and not love.

'You want me.' It was Blake's thick utterance of the words that brought her back to reality. That, and her own bitter mental acknowledgement that somehow he had aroused her, had touched a deep core of need inside her that none of Alan's gentle caresses had ever revealed.

'I *want* Alan,' she lied curtly, 'but since he's not here...'

Blake withdrew from her immediately as she had known he would. His pride would never allow him to be a substitute for someone else, but what did surprise Sapphire was that he believed her. But then he could not, as she could, compare her reaction to him with her reaction to Alan. She did love Alan. What she had just experienced in Blake's arms; that bitter tension that had made her body ache and her eyes sting with suppressed tears was just something left over from the past, that was all.

'Are we going to eat, or do you want to spend the rest of the evening in the car?'

The harsh words rasped over too-sensitive nerves. Sapphire pushed Blake's hand away as he reached out to help her with her seat belt, and knew by the tension in his body that she had annoyed him. How on earth were they supposed to live together, supposedly as man and wife, preserving the fiction that they had been reconciled when they reacted so explosively to one another? If only she hadn't made that stupid comment to her father, but he had looked so ill...and he had been so pleased, almost as though she had given him a reason to go on fighting to live. And so she had.

The restaurant was just as attractive as she remembered. The old barn had been sensitively restored, and while the atmosphere was not one of luxurious glamour there was something about it that Sapphire found more appealing than any of Alan's favourite haunts.

The Head Waiter recognised Blake immediately and they were swiftly shown to a table for two.

The restaurant wasn't a large one, the proprietors preferring not to expand and risk losing their excellent reputation. As they studied their menus, Sapphire glanced covertly round the room, wondering if she would recognise any of their fellow diners. A couple sat at one table talking and Sapphire stiffened as she recognised Miranda.

Four years ago this woman had been her husband's mistress, and she was still as beautiful as ever Sapphire recognised, and still obviously bemusing the opposite sex if her table companion's expression was anything to go by. Just as Sapphire was about to look away, she raised her head, her eyes narrowing as they met Sapphire's. Conscious that she was staring Sapphire tried to look away and found that she could not. A familiar nausea started to well up inside her, and she fought it down. She was over all that now. She wasn't going to let it happen again, and yet against her will her mind kept on relaying to her mental images of Blake and Miranda together, of Blake's long-legged, narrow-hipped body making love to Miranda's, in all the ways it had never made love to hers. The menu dropped from her fingers as she tried to stem the flood of images. She was over this; she had been over it for years... She knew now that most of her anguish sprang not from the fact that Blake and Miranda had been lovers, but rather from the knowledge that he had desired Miranda as intensely as he had not desired her. If Blake had made love to her she would not have suffered this torment; she and Miranda would have met as equals; as women, not as adult and child.

'Sapphire?'

She realised that Blake was talking to her; watching her and her face closed up. How much had she already given away? She glanced desperately at him but he was looking at Miranda.

Sapphire followed his look, tensing as she saw the other couple stand up and head towards them.

'Blake.' Miranda's companion held out his hand to Blake, who rose to shake it, but it was at Sapphire that he looked.

'Sapphire.' Miranda's greeting to her was coolly mocking. 'You've barely changed.'

The words were designed to hurt, but Sapphire chose to turn the barb back on its sender. 'In four years?' she murmured, 'How flattering. I must confess I barely recognised you.'

A blatant lie, but she could always use it to explain away her too lengthy scrutiny of the other woman. And she *had* aged, Sapphire noted now. Although she was still very beautiful, she was now more obviously a woman well into her thirties. She must be a year or two older than Blake. Her companion was in his forties, and although he looked pleasant enough, physically he could not compare with Blake.

'Sapphire, let me introduce you to Miranda's husband.' Blake's words were a shock. Her husband? Her eyes went automatically to Miranda's ring hand where a huge diamond solitaire nestled against an obviously new wedding ring.

'Jim is the Senior Registrar at Hexham General.' Blake told her. 'He and Miranda got married a couple of months ago.'

'What brings you back up here Sapphire?' Miranda questioned her.

She stared to reply but Blake beat her to it, drawing her hand through his arm, pulling her into the warmth of his side as he said calmly, 'We've decided to give our marriage another try.'

'A rather sudden decision surely?' Icy blue eyes swept over Sapphire, Miranda's tone intimating disbelief.

'Not really.' Blake's voice was as smooth as silk and for the first time, Sapphire was grateful for his ability to conceal the truth. 'It's been on the cards for some time. Sapphire just took a bit of convincing that's all.' His possessive smile was meant to indicate that he considered himself lucky to get her back, but Sapphire wasn't deceived for one moment. There was a subtle tension between Blake and Miranda which suggested to Sapphire that getting her father's land wasn't the sole reason Blake wanted a 'reconciliation'. Had Miranda married to spite Blake? To prove to him that if he didn't want marriage then other men did, and was he now retaliating by announcing their reconciliation? Even worse, had he known that Miranda and Jim would be here tonight?

'Well congratulations to you both.' Jim smiled warmly at them, and took Miranda's arm.

'Yes indeed, better luck this time.' The words were innocuous enough but Sapphire wasn't deceived. She read the venom behind them, and knew that Blake had too.

When the other couple had gone she sat down and picked up her menu. Eating was the last thing she felt like but she was determined not to let Blake see how much seeing Miranda again had disturbed her.

'I'm sorry about that.' His terse apology stunned her and Sapphire looked up at him. There were deep grooves of tension running from his nose to his mouth. 'I didn't know they'd be here.'

Sapphire shrugged dismissively, 'It doesn't matter. I didn't realise Miranda was married.'

'Why should you?' Blake was curt and abrupt, 'I didn't realise that...' He broke off, his mouth grim. 'Look I don't think coming out tonight was such a good idea. Let's leave shall we? I don't think either of us is in the mood for the type of celebration your father had in mind.'

'But what about Miranda?' Sapphire objected. 'If we leave now, she'll never believe what you said about us being reconciled.'

Blake shrugged, standing up to come round and hold her chair as she got to her feet. 'Does it matter what she thinks?' He sounded tense. 'As a matter of fact, what she probably will think is that we've decided we'd rather be making love than eating.'

'Because that's what you'd be doing if you were with her?' The words were out before Sapphire could stop them. 'Aren't you forgetting something,' she added bitterly. 'Miranda knows exactly how undesirable you find me. You told her—remember?'

'I told her nothing,' Blake grated back. 'She tricked that admission out of you, but if it worries you so much I can take you back to Sefton House right now and make you my wife in every sense of the word.'

'Thanks, but no thanks.' Somehow she managed to inject just the right amount of scathing indifference into her voice, but it was hard not to react to his words; not to shiver beneath the rough velvet urgency of his voice, nor to turn to him in blind acceptance of the pleasure it promised, but instead to simply precede him and walk out of the restaurant as calmly as though she were completely unaffected by his words.

Were he and Miranda still lovers? Somehow Sapphire didn't think so; there hadn't been the complicity between them she would have expected had they been. Instead there had been something almost approaching antagonism.

They drove back along the road they had come in a silence which remained unbroken until Sapphire realised that Blake had taken the turning for his own house instead of carrying on to her father's farm.

'Don't worry, I'm not kidnapping you,' he told her sardonically as she turned to him in protest. 'It's barely ten o'clock. If I take you home now your father will think there's something wrong.'

'And he'd be right.' Sapphire muttered the words under her breath but Blake heard them.

'This isn't easy for me either you know,' he told her grittily, 'but why should I expect you to realise that? You were never any good at seeing the other person's point of view.'

'Meaning what exactly?' The anger that had been burning inside her all evening burst into destructive flames. 'That I should have played the ''understanding'' wife and turned a blind eye to your affair?'

Light spilled out into the cobbled courtyard as Blake pulled up outside his house. He stopped the engine and Sapphire saw him tense almost as though he were bracing himself to do something. 'Sapphire, look, my ''affair'' as you call it never...'

'I don't want to hear about it.' She cut across him quickly. She didn't want to exhume the past; it was far too painful. Talking about his relationship with Miranda forced her to remember how intensely she had once longed to have those brown hands touching her body, exploring its contours, giving her the pleasure her feverishly infatuated senses had told her she could find in his arms. 'It's over Blake,' she reminded him determinedly. 'We're two different people now.'

'If you say so.' He unfastened his seat belt and opened his door. 'Hungry?'

Sapphire shook her head.

'Come inside and have a cup of coffee then, I've got a mare waiting to foal in the barn, I'll check up on her and then I'll take you home.'

He didn't invite her to go with him, and Sapphire stood forlornly in the immaculate kitchen of Sefton House listening to the sound of his footsteps dying away as he crossed the yard and entered the large barn.

Once she had been part of this world, and he would have thought nothing of inviting her to join him. Together they had shared the miracle of birth on many occasions in the past, but now she was deliberately being excluded. It baffled Sapphire that the anger she sensed churning inside him should be directed against her. Blake had no rational reason for being angry with her: had someone asked her she would have said he was incapable of feeling any emotional response towards her whatsoever.

More to keep herself occupied than because she wanted any she started to make some coffee. The kitchen was immaculate, but somehow impersonal. Presumably he had his own reasons for not replacing his aunt with a housekeeper. At least that was one complication she wouldn't have to face this time. Sarah Sefton had never made any secret of the fact that she considered her far too young for Blake. She had disapproved of her right from the very start, Sapphire mused, watching the aromatic dark-brown liquid filter down into the jug, and breathing in the heavenly smell.

'That smells good.' She hadn't heard Blake return, and she swung round tensely, trying to mask her automatic reaction to him by asking after the mare.

'She's fine. This will be her third foal, and we don't anticipate any problems, but like any other female she needs the reassurance of knowing someone cares.'

He said the words carelessly but the look in his eyes was far from casual as he added softly, 'Does Alan let you know he cares Sapphire?'

'All the time.' She managed a cool smile, 'I've made us some coffee, I hope your "help" won't mind my rummaging in her cupboards.'

'I'm sure she won't,' Blake responded equally blandly, 'but when my aunt retired I decided I preferred having the place to myself. A woman comes up from the village to clean; apart from that I'm self-sufficient.' He saw the assessing glance Sapphire slid over the immaculate kitchen, and said softly, 'I don't spend enough time here to make it untidy. In fact recently I've been eating as many meals at Flaws as I have here.'

'Yes, I haven't thanked you yet for taking on the responsibility for the farm.'

He smiled sardonically at her, as though he knew just how hard she had found it to mutter the words.

'That's what neighbours are for. Your father would have done the same thing for me had our positions been reversed.' He pulled off his jacket, dropping it carelessly on to the table, and then checking and picking it up again. 'One special licence,' he told her withdrawing a piece of paper from an inner pocket. 'Special dispensation from the Bishop of Hawick. I went to see him today.'

'So we'll be married...'

'The day after tomorrow,' Blake told her. 'In Hexham, everything's arranged, the vicar...'

'A Church wedding?' Sapphire's head came up, her forehead creased in a frown. Somehow she had expected the ceremony to be conducted in the more mundane surroundings of a registry office.

'It seemed less public,' Blake told her carelessly. 'Have you told your boyfriend yet?'

Sapphire shook her head. 'No, but he's coming up for his car, I'll tell him then, it isn't the sort of news I could break over the 'phone.'

'He's going to get quite a shock.'

Why should she think she heard satisfaction beneath the cool words? 'It's only for a few months, once I've explained the situation to him...'

'He'll wait for you?' Blake supplied sardonically, 'Get your coat on and I'll take you back to Flaws, I've got to be up early in the morning. We've got to get the sheep down off the high pastures, the weather's about to change.'

They didn't speak again until Blake stopped his car outside the back door to Flaws Farm. For a moment as she unfastened her seat belt Sapphire panicked. What if he should try to kiss her again?

But apart from opening her door for her Blake didn't attempt to touch her. He walked with her across the cobbled yard, both of them stopping by the door.

'I won't see you tomorrow,' he told her, 'but I'll be round the morning after. Our appointment with the Vicar is for eleven o'clock, so I'll pick you up at ten.' Giving her a brief nod he turned away and walked back to the car. He had reversed out of the yard before Sapphire had managed to pull herself together sufficiently to open the back door.

What was the matter with her, she chided herself as she prepared for bed. Surely she hadn't wanted him to kiss her? Of course she hadn't. So why this curiously flat feeling; this niggly ache in her body that was all too dangerously familiar? Stop it, she cautioned herself as she slid into the cold bed. Stop thinking about him.

IT WAS EASIER SAID than done, especially with twenty-four empty hours stretching ahead of her with nothing to fill them other than doubts about the wisdom of marrying Blake for a second time, no matter how altruistic the reasons.

She helped Mary with her chores, and spent the

afternoon outdoors, but although she kept her hands busy she couldn't occupy her mind. Her father noticed her tension when she went to sit with him.

'Worrying about tomorrow?' he asked sympathetically, closing the book he had been reading. 'Blake is a fine man Sapphire,' he told her gently, 'I've always thought so. In fact in many ways I blame myself for the break-up of your marriage.'

When she started to protest he lifted his hand. 'I wanted you to marry Blake, even though he thought you were too young. He wanted to wait, but...'

'But you dangled the bait of this farm,' Sapphire interrupted briefly, 'and he couldn't resist it.' She bit her lip as she realised how cold and unloverlike her voice sounded. Deliberately trying to soften it, she added, 'But that's all over now, we're making a completely fresh start. We're both older and wiser.'

She couldn't bear to look at her father. His fragility still had the power to shock her, but even so her mind refused to accept that soon he would be gone from her.

Downstairs she found Mary busily baking. 'Blake just rang to confirm that he'll pick you up at ten tomorrow,' she said cheerfully. 'Having a day out?'

Her curiosity was only natural and Sapphire forced a smile. 'Yes... In fact you might as well know Mary, that Blake and I are going to give our marriage another try.' She couldn't look at the other woman. 'I suppose it took something like my father's...illness to show us both how we really felt.' That at least was true, even if Mary was hardly likely to interpret her words correctly. The other woman's face softened.

'Yes I know what you mean,' she agreed. 'So you'll be moving to Sefton House.'

'Yes.' Sapphire swallowed nervously. So far she hadn't let herself think about the intimacy of living in such close proximity to Blake. No matter how non-sexual their relationship was going to be; the thought made her stomach tense and knot in anxious apprehension. What was she frightened of for goodness sake? Not Blake. She already knew that he felt absolutely no desire for her, but last night he had talked about taking her home with him and making her truly his wife. Sapphire shivered. Those had been words; nothing more; words designed to keep her tense and apprehensive; and in her place. No, she had nothing to fear from Blake. Or from herself? Of course not. She had suffered the agony of loving him once, it was hardly likely to happen again.

# CHAPTER FIVE

SHE AND BLAKE were husband and wife again; Sapphire could hardly believe it. She glanced down at the gold band encircling her finger. It was the same ring that Blake had given her once before. She had been stunned when she saw it. Somehow she had never imagined Blake keeping it, never mind giving it back to her.

'It saved the bother of buying a new one,' he told her sardonically correctly following her chain of thought. He glanced at his watch flicking back his cuff in a manner that was achingly familiar. It shocked her that her mind should have stored and retained so many minute details about him. 'We'd better get back. I take it you don't want to go out and celebrate our reunion?'

'Can you think of any reason why I should?' Her voice was as cool as his, her eyes locking with the gold blaze that glittered over her too pale face. 'I've married you for one reason and one reason only Blake—my father's peace of mind, and just as soon as...' she gulped back the stinging tears that suddenly formed, '...just as soon as that reason no longer exists our marriage will be over.'

The silence that filled the car on the way back to the valley was not a comfortable one. Sapphire sat back in her seat, her head on the headrest, her face turned dismissively towards the window, and yet despite her determination to ignore Blake, she was acutely aware of him. Every time she closed her eyes she saw his face; pictured the lean strength of his hands on the steering wheel. For a moment, unnervingly she even pictured those hands against her skin, touching; stroking... Stop it, she warned herself. Dear God what was happening to her? Blake no longer possessed the power to affect her in that way. She was completely over him and the childish infatuation she had once had for him.

'We'll drive to Flaws Farm and pick up your things first.' His cool voice broke into her thoughts. 'I've got the vet coming out this afternoon to look at the mare, so we won't linger.'

'The fact that we're married doesn't mean we have to do everything together,' Sapphire pointed out tartly, not liking the way he was taking control. 'I can easily drive myself over to Flaws. In fact,' she turned in her seat to look determinedly at Blake, 'in view of my father's illness and the fact that no-one knows that we've been divorced, I think it would be quite acceptable for me to remain at Flaws...'

'Maybe it would,' Blake agreed sardonically, 'if your daughterly devotion wasn't a bit late in coming, and I was prepared to agree. Oh no, Sapphire,' he told her softly, 'I want you where I can keep an eye on you. You're not running out on me twice. Besides,' he added, 'if you don't come back to Sefton House with me, your father's going to get suspicious.'

His last words were undeniably true. Biting down hard on her lip to prevent her vexation from showing Sapphire turned back to stare out of her window, relieved when she saw the familiar turnoff for Flaws Valley. This tension between herself and Blake wasn't something she remembered from the past. Of course, she had always been aware of him; but surely never like this, with a nerve-rasping intensity that made her muscles ache from the strain she was imposing on them.

'You're back early.' Mary greeted them without any surprise, but of course as far as she was concerned she and Blake had merely had a morning out together. 'Are you staying for lunch?' Her question was addressed to Blake, but his arm tethered Sapphire to his side when she would have slipped out of the room. 'We haven't got time, I've got the vet coming this afternoon.' He released Sapphire to smile down at her, his eyes so warm and golden that his glance was like basking in the heat of the sun. 'I'll go up and see your father while you pack.'

He was gone before Sapphire could speak, leaving her to face Mary's raised eyebrows and expectant expression. Sapphire couldn't face her. 'I...I'm going back with Blake,' she said hesitantly, 'I...we....'

'Your father will be pleased,' Mary assured her coming to her rescue. 'Look,' she added, 'why don't I make some coffee and then come upstairs and give you a hand with your packing. Not that you brought a lot with you.'

Sensing the speculation behind her words Sapphire said shakily. 'N...I had no idea then that Blake...'

'Still loved you?'

The words surprised her into a tense stillness, but mercifully Mary was too busily engaged in making the coffee to notice her startled response. It had been on the tip of her tongue to blurt out that Blake had never loved her, but fortunately she had caught the words back just in time.

It was over an hour before they were finally able to leave. Her father had been so pleased by their news. Sighing Sapphire tried to settle herself in the car, telling herself that her sacrifice must surely have been made worthwhile by her father's pleasure.

'I'm going to have to leave you to find your own way about,' Blake told her tensely when he stopped the car in his own farmyard. 'I want to have a word with the shepherd before the vet arrives. You'll have to make yourself up a bed I'm afraid—unless of course you prefer to share mine.' The last words were accompanied by a cynical smile.

'Hardly,' Sapphire told him crisply, 'I'm no masochist, Blake; nor am I a naive seventeen-year-old any longer.'

'No,' he agreed bitterly, and for a moment Sapphire wondered at the deeply intense timbre of his voice and the drawn expression tensing his face, before dismissing her impressions as false ones and berating herself for allowing her imagination to work overtime. Blake had no reason to feel bitter—unlike her.

As she let herself into the kitchen she was struck by the fact that despite, or perhaps because of its gleaming appearance the room seemed oddly sterile; not like a home at all. The mellow wooden cabinets which should have imparted a warm glow, looked too much like a glossy, cold advertisement; there were no warm, baking smells to tantalise or tempt. Blake's aunt had made her own bread, she remembered with unexpected nostalgia, and she remembered this kitchen best filled with its warmly fragrant scent. Of course if the smell of freshly baked bread was all it took to bring the place alive, she was more than capable of supplying that herself. Her culinary efforts so much despised by Blake's aunt had improved rapidly in the security of her own small home. Alan often asked her to cook for important clients and among their circle of friends she had quite a reputation as a first-rate hostess. Alan approved of her domestic talents; Alan! Her body tensed. What was he going to say when he heard about all this? She could well lose him. Why was she not more concerned at the prospect; after all she had been planning to marry him? Pushing aside the thought she opened the kitchen door and stepped into the square parquet-floored hall.

On the plate rack encircling the hall were the plates she remembered from the early days of her marriage, the smooth cream walls otherwise clean and bare. The parquet floor glistened in the bright March sunshine, but the table was empty of its customary bowl of flowers and she found she missed their bright splash of colour. Whatever her other faults Blake's aunt had been a first rate housewife, and she had obviously learned something from her Sapphire thought wryly, noticing the thin film of dust beginning to form on the hall table. The rich reds and blues of the traditional stair carpet carried her eye upwards. The house had six bedrooms and two bathrooms; a more than adequate supply for two people. Did Blake still occupy the master bedroom? It had been redecorated especially for them before their marriage she remembered, in soft peaches and blues that Blake had told her he had chosen with her eyes in mind. Her mouth curled into a sardonic smile. And to think she had been fool enough to believe him. The door handle turned easily under her fingers, but she stood still once it was opened. Everything was just as she remembered it; everything was clean and neat, but the room gave the impression of being unused.

'Re-living old memories?' Blake's voice was harshly discordant making her whirl round in shock.

She said the first thing that came into her mind. 'It doesn't look used.'

'It isn't.' His voice was still harsh, his eyes fiercely golden as they all but pinned her where she stood. 'Let's face it,' he added cynically, 'the memories it holds aren't precisely those I want to take to bed with me every night. I sleep in my old room, but you can have this one if you wish.'

His old room. Unwillingly her eyes were drawn along the corridor to the room she knew he meant. She had only been in it once. She had come with a message from her father and finding the kitchen empty and hearing Blake's voice had hurried upstairs. He had emerged from his room just as she reached it, a towel wrapped round lean hips, his body still damp from his shower. She hadn't been able to take her eyes off him, she remembered sardonically; and neither had she been able to speak. Blake had drawn her inside the room closing the door. 'What is it little girl,' he had asked tauntingly, 'haven't you ever seen a man before?' She had turned to flee but he had caught her, kissing her with what she had interpreted as fierce passion but which in reality could only have been play-acting...

'Sapphire, are you all right?' His voice dragged her back to the present.

'Fine,' she told him in a clipped voice. 'I might as well use this room. The woman who comes up from the village, when...'

'Three days a week, if you feel you need her more then arrange it. Don't worry,' he added sardonically, watching her, 'I don't expect you to soil your lady-like hands with housework, or cooking.' If anything his mouth curled even more cynically. 'I have too much respect for my stomach for that. I came up to tell you that I've brought your cases in. Once the vet's been, I've got to go out and check one of the fences, some of the sheep were found on the road...'

He disappeared, leaving Sapphire standing by the open door, her face still scarlet from his insults about her cooking. So he thought she was still the same useless, timid child he had first married, did he? Well, she would show him.

Returning upstairs, Sapphire quickly changed into her jeans and an old tee-shirt. A thorough inspection of the kitchen cupboards revealed the fact that they were surprisingly well stocked and within an hour of Blake's exit she had a large bowl of dough rising in the warmth of the upstairs airing cupboard—a trick she had learned in her London flat which lacked the large warming compartment of the old-fashioned stove at home.

She heard the vet arrive while she was making the pastry for Beef Wellington, but continued with her self-imposed task. Blake would soon discover that she was not the timid child she had once been, and she wouldn't have been human, she told herself, if she didn't take pleasure from imagining his surprise at the discovery.

She had half-expected Blake to bring the vet in for a cup of tea after he had inspected that mare—it was a cold day, and she was sure the older man would have welcomed a warming drink, but instead when they emerged from the barn Blake walked with him to his Range Rover. The two men stood talking for a few minutes and then the vet climbed into his vehicle and Blake turned back towards the stable, disappearing inside.

Sapphire had just put her loaves in the oven when the 'phone rang. Wiping her floury hands on a towel she picked up the receiver, recognising Miranda's slightly shrill voice the moment she heard it.

'Is Blake there?' the other woman demanded imperiously. 'I want to speak to him—urgently.'

'He's in the barn at the moment,' Sapphire responded coolly, suppressing the urge to slam the receiver down. 'If you'd like to hold on for a moment I'll go and get him.'

The interior of the barn, so dark after the bright sunlit afternoon was temporarily blinding. Sapphire was peripherally aware of the familiar barn sounds; the mare shuffling restlessly in her stall, the scent of hay, the rustling sound it made. As her eyes grew accustomed to the gloom she stepped forward calling Blake's name.

'Up here,' he called back, making her start tensely and peer upwards into the dimness of the upper hayloft.

'There's a 'phone call for you,' Sapphire told him curtly, not wanting to think she had come looking for him on her own account. 'Miranda.'

'I'll have to ring her back.' Blake was frowning as he turned back into the interior of the loft, and although she knew she was being foolish Sapphire couldn't quite control the sudden leap of her senses as she caught a glimpse of the tawny skin of his chest where his shirt had come unfastened. Enough, she berated herself, as she walked blindly towards the door. 'You don't even like the man—you loathe him, so how can you possibly…feel desire for him?' Somehow the words insinuated themselves into her mind and wouldn't go away, making her face up to the truth. Blake still had the power to disturb her; still held a sexual appeal for her, which although it had nothing to do with love, or indeed any genuine worthwhile emotion, did, nonetheless, hold a dangerously potent allure.

Deep in thought Sapphire recoiled with pain as she cannoned into one of the posts supporting the upper floor, the intensity of the unexpected pain almost robbing her of breath as she stumbled backwards.

She was aware of sounds behind her, of Blake's peremptory command and then the firm strength of his arm supporting her against his body as she slowly crumpled.

'Sapphire, are you all right?'

His voice was a roughly urgent mutter somewhere above her left ear; the heat of his body against her back drowning out her earlier pain and replacing it with a dangerous languor that reinforced every one of her earlier thoughts.

'Sapphire?'

This time the urgency in Blake's voice compelled her to make some response. 'I'm fine,' she told him shakily, 'it was just the shock… It took my breath away.'

'I know the feeling.' She could feel the reverberations of his words rumbling in his chest, but the dry tone in which they were uttered made her lift her head and turn round the better to study his face.

'Can't you feel what having you in my arms does to me?' he murmured rawly. 'I'd almost forgotten it was possible to feel like this.'

Sapphire didn't need to ask 'to feel like what?' Her own treacherous body was already reacting shamelessly to Blake's proximity. You fool, she protested inwardly, he doesn't care anymore about you than he did before; it's just another act, another scene of the charade he insists we play. He doesn't want you.

But Blake's body was telling her otherwise. More experienced now than she had been at seventeen, she could clearly read the tell-tale signs; in the dim light of the barn his eyes glittered dark gold, searching her face as he cupped her jaw with one hand and turned her round to face him. There was a tension in his body that was betrayed by the fine tremor of his muscles and the harsh control he exercised over his breathing.

The knowledge that she had aroused him was infinitely exciting; dangerously intoxicating, so much so that she was drunk on it. There could be no other explanation for the suicidal desire she suddenly experienced to trace the deep vee of Blake's open shirt with the tip of one finger, nor for giving into it.

Apart from one deep inhaled breath Blake kept absolutely still. His skin felt warm and surprisingly vulnerable, the difference in texture between his skin and the crispness of his dark chest hair deeply erotic.

She had never touched him like this in the past; had never dared to initiate any intimacy between them. A pulse thudded at the base of his throat, his fingers tensing into her waist as he looked down at her.

'Sapphire!'

Her name seemed to well up from the very depths of his soul, spilling into the silence of the barn as a tormented groan. Her shocked senses barely had time to register it before the hard fingers cupping her jaw were tilting her face up and his mouth was consuming hers, burning it with a kiss of such fierce intensity that her senses took fire from it, liquid heat running moltenly through her veins, making her melt into him with a feverish need to meld with him and become part of him.

When his tongue stroked her lips, coaxing them apart Sapphire surrendered willingly, an ache that was partly desire and partly pain flowering to life inside her. Never once had he kissed her like this before; like a man who had hungered desperately for the feel of her mouth beneath his; who burned with a totally male desire to conquer and possess.

His free hand stroked down her body, finding the soft curve of her breast his thumb finding the newly burgeoning peak and caressing it with a feverish intensity that was echoed in the taut tension of his body.

Everything in her that was feminine yielded beneath the force of such a rawly masculine need and as though his body sensed the responsiveness of hers, Blake slid his hand beneath her tee-shirt, searching for and finding the aroused swell of her breast.

Which of them made the small murmur of satisfaction Sapphire didn't know, all she did know was that by the time Blake's mouth left hers, to investigate the creamy curve of her throat, she was totally acquiescent; mutely encouraging the exploration of warm male lips and slightly calloused male hands.

'Sapphire if you don't stop me now, I'm going to end up making love to you where we stand.'

Blake groaned the words into her skin, using his superior strength to urge her against the hard arousal of his body, muttering thick words of pleasure as his hands slid down to her hips, moulding her against him, but his words had penetrated through the dizzying heat of desire welling up inside her and Sapphire pulled away. He released her almost immediately, the desire she had seen so recently in his face draining away to be replaced by sardonic comprehension.

'You forgot who I was, is that it?' he taunted, watching the emotions chase one another across her mobile face. 'You forgot that I wasn't your precious boyfriend, is that what you're going to tell me? Well I'll save you the trouble,' he told her. 'That was *me* you responded to Sapphire, *me* who set you on fire; *me* who you wanted to make love to.'

'Oh yes you did,' he insisted when she tried to speak. 'You wanted me Sapphire, whether you're honest to admit it or not.'

'Whatever there once was between us is gone,'

Sapphire protested, bitterly aware that he was right; she *had* wanted him and with an intensity that, now that she had herself under control again, shocked her.

'But you can't deny that you responded to me,' Blake pressed softly, watching her, making her feel trapped and tormented.

'I can't deny that I responded to your *masculinity*,' Sapphire agreed in a face-saving bid... 'I'm a woman now Blake, with all the desires and needs that that implies.' Heavens was this really her saying this? Inwardly she was trembling, praying that he wouldn't see through her pitiful attempt to deny the effect he had on her.

'Meaning that you would have responded to any man in the same way?' Blake asked her sardonically. 'I don't think so, Sapphire. In fact, judging by your response to me, there must be something lacking in your boyfriend's lovemaking. You responded to me as though you were starving for...'

'Stop it,' Sapphire interrupted his cruel speech. 'I won't listen to this, Blake.' She hurried to the barn door, wanting only to escape from him and the turbulence of her own emotions, completely forgetting the original purpose of her journey to the barn, until she got back to the kitchen and found the receiver still on the table. There was no-one at the other end and so she replaced it, busying herself in the kitchen, trying to find some balm to her disordered senses in the warm scent of baking bread that filled the room, but instead only able to remember the rough sensuality of Blake's mouth on hers; the urgent caress of his hands on her body; the unashamed arousal of his as he kissed and caressed her, but no, she mustn't think of these things. She must concentrate instead of remembering why she was here; how Blake had trapped her.

She was busily clearing away the remnants of pastry from the table when Blake walked in, checking on the threshold, frowning slightly as the warmly rich scent of her baking filled his nostrils. She ought to have been pleased by the startled expression on his face, but instead all she could think of was the way his mouth had felt against her own, and it took an almost physical effort to draw her gaze away from the slightly moist fullness of his lower lip.

'Bread?' he quizzed her, obviously surprised.

'Alan liked me to bake it for him,' Sapphire responded, knowing that she was deliberately invoking Alan's name as though it were a charm which had the ability to destroy Blake's powerful pull on her senses. Blake's face hardened immediately, as he strode across the kitchen and picked up the 'phone. Watching him punch in a series of numbers, so quickly that he must know them by heart, Sapphire was pierced by a feeling of desolation so acute that it terrified her. She mustn't become emotionally involved with Blake again. She had travelled that road once and knew all too well where it led; she wasn't going to travel it again.

Her desolation turned to sick pain as she heard him say Miranda's name. The other woman must have said something because Blake laughed, a deeply sensual sound that stirred up the tiny hairs on the back of Sapphire's nape, making her spine tingle.

'No, she must have forgotten to give me the message,' Sapphire heard him say, his eyes hard, his gaze unwavering splintering her with pain as she turned to face him. 'Umm…well how about dinner tonight? Yes I'll pick you up.'

Sapphire turned away, Blake was taking Miranda out to dinner? She glanced at the 'fridge where the pastry and fillet steak she had prepared for their evening meal lay, and her mouth compressed in a bitter line. Hadn't she already learned her lesson?

By the time Blake had replaced the receiver she had decided what she would do. Let Blake take his…mistress out to dinner if he wished, but she wasn't going to sit at home, moping, waiting for him. She would go over to Flaws and spend the evening with Mary and her father.

It wasn't until she heard the door close behind Blake that she realised that she had been holding her breath. Her lungs ached with the strain she was imposing on them, her body so tense that her muscles were almost locked.

Why on earth had she allowed Blake to kiss and touch her as he had? And why had she responded to him so…so ardently. She didn't love him any longer; but she still desired him; part of her still felt the old attraction; *that* must be the explanation. Like an amputee suffering pain from a limb that no longer existed she was still experiencing the pangs of her youthful love for Blake even though that love had long ago died.

SAPPHIRE WAS IN HER ROOM when Blake went out; she had gone there, deliberately avoiding him, and only emerged once she had heard his car engine die away.

Despite the fact that the heating was on the house felt slightly chilly—a sure sign that the threat of bad weather hadn't gone. In the living room a basket of logs stood on the hearth of the open fire, and Sapphire glanced longingly at them, acknowledging that it was pointless lighting a fire just for herself, especially when she didn't intend staying in. Why, when she knew where Blake had gone; when she knew how he had manipulated her, did her imagination insist on filling her mind with pictures of Blake as she had always wanted him to be rather than as he was; of herself at his side; their children upstairs asleep while they sat side by side by the warm glow of the fire; happy and content. Suppressing a sigh Sapphire walked into the kitchen, still redolent with the fragrance of her newly baked bread. On the table one of her loaves stood on the breadboard surrounded by crumbs. Blake had obviously cut himself a slice, and probably given himself indigestion she thought wryly, touching the still warm loaf.

Knowing that if she remained alone any longer in the house she would only brood, Sapphire picked up her jacket and headed for the Land Rover. Spending the evening with her father would stop her thinking about the past; about useless might-have-beens, she decided firmly, as she swung herself up into the utilitarian vehicle. She was just about to start the motor when a sound from the barn stopped her. Tensing she listened, wondering if she was imagining things, and then she heard it again; the shrill, unmistakable whinny of a horse in pain.

Blake's mare! But he had told her that the vet had said she probably wouldn't start to foal for at least twenty-four hours. Frowning Sapphire glanced towards the barn door, her conscience prodding her to get out of the Land Rover and go and investigate. She wasn't a stranger to animal birth; and as she hurried into the barn, snapping on the light, her experienced eye quickly took in the mare's distressed state and knew that the vet had been wrong. By the looks of her the mare was already in labour.

Despite her long years in London old habits reasserted themselves. Soothing the mare as best she could, Sapphire left her to race back to the house. To her relief the vet's wife answered the 'phone almost immediately. Quickly Sapphire explained the position.

'The vet isn't here,' she told Sapphire, 'but I know where he is. I'll 'phone him and let him know the position. I know he'll be with you just as soon as he can. Are you able to get in touch with Blake?' she asked worriedly, 'I know how much he thinks of that mare...'

It wasn't hard for Sapphire to find Miranda's telephone number, but she hesitated before dialling it. As she had half-expected, there was no answer. She ought to have felt a savage satisfaction that Blake was being repaid for his duplicity, but all she could feel was a growing concern for the mare, and concern at her own ability to handle the situation. The shepherd who might have been able to help was out on the hills with his flock; her father was far too ill to help and Mary... Mary was a trained nurse, Sapphire remembered excitedly, picking up the phone again and punching in the numbers quickly.

Mary listened while she explained the situation. 'I'll be right over,' she assured Sapphire. 'The vet may not be long, but it's better to be safe than sorry. This won't be the first birth I've attended by a long chalk.'

While she was waiting, more to keep herself busy than anything else Sapphire boiled water and scalded the buckets, finding carbolic soap, and a pack of clean, unused rope. If for some reason the foal was turned the wrong way they might need the rope. Hurriedly she tried to think of anything else they might need, rushing into the yard when she heard the sound of a vehicle. To her disappointment it was Mary and not the vet who alighted from the Range Rover.

'You've done well,' she approved as she followed Sapphire into the barn. 'But where's Blake?'

'He had to go out,' Sapphire avoided her eyes. 'I haven't been able to reach him.'

Fortunately Mary was too busy examining the mare to hear the slight hesitation in her voice.

'The foal's turned into the breech position,' Mary explained, fulfilling Sapphire's own fears. 'I'll try and turn it, can you hold the mare's head, try and soothe her?'

Her father had once told Sapphire that she had a way with animals, and Sapphire prayed that he might be right as she softly coaxed the nervous mare, talking to her in soothing whispers.

'This isn't her first foal,' Mary commented, 'but she's very nervous.'

'Missing Blake, I expect,' Sapphire murmured absently. 'Are you going to be able to turn it?'

'I think so.' Mary's face was strained with the effort of concentrating on her task, and Sapphire felt herself willing her to succeed.

'There...I think that's done it. Good girl,' she soothed the mare, adding to Sapphire, 'I think we can let nature take its course now, although I hope the birth won't be too protracted, she's already suffered a lot of pain.'

As the birth pangs rippled through the mare's swollen belly Sapphire found herself tensing in sympathy with her, and yet the mare did seem more relaxed as though she knew that they were there to help her.

'Quick, Sapphire, look.' Mary's voice was exultant as she pointed to the foal's head as it emerged from its mother's body. Deftly she moved to assist the mare, Sapphire immediately moving to help, remembering how she had assisted her father in the past.

The foal was a tiny bundle of stick-like limbs on the straw at its mother's feet when they heard the sound of a vehicle outside.

A door slammed and the vet came hurrying in bringing a gust of cold air with him, his anxious frown relaxing into a smile as he saw the foal. 'Well, well what have we here?' he asked gently, quickly examining the mare, nodding with approval as he inspected the foal.

'I'm sorry I couldn't get here before—an emergency at Low Head farm, but you seem to have managed well enough without me.' His smile was for Sapphire, but she shook her head, directing his attention to Mary. 'Without Mary's help I couldn't have done it.'

'The foal had turned,' Mary explained, 'but fortunately he was small enough for me to turn back.'

'Umm, quick thinking on your part to send for Mary,' the vet praised Sapphire, 'but where's Blake?'

'He had to go out.' Sapphire repeated the explanation she had given Mary.

'Lucky for him and the mare that you were here.' His eyes were curious as he inspected her, and Sapphire wondered if he knew that she was Blake's wife, and that they were back together again.

It was another two hours before Sapphire could crawl into bed. She had made supper for Mary and the vet, who had pronounced both mother and foal to be in perfect health, and by the time they had gone she had been almost too tired to sink into the hot bath she had run for herself. As she pulled the quilt up round her ears she glanced at her watch. One o'clock, and Blake still wasn't back. A bitter pain invaded her body. Was he at this very moment making love to Miranda, kissing her with the barely restrained passion he had shown her earlier in the day? They had not been lovers he had said to her, and for a moment she had believed him, but surely his actions tonight proved that he had lied?

She closed her eyes, willing herself to sleep. She *wasn't* going to lie here awake, wondering where he was, waiting for him to return as she had done so often in the past.

# CHAPTER SIX

A SURPRISE AWAITED Sapphire when she opened her eyes the following morning. It was the clarity of the light in her bedroom that first alerted her, and padding across the room on bare feet she flung back the curtains, bemused to see the white blanket of snow that must have fallen during the night. Everything was so quiet; the air so crystal clear it was almost like wine. She frowned; where was Blake? Had he even returned? She padded back to bed, picking up her watch and nearly dropping it as she realised how long she had overslept. It was gone ten o'clock!

Showering quickly she ran downstairs and opened the kitchen door. The room was empty but there was evidence that Blake had had some breakfast. The aroma of coffee hung tantalisingly in the air making her aware of her thirst. Deftly she moved about the kitchen going to stand by the window as she waited for the coffee to filter into the jug. The snow lay surprisingly deep in the yard, criss-crossed with footmarks plus those of a dog. Of course, the sheep! Sapphire gnawed at her bottom lip. Attractive though the snow was to look at it could spell disaster for any unwary farmer. She remembered her father's shepherd telling her that he had expected this weather. Had Blake got the ewes down to the lower pastures? If not there was every danger that the new lambs would be lost beneath the huge drifts Sapphire knew could form on the bleak mountain tops. Without consciously making any decision she found herself searching in the porch for a pair of suitable Wellingtons, mentally ticking off all that she would need if she was to be any help to the men. She could follow their tracks through the snow without any difficulty. Perhaps if she took them hot coffee and tea…

Fifteen minutes later Sapphire tramped through the farmyard, following the clearly defined footprints upwards. The snow had frozen to a crisp crust, her laboured breath made white plumes in the sharp morning air. At another time she would have found the atmosphere invigorating, but right now she was too concerned about the sheep to really enjoy the delights of the morning.

The baaing of the sheep and the sharp yelps of the dogs reached her first, carrying easily on the clear air, and she expelled her breath on a faint sigh of relief. Obviously some of the sheep at least had been brought down to the lower meadows. As she followed the footprints along a dry-stone wall Sapphire caught her first glimpse of her quarry, a rough shelter had been constructed in one of the fields, and men were busy unbaling hay from a tractor. The field sloped away slightly offering some protection from the wind and drifts, and as she got nearer Sapphire recognised her father's shepherd, busily at work. The other men she also vaguely recognised as general farmhands attached to Blake's farm whom he had no doubt taken from their other tasks to help with the all-important job of saving the sheep.

Tam recognised her face, a weary grin splitting his weathered face as he hailed her.

'I've brought you something hot to drink,' Sapphire called out as soon as she was close enough, adding anxiously, 'How's it going? The ewes...'

'Brought most of them down yesterday,' Tam informed her. 'Blake's gone looking for the rest of the flock. Shouldn't have too much of a problem with my Laddie to help him. Fine sheepdog.'

'Anything I can do to help?' Sapphire asked, handing out the thermos flasks and cups.

'No. I reckon everything's under control. Luckily Blake was running your dad's flock with his own, so we shouldn't have too many casualties. If this weather had come another two weeks on we could have been in trouble—the first ewes are due to start lambing then.'

'You don't think it will last then?' Sapphire asked, studying the snow-covered landscape.

Tam shook his head. 'Not more than three or four days, and we were prepared for it.' He nodded in the direction of the new shelter and the bales of hay. 'Blake knows what he's doing all right.' There was approval in his voice and Sapphire turned away, not wanting the shepherd to see her own bitter resentment. What time had Blake come home last night?

He could have had precious little sleep she thought revengefully. Had he arrived before the snow came or had the fact that she had not heard him been due to the fact that it had muffled his return?

What did it matter? It was no business of hers how he spent his time, or whose bed he shared.

She waited until the men had finished their drinks before gathering up the empty flasks.

'I'll keep this one for Blake,' Tam offered taking a half-full one from her and screwing on the top. 'He'll be fair frozen by the time he gets back.'

'Is he up there alone?' Sapphire frowned when the shepherd nodded. 'Is that wise?'

'Blake knows what he's doing.'

Tam had been right, Sapphire reflected several hours later when a noise in the yard alerted her to Blake's return. Snow clung to his thick protective jacket and the cuffs of his boots, his skin burned by the icy cold wind. She hadn't known whether to prepare a meal or not—there was still the Beef Wellington to cook from last night, and she had spent what was left of the morning making a nourishing hot soup, thinking that if Blake didn't return she could take it out to the men in flasks.

She had also been in to inspect the new foal, now standing proudly on all four spindly legs while his mother looked on in benign approval.

As Blake crossed the yard the 'phone rang. It was her father calling to enquire about the sheep. 'Everything's under control, Dad,' she assured him. 'Blake had already got the ewes down to the lower pasture and he's been up to the top to bring the rest down.'

'Yes, Mary told me I didn't need to worry, but old habits die hard.'

The kitchen door opened as she replied, and she could hear the sound of Blake tugging off his boots. 'Blake's back now,' she told her father, 'would you like to speak to him?'

'No, I know myself what it's like. He'll be frozen to the marrow and tired out—the last thing he'll feel like is talking to me. I'll speak to him later when he's thawed out.'

'Who was that?'

She hadn't heard Blake cross the floor in his stockinged feet and whirled round apprehensively. Exhaustion tautened the bone structure of his face, dimming the gold of his eyes to tawny brown. White flecks of snow clung to his hair and jumper.

'My father. Is it snowing again?'

'Trying to. God I'm tired. Is there any hot water?'

'Plenty. Would you like something to eat?' She saw his eyebrows lift and mockery invade his eyes. 'Quite the devoted wife today aren't we? What brought about this metamorphosis?'

'Nothing...there hasn't been one.' Sapphire retorted flatly cursing herself for her momentary weakness. 'I just thought...'

'Yes, I'm sorry.' Strong dark fingers raked through his already tousled hair. 'That was uncalled for—put it down to sheer male...' His glance studied her slim body in its covering of jeans and sweater and he grimaced faintly before adding bluntly, 'frustration... Deprivation of physical satisfaction does tend to make me behave like a churlish brute, and I haven't even thanked you for your midwifery last night...'

'Mary's the one you should thank,' Sapphire told him, turning away and busying herself filling the kettle. She wanted to scream at him that she didn't want to know the details about his relationship with Miranda or about his physical hunger for her. Was that why he had made love to *her* so intensely yesterday? In anticipation of holding Miranda in his arms? The thought made her feel physically sick, but what was even more shocking was the knowledge that she could feel so strongly and primitively about a man for whom she had already told herself she felt only the echoes of an old physical desire.

'Is something wrong?'

She could feel him approaching and tensed. 'No, nothing.' She couldn't bear him to come anywhere near her right now, not when her far too active mind was picturing him with Miranda, kissing and caressing her. The handle of the mug she had been holding in her hand snapped under the intensity of her grip, the mug falling to the floor where it shattered into fragments.

'No...don't. Leave it.' Her voice was sharper than she had intended, almost shrill in its intensity and she prayed that Blake wouldn't recognise the near hysteria edging up under it. 'You haven't got anything on your feet,' she added weakly. 'You go and have your bath and I'll clean it up. Are you hungry now, or can you wait an hour or so?'

'I can wait.' He too sounded clipped and terse, but Sapphire couldn't look at him to read the reason in his expression. Instead she waited until she heard the door close behind him and then carefully skirting the broken china went to get a brush and pan to clear up the mess.

She was putting the Beef Wellington into the oven when she heard Blake call out something from upstairs. Reacting without thinking Sapphire hurried up them, coming to an abrupt halt outside his bedroom door, wondering whether to knock or simply walk in. The dilemma was solved for her as Blake pulled the door open. He had taken off his sweater and shirt, and his skin gleamed silky bronze beneath the electric light. Her breathing, which hadn't been in the slightest affected by her dash upstairs, now suddenly constricted, her heart thudding heavily its beats reverberating through her body.

'I've scraped my back against a wall. I think the skin's broken.' Blake turned his back to her as he spoke and Sapphire saw the patch of broken skin, slightly swollen and discoloured with dried blood.

Farm accidents no matter how minor always had to be properly attended to; that was one of the first rules Sapphire had ever learned and she knew better than to accuse Blake of being too fussy in wanting the graze attended to. Neither would he be able to deal with it himself, positioned as it was just below his shoulder blade.

'I'll go and get some antiseptic and cotton wool. Your tetanus shots are up to date I hope?'

'Do you?' Blake grimaced sardonically, flexing his shoulder as he moved away from her, as though the muscles pained him. 'Funny, I had the distinct impression you'd like nothing better than to see me suffer.'

'Don't.' Sapphire whispered the protest, her face paper white, remembering the stories Tam had told her as a child about farm workers who had died from the dreaded 'lockjaw'. Fortunately, with his back to her Blake couldn't see her betraying expression, nor question her as to why she should feel such concern for someone she purportedly hated.

Why did she? She was forced to ask herself the question as she hurried into the bathroom for antiseptic and cotton-wool. There was nothing personal in her concern, she assured herself, she would have reacted the same way no matter who was involved. But she would not have reacted so intensely to the sight of anyone else's half-naked body; she would not have wanted to stretch out and touch the bronze skin and hard muscles, excitement gripping her by the throat as she visualised that same body… No…she was over all that. She no longer loved Blake, but for some reason her senses were playing cruel tricks on her, tormenting her with mental images of herself in Blake's arms; of Blake making love to her with all the fierce passion she suspected lay beneath his sardonic exterior.

Fool, fool, she berated herself as she hurried back

to the stark, functional bedroom Blake had chosen for his own occupation. As she walked in she noticed that the bed looked untidy and rumpled. When she had dealt with Blake's wound she would change the sheets and tidy up a bit. *Very wifely,* the inner cynical voice she had come to dread mocked her, *but it won't make him want you.* I don't want him to want me. The denial seemed to reverberate inside her skull, and then as though it knew how paper-frail it was that other voice taunted softly, *Liar.*

'Sapphire?' Blake's curt voice cut across her thoughts. 'Are you all right?' He was frowning, his eyes sharpening to vivid gold as they searched her face.

'I'm not going to faint at the sight of a drop of your precious blood if that's what you think,' Sapphire responded tartly, adding with a calm she was far from feeling. 'While you're having your bath I'll change the bed for you. You'd better sit down on it, otherwise I'll never be able to reach the graze.'

'If you just clean it up for now,' Blake suggested, 'that should do the trick.'

'It will need a dressing on it,' Sapphire protested.

'Which will get soaked through the moment I get in the bath.'

'Then I'll put it on when you've finished,' Sapphire told him tartly, complaining, 'Honestly Blake, I never thought you of all people would be so irresponsible.'

'Perhaps I'm just testing to see exactly how deep your hatred of me really is,' Blake taunted back.

Sapphire compressed her lips. 'I'm not a child any more, Blake,' she reminded him. 'No matter what my personal feelings for you are, I wouldn't want to see you take the risk of getting a bad infection through a neglected skin wound.'

'Which doesn't really answer my question does it?'

'Sit down,' Sapphire instructed, ignoring his probing comment. 'This will sting,' she warned him as he sat down on the edge of the bed with his back to her. His skin looked so warm and inviting that it took all the self-control she possessed not to reach out and caress it.

'And won't you just enjoy it,' Blake muttered under his breath, tensing slightly as Sapphire applied the antiseptic soaked pad to his skin, gently cleaning the graze, until the blood flowed cleanly from it.

She let it flow for a few seconds, and then quickly stemmed it with fresh antiseptic, hiding a faint smile as Blake winced.

'Give me a shout when you're ready,' she told him when she had finished, 'and I'll come up and put a dressing on it for you. It should start to heal by morning.'

'Yes, nurse,' Blake mocked, getting up off the bed and momentarily making her feel at a distinct disadvantage as he towered over her. 'Taking a risk aren't you?' he drawled, watching her. For a moment Sapphire thought he meant the temptation she had exposed herself to in being so close to him, and her face flamed until he added softly, 'Isn't it a well known fact that patients always fall for their nurses?'

'In that case I think I'm pretty safe,' Sapphire responded, struggling to appear calmly unconcerned. 'After all I already know how you feel about me, don't I?'

Blake walked out without responding, and when she heard the bathroom door close behind him Sapphire got up and went to the large, old-fashioned airing cupboard situated on the landing to get clean sheets for his bed.

She worked methodically, changing the sheets, tidying up automatically, filling the laundry basket with the items of discarded clothing she found scattered round the room. Blake was basically a tidy man and there was nothing really in the starkly furnished room apart from his clothes that had his stamp of possession on it. If anything the room was rather bleak, she thought, studying it, almost monk-like. Mocking herself for her thoughts Sapphire carried the laundry out on to the landing. Blake was no monk, as she had seen last night.

She had just finished preparing the table when Blake called. Guessing that he would probably be tired she had decided that they might as well eat in the kitchen. It was warm and cosy enough and the table was large enough to seat an entire family, never mind merely two adults.

This time she walked into Blake's room without thinking, coming to an abrupt halt as she realised that he was nude. Of the two of them she was the one to be embarrassed she recognised angrily, as Blake merely grinned mockingly at her, taking his time in reaching for the towel that lay discarded on the bed.

'Why the outraged expression?' he demanded calmly. 'I can't be the first naked man you've seen.'

He was the only one, but Sapphire wasn't going to tell him that. 'Hardly,' she lied, shrugging aside the frisson of awareness the sight of his naked body had given her.

'And we are married...'

'Maybe, but it isn't the sort of marriage that involves parading around naked in front of one another.'

'What a pity.' Genuine amusement glinted in Blake's eyes as he teased her, and Sapphire had to fight against responding, against remembering how much joy there had been in loving him before she discovered the bitter truth. Blake had always been able to make her laugh, and even now she could feel the corners of her mouth twitching in response to his droll expression. The towel was firmly in place around his hips now, but to her chagrin that didn't stop Sapphire from visualising the taut shape of masculine buttocks and long hard thighs.

'Something smells good.' Blake's voice jerked her out of her reverie, and Sapphire bent her head to hide her guilty flush of colour. What on earth would he think if he knew what had been in her mind?

Fortunately he didn't, she assured herself as she gestured to the bed and suggested that he sit on it.

This time she didn't allow herself to dwell on the supple texture of his skin or the masculine formation of muscle and bone that lay beneath it, finishing her self-imposed task with a haste she was surprised Blake didn't pick up on.

When the dressing was in place, she stepped away from him, tensing nervously as his fingers curled round her arm, preventing her from moving.

'Blake, let me go.' Her voice sounded sharp and nervous even to her own ears, and her anxiety increased when Blake refused to accede to her demand.

'I haven't rewarded you yet,' he told her softly, the hard grip of his fingers pulling her inexorably closer to him. 'All ministering angels deserve a reward, don't you agree?'

Whatever she might have said was lost as she felt the warm heat of Blake's body. She put out a hand to push him away, but the sensation of warm, sensuously silken male skin beneath her fingertips was so intoxicating that her resistance melted.

Dimly she was aware of Blake pulling her down on to his lap, and of the single bed creaking protestingly under their double weight.

She struggled to pull away out of his constraining arms, but Blake simply toppled her over on to the bed, imprisoning her against it with the superior weight of his body. His thighs pinned her lower body to the mattress, his chest hard against the softness of her breasts.

Sapphire felt vulnerable and helpless and yet the

sensations coursing through her veins and along her nerve endings whispered sensuously of pleasurable excitement rather than fear. Even so, she felt moved to protest shakily, 'Blake, let me get up, the dinner...'

Soft laughter brushed against her skin. 'Right now I'm hungry for more than just food.'

'Then perhaps you ought to give Miranda a ring,' Sapphire suggested tartly, struggling to push him away. She was glad she had said that, until that moment she had been dangerously close to giving way to the insidious pull of her too vulnerable senses.

'Why should I need another man's wife, when I've got one of my own?' Blake countered outrageously, following her squirming movements and refusing to let her escape. His towel, Sapphire realised, had become dislodged, and weakening darts of pleasure relaxed her muscles into a sensuous lethargy as she felt her body reacting to the male provocation of Blake's body.

'Kiss me, Sapphire.'

She looked at him with desire-hazed eyes, barely comprehending the softly whispered command as she fought to subdue the treacherous impulses of her body.

'No.' She mumbled the denial huskily, knowing that it was far more than a kiss that Blake wanted from her. She wouldn't, she couldn't play substitute for Miranda.

'Yes.' The silky affirmation was whispered against her lips, the warmth of Blake's breath stirring to life a thousand tiny drumming pulses. Against her will Sapphire felt her mouth soften, her breathing suddenly ragged as Blake touched its soft contours with the tip of his tongue, expertly teasing light kisses into the corners, tormentingly stroking her sensitised skin, until she reacted with a feverish protest, lifting her arms, and locking her fingers behind his neck, her body arching instinctively into the hard heat of his, as her mouth opened to capture the marauding torment of his tongue. The sudden fierce pressure of his mouth, searing into her skin, took Sapphire by surprise, making her realise the extent of Blake's self-control. The kisses he had given her before had been so lightly teasing that she had been lulled into a false sense of security, and yet there was a wild elemental pleasure in responding to Blake's hunger; a knowledge that they were meeting as equals, not child and adult.

When he eventually released her mouth it felt bruised and slightly swollen, and yet the sensation was a pleasurable one, her lips acutely sensitive to the light kisses he caressed them with as he murmured softly, 'Let me take this tee-shirt off, I want to feel you against me, Sapphire.'

His hands were already gripping the edge of her tee-shirt, and to her shame Sapphire knew a wild impulse to help him. Once she had fantasised about seeing their bodies intimately enmeshed; the paleness of her fair skin against the gold-bronze of his and now, treacherously, that memory resurfaced making her protest only a token one as Blake tugged the stretchy fabric up over her body.

Her figure had changed in the intervening years, she knew; her shape no longer that of a young girl. Her waist had narrowed, but her breasts were fuller, more mature, crowned with deep pink nipples, at the moment veiled from Blake's intense scrutiny by the lacy fabric of her bra.

'Beautiful,' he murmured huskily, his thumb stroking caressingly along the edge of the dainty lace and down into the hollow between her breasts.

Desire seemed to explode like fireworks deep inside her, stunning Sapphire with its intensity. She had desired Blake before, but surely never with this consuming, all-important depth, that pushed aside every other emotion as trivial and not to be considered. She wanted to respond to him with every feminine nerve ending; she wanted to feel his hands and mouth against every inch of her skin; and she wanted the freedom to caress and know him in exactly the same way. The knowledge that she could feel like this was shocking and yet exciting; freeing her suddenly from the fear she had always had that somehow she was not quite 100 per cent feminine; that the deep inner core of her was cold and unfunctioning. No other man had made her feel like this, certainly not Alan.

Alan! She tensed, suddenly shocked back to reality. Blake's fingers were curled round the lacy cup of her bra, his eyes so brilliantly gold as he stared down at her that she found herself blinking, half-dazzled by their glitter.

'Blake, I don't want...' She shivered as he cut off her protest by bending his head and brushing his lips provocatively along the delicate skin exposed above the white lace.

A tumult of sensations poured moltenly through Sapphire's veins. She made a small sound, meant to be a protest, but which emerged as a soft cry of pleasure as Blake's fingers eased back the lace and his lips followed the path they made until they found the aching centre of her breast, being teased into wanton erectness by the caressing movement of his fingers.

Awash with pleasure Sapphire was barely aware of Blake unsnapping her bra, and exposing her other breast until he repeated his tormenting caresses on it with a nerve-racking delicacy that left Sapphire shivering and aching beneath an onslaught of pleasure she hadn't believed could exist.

'You respond to me as though no-one's ever touched you like that before,' Blake muttered rawly, cupping her breasts possessively as he looked up at her. 'I expected you to be more blasé.'

As she shuddered in reaction, he moaned thickly, 'Don't do that, you make me go up in flames, just thinking about...' His sudden tension alerted Sapphire to the sound of a vehicle arriving in the yard.

'Damn,' Blake swore softly. 'The last thing I feel like right now is leaving this bed.'

His words brought Sapphire back down to earth,

making her shrink in self-disgust from her own behaviour. How could she have behaved so foolishly? She was lucky that Blake didn't appear to have guessed how much she still cared about him… Stunned, Sapphire stopped what she was doing. That wasn't true, she didn't care about Blake at all… But if that was true, why had she reacted to intensely to him…why had her body welcomed him as its lover? She *didn't* still love him; she *couldn't*…but deep inside Sapphire knew that she was only deceiving herself. If sex was really her only motivation she could have found that with anyone of a dozen or more attractive men whom she had dated since leaving Blake, but she hadn't wanted to. She had remained sexually cold to them. She still loved Blake all right, and deep down inside her she must have known it all along, even though she had tried to hide from the truth.

Sick at heart, too numb almost to pull on her tee-shirt, she heard someone knocking on the back door, and hurriedly completed her task.

'I'll get it,' she told Blake, too disturbed to turn and look at him.

The rich smell of their evening meal filled the warm kitchen as Sapphire hurried across it, her hair as uncombed and her face free of makeup, her lips no doubt still swollen from Blake's kisses. A flush of embarrassment stained her skin as she pulled open the door, and then came to an abrupt halt, stunned by the sight of the very last person she had expected to see standing there.

'Alan,' she managed weakly, staring at him, thinking how out of place his dark business suit and obviously new sheepskin jacket looked—and how alien he seemed to her. She had only been away from London for a few days, but already it seemed like another life-time.

'Your father told me you were here,' Alan frowned. 'I've been to make arrangements to get the car back. You really should have been more careful, Sapphire, and what are you doing here?' he demanded waspishly. 'I expected to find you with your father, instead he directed me here...or rather his housekeeper did. Not a very forthcoming woman, but then I suppose it's only to be expected from these country types. Aren't you going to let me in?' he asked her querulously. 'It's freezing out here, and what on earth are you wearing?' He surveyed her jean-clad figure with open disapproval. 'Sapphire, what's going on, I...'

'Why don't you tell him, darling?'

Blake's voice from the other side of the kitchen made Sapphire wrench her head round in open-mouthed disbelief. Clad only in a towelling robe, Blake stood by the door, arms folded, hair tousled, the sight of his bare chest and long lean legs making Sapphire go weak at the knees, treacherous, reactionary sensations warming the pit of her stomach.

'Sapphire, who is this?' Alan demanded.

'Blake,' Blake offered, answering for her, and walking towards Alan, proferring his hand, 'Sapphire's husband.'

'Husband!' Alan practically goggled, and watching him Sapphire knew that no matter how she might have chosen to deceive herself, when it came to it, she would never have married Alan. The emotions she felt for him were lukewarm nonentities when compared with the fierce, tumultuous feelings she had for Blake.

'Yes, Sapphire and I have decided to give our marriage another try,' Blake told him calmly.

'Marriage. You told me you were divorced,' Alan accused Sapphire. 'When did all this happen? Why didn't you say something when I rang?'

'I wanted to tell you, Alan, but...'

'I was hoping your father would put me up for the night. It's too late to drive back to London now, and there isn't a decent hotel in miles.'

'You can stay here,' Blake offered, stunning Sapphire with his offer. 'There's plenty of room. If you bring in your case I'll take it upstairs for you—it will give you and Sapphire a chance to talk.'

Sapphire had expected Alan to refuse, but instead he walked out to his hired car and returned with an overnight case. When Blake took it upstairs Alan demanded, 'What's going on? When you left London you were going to marry me, now...'

'I'm sorry, Alan, but I didn't want to tell you over the 'phone. I thought you'd ring again before coming up here, and everything's happened so quickly that...'

'By everything I suppose you mean going to bed with your supposed ''ex'',' Alan interrupted crudely.

'He's obviously got something I don't have... Oh, come on Sapphire,' he added angrily when she tried to protest, 'it's written all over the pair of you. Well I'm beginning to think he's welcome to you. You aren't the woman I thought, that's obvious,' he added in disgust, 'and if it wasn't for necessity, there's no way I'd stay here tonight. My sister was right it seems. She warned me not to get too involved with you.'

Alan's sister was a domineering possessive woman whom Sapphire had never liked and she sighed faintly.

'I've put your case in your room. The door on the right,' Blake announced, coming back into the kitchen. 'How long until we eat?' he asked Sapphire, 'I want to check on the mare and foal. Sapphire told you about her midwifery skills yet?' he asked Alan. 'She's practically delivered him all by herself. Messy business too—breech birth...'

Alan had gone green and Sapphire suppressed a momentary flash of irritation against him. Poor Alan, he couldn't help being so squeamish. If she didn't know better she would have thought that Blake was deliberately trying to show him in a bad light. She frowned suddenly, remembering which room Blake had given Alan. That was Blake's own room. Perhaps he had put Alan's case there because he knew the bed was freshly made up, and after all there were plenty of other rooms for him to sleep in.

'We'll be eating in half an hour,' she told him. 'Alan, the bathroom's first on the left if you want to use it.'

# CHAPTER SEVEN

IT WAS DEFINITELY one of the worst meals Sapphire had ever endured. Alan had lapsed into a sulky silence, punctuated by petulant little-boy responses to her questions, designed to reinforce her guilt, but what was even harder to cope with was the proprietorial, and very obviously male-in-possession, stance adopted by Blake, who remained sublimely indifferent to the killing looks she gave him, taking every opportunity he could to touch her, or to look at her with such blatant sexuality that if she hadn't known exactly why he was doing it, she would have been in serious danger of succumbing to them.

Afterwards both men accepted coffee, and the tense silence pervading the sitting room as they all sat drinking it made Sapphire heave a sigh of relief when Blake announced that he ought to go and do his final rounds.

'We go to bed early in these parts,' he told Alan blandly.

'Yes, I'm sure with the livestock and...'

'Oh that isn't the only reason,' Blake interrupted softly, watching Sapphire.

'I thought you told me you hated him,' Alan said

stiffly the moment they were alone, 'and yet now, apparently you're reconciled.'

For a moment Sapphire was tempted to tell him the truth, as she had been planning to, but what was the point now? It was kinder in the long run to let Alan have the pride-saving cleansing of genuine anger to sustain him, and it would be selfish of her to tell him the truth now, knowing that she could never marry him.

'I made a mistake,' she told him quietly.

'But not as big a one as I made,' Alan told her through his teeth. 'I thought…oh what's the use? I might as well try and get what sleep I can. I'm leaving here in the morning. I'll have your office cleared out and your things sent on.'

'Thank you.' How stilted and formal they were with one another. Sapphire sighed. She wished they could have remained friends, but sensed that Alan's sister would prevent that!

When she had finished clearing away from their meal Sapphire went upstairs herself. Blake was still outside, and a thin line of light showed under the door of the room he had given Alan, the bathroom door open.

After showering in the privacy of her own en suite bathroom Sapphire towelled herself dry, clicking her tongue impatiently as she realised she had left her nightdress on the bed. Thank heavens for central heating, she reflected self-indulgently, as she dropped her damp towel and walked through into the other room. The lamps on either side of the half tester bed threw a soft haze of peach light across the room, emphasising the subtle blues of the decor, her progress silent as she wriggled her toes luxuriously in the thick blue pile of the carpet.

She was just picking up her nightdress when she froze in disbelief as the handle of her bedroom door turned. Clutching the thin silk to herself she stared as the door opened inwards and Blake walked casually in.

'Blake!' Her astonishment showed in her voice. 'What are you doing in here?'

'I am your husband,' he reminded her tauntingly, 'or is the maidenly shock because you were expecting someone else—your lover, perhaps? Sorry to disappoint you, but unless he wants to share your bed with me as well as with you, he'll have to sleep alone tonight,' Blake told her crudely.

Sapphire was too stunned to be embarrassed about her nudity, anger heating her blood to boiling point as she stared at him. 'Alan would never...' she began, only to be interrupted by Blake who drawled insultingly, 'Oh surely that can't be true, Sapphire? He must have wanted you once at least for you to be lovers, but not under my roof, and not while you're wearing my ring, and just to make sure he doesn't, I'll be sleeping in here with you tonight.'

'You can't.' The protest was out before she could stop it, her eyes widening with shock. 'Blake, there are half-a-dozen bedrooms for you to choose from...'

'But I've chosen this one,' he told her grimly, adding, 'Oh come on, Sapphire, I wasn't born yesterday, you really didn't think I was going to make it easy for you do you? You alone in one room, him virtually next door? When did you arrange for him to come here?'

He was across the room in four strides, gripping her upper arm with fingers that bit into the soft flesh, surprising a gasp of pain from her lips.

'Blake, I didn't arrange anything. I was as surprised as you to see him. Oh I knew he was coming to collect his car...' Anger fired her eyes to deep blue-black as she added bitterly, 'Why should I defend my actions to you? There's no reason why I should be faithful to you, Blake, no reason at all.'

'No?' His face was white with anger. 'Then perhaps I'd better give you one. Why didn't you tell him you were coming back to me, Sapphire? Were you afraid he wouldn't wait for you, is that it?'

'I wanted to tell him in person, not over the telephone. Alan fully understands the situation,' she lied, urged to utter the falsehood by some only dimly conceived knowledge that if Blake thought she still loved Alan, it would in some way protect her from him. This afternoon she had come dangerously close to succumbing to the raw masculinity of him; of succumbing to her own reluctantly admitted love for him, she told herself. If Blake discovered how she really felt she had no guarantee that he wouldn't somehow manipulate her vulnerable emotions and her, using them to his own best advantage. She shivered suddenly, wishing she had not as her shudder drew Blake's attention to her nude body.

In the lamplight her skin glowed pearly cream, her hair curling wildly round her shoulders, still damp from her shower, her face completely free of makeup.

'How many times has he seen you like this?' Blake grated hoarsely. 'How many times have you slept with him? How long have you been lovers?'

'That's none of your business,' Sapphire protested, hot colour flooding her skin. 'I don't ask you about your...your love life...'

'Love life!' Blake laughed harshly. 'Now there's an antiquated term if ever there was one. I don't have a *love life,* my dear wife, I learned the folly of that years ago, but I do have all the usual sexual desires... Like me to prove it to you?'

'You're disgusting.' Sapphire flung the words at him as she pulled free of his grip.

'You didn't seem to think so earlier this evening,' Blake reminded her softly, going back to the bedroom door where he turned the key in the lock and then removed it, putting it in his jeans pocket. 'Just in case you have any ideas about going to lover boy while I'm asleep,' he explained tersely.

What was the matter with Blake? Sapphire wondered bitterly. He seemed to have a fetish about her going to Alan. What would he say if he knew the truth? That Alan wasn't her lover; that no man ever had been... She shuddered; her skin suddenly too warm, her body weak with the knowledge that there was only one man she wanted to make love to her. What would Blake say if she told him…if she asked him…

Shocked she pulled her thoughts back from the precipice on which they teetered. Hadn't she learned anything at all from the past? Once before she had begged Blake to love her.

'Don't worry, you're quite safe with me,' Blake drawled, watching her. 'Unless of course, you choose not to be.'

'Why on earth should I do that?' Animosity flared between them; tension tightening Sapphire's nerve endings.

'Oh any number of reasons,' Blake told her insultingly. 'You've been up here several days…and it can sometimes be hard denying oneself, when one's been used to…'

'Stop it!' Sapphire demanded, goaded almost beyond endurance, her cheeks scarlet with rage. 'How dare you suggest that…'

'That you'd be so hungry for sex that you'd turn to me?' Blake finished coolly for her. 'Why not? After all it wouldn't be the first time, would it?'

He turned his back on her as he spoke, calmly pulling off his sweater and unfastening his shirt, leaving Sapphire seething with temper and pain. How could he throw that in her face? He always had been a cruel bastard, she thought bitterly, but she had never expected anything like this…

'Go on.' His voice was amused rather than contrite. 'Why don't you throw something at me, if that's how you feel.'

'Go to hell,' Sapphire told him thickly. 'God, I hate you, Blake…'

'Really?' He paused in the act of unfastening his belt, sitting down on the bed, his eyebrows arching as he studied the warm curves of her body. 'Then perhaps you ought to have a word with your hormones,' he tormented blandly, 'they seem to be getting the wrong message.'

Sapphire had forgotten her nudity, and she froze to the spot, the image of her own body faithfully reflected in the long pier-glass on the other side of the room. Her skin glowed milky pale, her breasts full and softly feminine, crowned with deeply pink nipples that betrayed all too clearly the correctness of Blake's taunt.

'I'm going to have a shower,' Blake told her, standing up and shedding his jeans. Frantically Sapphire dragged her gaze away from the muscled contours of his body, not sure who she hated the most; Blake for tormenting her as he was doing, or herself for being so vulnerable to that torment.

'You can always join me if you want to cool down.' The mocking taunt followed him across the room as he closed the bathroom door behind him. Once he was gone Sapphire struggled into her nightdress. The fine pearl grey silk seemed to emphasise her curves rather than conceal them, the deeply decolleté, lace-trimmed neckline outlining the curves of her breasts in explicit detail. One thing she was

sure of. When Blake came back from the bathroom
he would find her deeply and safely asleep. As she
lay down and pulled the covers over her, keeping as
close to the edge of the bed as possible she wondered
bitterly if he had come to her room deliberately to
torment her, or if he genuinely did believe if he
wasn't there to prevent her she might have gone to
Alan.

Letting him think that she and Alan were lovers
was her only means of protection, she acknowledged, closing her eyes, her body tense. Once Blake
found out they weren't, it wouldn't take him long to
discover that she still loved him and then she would
be completely at his mercy.

Nothing had changed, she thought bitterly, forcing
herself to breathe evenly, and then a small inner
voice corrected her, one thing had changed apparently. Blake, for some reason, now seemed to find
her physically desirable. Or was his desire for her
simply a frustrated sexual longing for Miranda who
presumably now shared her favours between Blake
and her husband? Nausea, deep and wrenching, tore
into her as Sapphire pictured them together. No,
please God not that, she whispered squeezing her
eyes closed as though she could blot out the pictures.
She had been through all this once before and suffered all the torments of the damned picturing Blake
with Miranda, imagining their bodies entwined in the
act of love; sharing its heated ecstasy and its languorous aftermath—pleasures which had been de-

nied to her, and she wasn't going to endure them again. She *couldn't.*

She heard Blake come back into the room and tensed as he snapped off the lamp, and pulled back the covers. The sarcastic comments she had expected about the way she was huddled on the edge of the bed never came, and to her chagrin within minutes of getting into bed, Blake appeared to be fast asleep!

As she struggled up through dense layers of sleep the first thing Sapphire realised was that at some time during the night she must have turned instinctively towards Blake, because now, instead of lying with her back to him, curled up on the edge of the bed she was actually curved against his body, her head pillowed on his shoulder.

Luckily Blake was still asleep and therefore unable to witness her weakness. As she started to move away from him, the second thing Sapphire realised was that he was sleeping nude. Perhaps she ought to have expected it; but during the brief days of their marriage he had always worn pyjamas, the jackets of which he had invariably tugged off at some time during the night, she remembered. Lost in her thoughts; seduced into inert languor by the warmth of his body, she was reluctant to move, even while acknowledging that she should; surely there could be no real harm in indulging herself in these few brief seconds of pleasure. But her conscience prodded her, and unwillingly she started to move away.

'Going somewhere?' Blake's voice, still husky with sleep, rasped tantalisingly against her sensitive skin, making her shiver with a reaction somewhere between delight and dread.

'It's light,' Sapphire told him unnecessarily, trying to edge away from him without drawing his attention to what she was doing, and failing abysmally as he rolled on to his side, pinning her against him with one arm.

He was so close now that she could feel the intimacy of his body heat; the warm, muskily male scent of his skin clouding her reasoning processes, so that it no longer seemed quite so imperative for her to move. Much more pleasant to give in to the allure of remaining where she was.

'I thought you'd want to be out, checking on the stock.' Conscience made her make the feeble concession to saying what she felt she should, but Blake brushed her protest aside.

'The men will be doing that, because I did the last round last night—we're very democratic up here,' he drawled teasingly. 'I must say it was quite a surprise to wake up and find you in my arms. I seem to remember that last night you couldn't get far enough away from me.'

'I didn't know what I was doing,' Sapphire defended herself, 'I must have turned over in my sleep and when...'

'You're used to sharing a bed with someone? Like you do with your lover?' Blake accused harshly, 'Is that what you were going to say?'

'And if it was?' Sapphire flung back at him recklessly. Anything to keep him from discovering just how much she was affected by his proximity.

'Then there must be other things you're missing, beside a warm body in bed beside you at night,' Blake countered softly. Sapphire couldn't tell if it was challenge or anger that turned his eyes to molten gold, but even as she moved away from him, his fingers clamped into her waist, refusing to let her go. As she struggled to free herself her breasts brushed the taut skin of his chest and even through the fabric of her nightdress she was overwhelmingly conscious of the contact, closing her eyes against a sudden too-painful image of skin against flesh, of Blake stroking and caressing her.

'Open your eyes,' Blake demanded harshly, shattering the erotic bubble of her thoughts. 'You aren't going to pretend it's someone else who's holding you in his arms, Sapphire.'

'Who was it who taught you to be so arousingly responsive?' he muttered, his eyes on the swift rise and fall of her breasts, her nipples pressing urgently against the fine fabric of her nightdress, in wanton supplication of the caresses her mind had envisioned so very recently.

Sapphire felt a wave of shame course through her. How could she be behaving in such an abandoned fashion?

'Who?' Blake pressed. 'Your precious Alan, or another lover?'

'Does it matter?' Hot tears stung her eyes, caused as much by his cruel blindness as her own weakness.

He was the only man she had ever met who could touch the deep inner core of her femininity; he was the only man with the ability to unleash her desire.

'Perhaps not.' The heat had gone from his voice to be replaced by a cynical blandness. 'That it has been achieved at all is miracle enough I suppose. When I think of the way you used to shy away from me.'

Shy away? Sapphire stared at him. What about all the times she had willed him to make love to her? What about the times she had lain in this bed praying that he would stretch out and touch her?

'I think it's time we were getting dressed,' she told him hurriedly, trying to dispel her tormenting memories.

'So, you haven't changed completely,' Blake drawled. 'You still run away from situations you find unpalatable. Well, this is one occasion my dear wife, when you can't run. Unless, of course, you want me to pursue you, and carry you back to this bed?'

'Why should you want to do that?' Sapphire tried to sound sophisticated and amused but instead her voice was a breathy, hesitant whisper, Blake's smile telling her that she had not succeeded.

'Do I really have to tell you?' He leaned towards her, the fingers of his free hand curling round the strap of her nightdress and slowly sliding it down her arm. The bedcovers had slipped down to her waist during their earlier struggle, and Sapphire watched like a rabbit transfixed by the hunter as

Blake leisurely revealed the creamy slope of her breast.

'You've changed,' he murmured, studying her until the colour ran up under her pale skin. 'You're fuller here,' his thumb skimmed the outline of her breast, resting so briefly against her nipple that she couldn't be sure whether the caress was deliberate or accidental, 'and narrower here.'

His fingers touched her waist, and she shivered convulsively, her throat dry and tight with the aching need she could feel burning up inside her. She wanted to slide her fingers into the crisp darkness of his hair, to hold his head against her breast, and caress the male contours of his body. Shame and fear mingled into a stomach-tensing cramp as she tried to fight against her feelings.

'Do you like this?' Blake slid the nightdress free of her breast cupping it with his palm and stroking his tongue along the valley between it and its twin, his thumb making erotic patterns around its rosy peak.

'No.' Her denial was a choked, strangled lie.

'I think you mean yes.' Blake was so lazily self-assured that Sapphire started to tremble. 'Well, Sapphire,' he pressed, 'did you mean yes?' All the time he spoke to her he was teasing, nibbling little kisses closer and closer to her nipple. Heat coursed through her veins. Part of her wanted to flee; to get as far away from him as she could, and the other part wanted to be so close to him that not even the fragile thinness of her nightdress was between them. She ached for the feel of Blake's mouth against her breast; his hands on her body, but as though to punish her for her fib, his kisses stopped tantalisingly short of their goal, and with memories of past rejections to the forefront of her mind Sapphire could not, would not guide his mouth to the place she most wanted it to be.

'Well, then, perhaps you prefer this?'

She was eased out of her nightdress before she had time to object, the embarrassment of Blake's thorough scrutiny of her nude body outweighing all other considerations as she struggled to tug the bedclothes up over her, and Blake effortlessly restrained her. A mocking smile curved his mouth, but it was the showers of gold lightening glittering in his eyes that made Sapphire tense on a sudden spiral of excitement.

His fingertips stroking her hip and then following the line of her body downwards sparked off a showerburst of heady pleasure that she fought to conceal, swallowing the small gasp of delight that threatened to betray how she felt. She badly wanted to touch Blake as freely as he was touching her, to taste the warm maleness of his skin and feel his body come alive beneath her hands.

'You have the loveliest skin.' Blake was still touching her, drawing spiralling patterns against her thigh which transmitted an intensity of heat totally at odds with the lightness of his touch. His voice had a velvet, mesmeric quality that lulled her tense muscles into languorous relaxation. She wanted to purr almost, like a small satisfied cat, Sapphire realised on a stunned wave of surprise; she wanted to stretch and arch beneath those teasing fingers; to prolong the tormenting love play and instigate some of her own.

'Sapphire?'

The sound of her name made her turn her head to look at Blake, her eyes unknowingly a deep, dense purple blue.

'Open your mouth,' Blake commanded softly, 'I want to kiss you.'

It was heaven and hell, the zenith of pleasure and the nadir of despair. It was life and death; light and dark, and she was no more capable of resisting him than she was of denying that she loved him.

She clung to him, obeying the wordless commands of his mouth, responding with deep, driven intensity of emotion she had not known she could feel, abandoning every last vestige of pride and self-defence as her fingers locked in his hair and she clung with unashamed need to the greater strength of his body.

When at last he released her mouth, he studied its bruised softness for several seconds, his eyes eventually lifting to her bemused eyes, before he kissed her again, this time letting the moist warmth of his lips soothe the sensitive stinging skin of hers.

'You liked that.' It was a statement, not a question, rich with self-satisfaction, the long, lingering look he gave her body that of a man who knows exactly what effect he has had on the woman in his arms. His fingers traced a lazy pattern around and between her breasts, trailing downwards to her waist.

Excitement and urgency arched her body upwards, mutely seeking closer contact with his.

'I think you were right after all. It is time we got dressed.' His words were like snow being trickled down her spine. Sapphire couldn't believe she had heard them. She wanted to protest, to demand to know why he had aroused her so deliberately and turned away from her, but her pride would not allow her to. If Blake could behave as though what had just happened between them meant nothing to him; if he was completely unaffected by the explosion of love and need which had gripped her, then so was she.

# CHAPTER EIGHT

SAPPHIRE DELIBERATELY dawdled getting dressed, not wanting to face Blake. As she had hoped, when she walked into the kitchen half an hour later there was no sign of him, but the sight of Alan sitting morosely at the table, a mug of coffee in front of him brought her to an abrupt halt.

'So you "hate" him do you?' he sneered bitterly. 'Some way you have of showing it! And to think I held off taking you to bed because I didn't want to stampede you! Oh, it's all right, Sapphire,' he grimaced, the anger deserting him, as he raked tired fingers through his hair. 'He's told me all about it; how the two of you decided to give your marriage another try. I just wish I heard it first from you that's all.'

'I'm sorry, Alan.' Shakily Sapphire sat down, knowing that Alan had every right to feel angry and resentful. 'I didn't tell you over the 'phone because…because I didn't think it was the right thing to do. I didn't realise that Blake intended us to be re-married quite so soon.'

'You're happy with him?' His voice was abrupt, tight with a pain that made Sapphire's heart ache in sympathy.

'I do love him,' she told him, avoiding the question.

'And obviously sexually you're extremely compatible,' Alan shocked her by saying. 'Come on, Sapphire, I'm not a complete fool,' he told her roughly, 'when a man comes down for breakfast, looking like a well-fed predator, it isn't hard to guess what's put the smile on his face.'

She wanted to protest that he was wrong, but sensibly did not. Perhaps it might make it easier for Alan to accept the situation if he believed that she and Blake were lovers. Sadly she knew that their friendship was now over, and that once she and Blake had parted there could be no going back to Alan. She would miss him as one always missed good friends, but she did not love him, she acknowledged, her feelings from him came nowhere near to those she felt for Blake.

After he had breakfast Alan insisted on leaving. When he had gone Sapphire felt restless. On impulse she decided to go out for a walk, glimpsing Blake working in one of the snow-covered fields—just a small dark figure by a Land Rover, with something familiar in his stance that tugged at her heart.

Shivering in the cold wind she walked back to the house, still too restless to settle. She would go and see her father; she decided visiting him might help to keep her mind off her own problems.

Flaws farmyard was deserted when she drove in. Someone had cleared the worst of the snow away, and although the kitchen was redolent with the yeasty smell of baking there was no sign of Mary.

Terror, sharp and paralysing, gripped her for a second, a dreadful vision of her father, motionless, dying, rising up before her. The vision cleared and she hurried upstairs, her heart thumping; her pulses racing in aching fear as she pushed open the door to her father's room and came to a full stop.

Far from lying close to death's door on his bed her father was standing by the window, dressed in a pair of disreputable old trousers and a thick woollen jumper. He looked thinner than Sapphire remembered, but otherwise he was still very much the father of her late teens, his weatherbeaten face turned towards the window, his eyes on the distant snow-covered line of hills.

'Back already,' he commented without looking round. 'I'll just have a cup of coffee Mary and then...' He turned and saw Sapphire, shock and something else she couldn't understand leaping to life in his eyes.

'Sapphire!'

The room started to tilt and spin and Sapphire heard a roaring sound in her ears, increasing in volume until it drowned out everything else. Dimly she was aware of her father calling for Mary, of blackness coming down over her, and then a thick, suffocating darkness that seemed to press down all around her.

When she opened her eyes she was sitting in her father's chair, Mary standing anxiously at her side.

'My, you gave us all a shock fainting like that,' she told Sapphire worriedly. 'Are you all right now?'

'Dad…' Sapphire croaked unevenly, 'when I came in and everywhere was so quiet, I thought…'

Shock, and something else she couldn't name shadowed Mary's eyes. She was about to speak when the door opened and her father walked in. *Walked in,* Sapphire noted dazedly, carrying a mug of tea.

'Come on, drink this,' Mary instructed her. 'It will help allay the shock.' The 'phone started to ring and as Sapphire took the mug from her father Mary said briskly, 'I'd better go down and answer that.'

When she had gone Sapphire looked at her father. 'Sorry about this,' she apologised huskily, 'but you gave me such a shock…'

'Aye, I'm sorry too, lass.' Her father looked sad and disturbed. 'I thought…' He shook his head. 'No, we won't talk about it now, Sapphire. You're in no fit state. You stay here and rest for a while and I'll…'

He broke off as Mary came in her round face creased into a thoughtful frown.

'That was Blake,' she told them both. 'In a rare old state, wanting to know if we'd seen anything of you.' She looked at Sapphire and smiled. 'That must have been some spat the two of you had to generate so much concern, and the pair of you not a week reconciled yet.'

Knowing that her father was watching her Sapphire summoned a light smile. 'Blake wasn't too pleased when Alan turned up last night,' she told them, hoping she would be forgiven her small fib, but not wanting to let them guess at the real state of affairs between herself and Blake.

'Jealous, was he?' her father laughed. 'Aye well, I suppose it's my fault for sending the laddie over to you, but I thought it best.'

'He's gone now,' Sapphire told them, and explained briefly.

'I'd better get back,' she told her father. She couldn't put off facing Blake for ever. From somewhere she would have to find the determination to remind him that their marriage was a strictly platonic one. Not that he could really want her, she reminded herself bitterly.

'You stay right here,' Mary scolded her. 'You're in no fit state to be driving after that faint. Blake's coming to take you home. He's getting one of the men to drive him over in the Land Rover. He'll be here in ten minutes or so.'

Shakily Sapphire drank her tea. Why had Blake rung Flaws Farm? Had he perhaps gone back to the house this morning and wondered where she was? She frowned, and then tensed as she heard the familiar sound of a Land Rover engine.

'Here he is now,' Mary announced going to look out of the window. 'I'll go down and tell him where we are. No, don't you get up,' she told Sapphire sternly. 'I'm not too happy about that faint of yours. You must try and take things easy for a few days. Put on a few pounds, perhaps. I know it's fashionable to be slim but you seem to have been overdoing things.'

'Now she's back with Blake, she'll soon fatten up a bit,' her father prophesied. 'There's nothing like a happy marriage.'

Sighing Sapphire turned her face away. What would her father say if he knew the truth? But he mustn't know the truth, she thought in panic. She could already see the effect their re-marriage had had on his health; he was marvellously improved. It couldn't last for long of course, but she daren't take the risk of him discovering the truth.

She heard Mary go downstairs and then return several minutes later accompanied by Blake. Where earlier she had been shocked to see how much healthier her father had appeared than she had anticipated, now she was equally startled by the pallor of Blake's skin and the tense, bitter, brooding darkness of his eyes.

'Mary tells me you fainted.' His voice was almost accusatory.

'It was just the shock of finding Dad out of bed,' she told him knowing how feeble her explanation sounded, but not able to tell him in front of her father of her fears when she had entered the strangely silent house.

She started to get out of the chair, but Blake forestalled her, striding over and bending to pick her up, ignoring her protests.

'Let him carry you,' Mary placated. 'I don't want you falling down those steep stairs. No, she's perfectly all right,' she told Blake who had turned to question her, 'she just needs to rest a little and get her strength back.'

When he had installed her in the passenger seat of his car Blake started the engine, his face grim as he drove the car out of the cobbled yard.

'What did you want me for?' Sapphire ventured once they were out on the road. 'You rang Mary to find out if I was there,' she pressed when he turned to frown at her. 'You must have wanted me for something...'

'When I went back to the house and found you missing,' Blake told her harshly, 'it struck me that you might have decided to renege on our bargain.'

It took several seconds for the words to sink in. 'You mean you thought I had left with Alan?' Sapphire said incredulously, 'But...'

'But he wouldn't take you, believing that you and I are lovers?' There was a cynically bitter twist to Blake's mouth, his eyes as hard and cold as the snow-encrusted stone walls they were driving past.

'No! I...' Oh, what was the use trying to get through to him when he was in this sort of mood, Sapphire thought despairingly. Reaction from her faint had started to set in. She felt sick and tense; in no condition to cope with Blake's biting sarcasm. This was the Blake she remembered, she thought miserably; this hard, cynical man who seemed to be driven by demons she could not comprehend; who seemed to take pleasure in humiliating her.

The moment the car stopped outside the backdoor,

she reached for her seatbelt, but Blake was too quick for her, moving swiftly round to her door, and lifting her out of her seat, even as she protested that she could manage.

'What made you faint, Sapphire?' he demanded as he carried her upstairs to their room. 'No wonder you put up so little fight when I suggested we re-marry. But you weren't completely truthful with me were you? What happened? Wouldn't he marry you when he knew that you were carrying his child?'

She was too stunned to answer him. He dropped her unceremoniously on the bed, where she simply lay, staring at him.

'Oh, I confess you had me nicely fooled,' Blake said bitterly. 'It never occurred to me that you... We can hardly have our marriage annulled now,' he continued sardonically, 'and that being the case...'

He walked back to the bedroom door, calmly locking it and pocketing the key while Sapphire watched him in stupid disbelief. Blake couldn't really believe that she was carrying Alan's child, could he? If that had been the case she would never had consented to this ridiculous remarriage. Allan would have married her and willingly. Anger swept aside pain. How dare he accuse her of behaving so selfishly? She opened her mouth to tell him the truth and then closed it, her eyes rounding in surprise as he stripped off his sweater and shirt. His hands were on the buckle of his belt before Sapphire realised what was happening, her voice croaky and unsteady as she whispered, 'Blake, just what do you think you're doing?'

'If you're going to foist the responsibility for this child off on me, I might as well have some of the pleasure of fathering it,' he snarled furiously at her. 'It might not be my child, Sapphire, but you are my wife, and since it looks like this time I'm stuck with you, I might as well get whatever I can get out of it...'

'I thought all you wanted was my father's land,' Sapphire gritted back at him. 'I won't make love with you, Blake,' she warned him. 'I...' Her breath was trapped in her throat as he stepped out of his jeans, flinging them on to the floor. Clad only in dark briefs his body was that of a man used to an active life. Unwillingly Sapphire felt her glance slide helplessly over his broad shoulders, and down across the width of his chest. Dark hair arrowed downwards across the flat tautness of his stomach, and a mad desire to reach out and trace its erotic path rose up inside her. Quelling it, she tore her gaze away, shaken by the force of her reaction.

Two strides brought Blake to the edge of the bed. Leaning down he grasped the lapels of the cotton blouse she was wearing and Sapphire tensed, blue eyes meeting gold. Her breath stifled in her throat as Blake's fingers curled into the fabric, the glitter in his eyes one of dark menace as he jerked forcefully at the cotton. Buttons flew in all directions as the blouse tore, unable to withstand the violence he was doing it. Sapphire knew she ought to have felt fear; terror even, but what she did feel was a wild surging excitement; a primaeval emotion that seemed to spring from her innermost being and burst into life, fuelled by the dark determination she could read in Blake's eyes.

He found the waistband of her denim skirt, unsnapping it and sliding down the zip. She tried to push him away, tensing as she heard the almost feral snarl of anger he gave as he removed her clutching fingers and tossed aside her skirt.

Wearing only her bra and briefs she stared up at him as he loomed over her, willing her body not to communicate to his her unwilling arousal. Despite the rage she could feel emanating from him, she couldn't forget that this was the man she loved; and that the mere sight of his body was enough to bring leaping pulses to life inside her, fuelling a burning ache that instinct told her only his possession could assuage. She remembered how he had deliberately aroused her only that morning and her eyes darkened unknowingly, her tongue touching the dry outline of her lips. Above her Blake growled menacingly, and her eyes met his, reading the eternal message of rage and desire that glinted there.

'Thinking about him, were you? Pity you fainted so unpropitiously this morning,' he taunted, 'otherwise I'd never have suspected you could be pregnant. Despite it all you still have a look of…almost innocence about you.'

His eyes darkened over the last few words, almost as though they caused him pain, and mingled with her own resentment that he could so easily think so little of her Sapphire felt a thread of aching response.

She wanted to be in his arms, she acknowledged wistfully; she wanted the warm heat of his body against hers; his hands caressing her, his lips… A shudder seemed to tear through her, visible in the brief convulsion of her body, escaping in a faint sigh that was lost as Blake gripped her hair, tangling his fingers in it, forcing her face up so that he could look into her eyes as he muttered thickly, 'Forget him,' and then bent to silence her protest with the fierce possession of his mouth.

This was no tentative, explorative kiss, but an explosion of raw emotions, too strong to be confined in neat pigeonholes labelled 'anger' or 'desire', but instinctively Sapphire recognised and responded to them, unaware that her fingers were digging into the muscled smoothness of his shoulder, until Blake released her abruptly.

'No wonder he wanted you,' he told her hoarsely, his fingers stroking lightly down her shoulder and then erotically over the taut outline of her breast, his warm breath fanning her bruised lips. 'If you always react like that I'm only surprised that he didn't want to keep you—or was it the thought of the child that put him off? Is that why you were so quick to accept my offer, Sapphire? Because you knew he didn't want to marry you?'

Anger flared hotly inside her. 'You already seem to know all the answers, Blake,' she responded brittly, 'so why ask the questions?'

'Perhaps because I'm hoping I don't.' His thumb was rubbing lightly over the thin silk covering her nipple and Sapphire squirmed slightly beneath the tormenting caress, trying to clamp down on the feelings he was arousing inside her.

'What's the matter? Doesn't my touch appeal to you as much as his? I can make you want me, Sapphire.'

'No!' Her denial was meant as a plea for him not to carry out his threat, but Blake chose to ignore it.

'You think not?' he muttered into her throat, searching for and finding the fast-beating pulse that gave the lie to her denial. She could smell the warm musky scent of his body—inflaming her own with a subtle sexual chemistry that made her languorous and weak. The rough hair on his chest rubbed abrasively against her skin as he moved, biting delicately into her skin, making her shiver almost deliriously with pleasure. The fine silk of her bra and briefs was a barrier between them that tormented her, denying her the intimate contact of skin against skin that she now craved and when Blake's hands slid round her back to remove her bra she expelled her breath in a pent-up sigh of relief he couldn't fail to understand. Soft colour filmed her cheeks as he looked down at her, his smile tormentingly cruel.

'Still expect me to believe you don't want me, Sapphire?'

What could she say? That he had misunderstood her initial remark? She turned her head aside, not wanting him to see the betraying sheen of tears she knew wasn't far away and then gasped out loud as she felt the stinging nip of his teeth against the swollen curve of her breast. Hard on the heels on the initial burst of pain came a pleasure so intense that her eyes widened in acknowledgment of it.

'Don't expect me to believe you haven't been touched like that before,' Blake told her thickly, watching her, 'or like this.'

Ripples of pleasure spread shiveringly through her body as his tongue stroked and teased the aching fullness of her breasts, making her tense and arch in a mindless frenzy of need she hadn't known herself capable of feeling. She dimly heard Blake's suddenly harsh breathing in counterpoint to her own quick shallow breaths, and then his hands slid to her waist, gripping its slenderness until his mouth opened over first one nipple and then the other, tasting, sucking, tugging, while Sapphire felt she would explode with the intensity of pleasure building up inside her.

Unable to stop herself, she moaned Blake's name, reaching up to stroke the hard contours of his back with hands suddenly desperately eager for the feel of his skin against them, scattering wild, impassioned kisses over his shoulder, using her teeth to deliver delicate little nips that drew a hoarse groan of satisfaction from his throat.

All sense of restraint and commonsense abandoned, Sapphire didn't allow herself to think or reason. This was Blake who she still loved as desperately now as she had done when they first married; and if he had accused her so unfairly, well what did it matter now that she was in his arms and he was touching and kissing her with a hunger that her body recognised even if her mind could not. It was a hunger that fed and matched her own, his body whispering to hers that it too had starved and ached for this tumultuous pleasure they were now sharing. Despite the fact that they had never before made love, there was nothing tentative or exploratory in their embraces. Sapphire responded to the intimacy of Blake's touch as intuitively as though they had been lovers for years. Her lips brushed the flat hardness of his nipple and she registered the surprised shock of pleasure jolting through him. His eyes closed, his mouth warm against the indentation of her waist, as she lay half-pinned beneath him, indolently admiring the sculptured perfection of his body.

She ran her fingers lightly down the dark arrowing of hair, stopping when she reached his briefs. He tensed, and then demanded thickly, 'Touch me, Sapphire.'

She let her fingers stray exploratively over the thin cotton of his briefs, her touch slightly hesitant and unsure, her heart thudding violently in response to the small, liquid sound of pleasure emerging from Blake's throat. Heated, muttered words of praise and encouragement overwhelmed all her shyness and reserve. When Blake tugged off his briefs her breath caught in her throat, her eyes unknowingly widening slightly.

'A man could be in danger of forgetting that he's only mortal under a look like that,' Blake told her throatily, sliding his hand round her throat, his thumb under her chin tilting her face up to meet his.

Passion blazed into life as they kissed, her mouth opening willingly to admit the penetration of his tongue, seeking, taking all the warm sweetness she gave up so willingly.

Blake's free hand was resting possessively against her thigh, a heavy warm weight that tantalised and excited her, her own fingers stroking and cajoling the strong muscles of his back, sliding round to investigate the sharp angles of his hips, moving in restless, roving urgency as she responded to the hunger in Blake's kiss.

He released her to tease a chain of moist caresses in a line that investigated the valley between her breast and the slight well of her stomach.

The restless urgency in the pit of her stomach increased and in obedience to its commands Sapphire brushed her own lips against the firmness of Blake's belly, thrilling to the sudden tension in muscles finely tuned to her light touch. His skin tasted warm and slightly salty, its flavour almost addictive. Lost in the veil of pleasure touching him had revealed to her, she let her lips travel where they wished barely aware of Blake's harsh groan of protest until he snatched her up, rolling her beneath the constraining weight of his body, parting her legs with his thigh, muttering her name like a litany as his fingers touched her intimately, making her yield and ache for his possession.

Far beyond remembering the accusation that had

preceded their lovemaking, Sapphire wasn't ready for the unexpected burst of pain. Her muscles tensed immediately, shock mingling with hurt as she fought to understand the too-swift transition from pleasure to pain.

Above her she heard Blake curse, a fiercely bitter sound, his body withdrawing from hers. Suddenly the pain was gone, and shamelessly she clung to him, refusing to let him go, her eyes pleading mutely with him as her fingers dug into his shoulders, her soft, 'Blake, please...' dragging an anguished mutter of response from his throat as he tensed and then shuddered and her body melted in welcome to his, her senses singing with pleasure.

Never had pleasure seemed so tangible, her body was awash with it, glowing, so supremely fulfilled that she wanted to tell the whole world. Stretching indolently she turned her head. Blake was lying inches away, his eyes open, his expression sombre. Of course, this wasn't the first time he had experienced such feelings—not by a long way.

'There's never been anyone else, has there?' he asked the question in a flat voice that drained her pleasure as effectively as a tap being turned on. Sapphire shook her head.

'Then for God's sake why didn't you say so?'

No need to ask if he was regretting making love to her. It was there, written all over his face, etching into his scathing voice.

'I didn't think you'd listen.' She turned away from him, not wanting him to see how vulnerable she was.

Neither of them had mentioned love…but silently in her heart she had told him how she felt about him, just as her body told his how much it worshipped and adored him,

'So you decided to let me find out for myself?'

'I didn't think I could have stopped you.'

'Half-a-dozen words or so would have done it— ''I'm still a virgin'', for instance.'

Sapphire arched her eyebrows, turning back to face him. 'And you'd have believed me?' She turned away again. 'I'd better get dressed…'

'No.' Blake's voice was sharp. He swung himself out of bed. 'No, stay here and rest for a while, I'll go down and make you a drink.'

'I'm not an invalid, Blake,' she protested, flushing as his eyes studied her pale skin and slender body. Still bathed in the warm afterglow of their lovemaking she hadn't bothered to cover herself, but now she felt a need to do so, chilled by the way Blake was studying her. Was he comparing her to Miranda? She felt sick at the thought.

'You're not exactly in the peak of *health* either,' he told her still watching her. There was a dark, brooding quality to his look that saddened her. Was he already regretting what had happened?

She reached out towards him, her eyes unconsciously pleading, 'Blake, I…'

'Stay here and rest.' He had his back to her and was already getting dressed. Feeling dejected, Sapphire huddled beneath the bed-clothes. Plainly Blake didn't want to talk to her. She closed her eyes, knowing she should regret what had happened but knowing that she did not. Where was her pride? When Blake left the easy, weak tears of physical release flowed for a few seconds and then stopped. By the time he came back with her tea Sapphire was fast asleep. He stood watching her for several seconds with shuttered eyes, before turning to leave, his face grim.

# CHAPTER NINE

'SAPPHIRE, we have to talk.'

They were sitting in front of the log fire she had lit just before dinner. Blake had suggested they have their coffee there and now she tensed dreading what he might be about to say. She had been awaiting this moment with mingled apprehension and anguish ever since she had woken up this afternoon. Had Blake guessed that she still loved him? Was he going to tell her that what had happened between them had been caused by some mental aberration. That he would never have made love to her had he been in his right senses? Was he going to tell her about Miranda?

She risked a glance at him. He was sitting opposite her on a chair, his upper body leaning forward, elbows braced on his thighs as he dropped his head into his hands and pushed weary fingers through his hair.

A wave of love overwhelmed her. She wanted to reach out and touch him; to wipe away the lines of exhaustion fanning out from his eyes; to touch and caress him, to…

'Sapphire!' The tone of his voice warned her that

he knew her thoughts were wandering, his fingers steepled together as he watched her over them, the liquid gold of his eyes dulled, their expression almost stark.

'I never intended what happened this afternoon to take place,' he began abruptly, causing a thousand sharp knives to tear jaggedly at Sapphire's aching heart.

'I know that,' she interrupted curtly. 'I do have a memory, Blake, I'm well aware of the fact that you don't find me desirable. When we first married...'

'Don't be ridiculous, of course I find you desirable.' Angry fingers raked through his hair again. 'Hell, Sapphire,' he growled impatiently, 'you're not *that* innocent. If I don't desire you what the hell do you think that was all about this afternoon?'

Colour flamed momentarily in her face as she recalled the fierce intensity of their lovemaking; the feeling she had had at the time that both of them were suffering from the same driven compulsion; the same starving hunger. Quickly she reminded herself of the past, of the early days of their marriage. 'You may desire me now, Blake, but when we were first married, you couldn't bear to touch me; you...'

'I don't want to talk about the past.' His voice was clipped and brusque, defying her to continue the subject. 'We're living in the present now, Sapphire, and despite everything we said before we re-married, it must be as obvious to you now, as it is to me, that we can't live together platonically.'

Her muscles seemed to be seized in a paralysing

grip, her body totally unable to function, and then as the great wave of pain crashed down over her Sapphire knew her immobility was simply a defensive measure; a way of stopping the pain, only it had failed miserably. It seemed to fill every corner of her, drowning out pride and reserve. She wanted to cry out to Blake not to send her away; she wanted to plead with him to stay with her, but instead she remained unspeaking, dreading opening her mouth in case she voiced her anguished thoughts.

'Well?'

Blake was plainly waiting for a response, and when she didn't make one, said tersely, 'Come on, Sapphire, I know you...you were a virgin—and that fact alone merely reinforces what I feel—but you must know that sexually we're extremely compatible, almost explosively so,' he muttered half under his breath.

His words were so totally at variance to what she had expected to hear that Sapphire simply stared at him. 'Come on,' Blake demanded half-aggressively, 'Admit it Sapphire, when I made love to you, you enjoyed it. You...'

'Yes.' Her simple admission seemed to rob him of breath. 'I did enjoy it, Blake.'

Colour lay dark red along the ridge of his cheekbones, his eyes the flaming gold she remembered from that afternoon, their gaze trained on her, tracking every betraying expression that crossed her face. He breathed deeply, exhaling slowly, his chest rising and falling with the effort.

'Why were you still a virgin?' He was looking directly at her, and Sapphire knew an insane desire to laugh. Pure nerves she told herself, taking a deep breath of her own to steady her.

'At first when I left here I felt too bruised mentally to even think of loving anyone. Later...' she shrugged, 'Well, there just wasn't anyone I wanted, and then I met Alan...'

She paused, telling herself that it wasn't really lying to tell him the truth as she had believed it to be before realising that she still loved him. He didn't want her love, and if he knew how she felt he could easily send her away, when, in reality, all she wanted to do was to stay.

Ignoring the inner warning voices that told her she was courting even greater unhappiness than she had already experienced, she continued softly, '...I wanted to be sure that what we felt for one another was right. Alan felt the same way. Before I came up here we were planning to go away together for a holiday. We were going...'

'To be lovers? In some romantic, idyllic setting?' Blake demanded harshly. 'Mentally you were ready to make love, and because your boyfriend wasn't available you substituted me, is that what you're trying to tell me?' He looked so murderously angry that Sapphire knew a frisson of fear.

'Perhaps, subconsciously,' she lied bravely—anything rather than risk him guessing the truth. 'But no, I didn't consciously substitute you for Alan, Blake.'

THE SIX-MONTH MARRIAGE

'And am I also supposed to believe that we were good together because you thought I was someone else?'

Slowly Sapphire shook her head. She daren't risk trying to pretend that. Blake was angry enough already. Obviously she had touched some nerve of touchy male pride which it would be unwise to press on too hard. 'You're the one with the experience—not me,' she reminded him simply. 'Personally I don't think it would be possible to deceive oneself to that extent, but...'

'It isn't.' Blake's voice was so harsh, his face so shuttered and forbidding that she wondered what personal anguish lay behind the curt words, but could not bring herself to ask.

'So,' he told her, 'given that sexually we both agree that we're extremely compatible, I submit that we change the rules of our partnership.'

'Change the rules?' Sapphire was so surprised that she could only repeat what he had said, staring uncomprehendingly up at him. For an instant there was something in his eyes that warmed the ice-coldness of her heart, but it was gone almost immediately his voice crisp and businesslike as he said firmly. 'Yes. We agreed that our relationship would be a platonic one lasting just as long as...'

'My father lives,' Sapphire finished for him, her face white. For a few hours she had forgotten her father's condition. Mentally castigating herself she tried to concentrate on what Blake was saying. 'Now I'm suggesting that we lift that self-imposed ban;

that we make our marriage a real one in every sense of the word, to be...'

'Set aside when we no longer desire one another?'

'Is that what you want?'

His eyes narrowed as he waited for her response, and Sapphire felt a quiver of apprehension deep down inside her. Had he guessed how she felt? It was pride and pride alone that kept her from crying out that she wanted to be with him for ever; that she wanted to share his life and his bed for just as long as her life lasted. Instead she said lightly, 'Yes, of course.'

A mask seemed to drop down over his features, his eyelids lowering to conceal his thoughts from her. 'Very well then,' he said at last. 'If those are your terms, then for as long as our desire lasts, so does our marriage.' He stood up, stretching lithely, and completely changing the subject said calmly, 'Snow's melting. I'll just go out and check on the foal. Why don't you have an early night? You still look washed out.'

Very flattering, Sapphire thought wrathfully ten minutes later, luxuriating in a deep scented bath of deliciously hot water. She wasn't going to question Blake's abrupt volte-face, nor his suggestion that their marriage continue. Perhaps he was hoping to quench his desire for Miranda with her. Perhaps the fact that Miranda was now married broke Blake's own personal code of behaviour, Sapphire didn't know.

One half of her urged flight and safety, reminding

her of all the pain he had already caused her, while
the other whispered that life without him had been
arid, dead; and that perhaps his desire for her could
flower into something stronger and more permanent
if it was carefully nurtured and protected.

She lingered so long in the bath, deep in thought,
that the water started to cool. A draught from the
door as it opened made her shiver and she turned
round thinking it must have swung open.

'You've been in here so long I was beginning to
wonder if my suggestion was so offensive to you that
you'd decided you preferred a watery grave to another night in my arms.'

The sight of Blake standing beside the bath, looking down at her, was so unexpected and startling that
she could barely breathe. 'I was thinking,' she told
him huskily, shivering again as her skin chilled. 'I'm
sorry if you've been waiting for the bathroom.' How
formal her voice sounded, her expression hunted as
she looked past him to where she had left her towel,
trying not to think about the hunger that had started
to unfurl inside her at the thought of 'a night in his
arms'.

'It's large enough for us to share,' Blake drawled
reaching for his electric razor, and wiping some of
the steam off the mirror above the basin as he
plugged it in and switched it on.

'Blake, it's cold in here...' He was halfway
through shaving when she finally plucked up the
courage to remind him, albeit obliquely, that she
wanted to get out of the bath. He finished what he

was doing, rubbing his jaw experimentally. 'I thought you always shaved in the morning,' Sapphire muttered crossly. Why couldn't he take the hint and leave her in privacy to get ready for bed?

'So I did,' he agreed blandly, unplugging the razor and turning round to lean indolently against the wall, watching her, 'but married men, my sweet, always shave at night. It saves wear and tear on delicate feminine skin,' he pointed out, grinning openly when she started to blush. The colour seemed to start at her toes and wash up over her body until it reached the swell of her breasts, now barely concealed by the cold bubbles, 'and if you're cold, why don't you get out of the bath?' He saw her tense and instinctively try to submerge more of her body beneath the bubbles and leant towards her. 'Why so shy? You weren't this afternoon.'

How could she explain that that had been different; that then in the heat of passion her own nudity had not disturbed her, but that now in the small confines of the bathroom, with Blake still fully dressed, it did?

All she could manage was a cross, 'You seem to forget that unlike you, I'm not used to...to...'

'Living with someone? The only person I've ever lived with is you, Sapphire.' As he spoke he was unfastening his shirt buttons. When he had finished he tugged it off, revealing the tautly muscled expanse of his chest. Her breath seemed to lock inside her as Sapphire tried to drag her hungry gaze away from his body.

'Since you won't get out of your own volition, and since I'm too much of a gentleman to let you freeze, I'll just have to help you, won't I?' Blake drawled, and as he leaned towards her, Sapphire realised why he had removed his shirt, and tried automatically to evade him. The small tidal wave her hurried movements caused soaked Blake's jeans, but didn't prevent him from lifting her out of the bath. His chest felt warm and hard against her water-chilled damp flesh, a shivering that had nothing to do with the cold raising goose bumps over her sensitised skin.

'Blake!' Her half-shocked protest was ignored. 'You're soaking wet,' she pointed out breathlessly, trying to clamp down on her rising excitement and totally unable to do so. This close she could see the pores in his skin, the mingled scent of sweat and heat coming off it provocatively arousing.

'We both are,' he agreed, slowly letting her slide to the floor, while reaching for her towel with his free hand, 'but it can soon be remedied.' His eyes never left her face as he enveloped her in the large soft towel and then slowly started to rub her dry.

Within seconds of his touching her Sapphire had forgotten how chilled she had been. Her body seemed to be bathed with heat, consumed by it everywhere he touched her. She had never dreamed that something as mundane as drying her damp skin could be so unbelievably erotic but the gentle friction of the towel against her skin, in Blake's hands became an instrument of exquisite pleasure that delighted and yet intruded unbearably, stopping her from savouring the touch of Blake's hands against her skin—a touch she now burned and hungered for even more than she had this afternoon. He only had to touch her and she went up in flames, she realised shudderingly, almost lightheaded with desire.

'Blake.' His name was a muffled protest and a plea, lost against his chest as she gave in to an overwhelming urge to reach out and touch him, pressing trembling lips to the hard column of his throat, and glorying in his responsive shudder.

'Tell me you want me.' The hoarse command was one she couldn't resist.

'I want you.'

The towel fell away as he picked her up and strode through into the bedroom. Against her body she could feel the fierce thud of Blake's heart, pounding out an unmistakably erotic message, his body, hard and urgent as he deposited her on the bed, tugging off his wet jeans before joining her.

'Show me how much,' he demanded thickly, tracing an erotic pathway downwards along her throat, his fingers burning fiery brands of possession against her skin as he cupped the silky skin of her breast, delicately stroking the hard nub of her nipple. This time Sapphire responded immediately without hesitation, knowing with one corner of her mind that mingled with her desire and love was a tiny thread of desperation urging her to take as much of him as she could while she could—memories to store up to keep her warm on those nights when her bed would be cold and empty without him. As though her yearning hunger reached out and unleashed some deep core of need within him Blake reacted to her passion, touching her, kissing her with a barely restrained ferocity that left her weakly clinging to him like a drowning person to a raft. His touch, his need, the words of passion and hunger he muttered into her ear, took her far beyond the shores of love and out into an ocean so deep she knew that without him she would sink and never ever re-surface.

Fierce tremors of pleasure raced through her body, each lingering caress making her arch and invite with a sensuality that left one corner of her mind half-shocked. Could this really be her, touching Blake with a far greater intimacy than she had ever envisaged; stroking and kissing the taut male body until Blake cried out in a delirium of need, reaching for her, taking the fullness of one breast deeply into his mouth and laving it with the moist heat of his tongue.

Now it was her turn to cry out with pleasure and to experience the fierce shudder of pleasure slamming through Blake's body as he responded to that cry. His fingers stroked circles of fire along the inside of her thigh her body aching with the intensity of her need. He touched her intimately and she melted, twisting and turning, breathing in short, muffled gasps.

'It's no good, I can't wait any longer.' Blake's groaned admission echoed her own thoughts, her body wildly exulting in his swift possession and frenziedly responding to it. The world seemed to explode around them Sapphire crying out with pleasure at each powerful thrust of his body, her nails scoring heatedly along his back as she sought to prolong the contact her body craved even after the climax had been reached and the deep ache inside her soothed.

She felt Blake move away slightly and murmured an incoherent protest. 'Hush…' His mouth covered hers briefly, warm and moist and she was shocked to feel the light spiral of desire twist through her so quickly after she thought it had been sated. She tried to move away when Blake bent his head to suck lightly on her swollen and slightly sore nipples, but the pleasure of his touch seduced her into staying where she was, dreamily contemplating the smooth warmth of his skin, reaching out lazy fingers to stroke idly along the ridge of his shoulder.

When his lips grazed across her stomach she felt too indolent to protest, simply looking down at the thick darkness of his hair and wondering awedly that one person could be so vitally important to her happiness.

Blake's fingers touched her thigh, and she tensed as his tongue touched her so intimately that she almost recoiled from the shock of it, trying to pull away and yet at the same time consumed by the molten heat his intimacy engendered until she was giving herself up to it, abandoning herself completely to the sensual spell he was weaving around her, unaware that she was crying out his name.

This time their coming together was less tumultuous, more leisurely and prolonged; Blake's fierce

cry of exultation muffled by her kiss, her arms holding him locked against her body as she savoured the
sweet aftermath of their pleasure. She fell asleep still
holding him, waking during the night to discover
that their positions were reversed and that he was
now the one holding her, the heavy weight of one
leg thrown across her body, pinning her close against
him. Sleepily content she nestled closer to him gloat-
ing over the pleasure of being able to do so; of being
free to reach out and touch the matted hair on his
chest; to place her lips to the pulse thudding slowly
in his throat. Maybe he only wanted her, but she
loved him and hopefully, God willing, they could yet
build a relationship; a marriage that could last.

She fell asleep on that thought waking to find herself alone. Downstairs in the kitchen she found a
note propped up against the teapot and a small smile
tugged at her lips as she read it.

'Market Day,' Blake had written. 'Don't expect
me back until late—suggest you catch up on your
sleep!'

She spent the morning in a blissful daze, knowing
that she was walking around with a smile on her face
like a cat fed on cream, but unable to do a thing
about it.

After a light lunch she contemplated going for a
walk, and was just about to set out when she heard
the sound of a car driving into the yard. From her
vantage point in the kitchen she watched Miranda
uncurl her slender body from the driver's seat, her
face disdainful as she picked her way over the cob-

bled yard in spike heeled shoes. Her cream wool suit and expensive shoes were beautiful but surely completely unsuitable for farm visiting Sapphire reflected waspishly as Miranda knocked on the back door.

'If you want Blake, I'm afraid he isn't here,' she told her curtly, knowing she was being ungracious but unable to stop herself. It still hurt bitterly to think of Blake and this woman being lovers; to know that if Miranda hadn't married they still would be lovers. It did nothing to endear Miranda to her to know that at least some of Blake's desire for her must have been fuelled by the fact that he was missing *her* and Sapphire knew some of her feelings must be reflected in her face.

'It isn't Blake I wanted to see,' Miranda surprised her by saying smugly, 'Of course I knew he wouldn't be here. It's market day—we normally meet for lunch but of course since I got married...' She shrugged dainty shoulders. 'I've told Blake he can't have his cake and eat it. It's much pleasanter being a married woman than being a single one...'

'Despite the fact that you had to settle for second best,' Sapphire threw at her, regretting her impulsive comment the moment she saw the pale blue eyes harden.

'Hardly that,' Miranda drawled tauntingly. 'As a lover Blake is first-rate, but as a husband?' Her eyebrows lifted. 'Hardly. For one thing Jim is an extremely wealthy man, whereas Blake...' She glanced round the large kitchen disparagingly. 'Being a working farmer's wife is hardly my metier...'

'No, I can see that,' Sapphire agreed drily, 'But if you haven't come to see Blake why have you come here?'

Settling herself comfortably in a chair Miranda raised calculating blue eyes to Sapphire's darker ones. 'Oh I thought it was time you and I had a little talk—that er, shall we say...certain ground rules were laid down. You know of course that Blake and I are lovers?'

'I know you *were*,' Sapphire agreed coolly, hoping that Miranda would never guess how much the admission cost her.

*'Were?'* The thin eyebrows lifted tauntingly, 'Oh dear is that what he told you? And you believed him? Poor Sapphire,' she mocked. 'Blake is far too virile a man to give up what he and I have between us. Oh I grant you, you've grown up from the awkward adolescent he married, but Blake loves me, Sapphire, and all you'll ever be is a pale substitute. Your marriage to him won't last. Blake will tire of you again just like he did before.'

Her taunting words, the look in her eyes, and her own inner insecurities all combined to goad Sapphire into saying with desperate intensity, 'You're wrong; Blake wants our marriage to last.'

'You mean he wants to keep your father sweet to make sure he doesn't lose out on Flaws Farm,' Miranda derided. 'Oh come on Sapphire you know it's true. That's the only reason Blake ever married you, and the reason he wanted you back. Your father threatened to sell his farm elsewhere if he didn't. You'd better pray that he lives a long time if you're counting on seeing more than one wedding anniversary, just as Blake must be hoping that he doesn't.'

The cruelty of her gibe took Sapphire's breath away for a moment. With tears in her eyes she cried fiercely, 'That's not true, Blake knows that my father only has a matter of months to live... I...'

'What? What on earth are you talking about?' Miranda snapped obviously disbelieving her. 'Why only last month Jim was telling me how amazed he is by your father's stamina. It must come of coming from sturdy farming stock,' she added, her lip curling fastidiously.

'Oh I know he was seriously ill with pneumonia, but Jim told me he'd never seen anyone recover so quickly from it, never mind a man well into his midsixties. If he's told you he's at death's door, he's lying,' she told Sapphire positively. A gleam of suspicion darkened her eyes momentarily, her gaze narrowing as she studied Sapphire with insolent appraisal. 'So that's how he got Blake to take you back,' she breathed triumphantly at last, 'by telling him that he's close to death. Of course! It would work perfectly. Poor Blake, I wonder what he's going to say when he knows he's been deceived. I can't wait to see his face,' she purred viciously. 'I don't think he's going to be too pleased about the way you've trapped him into taking you back. Oh I grant you he's single-minded enough to stay with you until he's got what he wants, but that doesn't mean he'll ever really be yours or that he cares about you.'

She turned and left before Sapphire could retaliate. Not that she had anything left to retaliate with, she thought despairingly, staring helplessly out of the window. Everything fitted together too neatly for Miranda to be wrong. She had thought herself, the last time she saw him, that her father looked better. He had even been out of bed, she remembered. Dear God how could he have done this to her? How could he have put her in this position?

Perhaps Miranda *was* wrong, she though feverishly…after all she had only the other woman's word for it that her father had only had pneumonia. Frantically pacing the kitchen Sapphire knew there was only one way to find out. She was already dressed for walking, so pulling on her boots she stepped out into the yard closing the kitchen door behind her.

If Miranda was right Blake would have to be told. She shivered in the cold breeze. What would his reaction be? He had never made any secret of the fact that he wanted Flaws Farm, but there was a big difference in expecting to inherit in say six months' time and waiting perhaps sixteen years? After all her grandfather had lived to his mid-eighties and so had his father before him. Walking quickly to try and blot out her jumbled thoughts, Sapphire headed for Flaws Farm.

# CHAPTER TEN

'YOUR FATHER?' Mary responded in answer to Sapphire's query. 'Yes, he's in his room.'

'How is he today?' Sapphire watched closely as she waited for Mary's response.

'Oh much better,' the older woman beamed. 'In fact he's improving rapidly every day now. As soon as this cold spell breaks he'll probably be able to go outside. He's chafing at the bit now I'm afraid,' she smiled ruefully, 'not the best of patients, but then that's understandable when one thinks of the active life he's led.'

'But he will be able to get out and about?' Sapphire queried.

'Good heavens yes.' Mary looked surprised that she even needed to ask. 'Pneumonia is serious of course, but these days, with modern drugs, it's not dangerous, and of course your father is supremely fit.'

'Pneumonia... There weren't any other complications then?' Sapphire asked trying to sound casual while inwardly shaking with dread. So Miranda *had* been right after all.

'Not as far as I know.' Mary looked concerned. 'I

know you must be worried about him, but there really is no need you know,' she told her gently. 'For a while he did seem to have reached a plateau stage, but since you came back he's really made progress. I suspect the hope of a grandchild has had some bearing on that. Men hereabouts place a great deal of importance on continuance of the family line. I think when your father was ill he brooded rather a lot on the fact that he was the last male Bell, but he's definitely over that now. Why don't you go up and see him, he'll welcome the interruption. He's working on the farm accounts.' She grinned conspiratorily, 'And you know how he hates that.'

It was amazing what one could see when one knew what to look for Sapphire thought wretchedly, opening the door without knocking and walking into a scene familiar to her from her childhood.

Her father's dog lay curled up at his feet, swear words turning the air mildly blue as he bent his head over his ledgers. Seeing him now with her new knowledge, Sapphire could see that he had been ill and that he was recovering. There was more flesh on his bones for one thing and for another the colour of his skin was better. The door creaked faintly as she let it swing closed and he turned round, his welcoming smile changing to a frown as he saw her pale face.

'Sapphire.' He got up, coming towards her, but she avoided him, sitting down in a spare chair.

'I know exactly what's been going on, Dad,' she said quietly. 'I know you're not...not dying.' Her control broke as she cried out wretchedly, 'How could you do this to me…? How could you trick and deceive…?'

'Lass, lass, believe me I thought it best,' he interrupted sadly. 'Your place is here with your husband. I've always thought that.'

'You're free to think what you like, Dad, but to try to force me back with Blake by pretending…' She bit her lip, turning away from the remorse in his face.

'Sapphire, perhaps I shouldn't have meddled, but believe me I thought it was for the best. It was plain to me that you weren't happy in London. You loved Blake when you married him.'

'But he didn't love me, he only married me to get Flaws Farm. That's the only reason he took me back,' she cried wildly. 'Can't you see that? He doesn't really want me, he only wants your land, and the only reason he re-married me was because he thought it wouldn't be long before he inherited it. We made a bargain you see,' she told him wretchedly, 'peace of mind for you, and Flaws Farm for Blake. I agreed I'd sell it to him, once… How do you suppose he'll feel when he discovers how you've tricked him and he *will* discover it…'

'Sapphire, you've got it all wrong,' her father interrupted sternly. 'I've never deceived Blake. He knew exactly what was wrong with me. He wanted you back here as much as I did. Don't you see…Blake knew the truth…he knew, Sapphire…'

For a few minutes it was too much for her to take

in and then she burst out bitterly, 'I see…and how were the pair of you planning to resolve this grand charade—a miracle recovery? And to think I fell for it.' Unable to endure any more she wrenched open the door, ignoring her father's anguished cry, half-running through the kitchen and out into the yard. The afternoon was drawing in and the cold blast of air against her heated skin stung, but Sapphire ignored it, head down, hands stuffed into her pockets as she walked doggedly away from the farm, instinctively taking the path that had been her favourite as a child.

It led to a disused quarry, now overgrown and mossy. As a child she had discovered a moss-covered ledge halfway down one of the escarpments, and almost hidden from view by the lip of the quarry.

This had been a favourite refuge of her childhood, and now driven by an intense need to be alone she automatically took the path that led to it.

She could understand what her father had had to gain from deceiving her, but Blake… Had her father perhaps dangled the farm in front of him? Take Sapphire back, give me a grandchild and in return… Her mind shied away from the thought. No, Blake would never allow himself to be manoeuvred like that, he wasn't that type of man, but he was very fond of her father…and he did want Flaws' land…and he did find her desirable. Given that might he not decide that marriage to her was a reasonable price to pay, especially when he could still be Miranda's lover?

Round and round her thoughts circled, tormenting her with each combination that came to mind. There were so many imponderables for her to consider, so many differing combinations, and only Blake knew the real truth; exactly what had motivated him. But now it would have to end. She couldn't stay with him knowing what she now did. Humiliation seared her soul when she thought about their lovemaking; about the intensity of emotion she had put into it when he had merely been enduring it out of necessity.

On and on she walked, scarcely aware that it was starting to get dark, setting one foot in front of the other, wrestling with her thoughts.

By the time she reached the quarry it was almost dark, but logic and common sense had long since given way to an instinct for sanctuary which led her to seek out the treacherous path going down to her childhood hiding place.

She found it more by instinct than anything else, stumbling once halfway down and clinging to the quarry face for support as a tiny avalanche of stones crumbled downwards beneath her feet, to eventually splash eerily into the deep pool that had formed at the centre of the quarry crater. This place had been out of bounds to her as a child but it had never stopped her coming here. She shivered suddenly, coming out of the bleak despair that had driven her to seek out this place, swaying lightheadedly. Perhaps she ought to go back; her father would be worrying about her. Remorse overcame her earlier anger.

Of course he had been doing what he thought best; to him no doubt she was still the shy seventeen-year-old who had first fallen in love with Blake. And her father *was* old-fashioned. To him marriage vows were sacrosanct and not lightly to be set aside. Sighing faintly Sapphire started to turn round, freezing tensely as she felt the shale beneath her feet shift. The last time she had come down here she had been seventeen—a child bride looking for somewhere to escape the miseries of a marriage that had turned out to be so far removed from her childish imaginings of high romance that now it seemed to be a farce. Even then the path had been dangerous—something she had forgotten when she came down it tonight. She shivered again remembering the remoteness of the quarry and the unlikelihood of anyone guessing that she was up here. If she made it to the ledge she would be stuck there until morning when she might be able to attract the attention of one of the shepherds. If she made it, she thought wretchedly as another part of the path slid away to drop into the pool. The pool. Icy trickles of fear dripped down her spine. The water in that pool was freezing, its sides smooth and worn by time into a glassy slipperyness that made the pool a death trap for anyone foolish enough to swim in it. Closing her eyes and clinging to the wall of the quarry she inched her way carefully down to the ledge, easing her shaking body on to its grassy smoothness.

It seemed smaller than she remembered and as she edged back against the quarry wall, trying to sit down she realised why. Like the path, the ledge had been partially eroded away. Every time she moved she could hear the rattling of shale and small stones. How safe was the ledge? She could die here and no-one would be any the wiser. Would it matter if she did? Was life really worth living without Blake? If one judged life on its quality rather than its quantity then no. Without him her life had no direction; no purpose. Without his love... Wearily her body relaxed into a numbing lethargy that was almost a relief, her mind torturing her with images of Blake and on to the point where death lured her with its promise of oblivion.

Suicide had always been something she had viewed with horror—until she lost Blake, and now with sharp clarity she remembered those first months after she had left him, when she would have given anything not to have had to wake up in the morning. Now she was going to lose him again. The moon slid out from behind a cloud illuminating the still water below. It beckoned to her, casting a spell that seemed to reach out and enfold her until she could almost imagine she was already in its icy embrace. As though obeying the directions of a voice only she could hear Sapphire stood up, drifting like a sleep-walker towards the edge of the ledge where she stood poised, drawn by the inky black depths below, her powers of reasoning clouded by the greater force of her emotions.

'No!'

At first Sapphire thought the taut cry had been torn

from her own throat, but when it was followed by her name, called abruptly by a familiar male voice she started back from the edge of the ledge, staring up in disbelief to find Blake looking down at her.

Perhaps it was a trick of the moonlight, but his face seemed oddly white and drawn, his eyes burning as though he had looked into the fires of hell.

'Stand back from the edge Sapphire, and I'll throw you down a rope.'

She was too bemused to question how he had got there, simply obeying the commands he shouted down to her, feeling the coarse fibre of the rope bite into her waist as Blake hauled her back up the quarry face, until she was lying flat on her back, on the ice-cold grass, breathing in great gulps of air, like a landed fish.

Blake's fingers tugged at the knotted rope, unfastening it from around her. His head bent over his self-imposed task, Sapphire resisted the urge to reach out and stroke the thick darkness, but she couldn't restrain the brief quiver tensing her body when she remembered how they had made love.

'Keep still,' Blake's voice was terse, his hands clinically detached as they examined her body. 'Nothing seems to be broken... Come on, I'd better get you back and alert the rest of the team.' As she stood up Sapphire saw that his mouth was compressed, his eyes darkly bitter as they studied her.

'The team?' Was that really her own voice, soft and husky almost begging him to reach out and touch her?

'The Rescue Team,' he reminded her in the same clipped voice. 'Your father called them out when you didn't come back. Tom Barnes rang me and asked me to stand in for Geoff Plant—he's away at the moment. I had no idea when I set out that it was you…' He broke off and turned away from her, rubbing his forehead with tense fingers. 'I called at Flaws on the way to see if you were there—I thought you might have decided to spend the evening with your father…'

'In view of his ailing health I suppose you mean,' Sapphire cut in sarcastically, only to be silenced by Blake's brusque, 'Not now Sapphire. You realise your father's practically frantic with worry, to say nothing of how I felt…'

'And how did you feel Blake?' she asked bitterly, suddenly furiously and intensely angry, the adrenalin flowing fiercely along her veins. 'Worried that you might not get Flaws after all? Oh yes, I know all about how the pair of you deceived me. Your very good friend Miranda enlightened me. My father I can forgive because I know he acted in what he believed to be my best interests, but you…' Her heated words were silenced by the brief blast Blake gave on the whistle he was holding.

'We can discuss all that later,' he told her curtly. 'Right now, like the rest of the team, all I want to do is get home to bed. You do realise that if I hadn't remembered about this damned quarry, you'd have been there until morning, if not longer, don't you? And just what the hell were you playing at when I arrived, for God's sake?' he shouted at her, fingers clenching into her shoulders as he shook her roughly. Once given life it seemed as though his anger couldn't be quenched, and Sapphire listened in silence as it flowed moltenly over her. Blake was angry... It was a phenomenon she had never witnessed before. Before he had always been so cool and in control.

Other members of the team alerted by his whistle were hurrying towards them, and he stopped berating her, turning instead to assure them that she was quite safe.

'She slipped off the path and luckily for her landed on a ledge,' was the explanation he gave his co-rescuers, and after Sapphire had endured some well-deserved chaffing on the subject of her carelessness Blake started to guide her towards where he had left his Land Rover.

'I'll call at Flaws and let Simon have the good news,' one of the men offered. 'It's on my way, and you'll both be wanting to get back home. Hot baths and a good mug of toddy, put the pair of you to rights...' He winked over his shoulder at Blake, and Sapphire felt the warmth seep up under her skin as she intercepted the very male look they exchanged. And the worst of it was that deep down inside her she still yearned for Blake to take her into the warmth of his bed and hold her until all the nightmare details of the day faded into oblivion.

Instead she had to sit with him in the Land Rover, the tense quality of the silence stretching between them acting on her nerves with all the torment of a thumbscrew. When the Land Rover eventually came to a halt in the farmyard she was out the moment Blake cut the engine, shocked to discover how weak her legs felt as she clung wretchedly to her open door.

'You should have waited for me.' The terse, un-sympathetic words brought tears of weakness and pain to her eyes, but thankfully it was too dark for Blake to see them. She wanted to protest when he walked round to her and hauled her carelessly into his arms, but she knew that she just didn't have the strength to object.

Upstairs she lay on the bed where he had dropped her knowing that she couldn't endure sleeping with him now. Not that he was likely to want to. Her mouth twisted bitterly. Had he, like her father, hoped they might have a child—preferably a son who could inherit the rich Flaws acres he coveted? Was that why... Unable to endure the torment of her thoughts she gave a low moan, rolling on to her stomach.

'Can you manage to get undressed or...'

Until Blake spoke she had forgotten she was still wearing her outdoor clothes.

'I can manage.' Her voice was colourless and completely dry.

'Sapphire, we have to talk.'

Was that uncertainty and pain she could hear threading through the determined words? Anger hardened her heart. Whatever he might be enduring through guilt and fear of losing Flaws was nothing compared with her own agony. 'Tomorrow,' she told him briefly. 'I don't want to talk tonight Blake…I need to think.' It was a lie, but at least it got him out of her room.

When he had gone she struggled exhaustedly to remove her clothes, almost crawling into the bathroom. Her legs were bruised and scraped where they had rubbed against the rough stone of the quarry walls, the abrasions stinging with the hot water. Bathed and dried she went back into the bedroom, tensing as she saw Blake waiting there.

'I already told you, I don't want to talk tonight Blake,' she told him rudely. 'I'm tired, and so if you don't mind…' Glad that she had had the forethought to take her nightdress into the bathroom with her, she swept past him with magnificent disdain, hoping that he wouldn't guess how vulnerable and hurt she was really feeling.

'It's a bit late for this isn't it?' Lean fingers reached out and tugged at the fine lawn fabric. 'After last night…'

'Last night is something that should never have happened and would never have happened if I'd known…' Sapphire gasped out loud as Blake's fingers moved from the frill of her nightdress to the vee of its neckline, stroking softly over the upper swell of her breasts.

'You think not?' Blake's voice was soft, almost detached, but there was nothing detached about the look in his eyes Sapphire realised, her heart starting to thud with powerful, heavy thuds. 'I'm getting tired of playing "let's make believe", Sapphire,' Blake told her thickly. 'Last night you wanted me, and tonight I could make you want me again.'

'No!' The harsh denial was out before she could stop it and the moment it was said Sapphire knew she had made a mistake. It was almost as though something snapped inside Blake, some fine thread whose snapping unleashed a savage tumult of emotions that demanded expression.

Her moaned protest of 'Blake you can't do this', went unheard as he picked her up and carried her over to the bed, stripping off her nightdress with ruthless, hard fingers, his touch a thousand times removed from that of the tender lover of the previous night.

'I know you want me, damn you,' Blake muttered in a tortured whisper against her skin, bruising it faintly with the pressure of lips suddenly savage with pent-up emotions whose origins she could only guess at. His thumb brushed her nipple and Sapphire felt the unmistakable flowering of her body, her cry of despair mingling with Blake's murmured triumph.

As he bent his head to touch her treacherous body first with his tongue and then his lips Sapphire felt the first weak tears of broken pride slide from her eyes. In the darkness Blake lifted his head and stared at her, his thumb touching the dampness of her face.

'You're crying. Why?' If she hadn't known better Sapphire might have believed that the pain in his voice was real; that the anguish in his eyes was because he couldn't bear to hurt her, but she did know better. She turned her head away from him too weak to stem the tears.

'Don't touch me Blake,' she begged huskily, 'Please...just leave me alone.'

She closed her eyes and felt the bed shift under his weight. When she opened them again he had gone.

Sleep was a long time coming. She could hear Blake moving about in his own room; the noises of the old house as it settled into sleep disturbing tonight instead of vaguely comforting. Tomorrow she would have to tell Blake she was leaving him. No running away this time. She would tell him this time that she was going, and that she was never going to come back. A sob stuck in her throat and suddenly she was crying as she could not remember doing in a long time, tearing, painful sobs that left her chest aching and her eyes sore.

'SAPPHIRE, are you awake?'

Slowly she turned her head. Blake was standing just inside the door, his hair ruffled and on edge, his shirt half-unfastened, a cup of tea in one hand. 'I've brought you a drink,' he told her unnecessarily when she lifted her head from the pillow.

'What time is it?' Sapphire glanced at her watch, dismayed to see that it was midmorning. 'Shouldn't you be out working?'

It was obviously the wrong thing to say. Blake's mouth thinned, anger hardening his eyes. 'It's all

right,' she muttered huskily. 'This time I'm not going to run away. This time when I leave...' She
broke off stunned by the sudden blaze of heat turning
his eyes molten gold, which died just as quickly
when she started to finish her sentence. Surely Blake
couldn't want her to stay? Not for herself, she told
herself cynically, but perhaps for the farm. The
thought sickened her as it had done ever since it had
first come into her mind all those years ago.

'I'd better get up.'

'Sapphire we have to talk.' Blake's voice sounded
thick and hoarse, and now that she looked at him
properly she saw that beneath the healthy tan of his
face he looked drawn and tired.

'We can talk downstairs,' she told him reasonably,
feeling very much at a disadvantage in bed while he
stood, virtually fully dressed, in front of her. She
hadn't put another nightdress on after he had left her
and the remnants of the one he had torn off her body
lay on the floor at her side of the bed.

'No, now...' One stride brought him alongside the
bed, the mattress dipping under his weight as he sat
down next to her, one lean arm imprisoning her
against his side should she have any thoughts of trying to turn away.

'All right...' he admitted tiredly when she said
nothing. 'I know I shouldn't have done it...you've
every reason to hate me for it, God knows, I knew
when your father suggested it that it was a crazy
idea, but then when a man's as desperate as I was,
any idea, no matter how crazy, has its appeal.

'My forebears would be extremely flattered to know how eager you are to gain possession of Flaws' land,' Sapphire gritted at him. 'Such a noble sacrifice…' Some demon she had never suspected she possessed drove her on. '…even to the extent of giving up your mistress, but then that wouldn't have lasted would it? How long did you intend to devote your attentions to me? Long enough to get me pregnant—to provide my father with a grandson? And we both know what a sacrifice that would have been, don't we Blake? I should have remembered how much you loathed touching me, instead of deluding myself into…' She broke off as Blake wrenched the bedclothes away, squirming away from him, trying to cover her naked breasts by folding her arms.

'So I loathe touching you do I?' Blake muttered huskily, tugging her arms away from her body and then cupping the rounded warmth of her breasts stroking their pink tips with rough thumb pads. A deep sensual warmth burgeoned somewhere deep within her, increasing in intensity when she felt the fine tremor in Blake's hands. His eyes golden and fiery as the sun seemed to bathe her skin in molten heat, the expression she saw in their glowing depths as he bent his head to touch his lips first to one pink nipple and then the other making her wonder if she had suddenly completely lost her wits. 'Does this feel like I loathe the enticement of your skin beneath my fingers?' Blake demanded rawly releasing her breasts to spread brown hands possessively against her rib cage. 'Or this.' Hot damp kisses filled the valley between her breasts, his lips exploring the tender column of her throat, teasing the line of her jaw, his teeth nipping delicately at the fullness of her bottom lip until her lips parted and the fine tremor of his body became an open spasm of need, his mouth savagely hungry as it possessed hers, his tongue pushing past her teeth to explore its inner sweetness.

Unable to stop herself Sapphire caressed the firm muscles under his skin, stroking his neck and shoulders and feeling the powerful surge of his body's response.

'I love you so much,' Blake whispered as he lifted his mouth from hers, touching its swollen contours with his tongue as though unable to stop himself from doing so, 'that's my only defence. I nearly went crazy when you left me, hoping that you'd come back, telling myself that I'd find a way to get you back, and then when your father told me you were thinking of marrying again...' She felt him swallow and saw the unmistakable truth darkening his eyes, shining in the unexpected tears that shimmered in his eyes.

'You love me?' She could hardly trust herself to say the words. How could that be true?

'Always,' he averred.

'But you never made love to me, never...'

'Because you were so young,' he told her abruptly. 'Because I knew I'd taken advantage of what was little more than an infatuation, using it to bind you to me when you'd barely had a chance to taste real life.'

'I thought you didn't want me.'

'Not want you.' He closed his eyes, and swallowed hard. 'I wanted you so much I couldn't trust myself within a hundred yards of you, but I wanted you as a man wants the woman he loves Sapphire, not as an adolescent boy wants the first girl he falls in love with. I was terrified of frightening you away, and yet I knew that once I touched you I wouldn't be able to control myself; that I couldn't play the controlled lover…'

'And that was why you went to Miranda?' she asked in a low voice.

'I never "went to her" as you put it. Once, a long time before I fell in love with you she and I were lovers, but never since…'

'But the other night…'

'I wanted to make you jealous. To make you feel the same agony as I've endured over Alan. I spent the entire evening driving around in my car. After you'd gone out I rang her back cancelling the date.'

'But you wrote her love letters,' Sapphire told him, frowning as she remembered finding that incriminating evidence.

'Love letters?' Blake stared down at her.

'Yes.' Pain ached through her, her eyes clouding. 'When my father told me you married me because you wanted the farm, and after I'd seen what you'd written, I knew I couldn't stay… I saw the letter myself Blake, it was so full of…of need and love…'

She couldn't go on, remembering as though it had been yesterday how she had felt.

Suddenly Blake's frown cleared. 'Stay here,' he told her softly. 'Don't move.'

He was gone less than five minutes, during which time she had pulled the bedclothes back up round her body, but the first thing Blake did when he walked back into the room was to pull them down again. 'I love looking at your body,' he told her simply. 'It makes up for all the years when I couldn't. You can't imagine how I felt when I found out you were still a virgin.' His lips caressed one deeply pink peak, bringing it achingly to life, and then as though unable to resist the temptation, transferred to the other, adoration giving way to passionate need as he felt her body's unmistakable response and Sapphire arched achingly, longing to curl her fingers into his hair and hold him against her, but the paper he had dropped on the bed caught her eye and she tensed, causing him to stop and pull her into the warmth of his body so that she was leaning against his thighs her head cushioned against his shoulder.

'Is this what you read?' he asked her gently, offering her the close written sheets. Sapphire only needed to read the first few words to nod an assent.

'And because of this you left me? Oh! Sapphire...' His voice broke and she felt the damp warmth of his tears against her skin. 'I wrote them for *you*,' he told her brokenly, 'I wrote what I daren't tell you! What I couldn't in all honour show you... You're the only woman I've ever loved and when I saw you standing on that ledge, about to go over into the pool, I didn't know what I wanted to do most—strangle you or strangle Alan for hurting you so much that you felt you needed to end your life because of him.'

'It wasn't him, it was you,' Sapphire told him urgently. Right now it was almost impossible to take in the enormity of what had happened; but that Blake was telling the truth when he said he loved her she didn't for one moment doubt.

'After Miranda told me the truth about my father's illness I knew I couldn't stay with you—not when really you loved her, and yet I didn't know where I was going to find the courage to leave, loving you so much.'

'I've never loved anyone but you,' Blake interrupted fiercely. 'I think you were all of sixteen years' old the first time I realised how I felt about you. Miranda lied to you.'

Because she had been jealous. Sapphire now realised, but she had been clever as well, using her sophistication and experience to drive a wedge between them, no doubt hoping that Blake would turn to her once Sapphire had left him.

'So many wasted years,' she said sadly raising bleak eyes to meet his.

'No...not wasted. You *were* too young for marriage at seventeen,' Blake told her. 'I would always have felt guilty and uncertain wondering if I had stolen from you the right to make your own choice of husband, but now I know that you love *me*. You do love me, don't you?' he demanded thickly, when Sapphire remained silent.

Part of her longed to tease him just a little, but the rest of her responded eagerly to the plea in his eyes, her body curling into his as she kissed him, lightly at first and then with growing need, breaking away from him only to murmur huskily, 'So much... Blake if you hadn't arrived at the quarry when you did...' A shudder wracked her body and she felt him tense in response.

'Don't,' he commanded her rawly. 'Don't even think about it, just tell me you've forgiven me for lying to you about your father. I hated myself for doing it; for causing you pain—a pain I could see every time you looked at your father, but I was desperate to get you back; willing to do anything to stop you from marrying someone else.'

'And having got me back how did you intend to keep me?' Sapphire teased, forgiveness explicit in the look she gave him as she reached out to push the unruly hair back off his forehead.

'Oh, I'd have thought of something.' The old assurance was creeping back into his voice, but she didn't mind. Now that she had seen his vulnerability she could accept the macho side of his personality more easily. 'Such as?' she whispered, feathering light kisses along his jaw and glorying in his responsive shudder.

'Such as this...and this...' Blake's voice deepened, raw need underlying the husky words as he caressed her body, kissing her silky skin, words no longer necessary.

Now she really had come home, Sapphire thought contentedly abandoning herself completely into his keeping, revelling in the fierce thrust of pleasure seizing his body as he recognised her surrender, and she was never ever going to leave again. Closing her eyes she murmured the words of love she knew he longed to hear, for the first time saying them in complete trust that she would hear them back in return.

'The stock...' she reminded Blake weakly long, satisfying minutes later... 'You...'

'To hell with the stock,' Blake responded thickly. 'Right now I've got far more important things on my mind, like making love to my wife, unless of course she has any objections?'

A smile dimpled the corner of Sapphire's mouth. 'Only one,' she told him gravely, 'and that is that you're wasting far too much time in talk instead of action...'

Retaliation was every bit as swift as she had envisaged—and every bit as pleasurable, the words of love she had longed to hear for so long caressing her skin in silken whispers as Blake took her back in his arms.

# MURIEL JENSEN

## Bride by Surprise

### Three lighthearted stories of marriages that aren't quite what they seem…

If Charlotte Morreaux had gotten married, it wouldn't have been to her nemesis Derek Cabot. But fate and her stepmother contrived to force them both into a lie that snowballed uncontrollably.

When Barbara Ryan's boss, John Cheney, and a cluster of clergymen found her in his office—half-naked—he planted a kiss on her lips and introduced her as his blushing bride. And the new mother of his twin boys!

Patrick Gallagher was looking for money, not a wife. But marrying Regina Raleigh was a condition of his loan. Now on the run from a predator, they realized there was another problem confronting them—lust!

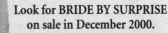

HARLEQUIN®
*Makes any time special* ™

**Look for BRIDE BY SURPRISE on sale in December 2000.**

PBR3BBS

# CELEBRATE VALENTINE'S DAY WITH HARLEQUIN®'S LATEST TITLE—

## Stolen Memories

Available in trade-size format, this collector's edition contains three full-length novels by *New York Times* bestselling authors Jayne Ann Krentz and Tess Gerritsen, along with national bestselling author Stella Cameron.

### TEST OF TIME by **Jayne Ann Krentz**—

He married for the best reason.... She married for the only reason.... Did they stand a chance at making the only reason the real reason to share a lifetime?

### THIEF OF HEARTS by **Tess Gerritsen**—

Their distrust of each other was only as strong as their desire. And Jordan began to fear that Diana was more than just a thief of hearts.

### MOONTIDE by **Stella Cameron**—

For Andrew, Greer's return is a miracle. It had broken his heart to let her go. Now fate has brought them back together. And he won't lose her again...

*Make this Valentine's Day one to remember!*

Look for this exciting collector's edition on sale January 2001 at your favorite retail outlet.

HARLEQUIN®

*Makes any time special* ™

Visit us at www.eHarlequin.com

PHSM

# *You're not going to believe this offer!*

### In October and November 2000, buy any two Harlequin or Silhouette books and save $10.00 off future purchases, or buy any three and save $20.00 off future purchases!

Just fill out this form and attach 2 proofs of purchase (cash register receipts) from October and November 2000 books and Harlequin will send you a coupon booklet worth a total savings of $10.00 off future purchases of Harlequin and Silhouette books in 2001. Send us 3 proofs of purchase and we will send you a coupon booklet worth a total savings of $20.00 off future purchases.

### *Saving money has never been this easy.*

---

## I accept your offer! Please send me a coupon booklet:

Name: _____

Address: _____ City: _____

State/Prov.: _____ Zip/Postal Code: _____

---

## *Optional Survey!*

In a typical month, how many Harlequin or Silhouette books would you buy <u>new</u> at retail stores?

☐ Less than 1     ☐ 1     ☐ 2     ☐ 3 to 4     ☐ 5+

Which of the following statements best describes how you <u>buy</u> Harlequin or Silhouette books? Choose one answer only that <u>best</u> describes you.

☐ I am a regular buyer and reader
☐ I am a regular reader but buy only occasionally
☐ I only buy and read for specific times of the year, e.g. vacations
☐ I subscribe through Reader Service but also buy at retail stores
☐ I mainly borrow and buy only occasionally
☐ I am an occasional buyer and reader

Which of the following statements best describes how you <u>choose</u> the Harlequin and Silhouette series books you buy <u>new</u> at retail stores? By "series," we mean books within a particular line, such as *Harlequin PRESENTS* or *Silhouette SPECIAL EDITION*. Choose one answer only that <u>best</u> describes you.

☐ I only buy books from my favorite series
☐ I generally buy books from my favorite series but also buy books from other series on occasion
☐ I buy some books from my favorite series but also buy from many other series regularly
☐ I buy all types of books depending on my mood and what I find interesting and have no favorite series

---

Please send this form, along with your cash register receipts as proofs of purchase, to:
**In the U.S.:** Harlequin Books, P.O. Box 9057, Buffalo, NY 14269
**In Canada:** Harlequin Books, P.O. Box 622, Fort Erie, Ontario L2A 5X3
(Allow 4-6 weeks for delivery) Offer expires December 31, 2000.      PHQ4002